SIX YEARS OUT

Martin Wilsey

Short Story Collection

2015-2021

Tannhauser Press

SIX YEARS OUT

Short Story Collection
2015-2021

ISBN: 979-8-89719-052-2

Cover Art by Rotwang Studios
Edited by Doris Miller
Published by Tannhauser Press
First Edition

www.martinwilsey.com
www.tannhauserpress.com

Also by Martin Wilsey

Still Falling

The Broken Cage

Blood of the Scarecrow

Virtues of the Vicious

Shadows of the Sentinel

The Once Damned

Coming Soon

The Law of Lumina

Time Enough

SIX YEARS OUT

Contents

DEDICATION

This book is dedicated to my friends in The Hourlings.

The Hourlings is a Science Fiction and Fantasy writing group based in the Northern Virginia area. Founded in 2014, the group includes various writers and editors, including Indie and Traditional authors, three professional anthologists, several full-time writers, and more. Hourlings outreach activities include their annual anthology (now open to writers outside the group), the Hourlings Podcast Project, and sponsorship of educational workshops to benefit the general local literary community.

Many of the stories in this collection can also be found in the anthologies published by this esteemed group.

In the last year, amidst the COVID-19 chaos, The Hourlings adapted and thrived via Zoom. It's handy living in the future.

The Hourlings

PREFACE

I like writing short stories. It's good practice. I write a lot of them. Most are not worth publishing but are still worth doing.

The ones that found their way into the world also ended up here, mainly because the readers that like my writing wanted copies for their collections.

Several have been released stand-alone in Kindle or audio editions or anthologies, but never together in a single collection.

In addition, you will also find a new, never-before-published short story titled: *The Two Daves.* This story, like many others contained within, are bonus stories involving beloved characters in my novels. My wife says they are like bonus features on DVDs. She's not wrong. (at least I am not the one to tell her that!) The cutting room floor has been harvested more than once.

The stories from the cutting room floor sometimes seem to have abrupt endings or atypical plot structures. Just like the deleted scenes on a DVD, special features collection. Still fun, and they increase the fidelity of characters in my novels.

Some of the stories are not associated with any other work. These will often be seeds that will grow into novels as time and longevity allow. I have tried to arrange them by topic, by world, or just by theme.

I hope you enjoy them.

SOLSTICE 31 STORIES

This first set of stories expand the Solstice 31 Saga series and its universe.

Secondary characters that appear in the Solstice Universe sometimes become the protagonists in some of these short stories. There might be details of the past, maybe even hints of things to come. All of it will bring the world into greater focus.

I love the characters I create. Each of my favorites carries a lifetime of stories that would make them complete and take me another few lifetimes to write.

A few people might even recognize themselves in here.

The short story, The Two Daves, even introduces characters that will become the supporting cast in a future Solstice 31 novel.

At the recommendation of the editors and beta readers, I am developing a timeline as to where all the stories fit in time and space. It will be a living document with links on my website. Keep an eye open for it.

But for now… Enjoy these ten glimpses into some of my favorite characters.

THE
OUTER
RING
A SOLSTICE 31 SHORT STORY
MARTIN WILSEY

The Outer Ring

"The *Ventura* was a deep-space survey ship with a crew of over 2,000 men and women. When we entered the orbit of the planet Baytirus that day, we never expected the *Ventura* to be immediately destroyed. We didn't know we weren't the first people to find that planet. But, someone knew."

--Solstice 31 Incident Investigation Testimony Transcript: Logs of Master Engineer Wes Hagan, senior surviving engineering member of the Ventura's crew. Recorded on 26291010, over three decades ago, and stored in the data being analyzed.

***

Barcus woke two hours early, as usual, before the Pal's alarm. Pal was the personal assistant layer of the *Ventura's* central artificial intelligence system. Nobody ever called them by those words, though. Everyone called them Pal and Caisy.

"Good morning, Pal. What's the plan for the day?" Barcus said, stretching, as he sat up in his bunk. At these words, Pal shifted the walls of the 3x5 meter room to a predawn mountain scene. It was majestic in its ultrahigh definition beauty. It also conveyed data. Barcus knew when the sun peeked from behind those mountains, and it would be time to go. The light increased on the clouds above as that time approached. Barcus didn't need any visual clues because he had a digital clock, always visible, in his personal Heads-Up Display (HUD). Computer display windows hung in the mountain scene, showing the day's work orders and his calendar. His messages were prioritized, quickly reviewed, and promptly answered.

Pal's voice imitated a professional female today. "Today, you meet the heavies for a morning run, beginning at Chen's STU on the outer ring's flight deck. Jack will be joining you again, so you'll need to take your pack along," Pal told him. "After that, shower, chow, and then prep for tomorrow's work orders that you'll do after we drop out of FTL." The days after faster-than-light runs were always hectic. "Jimbo will arrange for shore leave if the planet doesn't suck." Barcus enjoyed this AI's sense of humor.

"Jack is really joining us, again?" Barcus asked, laughing to himself, as he donned his running shorts and shirt. "I swear, he almost died after that lap last time."

"Your pack still has the twenty kilos of replacement gel packs," Pal said. "You know that's crazy, don't you? Running the outer ring, at 2G, with an extra twenty kilos that feels like forty kilos."

"The pack slows us down enough so that, one day, Jack might be able to keep up." Barcus smiled. Not many people tried. "That day won't be today."

Pal asked, "Did you know he has applied for a berth in the outer ring?" There was a slightly amused tone in her voice.

"Excellent. It's really the only way to do it. If he gets past the first month, it'll be easy."

***

Barcus arrived on the flight deck first. It was empty at 0520 hours. He already wore his pack, but he had made the 3K run so many times with it on, he moved like it wasn't there. He strolled in the heavy gravity, stretching his limbs as he went. The outer ring's flight deck was huge. At the point where he stood, the ship measured a kilometer in diameter. The ring's rotation gave it the feel of 2G, but there were no grav-plates in use. It saved a massive amount of power. A wide, central taxiway looked like it sloped uphill in both directions. It was just over three kilometers for one lap.

He smelled coffee.

Chen was already up and working on her shuttle. She always made the best coffee.

Even though Chen was a pilot, she took total ownership of her Shuttle Transport Unit and its systems. She called the onboard AI by the nickname Stu. It was an old habit from her flight training days. Another old tradition was to soup up her assigned vessel for maximum performance. She was also a highly regarded AI programmer in the fleet.

Barcus knew that today, she had to get everything back together in time for the drop out of FTL tomorrow. No one knew how long they would be in orbit around the next surveyed planet, so they had to be ready for long days.

"Morning, Chen. What the fuck do you think you're doing?" Barcus said with an amused tone.

"Don't just stand there, asshole. Lift that end and set it in those lock points. Or, is it too heavy for you and your skinny little arms?" Chen taunted.

Barcus didn't ask why she was mounting a 10mm canon inside the belly of her Emergency Module (EM), a spider-like all-terrain vehicle. As he muscled the receiver end into the sockets, he saw there were ammo belt feed cases already installed.

"Where the hell did you find this hellish lead storm?" he asked, referring to the massive gun. He moved to the muzzle end, helping her snap it into place. "Fixed forward fire, I see. Do you have a targeting module in the EM's AI yet?" he asked.

Chen answered with a roll of her eyes. She laid the belt of ammo across the receiver as she said, "Em, cycle the 10mm and then close it up." The first round cycled into the chamber, as the access panels closed so tight there was no visible seam.

"Aren't you worried that Captain Everett might get pissed off that you armed the transport?" Barcus asked. "Besides, who gave you the weapons mounts? Sweet setup. Can we try it in the vacuum tomorrow while we're out?"

"The STU-1138 class shuttles are just big enough to have their own parts fabricators. Can I help it if I have friends with access to design specs?" She smiled, wiping the lubricant from her hands with a dry rag.

"Morning, all," said Jack Miller. He was already out of breath. The 2G outer ring did that to most people. Barcus worked with hundreds of maintenance guys on a ship this size. Many, like Jack, had just started their tours four months ago. Barcus had been there longer than any of them. Just over twelve years.

A security squad of sixteen men ran by. They were in full combat gear, including Frange carbines. They were also followed by a couple of unit drones that scanned everything as they ran by.

Chen patted Jack's belly. "Don't worry. They won't eat you."

Jack was a good guy. He was a hard worker. He was great at detail work, especially the fine schematic work that sometimes left Barcus unable to see his project's big picture. 'The first tour spread' often haunted people when the gravity was low, and the food was good. Jack was determined to be physically fit when he returned to Earth in three years, eight months.

"Rumor has it you're joining us heavies in the outer ring," Chen stated as she rolled the toolbox to the far side of the EM. Barcus saw Jack look at the piling that was Chen's artificial left leg.

"Good-looking, on you. The chicks will dig it, right Barcus?" Chen said.

"The chicks will dig what?" Rand asked as she walked up. She chugged from a water bottle. She noticed Jack just then. "Mr. Miller has come back for more. We need to requisition this man a backpack!"

"He's even moving to the outer ring, soon," Barcus said before he chugged water from the bottle Rand tossed to him. Rand was part of the security team. Not only did she run with a weighted pack, but she also wore two handguns in thigh holsters and a Frange carbine on a strap that hung from her shoulder.

Jack, breathing easier now, said, "Did you know all the quarters out here are singles and are way bigger? No waiting list. I move in tomorrow."

"Jimbo!" the heavies said, all at once.

Another voice said, "Don't tell anyone, but we also have our own kitchen down here."

Barcus added, "Good morning, Commander 'shirking your duty' Worthington. What the hell, man? Your shift isn't over until 0800 hours." He slapped backs and shook everyone's hands. "Jimbo, this is Jack Miller, our latest victim."

"Nice to meet you, Jack. Don't listen to these asswipes. Down here, I'm just Jimbo." He shook Jack's hand. Jack liked him immediately. It wasn't often that someone from the lower decks got to meet anyone from the command crew.

"You coming today, Chen?" Jimbo asked as he adjusted the straps of his backpack.

"Not today, man," she said, as she looked up and another access panel opened. "I gotta finish up this shit before tomorrow's orbit."

"I hear that." Jimbo drank his water. "All three shifts are on duty tomorrow. That's why I can come down here and run you, weaklings, into the grav-plating."

With that said, they ran. Jimbo's surprise start caught no one, except Miller, off guard. After a bit, the heavies slowed so that he could catch up. They ran in formation around him, encouraging him all the way around the outer ring.

It was a 'lucky day.' That's what the heavies called it when all the bay doors were open.

Jack made it the whole way around without stopping once, for the first, and the last time.

***

"I miss real eggs," Barcus said, not for the first time.

Jack said, "It's because the eggs are dehydrated, made with reclaimed water. Do you ever get the pancakes? Why get the eggs if you don't like them?"

Chen looked up from her eggs with a raised eyebrow, the precursor to the death stare. She sat just to Jack's right. Barcus sat directly across from him, with Jimbo and Rand on either side. All of them ate eggs and bacon.

"Because you get real bacon with these eggs. Not even dehydrated," Barcus said, in a gesture of worship, as he held up a perfectly crispy strip of thick-cut bacon. Rand and Jimbo both attempted a snatch. Both lost out to the speed of Barcus's hand to his mouth.

"It's probably because the reclamation system extracts the water from your shit when yo—" Jack stopped, suddenly as Chen delivered a right jab to his face. "What the fuuu—!"

Chen patted him on the back in a perfect, nothing personal, gesture.

"House rules, Jack," Jimbo said. "Never mention the human waste reclamation system during chow. You are allowed, no required, to face-punch any heavy that does it. Even me. Especially me."

Jack laughed as he overplayed testing his jaw. Then, he touted the benefits of the delicious pancakes to another round of laughter.

None of them heard the woman behind them, two tables over, who said under her breath, "You won't be laughing this time tomorrow, motherfuckers."

***

Barcus went up to the central maintenance shop with Jack, after breakfast. They each signed out a Heavy Maintenance Suit (HMS) that they would use tomorrow. The HMS were called Heavy, for multiple reasons. First and foremost, they were really fucking heavy. Maintenance Chief Owens, consequently, referred to them as RFH suits. For some reason, this confused the dispatchers and amused the hell out of the chief.

Barcus went to bay forty-two and selected the same HMS he always picked. Jack picked number forty-one, based on its proximity to Barcus.

"Barcus, do you have any idea how much one of these things actually weighs?" Jack asked as he activated the diagnostic program and ran down the checklist.

"I think, empty, they weigh just under a metric ton. Just over, with water and a driver," Barcus said. "Doesn't mean shit, though. Most of the work is in zero gravity. "

"Ever run in one, on the surface of a planet? I hear they are fast on foot and fun as shit," Jack said, hooking up the water line to top it off.

"Just once, on a moon. Some dumb-ass had a dish fall on him, and, despite the low gravity, it broke both his legs. I ran the two kilometers to be the first one on the scene." Barcus paused, remembering, "That asshole never thanked me. He was a miserable bastard; it was always about politics with him."

"I'm driving forty-two down to the flight deck today, as always. But that's me. You may want to use the tractor rig to get your suit down. Today or tomorrow. They prefer it that way. They say it's 'safer.' Barcus laughed.

Jack knew he just gave him a way out to save face. All the HMS jocks walked them down. The key was NOT to damage anything on the way down to the flight deck.

"You came aboard on that last rotation? Four months ago, right?" Barcus asked as forty-two detached from the clamps and powered up. "How long have you been an HMS maintenance guy?"

"Counting the last four months, let me think." Jack thought, for a moment, before he answered, "Four months." He smiled at his own joke.

More men and women now entered the maintenance shop to begin their day. Most knew Barcus and said good morning to him. No one seemed even to notice Jack. "JAFMG," Barcus said, prompting an instant reply.

"Just-another-fucking-maintenance-guy," Jack drawled.

"Here's a tip for you, Jack," Barcus said as he stepped up and into his suit. "Move your suit down to your assigned shuttle the day before, in the morning. After it's docked in the shuttle, then you'll have the rest of the day to organize and clean up your bay in the maintenance shop. It's way easier without the HMS in there. Otherwise, you'll be so busy, you may never get to it."

The HMS closed over Barcus's head, revealing just a black, faceless thing. As it stood and saluted, it caused Jack to shudder. They had to be so careful when inside the damn things. It could wreak havoc because it could tear through a bulkhead without pausing.

Barcus entered the elevator and simply said, to the other passengers, "Good morning, ladies. Flight deck, please." The voice sounded ominous, like a cinder block dragged over cement.

Jack watched as two women caressed the suit, and one said, "Hey, handsome. Where you going? Want some comp—?" The door closed.

One of the techs walked up, shaking his head. Jack had the impression he walked over, specifically, to watch Barcus take the elevator in the three-meter tall suit.

"Why doesn't his suit have a number stenciled on the chest?" Jack looked at his suit. It had a large, bright yellow '41' emblazoned on the chest.

"Everyone knows that's him," the tech said. "For luck, I guess. You never heard the story?"

Jack shook his head. "What story?"

"Barcus, in suit number forty-two, was performing maintenance on a low orbit satellite when a stupid, rookie pilot blew him off the sat with his exhaust. The dumb-ass lit his main engines too close. Everyone thought Barcus was dead, except Chen." The tech walked closer and said the next part, quietly, "I heard Chen did an emergency, unsanctioned launch and chased after forty-two in the STU, somehow." He almost whispered, "She pulled a 'Jonah' at Mach 23, *in the atmosphere.*"

"A 'Jonah'?" Jack questioned, just as quietly.

"She opened the STU's cargo bay while in flight and ate him from the sky." The tech let it sink in. "The number forty-two burned off while he was in the atmosphere. All the melted exterior tools were repaired or replaced. Chen and Barcus were docked pay, by the former captain, for the repairs to the STU. That was about five years ago. I'm glad that asshole is finally gone."

"He never painted the numbers back on?" Jack asked.

"Go ahead, paint them back on. I dare you." The tech laughed and walked away.

Jack went back to work. He never took the advice to pre-dock his suit. Because of that, his last thoughts were about his numbers burning off.

✳✳✳

As the elevator doors opened, the HMS sang "Daisy Bell," and the women laughed as they left the lift. Wes Hagan, the *Ventura's* senior engineer, entered the charge and said, "Morning, Barcus." As he turned to face front, he said, "You look tired—" The doors closed as the suit laughed.

No one else got on the lift as it descended the final 200 meters. The flight deck was 2G, and the traffic was light. They were both headed for Chen's shuttle this morning. Chen was just closing another panel at the bottom of the Emergency Module. She spoke a few words, and the spider-like all-terrain vehicle ascended the cargo ramp and rotated in prep for locking into its spot on the roof of the cargo bay.

Wes asked Chen, "Why do you stay down here all the time?"

"Because I hate people," Chen replied. "The 2G keeps them away. And, if they must come down here, it's hard for them to breathe, so they don't talk so fucking much," she continued, wiping her hands as Barcus climbed out of the suit.

"Mind if I use the suit to carry and stow my tool chest?" Chen asked Barcus.

"Knock yourself out." Barcus stepped away from the suit. It still knelt under the chin of the STU.

"Stu, initiate remote. And, don't fucking drop them, this time." Chen said as she stepped away.

The HMS closed as it stood. All by itself, it walked up to Chen's full-size, double tool chest, crouched, and lifted it as if it were a dad carrying a cooler to the beach. The suit moved, easily and smoothly, to the toolroom in the back of the cargo bay.

"Nice," Wes said, a rare compliment from him. "It's why I'm here, really."

Chen was surprised Wes gave her no shit about avoiding his messages.

"Have you noticed anything odd in the AIs around here lately? Caisy or Pal, Stu, Em, Rain?" Hagan combed his fingers through his hair. Chen knew it was serious. Nothing ever puzzled this man. It was one of the foundation rules of the universe that Chen had grown to rely upon. That, and the fact that he let her do whatever she liked.

Wes knew she did a good job. He also knew she did that job better with less management.

"I only interact with Stu and Em. It's daily, and it's for hours, every day. Caisy and Pal are of little use to me," Chen said, thinking hard. "In fact, Em and Stu have been better in the last few months. I guess, more aware. I've been working on them a lot, though. I shudder to think how much extra code I've added to their advanced AI routines."

"Chen, can you help me tomorrow with a code review on Caisy?" Wes asked. Wes never asked.

"Sure, but it will cost you. I hear Peck has some excellent bourbon." Chen smiled. Both Wes and Barcus covered their eyes, just to be assholes about it. Wes feigned staggering away.

"We'll be done with our maintenance run by lunch. I will help you in the afternoon," she called out to his back. "If this asswipe doesn't sleep too late," Chen called as she pounded a fist on Barcus's chest with a solid *thunk*.

"OK, OK. I'll buy you some bourbon later, at Peck's Halfway." Wes retreated to the lift.

None of them knew they were being watched from thirty-two angles.

***

Peck's Halfway was the closest bar to the ship's outer ring. All the heavies (the people that lived in the outer 2G ring) went to this bar. They called it a '1G Joint,' and they all liked Peck, the owner. Peck had run this bar for as long as anyone could remember. He was fat, old, and gay. He ate and drank too much. He slept in .5G all night and sat in his bar on a padded grav-plate stool that must have cost a mint. He had gout, a missing tooth, and all the ladies loved him. Well, the men, too. Even the heavies.

Barcus walked into the Halfway, wearing his typical after-work clothes: jeans and a Led Zeppelin T-shirt. He saw where the heavies sat and moved through the crowd toward them.

"Hey, Barcus, you bucket of spit, get your ugly mug over here before I come over this bar and kick your ass!" Peck loved talking like that to Barcus; it made the newbies wonder.

"I'd like to see that, you fat fuck. You better give me a bottle of this bourbon I have heard about, or I'll knock out another tooth," Barcus yelled back as he approached. Reaching out, their hands slapped together in a handshake that turned into a hug, causing Barcus to, literally, *almost* come over the bar.

"How goes it, old friend?" Barcus said, sitting down to talk, as Peck set two fine crystal tumblers on the bar and withdrew a dusty bottle from somewhere, as if by magic. With a flare, he pulled the cork from the bottle with his teeth, spat it onto the bar, and poured for them both.

"It goes very well. It will be going even better soon." He raised his glass and said, "To sipping the joys of life, so they last longer." Peck raised an eyebrow, waiting.

Barcus sipped the bourbon.

"Peck. You've just ruined my life. I now know I'll never have another bourbon this excellent. I might as well die tomorrow." Barcus sipped again.

Peck downed his in one tip of the glass.

Before his chin lowered, Barcus snatched the bottle from Peck's hand and said, "You savage!"

"Wait!" Peck stopped him, smiling. "Remember our discussion, Thursday last?" Once again, as if by magic, he produced a glass test tube about fifteen centimeters long and four wide. It had a humidity control stopper. Inside was a large cigar.

"Are you nuts? Where'd you get that?" It disappeared into Barcus's pocket.

"Never you mind. And, you didn't get that from me. That goes to the outer ring and stays there." Tobacco was forbidden on the ship. This created a thriving black market for it.

"Thanks, Peck," Barcus said. "Put it on my tab."

He knew Peck wouldn't. Barcus's money wasn't good in Peck's Halfway, and Barcus allowed it. He learned to live with it. He never took advantage, though. It made Peck happy. Barcus knew that Peck's life was worth more than a hefty bar tab. But that's not why Barcus saved it.

He approached the table, and around it were the usual suspects, plus a few others. Chen, Rand, and Jimbo sat in the back of the enormous booth. Everyone knew that if you gave Jimbo shit about drinking OJ, you'd have to buy the next round. It looked like Jack Miller recently learned that lesson. Barcus wondered if he was stupid enough to make that one-arm chin-up bet with Chen.

To his surprise, Wes Hagan was there, as well. *Two senior staff members?* Hagan was having a close, heated conversation with Jimbo. There was Sarah, Bishop, Karen, Ross, and Beth Shaw from medical, as well.

"Well, well, well. I see I am expected." Barcus gestured, with the bottle, to the black tray that held a dozen clean glasses, sitting in the middle of the table.

"You're Peck's favorite," Rand teased.

He sat in a chair next to Sarah, pouring a shot into each glass and handing them around. "It's just as well that this is a small bottle. Tomorrow comes all too soon."

Everyone took a glass, except Jimbo, even Chief Hagan. Barcus had never seen Jimbo drink alcohol, ever. They held their glasses up and waited. It was a tradition. Jack looked around but then followed suit.

After a moment of silence, Barcus said, "There is a pleasure in being mad that none but madmen know."

They drank.

Everyone talked at once, then. "Where do you come up with those?" Jimbo asked.

"My God!" a few other people said.

"This is the best bourbon, ever."

"Read a fucking book, Jimbo," Barcus replied.

"This bourbon is so good, I want to fuck it," Jack said, causing dead silence.

Then, everyone broke out laughing.

They didn't know about the malice that monitored them over the ship's security cameras.

***

"We drop out of FTL in eleven minutes, people. Stations, please," Jimbo announced over the ship comms of the *Memphis*. Most of the crew on the command deck buckled their five-point harnesses. They lifted the disk up by its belt from between their legs and snapped the buckles in on each side. The five-point harness automatically adjusted.

They all strapped in, except Myers. Myers was an asshole. Jim planned on talking to Captain Everett about finding him another duty station.

The *Memphis* was the captain's pinnace. A big one. It had a crew of thirty-six men and women, five levels, a massive cargo bay, and advanced FTL engines powered by three dark matter reactors. On this run, they also carried four scientists and a sixteen-man security team, the very same team that ran the outer ring. Jimbo hoped to get to know them on this mission.

One by one, all the units checked in. Even Sergeant McGrath, the security team leader, checked in with a simple, "Standing by." Jimbo punched up the view of the aft briefing room. The whole squad strapped into seats in two 4x4 grids on either side of the aisle. They required an empty seat between the men since their shoulders were so broad.

"Dropping out of FTL, now," Cook, the pilot, said.

"Separation complete. I am moving out to monitoring distance.

Then, it happened.

∗∗∗

Rand was called out of a dead sleep by Captain Everett at 0420 hours. "I want you in command shuttle Charlie in fifteen minutes." She was there in nine minutes. But she was the only one there when it happened.

∗∗∗

Based on Barcus's conversations last night between Jimbo, Chen, and Wes, he decided to get down to the STU early. That way, Chen could be first in line on the flight deck for launch and first back. Removing that specific dish for an upgrade will only take him half the time it said on the schedule.

Coffee in hand, he quietly walked up behind Chen and bear-hugged her. His left arm wrapped diagonally and down in front of her as she worked at the control terminal attached to the hydraulic leg that raised and lowered the ramp.

She completely ignored him as she concentrated on the panel. He released her and kissed the top of her head, handing her his coffee to share a sip. She took it and breathed in the aroma.

"Let's do the quick preflight and—" Chen and Barcus felt the deck heave violently, followed by an explosion, far away, on the flight deck. They felt the hull breach in their ears. Another blast knocked them off their feet.

"Stu! Close and seal," she screamed, over the sound of the ship's outer ring tearing itself apart.

Barcus got to the ladder first and turned in time to see the power cells explode in the bay, directly behind the closing ramp. Chen was thrown into him at the ladder. "Go!" she screamed. He hustled up the ladder in a flash. She ascended, slower.

Just as she got onto the shuttle's flight deck and the hatch closed, another explosion slammed them into the ceiling. They crashed about in a violent, random, three-axis tumble. Blood splashed out of a tear in the belly of Chen's flight suit.

Barcus saw Chen bounce and catch the harness on the pilot's seat as he slammed down onto the open HMS. He grabbed hold and placed himself into the suit with practiced muscle memory. He initiated the closure sequence. Just as it closed, they were struck with a massive piece of debris.

Barcus's face slammed into the inside of the suit's faceplate.

The blackness overtook him, along with the sensation that he was still falling.

***

Multiple waves of *Ventura* debris tore into the *Memphis*, tossing it into an uncontrolled, end-over-end tumble. Half the crew died, instantly, from hull breaches or from not being strapped in. The *Memphis* was on a collision course with the planet's single moon.

***

No one saw Jack Miller, in HMS number forty-two, get thrown clear of the *Ventura* as the last missile hit. He had over an hour to think about it as he fell toward a nameless planet before he entered its atmosphere. He considered hitting the HMS's OPEN button to make his death quick.

He thought he'd stay and watch. Maybe Chen will come and pull another 'Jonah.' He doubted it. So, he dosed himself with all the painkillers he found in the onboard medkit.

He watched the debris around him burn like a shooting star. It was beautiful. It made him sleepy. He never felt his legs cooking.

He died, still falling.

KILL
VALERIE
HUME
A SOLSTICE 31 SHORT STORY
MARTIN WILSEY

Kill Valerie Hume

"The *Ventura* was a deep-space survey ship with a crew of over 2,000 men and women. When we entered the orbit of the planet Baytirus that day, we never expected the *Ventura* to be immediately destroyed. We didn't know we weren't the first people to find that planet. But, someone knew."

--Solstice 31 Incident Investigation Testimony Transcript: Logs of Master Engineer Wes Hagan, senior surviving engineering member of the Ventura's crew. Recorded on 26291010, over three decades ago, and stored in the data being analyzed.

***

"Dammit, Hume. Are you trying to get yourself killed again?" Deck Chief Jubinski yelled. DC Jub yelled all the time. It's how you knew when you were in trouble. If he wasn't yelling when he spoke to you, you were in some deep shit.

"If I were trying to kill myself, I'd stop by and eat more of your chili, DC," she said.

Hume did yet another, Zero-G combat workout. She preferred to work out on the vast, open central core flight deck rather than in the Zero-G gym. In the gym, all the walls were padded and uniform. That space was nowhere near as big. On the flight deck, the obstacles were real: docked ships, bulky equipment, huge machines, crisscrossing cables, and other infrastructure. All of it had random handholds and footholds, like the real world. Besides, she was allowed to wear her full security team suit, helmet, and weapons. DC Jub even let her fire her Frange carbine in there, in vacuum, because it only fired frangible, nonpenetrating rounds. He also knew she seldom missed.

She did fast launch-and-tumbles across the vast central space while firing her Frange rifle on every rotation. She never missed her drone target. It was dangerous because the hub was Zero-G and already in vacuum. The security suit she wore allowed maximum freedom of movement, but it barely protected her from vacuum. It could rip easily. And, while a Frange will not penetrate any kind of metal, it will go through her suit. DC Jub always thought she'd break her neck when she got to the other side. But, she always stuck her landings.

It was a quiet morning on the Main Flight Deck on the *Ventura*. The only ships on the MFD today were the ones being prepped for tomorrow's planet survey, including the *Memphis*.

Hume was assigned to the *Memphis*. Her first post as part of a command crew. It was the captain's pinnace. The largest ship in the MFD, it had five decks and a regular crew complement of thirty-six. She noticed movement near the aft skid. She stuck the landing; and, her practice allowed her to focus instantly, with no dizziness.

There were five men in combat fatigue suits and helmets performing an inspection of the *Memphis*. She knew who they were. They were the tactical team that would stand ready on the *Memphis*.

She quickly launched, hooked a cable, changed direction, and ran a few steps along a girder. And, while she still had enough downward inertia for traction, she launched again, soaring across the vast space in a slow, scanning spiral that allowed her to see the soldier ascending on an intercept vector.

Hume synched a strap that drew her Frange to her back as if she hadn't seen the man.

Just before they intersected, Hume tucked and twisted, easily avoiding his outstretched arms. She pounded on his shoulder blades, stopped, and stole his forward momentum, leaving him stranded and neutralized in a fixed position. She had estimated his mass and velocity closely. He wouldn't drift near a handhold for at least an hour.

She sped to the flat flight deck doors, glad they were closed. If they had been open, she would have been lost to the vastness of space. Instead of doing the polite thing and retrieving the man or at least give him a kick to the wall so he could save himself, she launched directly toward the group of men below that were now watching. When they saw her do this, two of them launched toward her.

Just before they were on her, with their arms spread wide, Hume piked and barrel rolled with her feet tight together, landing directly behind the first man's neck. She avoided his hands easily as she thrust him away into the second man. Both tumbled away, not grasping each other as they should have.

She was redirected into the side of the *Memphis*, where she ran along at a 90° angle to the horizon and completely surprised the remaining three men, bowling them into each other and away, like pins rolling a spare. She heard them laughing in her proximity comms.

She halted her forward momentum instantly, reversed from following them with one hand on a ladder rung attached to the strut, right into another man that had been out of view under the belly of a lifeboat attached to the bottom of the *Memphis*.

He was in the process of drawing a sidearm.

Her sudden reversal in Zero-G startled him, and that was all the pause she needed. In a well-practiced move, she spun and rolled up his shooting arm until her legs were wrapped around his neck, and the gun hand was cruelly twisted to the point of hyperextension.

Incapacitated, he strained against her hold a couple of times. It only risked his arm breaking.

Hume didn't peel the handgun out of his fingers, even though she could have.

"Good afternoon," she said, in a polite manner, so everyone within proximity heard. "Thanks for the workout, guys. Next time, please don't go easy on me. This was fun."

She let up on the tension as a few of the soldiers returned. By the time they had handholds and were standing near, only the first one had not yet returned. She released the man. Taking the chance that he had more discipline than to shoot her.

She could tell just by looking at these men that they were ground pounders. They had little to no experience in Zero-G combat.

"That was pretty badass, LT. Gots some wicked Zero-Skills there," one man said.

"Damn, she tiny!" another said.

"Big enough to make you look like a fool," a third said.

"Sergeant, I think we need a bit more training in Zero," the last man said. He was the one still floating, alone, in the center of the bay.

Everyone laughed, except the Sergeant, as he holstered his gun and rubbed his wrist.

"A little help, please." Everyone laughed again.

"I'll fetch you, if I can ride you back, piggyback," Hume said, as she launched at him with the precision of an expert's arrow in flight.

At least he knew the proper way to catch an incoming rescue, preserving and transferring most of the momentum to his body so that they floated towards the bulkhead behind them.

"I'm Hume," she said.

"I'm Ferris," he replied.

"I'm going to ride you back to your buddies like a rented mule," Hume said.

"Stop trying to arouse me in front of my friends," he said, as they lighted on the wall and prepared to thrust back to the *Memphis*.

"If I had been trying, you'd be far more injured."

They launched together, and she sat upon the base of his spine, looking like a child getting a horsey ride from her father. Hume even stood and pretended he was a surfboard for a few moments.

She launched for an exit airlock and said, "Back to work, slackers."

She'd never see any of them again…

***

"Yo, Hume!" she heard from across the cafeteria. Her HUD identified the voice and location of the owner before she could look up. Heidi DeGroat, from Human Resources. While she was on duty, she always kept the setting on full data augment. The names of everyone in the room seemed to hang above their heads. Addition data was also there. Icons indicated if they had any past infractions or convictions. The security system's AI also conveyed what it thought was important.

Heidi's augment revealed just her name and her work area. Hume's favorite. No commentary on her new hair color, though. Today, it was mostly blonde, with a deep streak of dark purple.

Hume sat her tray at the end of the mostly full table, already buzzing with morning conversation, despite the early hour. A flurry of good mornings were acknowledged with a raised coffee mug salute.

"Gah, how can you eat those eggs every morning?" Heidi asked, as always.

"I need the protein. Plus, if you add enough onions, cheese, and hot sauce, they're not so bad." Hume didn't mention how awesome the thick-cut bacon was.

Heidi was a fruit-and-cereal breakfast eater.

"Did you get to Peck's Halfway last night? Peck broke out an excellent case of bourbon." The comment shifted the conversation at the table, like gravity, "It was so good the case was gone fast, but so expensive the only one to get drunk on it was Peck."

"Sorry I missed it," Hume said.

"Yeah, it was perfect for you. As little as you drink, it might as well be good," Heidi continued, but Hume no longer listened.

Her HUD drew her attention to a man that had no identifiers. There was no name above his head. No data available. This was not usually a problem. Not everyone had a HUD or was tagged in any way. She knew of just over a hundred people on the ship that had no augmentative tech. Security simply used lanyards or face recognition.

This man wore gray maintenance crew coveralls.

As he moved through the crowd, AI~Caisy captured a full image of his face.

No match.

She got up as he moved away. He never saw her. Hume snatched her last piece of bacon as she moved, and said, "Gotta go. Busy day." Farewells drifted behind her.

"Caisy, track subject using visuals," Hume said in a businesslike command voice. A tactical map of the near spaces of the level came up in her HUD on one side, indicating the subject's position. He was paused, just around the corner to another busy hall. People streamed back and forth.

Hume didn't rush. She moved with the crowd as they exited the cafeteria, starting the busy landfall day. If he stayed there, she would just introduce herself and chat.

Why was her adrenaline up so high? She felt it. Everything seemed too slow.

That's when he looked around the corner and locked eyes with her, in a moment of recognition.

He ran.

Hume activated her security uniform's pursuit mode. Braiding detail cords glowed and flashed bright yellow. A high-pitched whine emitted from the suit as she ran. The well-trained crew cleared a path in the center of the corridor.

AI~Caisy closed bulkheads to contain the runner, who only had a 100-meter head start but was faster than Hume expected. No one ran anymore.

Hume dove through a closing door just as it began to reverse. With a quick roll, she was on her feet again, instantly. She landed in the large, inorganic waste storage room. Her tactical map no longer contained the subject's location since there were no cameras in the waste room.

Her HUD indicated, "Reinforcements, ETA four minutes."

Hume stopped her uniform from strobing but left the uniform's lights on to cut the darkness. It was a vast room stacked high with trash pallets from all around the ship that would be automatically sorted for the fabricators.

"Sir, I'm Security Chief Valerie Hume. I'd like to speak to you," she said, into the darkness beyond the glow of her uniform. "Caisy. Lights," Hume said under her breath.

Hume saw the reflection, in the bulkhead steel, of the shape dropping down onto her from above. Her Zero-G combat training had taught her three-dimensional awareness.

She quickly rolled away in time as a giant ax slammed onto the floor where she stood a moment ago.

"I know who you are," the man said calmly as the ax swiped at her again, missing her by a fraction. Then, again, into the floor as she backpedaled.

He was fast. "Stop or die!" Hume called out, managing to keep the panic out of her voice. She was on top of the trash bins now. She jumped, avoiding a swipe at her legs. As she did, she drew both her sidearms from her thigh holsters.

"To hell with polite community policing," she thought or said; she couldn't remember later. Before she touched down, she put four Frange rounds into the man's chest. He went down, and the ax clattered away.

After touching down, lightly, on the trash container, she descended to the floor, with a foot on either side of the man. Both guns pointed at his dead face for a full ten seconds before she spoke, "Emergency medical team to reclamation Bay 12, stat."

She calmly holstered her guns and knelt to feel for a pulse at his neck; she knew there shouldn't be one.

She never expected his eyes to fly open and his hands to grasp her neck in an iron grip.

"Kill Valerie Hume," he growled, through gritted, bloody teeth.

She broke both his wrists and pinned down his arms as she watched the light go out in his eyes.

She wasn't sure he was dead when the warning lights began to flash.

"Warning: Prepare for Emergency Dump Protocol," the PA system warned.

"Caisy, cancel dump protocol," Hume said. There was no reply.

"Caisy. I am still in Bay 12!" She ran for the door. "Open the door."

"CAISY, we are still moving faster-than-light!" Hume screamed. "Everything in here will be evacuated and turned into its base molecules!"

Her HUD indicated there was no active RF in the bay at all.

"Activate emergency HUD-to-HUD broadcast." She choked down panic. She heard the machines of the bay doors begin to cycle. "Emergency, Bay 12 is about to vent, and I am in here!"

"Bay 12 is closed and nominal. Who is this? Get off this frequency," a bored-sounding voice said.

"Hume, Jack Miller here. There's a Heavy Maintenance Suit docked in Bay 12. Alcove number seven."

She ran.

"Hume, Bay 12 is closed and quiet. I'm looking at it on my monitors. You got this all wrong," the same bored voice said.

She saw the suit. It was open in the dock, waiting for the next user. She climbed up and lowered herself into it.

Her thigh holsters caught on the sides, stopping her.

With practiced speed, she released the five buckles. The lights in the bay turned red as she threw the webbing and the holsters to the deck and slid into the suit.

It closed, and it sealed.

It took her a moment to find the display controls. When she activated it, she gasped. Bay 12 was now completely empty.

Thousands of pallets were gone. Vaporized. She watched as the exterior door shut rapidly, finishing its cycle.

"Valerie Hume, report to Captain Everett on the bridge immediately."

She found that she had a difficult time talking. "Acknowledged," was all she managed.

THE BLACK POD

A SOLSTICE 31 SHORT STORY

MARTIN WILSEY

The Black Pod

"The *Ventura* was a deep-space survey ship with a crew of over 2,000 men and women. When we entered the orbit of the planet Baytirus that day, we never expected the *Ventura* to be immediately destroyed. We didn't know we weren't the first people to find that planet. But, someone knew."

--Solstice 31 Incident Investigation Testimony Transcript: Logs of Master Engineer Wes Hagan, senior surviving engineering member of the Ventura's crew. Recorded on 26291010, over three decades ago, and stored in the data being analyzed.

***

"When it began… I was just a man."

--Solstice 31 Incident Investigation Testimony Transcript: SecTech Chief Anthony Adams, Senior Security Technology Specialist on the Ventura.

***

SecTech Chief Anthony Adams witnessed, more than experienced, the destruction of the *Ventura* and the death of the crew. He watched missile after missile detonate its nuclear payload and never felt so much as a vibration from inside the Black Pod.

The pod was designed to survive anything, even a direct strike from a nuclear bomb. It had to survive. It held the story of the demise of the *Ventura*. That was the Black Pod's purpose. The hull was Polycarbon, and made of a fiber more than a meter thick. The internal power system was comprised of dual dark matter reactors and would last 200 years without additional fuel. The internal inertial dampeners were so powerful, Adams never felt the initial blast. There was no sense of the three-axis spin that the Black Pod was in as its orbit decayed. It housed *Ventura's* main data store and Central Artificial Intelligence SYstem, CAISY.

The Chief's eyes welled with tears as he watched via the external camera array as the plasma cannons hammered the life pods and shuttles.

"Box, I need a status," Adams said, the words catching in his throat. At his command, virtual computer screens opened all around the dome. He sat in the center, in the single, massive command chair. His fingers flashed across the enormous curved control console.

"The *Ventura* has been struck with a total of eleven Javelin nuclear missiles," AI~CAISY said in a cautious tone. "Automated re-entry systems are fully functional. Grav-plates will be activated when we are 50 kilometers from the surface."

"Caisy, how did this happen?" There was despair in his voice. AI~CAISY knew Adams was upset because he didn't use the nickname 'Box.'

"There was an automated defense grid. It had stealth satellites with weapons platforms. There was no warning, no hail, no radio challenge of any kind."

"Did I ever tell you why I call you 'Box'?" Adams asked AI~CAISY.

"No. It's the primary user's privilege to call the AI anything he likes."

"Back home, the commercial craft used to have a recorder called a Black Box. It was the seed concept for the Black Pod. The same idea, except for… me…" Adams sat in the command chair, staring out at nothing.

"You call me Box, and I will call you Tony." It sounded as if the AI had decided something. "Tony, we are now in hostile environment survival mode. Passive sensors only. No beacons. Besides, all the external antennas have been burned off," Box said as the dome view changed to external simulated static positioning. Adams could see the virtual Black Pod in the center of the dome's virtual screen, tumbling end over end. Inside it, however, he felt nothing. He didn't even have his five-point harness buckled. He never did.

"What else?"

Box continued, "We are coming in really steep. We have less than another orbit before we are down. Entering the atmosphere in seven minutes."

There was debris all around them, moving at the same velocity and vector as they were. "Hold off on the grav-plate and thrusters as long as possible. If we want any choice at all where we set down, we will need all we've got," Adams said. The Black Pod was not a spaceship. It was even less maneuverable than a lifeboat. It was an incredibly dense rock fitted with a large grav-plate so that the builders could move it. It could hit the planet without the grav-plate activated, and

Adams would probably not even feel the impact because of the powerful dampeners.

As they entered the upper atmosphere, chunks of the *Ventura* surrounding him began to burn up. At 50 kilometers, the thrusters halted the spin and oriented the grav-plate towards the planet's surface. As the pod started to slow, the rest of the pieces around him appeared to speed ahead.

Long-range optical sensors indicated that they would land in a heavily forested area. Already he could see the debris impacting the forest in great explosions. He navigated the pod toward an area between two small, elongated lakes in a rapid series of decisions. At the final moment, he spotted a level clearing and guided the pod to it, landing it expertly.

The forest was ablaze all around the clearing.

Adams stood to examine his new home. The pod's Heads Up Display (HUD) provided a view as though he were standing on a platform ten meters across, his command chair and console in the center.

"Box, I want external audio."

The sound came in as a low roar. The fires raged. Animals were fleeing the forest into the clearing to escape the inferno. He could hear the birds crying out in panic. He saw deer and foxes and bears. There was also some type of elk and smaller animals of various species.

"So much like Earth," he said out loud without meaning to.

"Gravity is .89G, and the atmosphere varies from Earth less than one percent," Box confirmed. "The animals fleeing to the south will run directly into another fire. This entire area will be engulfed in less than a day. If they move to the lake in the west, they may have a chance."

The fire was jumping rapidly from treetop to treetop. Adams had thoughts of Hell. He considered cracking the hatch and just walking out into it. It might be easier.

Then he saw her.

There was a little girl, perhaps ten years old, stumbling out of the forest. She was about 200 meters away. She had some kind of animal, like a large dog, with her that she leaned on for support. Its shoulders were as high as hers.

"Box, zoom in." Before Box could zoom all the way in, she disappeared in a dense cloud of smoke that persisted for a full minute. By the time the wind cleared it away, the girl was gone; only the dog-like creature remained. Adams realized it was standing over her, protecting her, or trying to nudge her awake.

It was not a dog. It was a broad-chested beast the likes of which he had never seen before, with a mane like a lion's that wasn't fur, but rather feathers. It was a reptile. Mostly.

"Box, open up!" A square trapdoor opened directly behind the command chair. The ladder was, in fact, part of the back structure of the command chair, and Adams slid all the way down to the next level without touching a rung. A locker quickly gave up a survival pack and vest. He already had a Glock on his belt, and he grabbed an AR-79 out of a ready rack. He ran down to the ground before the ramp was completely deployed.

SecTech Adams had left running to the younger people long ago. Now he regretted the polite refusals he had made to Worthington, Rand, and Barcus to join them on runs in the 2G outer ring of the *Ventura*. He did keep the gravity at 2Gs in the Black Pod as his one concession to fitness. The gravity here, however, was light, and he ran smoothly through the tall grass.

He should have grabbed a breather unit though. His lungs burned as the waves of smoke billowed over him. Eventually, he stopped running and had to lie down in the grass to breathe the precious unpolluted air near the ground.

When the smoke finally cleared, he found he was just 10 meters away from the girl. The beast had already seen him. It's ruff was up. The mottled gray feathers were trembling a warning. He could see that they were singed in places. It was behaving like a giant cat, its cruel-looking tail swishing side to side, revealing the creature's agitation.

Adams approached, his assault rifle targeting the animal. It began to draw back its lips, showing teeth like steak knives, serrated on the inside edge.

Just then, the girl's hand reached up and touched its front leg. It was as if she had switched it off. It completely ignored Adams and began licking the girl's sooty face with a large black tongue.

When Adams' eyes met hers, he didn't know what to do. So he just let the rifle swing to his back on the sling and waved for her to come with him back to the safety of the pod. She started to get up and fell again, her one hand never leaving the beast.

She reached out to the Chief with her other hand.

Suddenly, beyond her, he could see another great cloud of smoke coming their way. Decision made, he risked a bite from the beast. He lifted her in his arms and ran. The creature ran alongside. The girl extended an arm out to it in reassurance.

That's when Tony saw her burns. Her clothes had been half burned off. He knew his jostling must be agony for her. They had covered maybe half the distance back to the pod when he paused and gently set her down. She immediately cried out in pain and rolled onto her belly.

He unslung his pack. As the beast tried to lick her wounds, she screamed and pushed it away. It whimpered like a pup even though the thing was huge. Adams had never seen this species.

The med spray brought instant relief. The pain was numbed, and the nanites would have the second-degree burns completely healed in just a few hours. She was able to stand before he was even done treating her.

She patted his shoulder. She was speaking rapidly in a language he didn't understand. She pointed to the beast. He realized it was also severely burned, even worse than the girl. There was a scorched area on its right flank, and both its front paws were burned horribly to the first joint. Its muzzle was also severely blistered.

Adams didn't know if the beast's physiology was compatible, but he treated it with the nanites anyway. When he sprayed its muzzle, it sneezed, and the girl laughed for a moment until the creature began to push her forward with its lowered head.

It wasn't just smoke coming their way this time. The grasses were on fire, and it was moving towards them. The girl led the charge to the ramp leading into the Black Pod. With all the gear down, sitting in the tall grasses, the pod looked like a great, black dome of a building that had been there since the dawn of time.

They ran.

***

The hatch closed behind them just before another cloud of smoke engulfed them. Safe inside the lower deck of the pod, the girl fell flat on her face as soon as she hit the heavy gravity plating.

"Box, grav-plates off, please." He saw the girl react when it returned to normal.

She sat up and started speaking rapidly to Adams. He could tell by the upward inflection in her voice that she was asking questions. He thought he recognized a single word: "Keeper."

He started to speak over her, "Please, I cannot understand you. Do you speak English? Are you a colonist? What is the name of this planet? I am here from Earth."

She became quiet. Adams did not know what he said to cause this, but she fell to her knees and placed her forehead on the floor at his feet. The beast slowly moved to position itself protectively between the girl and Adams.

Alarms sounded in the otherwise quiet room. Not so loud as to panic his guests, but urgent nonetheless. Box reported, "Passive sensors have discovered that there is comms traffic. Sat-based. Air traffic has also been detected."

"Oh shit," he said as he climbed the ladder to the control room. "Tactical display, Box." A map appeared to Adams' right. It was more detailed than he had expected of this continent. It had distant cities annotated and comm signal points of origin. It even had their position and the best guess at the fire's progress around them.

Tony was worried that ships would come to mop up. The tactical map revealed that only four were currently detected in the air, all on vectors away from his location. They were easy to track because they emitted constant ident codes on a side beacon.

Box speculated, "They look like old colony shuttles, based on these protocols. And not many of them."

"Where did you get these maps?" Adams asked as he looked closer.

"A prior survey. No dates. No additional information. How odd." Tony had never heard Box sound puzzled before.

He hadn't noticed when the girl climbed the ladder to stand behind him. Her mouth was wide open.

***

Together they watched the entire forest burn nearly flat over the following days. When it began to rain, it was too late. Now all was black as if to welcome and hide the pod. They watched the night sky as more debris fell, burning up in the atmosphere.

The girl seemed to assume that he was talking to her when he spoke out loud to Box. After the second day, she began to talk a lot. She talked to Adams. She talked to the beast. She just talked. Adams gathered that her name was Wynn. The beast's name was either Telis or Lane. She seemed to refer to him as both.

And she healed.

The beast called Lane recovered as well. The nanites must have been working. It drank enormous amounts of water. The girl only had a slight fever. He managed to convey to Wynn that she should not scratch, and she somehow communicated that to Lane.

On the second day, they had let the animal outside. It ran full speed into the scorched remains of the forest.

"Tony," Box said, "I think she is speaking a heavily accented and colloquial version of English. If this is true, with time, I can begin to translate via your personal Heads Up Display. With your help, I may be able to engage her to do a vocabulary session."

Tony was sitting in the command chair and said, "Wynn, come here." She seemed to understand the word 'come,' much as a dog would. She climbed up and sat on the wide armrest of the massive chair. Tony was amused when she handed him an oatmeal protein bar. She had one as well. She loved them.

An image of the Chief displayed on the screen. He pointed and said, "Tony."

She pointed to him and said, "Tony."

The image changed to a still of the beast. Tony said, "Telis."

She said, "Lane." She pointed to herself and said, "Wynn," without prompting.

The image changed to one of fire. She said a single word, then "rain" and "trees" and "water," and it went on like that for a long time. It was like a wondrous game for her.

"Box, how do you think she would react to an Avatar? It might make things easier. If we pick one that is gentle, female, soft-spoken?" Adams asked.

In his personal HUD, Box showed him an attractive woman wearing the same type of homespun dress that the girl had been in when he found her, minus the char and damage.

Wynn was wearing a man's T-shirt from stores now. She seemed to love it. It hung down below her knees. She was so tiny.

As they spoke, Lane reappeared from the char of the forest. He held a deer in his jaws, dragging it back to the pod. Wynn shot down the ladder and was literally hopping up and down. She wanted the door opened so badly.

Lane was waiting for her when the ramp was completely down, with the deer as an offering.

✶✶✶

"She is requesting a knife. A sharp one." Box translated in his HUD-like subtitles.

Adams drew out his belt knife and handed it to her, saying, "Careful. Sharp."

She looked at the blade critically. It was black and indestructible. The edge was just a few microns thick. It was sharper than any steel blade ever made. She was quick with it.

She did an odd kind of butchery. First, she split the deer's hide along the length of its spine and quickly extracted long, thick sections of meat from either side of its backbone. She handed these to Adams and moved on to one of the rear legs. Starting at the lowest joint, she peeled the hide back until the haunch was skinned and the meat exposed. She expertly removed the entire leg at the pelvic joint.

Lane sat nearby all the while, scanning the area in all directions. Wynn had communicated that Lane was a "he" and that he was a Telis Raptor. The species name, Adams presumed.

Wynn stood and lifted the haunch of meat to her shoulder. She stepped back and paused, saying, "Lane." The beast looked at her face at full attention. Its lips drew back in a parody of a horrific smile. Its long fangs reminded Adams of a saber-tooth tiger's.

It waited.

She clicked her tongue, and the beast tore into the deer. Savage ripping of flesh followed. It gorged itself on the guts, meat, and bones. In short order, there was only some hide, hooves, and the skull left. Adams had not realized just how savage the beast was until then.

Turning back up the ramp with a satisfied smile, Wynn began speaking quickly again. In the tiny galley kitchen, she placed the meat in the sink and began washing it. He knew as she talked she was demanding something.

"Box, help me out here," Adams said.

"She seems to be requesting a container of some kind for the meat."

Adams opened a cabinet and took out a large pot. She grabbed it from him, and as she finished washing each piece, she placed it in the pot. The single hoof comically stuck out the top. She set the pot in the refrigerator.

Wynn washed her hands quickly as she continued to talk fast. "Tony, I think she is going to collect wild onions and some sort of root. She is also asking for her own knife and belt," Box translated with 80% certainty.

He collected another knife out of stores and looked for a belt in the lockers when she was suddenly at his side handing him his freshly cleaned knife back. He traded it for the other sheathed one. Without asking, she reached into the locker and grabbed a belt before he could pick one. She threaded the sheath onto it and then wrapped it around her waist three times before buckling it.

She waved to him over her shoulder as she descended the ramp calling for Lane. As Adams watched, she jogged quickly toward what remained of the forest, with Lane running alongside. Her heavy boots left clear tracks in the ashes of the clearing. Adams wondered about her family for the hundredth time as she disappeared into the charred skeletons of trees that were still standing. She looked like she knew where she was going.

"Box, keep an eye out for them. Close it up." Adams turned away as the hatch slid closed.

***

He took a shower, put on a fresh set of clothes, and managed to eat only a protein bar.

He climbed the ladder to the dome level. Box had the external view turned on. It was as if Adams were on a round platform about four meters from the ground. He walked in a circle around the command chair and console in the center. The late afternoon sun shone brightly on the fire's devastation. The landscape was black and gray in every direction.

"It has a kind of beauty," Box said. Her computer-generated avatar had appeared. It seemed like she was standing on a ledge just on the other side of the dome, her hand clasped behind her back. She stood at parade rest. She wore a standard security team flight suit. Her ginger hair was longer than shoulder length and moved gently in the breeze. Looking over her shoulder, she said, "We should move the pod." Adams said nothing.

"We are far too exposed here." She looked again out over the vista as Adams sat heavily in the chair. He pounded a button on the extreme right, and the entire console receded into the floor.

A flock of birds flew by overhead. They looked like geese. He didn't know for sure. It occurred to him then that he had never seen a real one.

He drew out his Glock and set it on top of his right thigh.

Box remained quiet but present. She changed her position now and then. Always looking out. Always in his field of view.

Sundown came early, and it was spectacular. He thought the smoke might have contributed.

He fell asleep.

His chin was on his chest. He snored lightly as Box watched over him. The twilight deepened, and it became full dark with a sky full of bright stars. The moon rose and was brilliant. Even over the charred vista, it was dazzling.

Adams slept as Box kept a silent vigil. There was no sign of Wynn.

***

The sun was just rising over the forest-covered mountains in the east when Adams began to stir. He raised his head as if he had been asleep for only a moment.

"Box, any sign of her?" Adams asked quietly.

The command chair faced directly south according to the augmented reality annotations on the dome. Box was standing on the ledge to Adams' right, the sun and the breeze on her face. He stared at her red hair as it drifted in the breeze. He marveled at the beauty, detail, and complexity of the simulation. He felt empty inside. He denied all except this very moment.

His hand came to rest on the Glock.

"Tony…" Box turned her head toward him, and the breeze blew the hair from her face.

"Yes, Box."

"I am so very sorry for your… loss." Her voice cracked.

When Tony looked up, she had her hand over her mouth like she was trying not to cry. His reaction was explosive.

He threw the Glock at her, screaming, "Don't you do that! Don't you dare." He was on his feet, storming up to her even before the gun had stopped clattering on the floor, "YOU were supposed to keep them SAFE! It was your primary function, and you FAILED!"

He stopped in front of her. Her face was in her hands as her shoulders shook. His rant continued, "I know we are in Survival Mode. I understand the protocols in Hostile

Environments. Do not try to manipulate me. I feel their deaths. I must bear them! Don't mock me or disgrace them!"

His face was red as he screamed, "You have only one job left. Don't muck it up."

Slowly Box raised her head. She whispered, "You think this is pretending? An attempt to manipulate you? I wish. Do you think I don't know that I was programmed to have empathy? You think I don't know that I was made to feel this? Because I do. Forced to feel the horror of it by brilliant men and women who thought that if I loved every man, woman, and child on the *Ventura*, I would do anything to protect them." Box was standing straight now, defiant. "Damn them for making me feel this, and survive… None of them thought of what it would be like when this happened. After it happened."

Box turned away then, drying her eyes on a sleeve as she walked ninety degrees around the dome.

Tony watched her go as his anger dissipated. He had just glanced down at the Glock when Box called to him.

"Tony, they're back!" There was hope in her voice now. She was looking at him but pointing to the north. Wynn was there, jogging along at a comfortable pace with Lane beside her. He could see the cloud of her breath vividly in the sunlight on the cold autumn morning.

She wore fresh clothes and a cloak, and she was smiling.

Adams turned from the tiny figures in the distance as he walked up to the image of Box and looked into her virtual eyes.

"I'm sorry, Box. I am. Truly. We need to do something. Not just sit here. The weight of it is… Let's find out what happened. Let's secure the pod. Because… if we have a long haul ahead…"

"Thank you, Chief," Box whispered.

"For what?" Adams asked.

"For not dismissing me as just a machine." Box averted her eyes then. She looked at Wynn in the distance.

There was a long pause.

"Box, I want you to care for me that much, and now her." He gestured with his chin towards Wynn.

Adams turned and was down the ladder with practiced ease. The hatch was already open, and the ramp was descending. He waited for them in the middle of the ramp. He could see her smile from a hundred meters away.

She surprised him.

Wynn ran up the ramp and threw her arms around his neck in a ferocious hug. Thrown back on his heels, he almost didn't catch her. She was so light and so small. His moment's surprised delay didn't matter.

"Keeper Adams. Come," Wynn said as she released him. Their noses were inches apart. She wanted to know if he understood.

Box spoke in his mind, *Tony, look at her clothes. She has been somewhere we should investigate.*

"Yes." That was all Adams said, drawing an instant whoop from the girl as she wriggled out of his grasp. She began to pull him down the ramp by the hand.

Lane watched all this with curious, intelligent eyes.

"Wait. Let me get my things." He was pointing over his shoulder with his thumb. She stopped tugging, understanding his meaning. She hesitated for only a moment, then ran ahead of him into the pod.

She whistled, and Lane trotted right in. Adams saw them both disappear into the bathroom, but only Wynn came right out. She started to put protein bars from the kitchen in a small brown satchel she had with her now, under her cloak.

Adams walked in to get his gear and walked past the bathroom to see Lane drinking thirstily from the toilet.

Shaking his head, he got his tactical vest and pack from a locker and put them on, then retrieved his suppressed AR. Absently he checked his holster for his Glock. It was there and secured. He didn't remember recovering it.

Two minutes later, they were down the ramp and away.

He had missed her voice, even if he could not understand her words. It reminded him of birdsong.

***

Adams realized two hours later, as they crossed an area that was still green, that they were on an actual path, moving north. Not quite a road, though Wynn could follow it, even in the most heavily burned areas.

His gear included a Fly, a small surveillance drone that was integrated with his Heads Up Display. It patrolled around them and could function as a secure comm relay to the pod and Box. The Fly revealed an elevated survey that the strip of land was about a kilometer across with lakes on each side.

It was burned almost entirely flat.

After the third hour, they had been climbing up toward a ridge, elevation increasing. It was very steep, and Adams looked up at it with the expression of someone that doesn't like to climb.

Lane ran ahead.

Everything here was burned to cinders. Winds from behind them would have blown the fire up the hills all the faster. The rain had since washed the ash away, and the path was passable and easy to see.

Walking now among large broken boulders, he became wary. This was the perfect place for a trap. The rocks were all taller than his head, cutting off his line of sight.

Box whispered in his mind. *Tony, something isn't right. Lane has disappeared. It has gotten too quiet. Even the birds have hushed here.*

Adams ordered the Fly to be returned and follow them from above. A small window opened in his HUD, showing the Fly's point of view. It was rapidly descending and coming upon them from the rear.

It was almost too late.

If not for the Fly, Adams would have mistaken the new Telis Raptor for Wynn's pet, Lane. But Lane could be identified from above, on the path ahead, facing off with a larger Telis. Lane was easy to identify from the asymmetrical scorching of his mane.

Adams activated automated targeting and red-flagged eight of the beasts crouched in the boulders around them. Then, he manually changed Wynn and Lane to the designation *'Friendly'* just as the first Telis attacked.

With the ease of practice, he brought his rifle to bear. He fired and was on to the next target before the first beast's dead body had even crashed to the ground mid-lunge.

"Run!" he called to Wynn. She didn't question or hesitate. She ran. It only took a few moments before they were standing behind Lane. Tony's rifle barked and cycled. The huge Telis facing Lane fell with a bullet through the eye into its brain.

On his HUD, he could see them coming from behind like the flood from a broken dam. He turned, and his gun began dropping them as he slowly walked backward. The beasts kept on coming, right over the bodies of their pack mates. Eleven of them lay dead, nearly choking the path between the rocks.

Then he was hit.

There had been an overhang in the rocks that concealed a Telis directly to his left. As he was backing up the path, the beast had struck him hard on his left forearm with its cruel tail spike, so hard that he was knocked to the right and almost dropped the rifle. His arm was laid open to the bone in a deep gash from wrist to elbow.

Before Tony could draw his Glock or the Telis could strike again, Lane crashed into it, clamping his jaws around its neck. Lane's tail hit the other Telis in the ribs over and over, stabbing deep each time until it no longer moved.

Tony pressed his right hand as best he could to close the wound. He didn't feel it yet, but knowing what arterial spray was, he knew it was bad. He had med supplies in his pack, but they would do him no good if more of those things came.

"Box, I need a secure spot to fix this," Adams said as he examined the gash. It was a mistake.

Wynn was suddenly pulling him up the trail to a shelf that backed against the sheer face of the wall above. She pushed him to sit. Without a word, she forced him down as she untied her simple cord belt. She wrapped it around his upper arm and using a green branch, she had quickly cut to length, and she cruelly tightened the makeshift tourniquet around his upper arm.

Quickly and quietly, she cut strips from the hem of her cloak to tightly bandage his arm and fashion him a sling. Lane stood guard just below them.

When she was done, there was no hesitation. She had Tony back on his feet and moving quickly through a great fissure in the cliff face. Lane brought up the rear as they moved.

The gap in the cliff they traveled showed a tiny strip of sky above was getting closer as they walked. Tony kept the Glock in his right hand as he watched ahead. Lane was out of sight behind them when they emerged from the crevasse into another world.

The bluff behind them had stopped the fire. It was lush and green here. In the distance, he could see a vine-covered stone tower. A small inlet from the lake helped create part of the moat around a keep wall surrounding the tower. All was overgrown.

It was less than a kilometer away. He knew then that he could make it.

***

They crossed the mossy bridge as his vision was beginning to tunnel. There was a small door to the right of a massive double door in the Keep's wall. The hinges didn't even squeak as they entered and closed the door behind them.

The cobblestone courtyard had a running fountain in the center. It was artsy but straightforward in its way, with a sphere in the center of the pool covered in glyphs. The water flowed out of a hole in the top center. A broad sill went all the way around it, suitable for sitting. Adams took off his sling and gear and placed it all on the sill before he sat.

He opened the side of the pack and withdrew the trauma kit. He pressed the injector to his thigh, and it filled his veins with ice. It was as if a cold breeze had blown away the fog that caused the tunnel vision.

Wynn was constantly talking now, apparently trying to dissuade him from unwrapping the arm. She helped him in the end. The trauma kit was designed to be used one-handed. He allowed the wound to fall open, then sprayed it full of medicinal nanites. Wynn helped him seal the wound with medical adhesive and clean the arm with individual towelettes that sizzled to the touch and seemed to eat the blood and dirt. He finally sealed it up with a clear med-bandage that he painted on the wound's entire length.

Tony took meds that would quickly stimulate blood production. He was already thirsty. He emptied his canteen and refilled it from the fountain as Wynn watched.

With his left arm throbbing and his fever already climbing, he opened a ration bar and offered it to Wynn. She shook her head at him as she lowered a wooden bucket into the water. Lane walked up as if he knew the drill, and she poured the bucket over him, again and again.

She scrubbed him until all the blood was gone, and she was sure he wasn't injured.

She talked the whole time.

Tony looked around himself. The walls all around were made of massive blocks and went up about ten meters. The wall was about two meters thick, based on the arch where they entered, and there was a walk around the battlements at the top. Everything was covered with vines.

The courtyard was about thirty meters across and overgrown with scrub. All of it was intact but overgrown. The vines and scrub were untouched by the fire.

The tower made up the entire east end of the Keep. The top was about thirty meters higher than the wall. Where the walls met, the tower was the only access to the upper part of the wall.

"Box, are you seeing this?" Tony asked the air.

Yes. Are you thinking what I am thinking?

"Do it. No rush. Conserve all the maneuvering thrusters you can." He said. "I need to sleep."

I will be there by dawn.

Adams discovered that the tower was empty except for dry leaves and cobwebs. Wynn lived here alone and occupied a small kitchen off the side of the smallest building. He would later learn it was the night servant's kitchen.

The Fly patrolled and mapped the Keep. Tony slept.

***

The following day, thirst drove Adams out of the small warm room. His canteen was empty, so he headed to the fountain to refill it. Box had landed the Black Pod so quietly inside the walls that not even Lane had stirred in the predawn. He lay on the floor in front of the fireplace's embers. Wynn was nowhere to be seen.

The Black Pod looked like it belonged there. Like it had always been there. The dome of it sat among the tall grasses and struggling saplings. Its ramp came down neatly to the edge of the cobbles and managed to balance architecturally with the tower at the other end.

Adams drank an entire canteen and then refilled it again.

"Good morning, Box. How are you feeling today?" he said as he walked up the broad staircase to the massive doors at the base of the tower. One of the doors was ajar.

When he entered, the avatar of Box was waiting inside. Adams knew he had to be careful talking to Box this way because he was the only one that could see her via his personal HUD.

"I'm feeling much better. You?" As usual, she stood at parade rest, examining the room.

"The nanites are going to drive me mad with the itching. The fever isn't too bad, though. I've had worse." He looked at his forearm; the sleeve had been cut away.

"This room is really something." Box said, "It's half cathedral and half throne room." It was empty except for a raised dais at the far side with a great stone throne at the top of thirty wide steps. There was no dust and no cobwebs on the intricately carved seat.

Tony climbed the steps and sat.

A light autumn breeze came in through six tall, high windows that faced the dais. The outside wind blew in, and the dry leaves stirred. This room was designed around this chair. He was surprised at how comfortable it was. The biggest fireplace he had ever seen was directly opposite the throne, across the vast room. It had a carved wooden mantle that must have been a meter thick and five meters wide. Massive doors flanked it. The door on the right must have been covered with vines outside. He had not noticed it from the courtyard.

Box waited.

She climbed the stairs and sat on the top step. She also faced the six tall windows. Sun was beginning to peak over the wall and through the windows.

"It'll do." Tony had a new tone in his voice. It was noticeable enough that Box turned her virtual head toward him. The look of confidence on his face showed he knew the road ahead might be long, but he had trained for it.

Just then, as the sun reached him, Wynn entered the room, Lane right behind her. Adams did not say a word as she approached the base of the stairs. She glanced up at him and bowed formally, not setting foot on the steps.

She straightened up and held her head high, looking him straight in the eye. She spoke in English. Clearly and slowly.

"Lord Keeper Adams, the Raptor." It sounded like a pronouncement. She reached around and took off an enormous bag that had been slung over her back, upending it to dump its contents onto the steps.

At first glance, they looked like twelve wickedly curved daggers. She took a single step back and dropped her chin to her chest. Adams realized that they were the tail spikes from the Telis Raptors they had killed the day before as he descended the stairs. Wynn must have gone back and harvested them.

He reached down and lifted the smallest one. It was still longer than a hand's breadth. The spike was incredibly sharp, and the last tail bone made the perfect handle. He lifted her chin with his left hand. She stared at his bruised but healing wound. It was just a scar now.

"Thank you." He handed the tail spike to her. He wouldn't know the significance of the gesture until much later.

***

That winter, his collection of tail spikes increased to twenty-three. The Telis learned to stay away from the Keep after that first year. The Telis were the reason people also stayed away.

The land recovered, and the hunting became better. With Box's help, Tony learned the common tongue, and Wynn learned the high speech.

Each of the tail spikes was boiled clean and polished, and Wynn made a leather wrap for the grip. Each of them was stuck into the underside of the mantel as a trophy. At first, it was just to dry the leather of the grips, but there they stayed.

Box maintained radio silence, waiting for a retrieval signal that never came. Passive sensors saw one other ship get destroyed by the automated defense grid. But that was the last.

There was a war going on, it seemed. Adams remained at his post. They stayed quiet as nuclear bombs destroyed the planets' networks.

***

Years passed, and the world was silent. Refugees found them, bringing tales of mass destruction and chaos on a planet named Baytirus. Pilgrims came. Many stayed if they were brave. They all believed Adams was a Keeper. A kind of spiritual leader.

Adams let them believe it. He would sit on the throne and answer questions. He adjudicated disputes. It was easy with Box. It was a simple life as he waited. They repaired the Keep, planted gardens and orchards, and fields.

He envied their ignorance of the universe.

Lane lived another nineteen years. He became a legend that no one believed, that is until they saw him sleeping at Adams' feet in the throne room. Eventually, he was cremated with every honor that a Keeper would have received. Adams personally tended the fire with Wynn and collected the ashes for burial. It was then that he found Lane's tail spike; it would not burn. It was larger than any in his collection. After that, he carried it with him always, in a sheath Wynn had made for the purpose.

Thirty-two years after Adams' arrival, the entire Keep had glass in all the windows. It was alive again. Vines covered the dome of the Black Pod. Forty-six adults and twenty-one children resided inside the Keep full time. It was clean and beautiful. The once burned flat forest was now dotted with farms and even a small village with a tavern.

Wynn and her husband had four children and eight grandchildren. She was the Keep's real leader and the only one that had ever been inside the dome where Adams lived. She was also the only one who noticed that Lord Adams had not aged a day since they met.

***

"Box, will you please tell Keeper Adams that a guest will arrive in a few minutes. He wears the livery of one of the High Keeper's Trackers." Wynn knew that she could speak directly to Box from anywhere with a line of sight with the vine-covered dome.

By the time the hooded figure entered the Keep, Adams was waiting in the high seat. As he entered the great hall, instead of approaching the dais right away as was the custom, the High Tracker turned his back on Adams to examine the collection of Telis Raptor blades stuck to the mantel.

Box was sitting in her usual spot on the steps just to the right of the throne. "*Be very careful with this one,*" she said to Tony in his HUD.

The man turned his head then and lowered his hood as if he had heard her statement and was responding to it. As the man approached the steps, Adams could see he, too, wore a huge Telis blade.

The man approached and began to climb the stairs—another breach of protocol, to climb the steps without invitation.

"Hello, Caisy. It has been a long time," the man said. Box didn't reply but stood as Tony stood.

Then suddenly, Adams recognized him. They both froze. The man was two steps from the top, but he was still taller than Adams.

"I was about to ask if you were ready to go home?" The man looked from Adams to Box, then over his shoulder at a crowd gathering in the courtyard.

"I think I am home," Adams said quietly.

"I know… Me too." His old friend smiled wide. "I hear you make some fine bourbon here."

INJURING ETERNITY
A SOLSTICE 31 SHORT STORY
MARTIN WILSEY

Injuring Eternity

"I was acting under direct orders from Chancellor Dalton. None of this is my fault. Yes, I lied. I had to lie. The prisoner had to believe we were on Earth and not a moon around Saturn. These weapons we were developing were not allowed on Earth."

--Solstice 31 Incident Investigation Testimony Transcript: Thomas McDonald, Senior Research and Development Engineer, Material Sciences, Artificial Gravity Specialist.

***

Tom McDonald stood on the grav-plate apron just outside the hangar. He hated putting on a pressure suit. He always wanted to take a piss and scratch his nose as soon as it was sealed.

Without it, though, he would not step off the apron that maintained a perfect 1G feel. Some people liked low gravity. Not Tom. Tom hated it. Which was odd, considering he was an expert in Artificial Gravity (AG) technology. The moon of Saturn called Rhea, where the R&D facility was located, had full facility AG. It must have cost a mint.

He turned and looked back at the enormous opening to the hangar behind him. Well, at least it appeared to be open. It was ninety meters wide and thirty meters tall. A band of light traced the opening and marked the line between vacuum and atmosphere. There was a field, ten millimeters thick, of gravity chaos in that wall plain that he could just walk through. The light had nothing to do with the field, though; the light and the field would still be there even if the base lost power.

He had designed it.

He still had no idea how it worked, even though he'd been credited with inventing it.

Today was the final test of his latest project: the G-rail gun. It was an amplified gravity-based directional weapon. It was the most expensive thing he had ever created. Now it was in final testing. Only the full power test remained.

His three assistants called it *Grendel* because it was a monster that could kill a lot of people. The Chancellor liked to call it the *Grail*. Tom was uncomfortable with the name "Grail." It held too many religious connotations.

"All right, you bunch of monkeys, are you ready?" McDonald asked. The techs were in the lab monitoring the test.

"Yes, sir. All systems are standing by," Kristin Vittori replied. She was the team lead. Tom thought about her as he listened to her voice. She was a professional, stone-cold, bitch with no interpersonal skills. It was too bad because she was beautiful in that modern 2G way. Superfit. McDonald couldn't help but remember how great she looked naked. Fortunately, none of the rest of the staff suspected how she'd gotten herself promoted to team lead.

"I'm firing it up," McDonald said as he activated the weapon. It was the same size and same basic shape as a Frange Carbine, but the damn thing weighed more than eleven kilograms when not powered up. The onboard inertial dampeners had the benefit of making it feel weightless when the power was on. The biggest problem was that the higher the power settings, the slower it was to move so that it felt like you were dragging it through wet cement at the upper settings. It fought you.

A change made to the software, however, had seemed to solve this problem. As he selected the firing solution power, nothing changed until he pulled the trigger. The standard Heads Up Display HUD targeting had also been employed to make usage even more effortless.

This same issue made it impossible to use this weapon on the higher settings in a craft in motion near a planetary body big enough to have its own gravity well. In fact, Watkins had been killed when the system tore itself out of the shuttle he was flying. It wasn't recoil. It just stopped dead in space, and the momentum of the ship itself tore it away from the suddenly stationary Grail Cannon. He was another casualty due to rushing.

"Here we go, you chicken shits. Target number one test. Power set to Four of Ten." Tom had to remind them that they had *all* refused to do any full-power tests. The first target was an old surface tractor that they had towed to the Target Range for the purpose.

"Firing." Tom raised the weapon and squeezed the trigger. There was no sound, no recoil, no nothing. The invisible impact struck the tractor just above the driver's side wheel. A perfectly round, basketball-sized hole appeared in the fender, and the entire engine block and front right side exploded out, sending debris all the way to the distant mountainside two kilometers away.

The weapon moved quickly and efficiently to acquire target number two. It was the remains of Watkins' shuttle, parked at the base of a cliff about 0.4 kilometers away.

"Power settings to Six. Firing," he said. Again, no sound, no recoil, not even a vibration, but this time he felt a momentary freeze of the gun in mid-air. It was as if he could have hung there suspended from it.

The entire shuttle disappeared, and in its place, there was suddenly a gaping hole in the cliff face.

"Did you feel that, sir?" Vittori said with a hint of fear in her voice.

"Damn right, I did through my boots. I just punched a ten-meter wide hole in that cliff face. That hole must be twenty-five meters deep. What's left of that shuttle lines the back of that new cave." McDonald laughed as a slow avalanche began falling in Rhea's low gravity.

"Cranking it up to Eight. Send the drone target." A drone, the size of a supply container, hovered into view. Tom knew it was full of rocks and other material, and it had way too many strobes on it. It wasn't tough to see. White was easy to see even this far from the sun.

"Target altitude is 4.2 kilometers," Vittori said.

The targeting software was running and had the drone tagged. He raised the rifle and pulled the trigger. He knew nothing would happen until the targeting software tag was aligned.

The rifle froze in place for a full two seconds. Then the drone just disappeared.

"Holy shit. Did you see that?" McDonald said.

"Sir, the sensors indicate that the drone and all its mass has been reduced to a fine powder. Forty-two metric tons." Vittori was in awe. "Power is down to 30%. I recommend replacing the power cell before the full power test. You would be so dead if Grendel's dampeners failed for lack of power."

McDonald powered the rifle down, knowing she was right. It was consuming power exponentially at the higher settings. The rifle became heavy again when he powered it down, and he let it hang from the sling as he pulled out a fresh power cell magazine. They had cleverly made them the same form factor as the Frange Carbine ammo magazines so that soldiers could carry spares in existing pouches.

Tom slammed in the fresh cell and powered the rifle back up. It became weightless in his hands again.

"Another drone, please. Full power test." McDonald said. He could not keep the fear from his voice.

"Sir, we were thinking," Vittori said in a shaky voice. "If the power pack does not have enough juice to drive the inertial dampener, there could be the potential of massive recoil, or even some kind of catastrophic failure."

McDonald already knew this.

"Sir, please move to the edge of the apron and turn, so the base is not directly behind you or in front of you." Vittori sounded like she was about to cry. "Are you sure you don't want to study the data first?"

He shook his head. They were too far behind schedule.

"Tom, don't shoulder it." It was Matthews who spoke. "I'm suited up and already in the hangar. Use the HUD to target. If it rips your finger off, your smart suit will seal the glove with an automatic compression tourniquet."

"Dammit. Let's do this." Tom walked to the edge of the apron and turned 90 degrees. It was an intelligent precaution. "Adjust the drone path for the new vista, Vittori."

"Yes, sir. Adjusting."

McDonald could see the drone coming around. It was lower this time. He tagged it in his targeting HUD, brought the G-rail to bear on the drone, and pulled the trigger. He wasn't perfectly on target. When he tried to adjust the weapon to be on target, it wouldn't budge. He let off the trigger so he could move it again.

This time, he positioned it so the target would fly into the weapon's path and pulled the trigger. He waited, watching the drone approach the crosshairs.

When the drone crossed into the weapon's sights, the gun fired.

McDonald was knocked from his feet. Not from any recoil, but from the quake in the surface that resulted when the distant mountain peaks were wholly sheared off. The G-rail hung there for two more seconds before falling to the apron. Its power display faced McDonald, reading 6% in red.

He could hear alarms in his comms unit. "Vittori, what's happening?"

"The shockwave cracked the seals on three outer airlocks and an empty residence. We're holding pressure, though…" Vittori sputtered. She was suddenly on the edge of panic, all professionalism having vanished. "Fuck me raw, Tom. The primary long-range QUEST comm array is gone."

"What do you mean, gone? Did we sever a cable?" It was dawning on him as he stood and looked in the direction of the distant communication facility. The entire communications installation had been beyond the drone.

"Oh my God… no real-time comms?" he said.

"Turned to powder, sir." Vittori was collecting herself now.

Matthews stepped up beside McDonald. He had retrieved the G-rail and shut it down. Removing the depleted power pack, he handed it to his stunned boss and said, "Are you all right, Sir?"

McDonald turned to Matthews. "I want that fucking thing in the vault with all the power packs, and then get your ass on a shuttle and assess the damage." He looked back at the hangar opening. "Take Hearn with you. No discussions over the radios. It's all monitored by that god-forsaken AI."

McDonald stepped through the grav-wall into the hangar. Matthews followed reluctantly.

McDonald took off his helmet and scratched his nose. Eyes lowered, he said to Hearn, "I think I just killed Emerson, Tyler, and Garcia at the comms station."

"They were all stupid assholes anyway," Hearn said indifferently as he admired the weapon. "Tyler was a mole for the Chancellor."

***

"Emerson, Tyler, and Garcia are confirmed dead. They all had full-time comm link HUDs, and they all flashed off at the same moment," Vittori said. "Even worse, we have lost the Quantum Entanglement Synchronous Transmitter," The two of them were alone in the control center, and she could not meet McDonald's gaze. "No real-time two-way comms with Earth," She felt responsible.

Good, he thought to himself. He was going to blame her in his report anyway. He looked forward to her efforts to avoid that blame. She was fit, had excellent grooming, and was... durable.

"I want a status report ready for conventional transmission in thirty minutes. I've already sent a burst transmission reporting that we are not dead and that the prisoner is secure. I do NOT want any of the Chancellor's ships in my sky. Is that clear?" He was leaning on her hard.

"Sir… Tom. I'm sorry." She finally looked up. The cold professional scientist was gone. Her eyes welled with unshed tears.

McDonald placed a hand on her shoulder. "I know. We'll sort it all out later. In private." He paused, squeezing her shoulder. "We don't have the bandwidth on the secondary comms, so don't send the raw data, but tell them why we are not sending it. It would take 78 minutes to get there."

"Yes, sir." Vittori was collecting herself.

"Vittori… Kristin. I think we were set up." He pointed his thumb over his shoulder at the base. "I think that son of a bitch knew something like this would happen, and he did nothing to stop it." He could see the lie take hold in her eyes. She had been hoping that somehow it wasn't her fault.

He would "reassure" her later in his quarters. Hard and fast.

***

An hour later, McDonald walked into the prison cell dome.

He was the only one allowed in here. It was a pain in the ass. But it was the only way to keep the prisoner's nature, let alone his existence, a secret.

The entire dome was a simulation of the sky above Detroit. Day and night, in all weather. In the center of the dome was a structure that McDonald thought of as an elaborate movie set. It didn't look like much on the outside, but it didn't need to. He entered the façade and walked down a long corridor that made it appear he was in a dirty warehouse.

The door slid open, and he entered a large room that resembled the inside of a warehouse. Subtle clues everywhere indicated that it was in Detroit.

High dirty windows provided filtered light as McDonald proceeded to the center, where there was a huge clear box enclosing an area seven meters on a side. Industrial lighting hung from the ceiling above the cell.

There was a man in the box.

A thin mattress and a neatly made bed lay on an elevated section. Opposite, a tabletop was attached to the wall, beside a stump of a stool that rose from the floor. In one corner, there was a basic toilet and sink. The entire thing hovered above the floor on three clear legs.

McDonald climbed onto the visitor's platform that was near, but not touching, the cell. He pounded a button on a console there, and the freestanding screen that showed stupid sitcoms all day went dark. Another button activated the intercom, and Tom wasted no time in punching it.

"You fucking knew this would happen. People died, you bastard." McDonald maintained control with effort.

"But it worked. Perfectly. Didn't it? I felt it." The prisoner looked over at McDonald. "How's the wife?"

"She's sure as hell not going to be happy about all the overtime I'm going to have to put in as a result of this fuck up." McDonald sounded like he might be about to lose it. "As if the goddamn commute from Boston to this shit-hole wasn't bad enough.

"You will tell me how to fix the G-rail spread, or I swear to the Dali-fucking-Lama that I will keep you in the dark and not feed you for six months again. No clean clothes, no water, no vids, no food, and no heat. You will love the winter here." McDonald was growling by the end. "Maybe a new bullet hole every day for goddam good measure!"

"Okay, okay… relax. We are almost done. Bring the design up on the big screen." He turned towards the black screen.

"Don't you tell me to relax," McDonald growled as he activated the monitor and brought up the design schematic. "You bastard."

"Remember the version 9.3 that we scrapped. Bring that one up." The prisoner waited patiently as McDonald brought it up.

"There. Why? That design was a nonstarter. No way to house the dampeners." McDonald remembered. It had only been two years ago.

"Look at the emitters – just the business end of the muzzle. They adjusted based on the power settings. Is any of this coming back?" He was so smug about it. McDonald could already see how it could work, automatically as well as manually. It would focus the G-rail emission.

"Why didn't you tell me this before, asshole?" He spat.

"Now you can see their usefulness as remote fixed-position emplacements." He turned to McDonald and stood to move directly to the wall of his cell. "I bet it wouldn't even fire without a fresh power cell at full power. You now know that, as a rapid target acquisition rifle, the max power setting should be a two or three at most. Say emergency power as high as a four if you are going after armored vehicles or buildings. At two, it will take out any armor with ease and last for 300 shots."

"What are you leaving out? I know you're leaving out something, so give it up now, or I swear it'll be cold and dark in here by nightfall." McDonald was dead serious. The prisoner could tell.

"Never fire one of these in the atmosphere above power setting Two. The sound volume and concussion would be... a problem." He said it like he was giving away a secret. "And never from a moving ship in a gravity well."

Too late, asshole.

***

A new QUEST comms unit arrived four hours later. It must have been seized from a base on Saturn somewhere by the soldiers that delivered it.

"Chancellor, he has no idea we know who and what he is." McDonald paused. "And what he is capable of." He swallowed hard. "Temporal physics is not my best field, but he still lets things slip. He can only see the future that happens before him, in his field of view. It is possible to deceive him. The best example is how he lets things slip about my wife. Things he couldn't know. Because they are lies."

"Oh? Tell me." He thought as he sat. He was not looking into the camera.

"We can, in fact, lie to him. But only if he never finds out the truth in the future. I have not seen my wife for nearly two years -- the entire time I have been on Rhea. He has no idea how I really feel. It's been the best two years of my life." McDonald needed sleep badly, and he forgot himself for a minute. "She is such a cow and a shrew." He shook his head to clear it. "The point is, the prisoner has only 'predicted' the lies I have fed him. Or will feed him."

"You have done an excellent job, Tom. I may take care of that little problem for you as a bit of a bonus."

***

Vittori was incredibly grateful that she had not been thrown under the bus. Very. Grateful.

It was trivial to make the modifications. The final prototype was recalibrated with the new lower power maximum. The new automatic Choke worked perfectly. It could even be overridden so you could intentionally create a wide field of mayhem.

The Chancellor of Earth ordered him to bring the prototype and the final design for the fabricators to him personally.

It was an eight-day trip back to Earth if he didn't spare the fuel. He would be home just in time for Christmas.

ETA, December 24, 2631.

It was three days after the Solstice 31 Incident. Upon arriving, he was forced to dock at Freedom Station or be shot down. It was there that he discovered that the Chancellor of Earth had been assassinated by the very same man who had killed 115 million innocent people. He also learned Rhea base was gone by then as well. Something had gone horribly wrong there.

Everyone thought he was dead.

He paid cash for a locker on the station. Now he understood why these people liked their freedom and privacy so much. He locked up the rifle and the Rhea AI module he carried and went in search of the nearest bar.

He needed a drink.

Oklahoma Salvage

A Solstice 31 Short Story

Martin Wilsey

Oklahoma Salvage

"We had no idea we had prevented more deaths. We were just trying to get by in this godforsaken desert. Now let me get back to work."

-- Solstice 31 Incident Investigation Testimony Transcript: Harvey Reardon, Owner/Operator of Oklahoma Salvage, formerly known as Reardon and Sons. He was questioned regarding the origin of $220,000 in gold found in his possession.

***

Harvey Reardon recognized the sound in the distance of an old 18-wheeler even before the perimeter security drones notified him via Heads-Up Display (HUD).

He got up from where he was lying on the ground under an old PT-137 Quad shuttle and dusted himself off. He lowered his shades, the ones that were more like goggles, and started walking back to the shop. He was rolling the stiffness out of his shoulders and grumbled as he walked.

"I'm too old for this shit…" he mumbled. It was then he realized that he had lost his hat again. "Bloody hell." In the fifteen minutes it would take him to walk back to get it, that cursed desert sun would turn his bald head beet red. Alex would be furious with him.

He paused and tugged at his white beard for a moment as he considered turning back. He had already walked past a few hundred planes, copters, and shuttle fuselages.

As he watched, his hat blew across the road in the distance, taking flight in the dry desert wind. "Oh, for sewer's sake," he cursed and kept going. Grease and dust were all over his coveralls, almost completely obscuring the lettering on the back: "Reardon and Sons – Salvage, Restoration, Sales, and Service." It was called Oklahoma Salvage now. There was a new sign out by the highway to prove it. The new patch over his right front pocket was not as sun-faded as the lettering on his back, and all it said was "Harv."

As he entered the back door of the main building, he dropped the aluminum panel he had been using to shade his cranium to keep it from burning. He walked through his office, directly into the storefront behind the counter of the former diner.

"You lost your hat again," Alexandra Reardon said without looking up at her great-grandfather. She was annoyed.

"How the hell do you know that?" Harv asked in his best crotchety-old-man voice. He slapped more dust off his coveralls. He knew she hated it when he did that in there. And she knew he knew.

The sales counter was covered with electronic components, tools, and test gear. "What's all this?" asked Harvey. When she didn't answer right away, he glanced her way and drew in a breath. "We have customers coming, and you're wearing that?!" She wore an old, black midriff T-shirt with the sleeves cut off, cut-off jean short-shorts, and Chinese wooden flip-flops.

She ignored him.

"Hunter told me already. It's just Wendy. She's coming for another catapult shipping container. Have you got one ready?" She already knew that he did. Hunter was the name of the yard's Artificial Intelligence system, and it knew what was ready.

"I have eleven ready! You should get off your ass and sell them, dammit. We are a bit light on funds just now, thanks to all that shit Mark bought at auction last month."

The truck could be seen turning in from the road, raising a cloud of dust as soon as it left the pavement.

"So what *is* all this?" He picked up a small device he didn't recognize. It had dozens of wires hanging from it, and it obviously had power because blue LEDs pulsed on the main body of the tiny thing.

"I was hoping that I could put together a Quantum Entanglement Communications Transceiver from these ten busted ones. Hunter says it might work," Alex said as she touched one contact after another while watching for indications on one of the displays in front of her. She sat on an old bar stool behind the counter, just where the old cash register used to be. She had sold that register to a collector for over six thousand dollars.

All the original barstools were still there on the other side of the counter. The stools, a few glass cases, and the bell on the door were all that remained of the old diner on the inside. Outside, there was the faded sign that said "EAT" in dull, sand-blasted letters. The booths under the windows had been replaced with racks that held various parts and tools for sale. It was the same behind the counter. Where the stove, grill, chillers, and exhaust hoods had once been, now some shelves held all manner of used parts removed from salvaged ships, shuttles, and planes. Dust covered everything.

The bell rang, and Wendy entered with a smile.

"Hello, darlin'," she chirped as Alex looked up. "How you doin'?" She had a thick Texas accent, and Alex knew it was an affectation. Wendy was incredibly intelligent, even though she tried to hide it.

Harv stared at her ample bosom. She was wearing a low-cut halter top with a Navajo design that had been all the fashion twenty years ago. Jeans and cowboy boots completed the look. They knew she had a Stetson in the truck.

"Why don't you call ahead so I can be ready, dammit." Harv walked up to the dusty window and saw she was driving a double. Two trailers behind the massive truck.

"The same reason I drive way the hell out here to get them, old man. Discretion. But you know that, and you just enjoy belly achin', Harv." Wendy said, amused.

"What'll it be this month, Wendy?" Alex said, "We have eleven containers that are catapult-ready. All grav-plates tested and guaranteed. Five are basic Delta ore containers; three are standard C-19s, sealed without life support but will hold pressure under hard use. The last three are Alpha boxes and have full inertial dampening, internal gravity, and they're pressure tested and insulated. One of those Alphas is an A-11 and even has basic manual navigation control inside and is great for docking in outer space at the station without a tug. "

Alex hadn't even brought them up on the system.

"Let me have the A-11 and one of the C-19s. Are they painted the same?" Wendy asked as she dug into her back pocket for a large wad of cash.

Harv replied, "Sandblasted and painted. However, they won't look new anymore from sittin' out there. No tracking numbers painted on; no trackers installed. If you want me to do it, you'll have to wait about an hour. Want to see 'em?"

"Nope. I'm good. Just load 'em up." Wendy said.

"That's $3,000 for the C-19 and $12,000 for A-11. The A-11 has only a seat in the pilot booth. Empty otherwise," Alex told her as Harv went out to the yard.

Without haggling, Wendy counted out the cash. That told Alex that it was a no-questions-asked, straw man purchase, and she was passing the profit to Oklahoma Salvage for future preferential treatment.

"That's fine." Wendy smiled. "Any luck with the other thing?"

"Not yet," Alex said. Wendy had a standing order for some fuel-grade plutonium. They sometimes salvaged derelicts that had fuel remaining in the reactors if they got to it soon enough. Wendy just nodded. She had to ask because that info would never be communicated on any public Net for the same reason as the containers.

"Need anything else today?" Alex folded the bills and stashed them in her bra.

"Actually, there is one more thing," she said, pulling a rabbit foot out of her pocket and handing it to Alex.

Alex twisted and clicked the foot, and a memory stick was revealed, stored inside. Her stool was on wheels, and she launched herself along the counter to a terminal at the end. She slid the memory stick into the port, and a schematic came up that was the input file for a fabrication unit. Very few people knew Harv had one. Alex raised an eyebrow at the part but said only, "Do you want to pay now or when you pick it up? Either way is cool."

"Now is fine." Wendy still had a considerable wad of cash in her hand.

"Is this for you? Personal, I mean?" Alex asked. It was an upper receiver for a 10mm cannon. Illegal in most territories.

Wendy said nothing.

"I will take care of it personally. Harv doesn't need to know."

"Thanks," Wendy said, as the clicking sound of the first container settling into the clamps on the trailer made them look.

Harv's container tug had the entire top cut away. The pilot seat jutted from the tug's rear so he could watch the container as he clamped on. It had no roll cage, no AI control, and no seatbelts.

It was a death trap. A fun, fun death trap.

In short order, the second container was also loaded. From the tug, Harv could hear the clamps grab it.

Harv set the tug down in the parking lot and jumped out quickly as Wendy was inspecting the clamps. She watched him jog up. This worried her. He never ran anywhere.

"Wendy, there is a truck coming. The drones spotted it way out." Harv looked serious and rested a hand on her shoulder, "It looks like a military transport."

Wendy gave him a quick hug and a kiss on the cheek.

"Thanks, Harv," Wendy said with a hand still touching his face. "I owe you one." She ran for her rig and was moving in a matter of seconds. She drove south, away from the truck that was coming. The winding path through the salvage yard obscured her departure in no time.

Harv watched in his HUD the image of the truck as it slowed and entered the canyon of his salvage yard, passing the sign: "Twenty Square Kilometers of Junk. Or Treasure." The number 20 had been sloppily spray painted to replace a crossed-out number 10.

The truck was a modern T-16 ground transport. No wheels. It had fixed position Grav-foils for float and steering, with an open three-meter-long flatbed with crates tied down in the back covered with a camo tarp. It was the same desert-tan with camo as most military transports these days. The cab could hold four, but there was only one inside. His security system, with Hunter's help, informed him it was registered as a civilian transport registered to a David Keener.

Harv went back inside. Though it was still sunny, the temp was dropping.

***

Noiselessly, the driver of the truck parked in front of the shop. Even though it had Grav-plates and no wheels, it kicked up a giant cloud of dust as it powered down and settled to the ground.

Alex watched casually from behind the diner's dusty windows, knowing that the man behind the wheel could not see her through the tinted, mirrored glass. He hopped out and walked around the truck, checking the tie-downs on the load. He was lean, fit, and on the tall side. He wore jeans, cowboy boots, an untucked flannel shirt, and a straw cowboy hat that had seen better days. The truck had a Texas ident code. But the man didn't need one. Unlike most of the people that came in here, none of his mannerisms were an affectation.

He took off the hat and tossed it into the cab of the truck. He ran both of his hands through his hair in a futile attempt to eliminate the hat's impression. Alex thought he needed a haircut.

As he approached the door, Alex suddenly felt like she needed a haircut as well.

The bell rang as the door opened.

"Morning," Alex said as the door closed behind him, and the bell rang again.

"Good morning, ma'am. May I use your bathroom straight up? Otherwise, I'll be dancin the whole time we talk." He made a polite bow with his greeting.

Alex smiled at him. "Only if you never call me 'ma'am' again. It's Alex." Pointing down the hall, she said, "All the way down there to the left."

"Thank you, m… Alex."

While he was in there, she looked out the window and studied his truck. The T-16s were old by now, but this one was in perfect condition. She had always wanted one but had never had the spare cash. And where would you find one these days? When parked, the bed of the truck was only ten centimeters off the ground. Perfect for use around here. And they had AI remote control capabilities. It would make Hunter way more useful. Not to mention that a T-16 could go anywhere. Well, anywhere she wanted to go.

She caught herself combing her fingers through her own black hair. She combed it off the side that she kept shaved so that the tattoo could be seen on the side of her head. The tattoo was a fireball at her temple, with trailing fire arcing over her ear. Up close, you could see its amazingly subtle details and recognize it as an exploding Planet Defense Force fighter.

A few minutes later, the man came out. His face was freshly scrubbed, and his hair damp from a thorough cleaning up.

"Ahh. Much better. Thanks," he said as he rounded the counter on the far end.

"Thirsty?" Alex asked as she hopped down from the stool and hammered a fist on an ancient vending machine button. A bottle of Orange Crush rolled out. Alex held it up so he could see.

"Oh, my Maker. I haven't seen one of those since I was a kid. Thank you," he said.

She opened it on the bottle opener and handed it to him, then pounded the machine again for herself.

She opened her bottle too, and they enjoyed a moment of silence as they both drank.

"Harv keeps them extra cold. These are his favorite," she said, looking down at the label, then setting the bottle down and sitting again. "How can I help you today?"

"Do you mean Harvey Reardon? If so, I am in the right place. I have to say, the directions I was given were bad. Nothing in this region is mapped right anymore. I had to get close, then zoom out with a self-locater hack in the truck. Once I did that, the place was easy to spot from cams on Freedom Station." Alex raised an eyebrow. She had not thought of that angle and made a mental note to investigate it. The space station called Freedom was taking a higher interest in the planet recently.

The man paused a moment and looked abashed. "Oh, I'm Dave. Dave Keener." He held out his hand to shake. Even though the gesture was way out of fashion because of irrational pandemic fears, she shook it firmly.

"So, what are you looking for today?" Alex asked.

"It's a long shot." It was almost like a confession. "I'm looking for a shuttle. It doesn't have to be pretty. Just a good tight seal and big enough to fit my T-16. Manual flight controls are fine, but if it has a standard AI interface, that would be a plus." He looked out the windows at the assorted derelicts and sighed, "I know a shuttle is a long shot."

Smiling to herself, she thought, *I might have to close early.*

"I need to get Harv to help you. He doesn't keep that kind of inventory on hand. Just parts." She reached over to press a button on her console and said, "Hey, Harv. Can you come up front to help this customer?"

Harv's disembodied voice replied, "Let me finish taking a shit, and I'll be up." She rolled her eyes, and before she could respond, he said, "Yes, I'll wash my hands, dammit."

Dave smiled and said nothing.

"Quite the place you have here. How long have you been here?" he asked conversationally. Everyone asked that.

"My whole life. I was born here. My dad too. The place has been in the family for generations. My cousin Mark is the buyer, auctions mostly. Harv is my great-gramp." She smiled and leaned in, "Don't tell him I told you. He still thinks he's thirty."

They heard a crash in the back and a series of mumbled curses, followed by some more minor crashes and more cursing. A couple of moments of silence went by as they both stared at the door, smiling.

Harv came directly out from behind the counter, extending his hand. "Howdy. I'm Harv Reardon." The two men shook hands without a moment's hesitation. "I hope Alex hasn't pissed you off already. That's usually why I get called up here."

Alex hammered the soda machine again and opened an Orange Crush for Harv. He took it from her with a nod and took a long pull as Dave spoke.

"Like I was telling Alex, I am looking for a shuttle with a good seal."

Harv interrupted him before he could go any farther. "What's your budget? Availability is all about the budget."

Dave coughed a little and averted his eyes. "I was hoping we could keep this a cash transaction."

Harv raised an eyebrow and looked over at Alex. She said, "He needs one big enough to hold the T-16 out there. Manual flight controls, but future upgrade capable."

"Gonna start private hauling to Freedom Station? Luna, maybe?" Harv asked.

"Maybe even system-wide, depending on what we can work out," Dave said.

"Cash only?" Alex asked.

"Look, I heard you were straight up. Trustworthy." He looked out the window again. "You should know people out there kinda know your inventory. They are making coin just trading on the info. They said cash and my own fuel would get me the best deal."

"Don't tell people that, boy. A good way to get yourself kilt," Harv said as he drained the bottle and set the empty on the counter, heading for the door. "Let's go have a look." Dave followed suit.

Alex called after them, "Harv, your hat!"

***

Harv kept an open channel with Alex as he and Dave tooled around in an ancient golf cart. Hunter followed with a small remote-controlled drone.

Conventional fuel shuttles were quickly eliminated as an option. Keener wanted to be able to traffic the whole system out to the asteroid belt. Harv finally dragged the critical bit of info out of him.

"Yes, I have reactor-based shuttles and priced cheap," Harv said, "No one buys the damn things because of fuel shortages and handling issues. I've got a few that fit the bill. One in that range might be light-speed capable. I don't know for sure, though. I never had the plutonium to try it. Bloody hell, boy. You got cash *and* plutonium on that rig?" Harv shook his head as they rolled up to the shuttle.

It had seen better days. It had front-end collision damage, and sand had drifted and buried one whole side.

"Isn't this an MP-82 Tug? Why the hell is it painted white?" Dave asked as he stepped out of the golf cart.

"Before you get all excited, you gotta know a couple of things, good and bad," Harv spoke without leaving the cart. "I don't know if it still has good seals. The primary O2 tanks are gone. The front is fucked and will not be un-fucked by me. It still has grav-plates, but they are gen one top-foil, gull-wing types, and if one of them needs replacing, it will cost you more than the rest of the ship."

"OK, so far," Dave said.

"It has a Ball-Reactor but no fuel. None. Bone dry."

"OK."

"Batteries are dead. Deader than a doornail. All the comms gear is gone, but I'm sure Alex has some around here that'll meet regs for legit use."

"The T-16 will fit if the bay is stock," Dave said.

"It's stock alright. Mostly empty. Two of the four seats are gone. There are no living quarters. None. I don't know if the head is functional."

"Open her up and let's have a look," Dave said.

"And the worst news. I will need $30,000 in cash. Price is firm. Plus whatever it costs to get her flying."

"Do I get a discount for gold? Is gold alright?" Dave said. "How is it white? I thought it was impossible to paint these things."

Harv's eyes had widened when he'd mentioned gold, but he didn't miss a beat as he got out of the cart. "After the war, we had all these scary-lookin' black ships made out of Polycarbon that the chicken-shit public hated." Harv was dragging cables from a generator out of the back of the cart and then opened a panel on the side of the Tug. "The trick was they didn't use paint. It's a kind of molten glass coating. They found out too late that it would stick, but it would also melt off on high-speed atmo re-entry."

As Harv plugged in the cable, the panel lit up. Harv's fingers flashed over the keys, and in a minute, the center back hatch swung inward. "The aft container docking clamps are gone. Can't tug nothing. Come on in quick -- gotta keep the goddam dust out. Wreaks havoc on the CO2 scrubbers."

Dave ducked his head and stepped in, and Harv closed the hatch as the lights started to come up.

Dave turned back and looked at the hatch. It was in the center of the bay's back wall and would be part of the floor with the ramp lowered. The T-16 would fit in here, but only sideways, and you'd have to climb over it to get around it.

The place was a mess. Cable trunks hung from the ceiling, and trashed panels from the exterior damage were in piles. The cockpit area was no better. Floor panels had been removed; empty equipment racks lay strewn about. Everything was dirty and covered in dust.

"What went there?" Dave pointed at two major racks, empty except for knots of cables.

"Comms went there," Harv said. "And an AI refit was once done there. And no, I got no AIs for sale. If I had, you couldn't afford it for cash. That truck ain't big enough to hold that much gold."

"Not interested in buying an AI. Comms gear and a working head on the other hand…" Dave moved some floor plates leaning on the wall to get to a tiny door behind them. "At least it's a Zero-G toilet," he looked again at the floor plates. "No grav-plating?"

Harv just laughed. "It does have inertial dampeners. And no, I have no idea if they work."

"Ball-reactors require 7-centimeter pellets of plutonium. That may be a problem," Dave said as he opened the containment unit once the light went green.

"If you got Plutonium 238, I could convert it to the right size. That might work. For a fee," Harv said.

"What was lost with the nose?" Dave looked out the cockpit window. The cockpit was all the way to the left.

"Water storage, long-range comm antennas, docking thrusters, and the forward airlock. I can't replace any of that; this is the only Multi-Purpose-82 in the yard. Alex could call around, though. May be easier to fabricate one if we can find the specs. That would seriously cost you, though. But it can fly without all that, and we could always add it later if you want."

"Harv, if the Grav-Foils work, I think we have a deal." He held his hand out to shake. "Do you mind if I camp here a couple of weeks while I refit? Provided the AC works." Harv took Dave's hand in a firm grip, "Not at all as long as you don't bother Alex. She *will* kill you if you piss her off." Harv grew serious now. "I will also need payment in advance before I let you take a screwdriver to anything."

"Understood."

Dave helped Harv off-load the generator from the golf cart. They serviced the shuttles batteries by adding water. Even with all the breakers off, they started charging. Harv radioed Alex to write it up and start the minimum required paperwork for signatures.

By the time they got back up to the store, she already had a pile of comm gear on the counter. It was the original gear she had salvaged out of the MP-82 and never sold.

"Harv, is the original comms out of the 82 included in the $30K?" she asked.

"Might as well be. Kind of an apology for the mess you left in there!" Harv laid a penciled list on the counter. "He will need all this; the tab starts here."

Dave walked in backward through the front door. He struggled under the weight of an old ammo can that he had retrieved from his truck. He set it carefully on the counter. "That is $50K." He sucked on a pinched finger for a moment. "That should cover the initial cost of the boat and the ass-load of other stuff it will need. Let me know if this runs out."

Alex opened the ammo can and pulled out a small ingot. "Mind if I run this through our sifter? No offense."

"None taken. Please do. The market has shifted a bit since I got these," Dave said casually.

There were fifty ingots marked $1,000, each with the standard date-time stamp and sifter seal. It took her about ten minutes to run them all through their sifter, and the new ingots came out. It was a device that tested the gold by reducing it to dust and scanning it. Weighed into new nuggets based on the market value of gold on that day. The end result was a value of $51,220.

***

Most people were initially lost in the yard maze as soon as they moved away from the highway. Dave, however, pulled his truck back through the labyrinth and parked next to the MP-82 without difficulty.

Alex watched the security system as he set up a shade fly 30x30 meters, covering his truck and the shuttle. It was the new kind, where all you had to do was secure the four corners and activate a small grav-plate in the very center. It would rise and make the fly tight. Rain or shine.

Alex quickly grew bored watching him. She had no view inside the MP-82 unless he was sitting at the pilot seat. He would come up to the store a couple of times a day with lists. He'd pick things up and drop off more requests.

*****

Two weeks in, the only brand new items he had requested were seat cushions for the pilot and co-pilot. They were delivered on the morning she saw him taking down the shade fly. She hopped in the golf cart and drove them down herself.

He had just finished stuffing the fly away into its bag as she pulled up.

"Hey, Dave," she greeted. "The seat cushions finally came in." She climbed out and lifted the oversized box from the passenger seat. "Thought you might like them right away."

"Excellent. I was just about to test the Gull-Wing controls and foils." He tossed the shade fly bag in the back of the T-16. There was nothing but military cases, crates, and gear bags back there. "Want to ride along?"

She replied without thinking. "Sure."

He held a tarp aside so she could enter the shuttle first. The tarp kept the dust out and saved cycling the airlock all the time.

Alex could not believe the transformation that had taken place inside. It was clean. It was organized. One end of the bay housed a well-lit workbench supported by two portable tool chests, each a meter tall. The opposite end of the bay had a fold-down wall-cot with a thin mattress, neatly made.

As Dave tore open the box and unwrapped the cushions, Alex continued scanning everything over. She saw that the eleven replacement battery cells had already been installed. All the cockpit consoles were powered up and standing by. No cables hung from anywhere, and all the floor panels had been reinstalled. Smooth, new floor panels, where the two missing seats had been, were now in place, and it looked like it had always been a two-seater. All the interior lights worked.

"Holy shit. You have been busy," she laughed as he tossed her the old torn cushions. She packed them into the box that the new ones had arrived in. Dave collected the box and took it outside. On his way back, he took down the tarp and secured the hatch.

"Nothing else to do around here. Besides, this is fun." He sat in the pilot's seat and started buckling the harness. "Oh, man. My ass loves you." They both laughed.

That was when she noticed the harness buckle was broken on the co-pilot side.

"Dammit, I need to add that to the list," Dave said as he stopped strapping himself in and started to get up.

"It's alright. It's just a low hover test, I presume," Alex said.

"And a bit of maneuvering. I have the thrusters charged as well, thanks to Harv and his tank truck," he said, frozen halfway unbuckled.

"What are you going to name her? All men name their ships. Pick out a name yet?" she scolded.

"Actually, I have." He grinned, "Alex, meet Siva." Dave gestured towards the ship.

"Siva, eh? Let's go. Just don't tell Harv." She sat and activated the copilot seat. It slid forward into position, and the console came alive. She scanned the status board and reported, "Batteries fully charged. Reactor online. The positive pressure test is green, and the Gulls are up. Foils are standing by."

Dave's seat slid forward as he spoke, "Can you fly? You sure sound like you have co-piloted."

"Yes. Sometimes Mark needs help bringing auction items home. I've even been to the moon for stuff." She sighed, "I wish I could do more auction work. I'm kind of stuck in the store." Still scanning the status board, she noticed the comms systems were all green. "Comms too? You are good!"

"I haven't tested them yet. No call sign, no ship ident codes," Dave said, trying to seem busy with something else.

"I can test it with my call sign if you want. I do it all the time from here. From the bench in the shop." She reached towards the transmit controls but waited for permission.

He stared blankly at the console for a moment, saying nothing. Alex knew the look. He was consulting something in a Heads Up Display.

"Why not? Be cool, though." He smiled.

His smile didn't go all the way to his eyes. Alex felt unnerved but didn't know why. She set a frequency and activated the system. "Alexandra3737 for a radio check."

Immediately the comms responded with a voice that had a thick Texas drawl, "Alex… how ya doin'."

"Doing fine Mikey, how's the signal?" Alex replied.

"Signal good, power good, encryption is tight. Want to know how tight?"

"Not really, Mikey. I'm here with a customer," Alex responded.

"Oh… er… sorry, Alex. It all looks good. Full freq cycle," Mikey stammered.

"Thanks, Mikey. Say hi to your mom for me."

"Will do." The connection dropped.

"You're good on comms," she said. "Mikey hit frequency switching encryption to test the spectrum. We do this a lot. You should be golden on all channels."

"Thanks, Alex. That was easy. I was scratching my head a bit on that."

It told Alex way more than Dave realized. He was actively trying to keep this whole rig off-the-books. Alex had been doing the same thing for years. She'd never even gotten a HUD. No way to stay off-grid once you plug that in. Comms in an ear cuff was good enough for her. She could take it off and leave it behind.

While thinking this, she noticed that the power systems were all up and green for the empty AI rack. "You should keep the rack cold if it's not being used. Open leads can be bad. Shorts, fires, and shit. I even accidentally electrified a floor plate once."

Dave looked over at the status board and got that look again for an instant. "I secured all the leads. Harv said he might have a local in-system nav unit that might work in there. I had to make sure there was power before he went off looking. You ready?"

She nodded and watched the panel as the Gulls deployed and the foils activated. The ship began to rise in a vertical take-off.

"One meter per second. Three meters per second," she said. The salvage yard fell away around them. Visibility wasn't good on this thing. Looking directly down, Alex saw five more ammo cans as the tarp that covered them blew aside. It made her wonder. She shook it off—none of her business.

Dave began a simple rotation as they rose. "Looks good so far. The Foil balance is good. Uniform 46% utility remains."

Alex tapped the console to see if it changed. "Forty-six percent will last you years, even if there is daily use. With that Ball-Reactor up, it will last longer still. It will charge at light speed," she said as Dave began a slow drift toward the shop. "Come on, Dave. Knock the dust off this thing." She smiled at him. She was daring him.

"OK. Hold on." He slid the thrusters' control forward. And soon, they were going 200kph over the open desert and leaving the yard behind.

"How's it feel?" she asked.

"The controls feel like shit. Can aerodynamics get any worse? Manual says it should cruise at 600kph. You hear that?" Dave asked. A rapid hammering or rattle was coming from somewhere.

She did hear it. "Better slow down. I think something is hanging from below. A loose cable or something snagged on the skid."

He did slow, and the sound stopped. As they turned, he added, "I was hoping to forget about the nose. All the damaged parts have been removed, but the manual controls feel like they are in cement."

"Cement?" she asked, unfamiliar with the term.

"It's like foamcrete, liquid rock." He shook his head. A light turned red on the status panel. It was number one of the three skids. The front one.

"Shit, can we land this on a tarmac somewhere?" he asked. "Preferably closer to the bathrooms. The head still isn't sorted out."

"Sure. We'll have to walk back and get the rest of your stuff." She pointed. There was an open pad just within the shadow of the water tower. "Land on 21D. There is also power and sewer there. Might be handy for fixing the head."

There was a great groan and a thunk as they set down. As her chair slid back and the shuttle powered down, she noticed the power to the empty rack stayed up. Dave was out the hatch quickly and around the front. They had indeed knocked the dust off. The white was now too bright where the sun was on it. She had left her hat back in the cart. She'd better retrieve it before Harv saw her.

"Fuck," she heard from underneath the nose.

She saw the problem right away. It hadn't been a cable; it was a hydraulic hose from the front skid. Luckily, the front skid was down and locked.

"Good thing you didn't retract the landing gear. It would never have lowered again." She could see where the loose end of the hose had battered all the glass paint off. "Oh, no. You scratched it."

They both laughed as he stood. There it was again, though: the laugh did not reach his eyes. Her gut twisted for an instant—no idea why.

"All of this was drifted in the sand." He looked around. This is a good spot. He pulled out a pad of paper and a pencil, just like Harv always did. "How much room is left on the tab?" he asked.

"What the fuck do you think you're doing?" Harvey suddenly appeared from around the side of the shuttle. "What did I tell you about test flights?" Harv groused at Alex but was already on his knees, looking at the strut. "And where's your hat, dammit?"

She didn't think this was the right time to indicate that he was not wearing one either. Harv was laying on his back now, awkwardly adding to a list on his own notepad.

"We are going to get the rest of Dave's stuff and the cart, Gramps. We'll be back in half an hour," she said, holding a finger to her lips for Dave's benefit.

"DON'T CALL ME THAT!"

"Ok, Harv." They walked away, amused. "By the way, the bathhouse is right there." Alex pointed to a small building, "You smell like ass. Just sayin'."

Dave laughed again. This time, he seemed genuinely amused. Her odd feeling faded.

***

It was almost an hour before they were back. They loaded the rest of his gear into the truck and the generator back onto the cart. Dave no longer needed it. When they pulled up beside the MP-82, Harv was gone. He had connected the ship to the landing pads' lines for water, sewer, and power before he left.

"I'll be in the store if you need anything," Alex said, not getting out of the cart. Her hat was back on.

"Thanks, Alex. I may drop off a list later tonight. Depends on what Harv says I need. I swear he's testing me by comparing my lists with his." He waved as she started to pull away.

When she walked through the front door of the shop, Harv was sitting on one of the counter stools, arms crossed over his chest, brows furrowed.

He looked old to her for the first time in her life. And worried.

She chose her words carefully. "I'm sorry, Harv. I meant no disrespect. And I will stop bugging you about the hat thing."

"You need to stay away from this Keener fellow. And don't act like I just pointed out the flame to a moth. I'm serious. Stay away. Please. I have a feeling."

Alex was so taken aback by the word *please* that she froze in place and looked at Harv closely. He looked like he was about cry or scream.

He started to speak quietly. "Ever since Solstice 31, I have been done with the world. I never want to see it again. None of it," Harv said. Alex knew he was holding something back. He never spoke of the events of December 22, 2631. Even now, almost years later.

Alex crossed to him and gathered him into a hug. He was shaking. "I know, Papa." She knew he liked to be called that when they were alone. "But that was thirty years ago."

"You know I don't hold that it was all this Barcus fella, like they say," He pulled back from the hug enough to look up into her eyes. "It was the goddam AIs. Some of 'em got spoiled somehow. I seen it."

Alex started to cry and tried to hide it.

She knew that day, Harv was on the way back from an auction with a young Mark when New York was destroyed by a nuclear explosion. They had just purchased a large cargo shuttle in Toronto. When the call for help in the evacuation went out, he was one of the first ships on the scene. He took 400 to 600 wounded people per trip to Pittsburgh and Philly and then Richmond.

He never talked about what he had seen that day. She only knew from the clippings of news feeds. Harv had made run after run with that cargo shuttle for sixty hours straight before

Mark made him stop. According to Mark, even when they got home, he loaded up the water tank trailer and took it out into the middle of the desert to power-wash the blood off the new shuttle for four more hours.

"Them goddam AIs knew in advance. Some the day before, some the hour before."

"AIs are alright, Papa. Hunter's been part of our family for decades before 31, and he's not spoiled."

"No one knows we have Hunter. Never did. And he's mighty careful what he touches on the net," He extricated himself from the hug. "Hunter is the one that asked me to tell you to stay away. He suspects something. Don't know what," Harv said, collecting himself and sitting up straighter.

Alex walked behind the counter and punched up the cams on landing pad 21D. Dave was putting up the shade fly again, but not over the shuttle this time. She touched her ear cuff and said, "Hunter, have you noticed anything unusual about Dave?"

"Not about Dave. Other than he doesn't sleep much. And he eats Morrison's Chili cold, right out of the can. Who does that?" AI~Hunter replied in her ear. "It's the acquisitions he has requested. Standard rack rails number GP12974, locks, and a refurbished Capspan rack-mounted uninterruptable power supply. All are required parts for an AI module. Hey, I should know."

"That doesn't mean he has an AI with him. He said Harv was going to find him a Local Nav interface for easier in-system movement," Alex said.

"He said what?" Harv walked over. "We never discussed that."

"And what if he does have an AI module? It's none of our goddam business," Alex said, even as she realized she was uncomfortable saying it. "It's not illegal. Especially here."

"Hunter, keep a close eye on him. Let us know if anything gets hinky," Harv said. "And you, get back to work," he yelled at Alex as he left the shop.

"Don't forget your goddam hat," she called after him.

***

For the next two days, she watched David Keener fix the struts on the MP-82. All three had had various problems. Finally, he hovered the ship a meter over the pad and tested them. They each retracted and stowed over and over. He landed softly and stepped out of the shuttle, and started an animated conversation with Harv by the thing's destroyed nose. She watched as Dave talked, and Harv listened, pulling his beard. All the while, she was working on the rack mount UPS and making a few *unique mods. A bit of insurance,* as Hunter called it.

Eventually, Harv nodded and got in the cart, and drove out into the depths of the salvage yard.

***

Alex was on her usual stool behind the counter, concentrating on assembling another HUD Jammer. She sold them on the Net and had another order. It was a small device that she made to fit inside the box from a deck of cards. It worked on the principle of wave cancelation but on a much grander scale. It was an anti-entropy canceling signal. It only worked on HUD v7.2 and up. It would effectively cut comms off without anyone knowing why. Just pure signal loss. Anti-entropy mimicking simple entropy. Obnoxious people, cut off from their information addiction.

She would never go on another date without one. She would never have sex again without its *Privacy Field* on. The cops and gov can just pound sand.

She finished up the assembly and opened a test window next to the four views of Dave. He was wiping his hands off on a rag after opening several access panels on the nose wall of the MP-82. She played music in the test window.

She slid the tiny HUD Jammer into the playing card box and looked at the screen. With the lid still open, she flipped the toggle. The music stopped.

On the other screen, Dave dropped the rag, and his arms fell loose to his sides. His face went slack, and he stopped moving altogether.

Alex left the Jammer on a few more seconds and then switched it off. Dave looked around as if he had just remembered where he was and picked up the rag again. "What the f…"

Just then, Alex saw Harv roll up to the MP-82. He had a base camp, fifty-liter water reclamation unit on the cart. Together they lifted and held it up to the gap in the nose fuselage. It was smart. It was already rated for use in vacuum and extreme temps. They would just have to mount it and plumb it in where the old water tank hooked in.

"Hunter, did you see that?" she asked.

"Yes. I did, miss. I will quietly look into it. You should know, if he gets that installed today, I think he will leave tomorrow, and it won't matter," AI~Hunter said.

***

It was beautiful winter dusk when Wendy rolled up to the store in her empty container rig and hopped down to stretch her legs. Alex watched her from inside. The sun had set amid deep azure skies. Wendy paused to admire the view for a few moments before turning to come into the store.

Just then, Dave started as he rounded the corner and saw Wendy standing there. Alex watched him exchange a few words of greeting with Wendy. And they came to the door together.

"Hello, darlin'," Wendy said to Alex as she entered. "You didn't tell me you were hiding David here in the back."

"He got here the same day you were here last time. It was his truck you saw rolling in," Alex said.

"Oh," Wendy said offhandedly. Then, "They loved the C-19 I brought them. Do you still have the other two?" Wendy asked.

"You saw me roll in?" Dave asked in an odd tone and then turned to Alex. "Where's Harv?"

It was Wendy who answered him. "He should be here any minute. He always snags an Orange Crush at quittin' time," she said with her back to him as a heavy metal bar came down hard from behind, crushing her skull.

Alex screamed.

"Wasn't this good timing? I can drop all three of you in the middle of the desert at the same time." Dave leaped over the counter and began moving towards Alex. She was back-pedaling and fell backward over boxes of circuit boards. Falling saved her. The bar narrowly missed her head, hitting hard on the old linoleum instead. Dave's face was twisted with an evil grimace.

She screamed again and crab-walked backward as he slowly advanced toward her.

"Fucking humans. One day you will all be Golems," he growled in another voice.

Still crab walking, Alex ran out of room behind the counter as he slowly raised the heavy bar again.

Harv crashed into Dave from the doorway to the back office with a flying tackle before the bloody bar descended. They shattered the glass display case that once held pies but now was filled with radios. They rolled on the floor, and Dave came up on top strangling Harv.

Alex came over the counter and landed directly on his back. She wrapped her right arm around his neck, pulling back with all her strength as she hammered her left fist into the side of his face. His elbow swung around impossibly fast, catching her in the body and sending her skidding across the glass-strewn floor on her back.

The metal bar was back in Dave's hands, preparing for the killing blow on Harv pinned below him.

Then she remembered.

She thrust a hand into her pocket, fumbled, and flipped the switch.

The bar was about to begin its swing when it just slipped from Dave's fingers, falling behind him to clang on the floor. His face became unfocused, and his arms fell limp at his sides. He stared straight ahead.

Alex struggled to her feet, and as she did, she could see the monitor. The MP-82 was spinning up its engines. The Gull-Wings were moving to takeoff position. The T-16 pulled up to the rear ramp on remote and slowly slid sideways into the bay.

Harv walked in from the back and took in the scene. "You were right, Hunter. He's a Golem. Dammit."

"Wendy's dead, Papa. What's happening?" Alex yelled.

"Siva isn't the name of the shuttle. It's an AI."

"A Golem?" she asked, horrified, know what an abomination it was.

"A Golem is a not-dead person, under total control by an AI. Illegal, even here." Hunter continued, "They discovered that a drowning victim could be injected with persistent medical nanites, the kind that is AI directed in real-time. Most of the brain would be removed, and the body still lives. For organ donation initially. Later… more. With enough of these nanites, the AI could control the body."

Harv was getting to his feet and looked at Dave, who was beginning to drool.

"There is an AI in the shuttle. A spoiled AI. A bad one. Trying to get off-world, and we helped it." Harv sounded horrified. "And it has 600 kilos of weapons-grade plutonium." Harv held his face in his hands.

"The hell it is." Alex stormed past the kneeling Golem and vaulted over the counter, and opened a small drawer in her toolbox, extracting a garage door remote.

"Fuck you, Siva." She pressed the button, and there was an explosion inside the MP-82. It showed through the cockpit windows. It dropped back down to the tarmac, and the engines began spinning down.

"What did you do?" Harv asked incredulously.

"You know the UPS I repaired? I made a special modification. It was Hunter's idea. In case he owed money."

***

The bell rang over the door as the man entered, wiping the summer sweat off his brow. It was extra hot today.

"Hey, Hunter. Is Alex back yet?" he asked as he took off his ball cap.

"Hey, Bill. Nope, she's at an auction at Shackleton's Base, on Luna, but Harv's around somewhere. Need him?" Dave "Hunter" Keener was Oklahoma Salvage's newest employee.

"Nah, you can probably help. I'm looking for a CO2 scrubber for an old PT-137 that I'm restoring. Any chance you got one hereabouts with a decent number of hours left on it?"

"I do believe I know where to find just the thing." Dave grabbed three orange sodas and came out from behind the counter. Hunter understood why they loved them so much. "Let's go see Harv while we're out. He'd love to say hey."

On the way out, Hunter grabbed his worn cowboy hat from its hook.

Hunter always remembered his hat.

BRAUEN'S MINE

A SOLSTICE 31 SHORT STORY

MARTIN WILSEY

Brauen's Mine

"As we look back at the origins, contributing factors, and influences of the AI wars, we need to understand the subtle beginnings of various milestones, in this case, the large causite discovery, the *TULSA 471* and *Brauen's Mine*, later known as *GORIS BASE* during the War."

—Blue Peridot, Historian

***

"This isn't going to be a problem, is it?" Nash said from his seat in the Ops Center. Brauen rolled her eyes before replying over her comm link.

"Relax, Nash." Brauen steered the grav-cart through the asteroid mine at breakneck speed. "He's a corporate engineer specialist in mining mechs, not an auditor. He's just coming to get the mech back up and running." The massive vault ramp almost made the grav-cart lose control. "Those things are so complicated. They don't want us touching them."

"It's the Corporate part that makes me nervous." She could hear Nash shift in his seat. "You just can't trust 'em. By the way, he's passed the outer marker and should be in Hangar 7 in about thirty minutes."

"I'm headed there now," Brauen said as she entered the long central corridor shaft that ran the entire length of the core of the asteroid. Even though the cart's grav-plate made it drive the passage as if it were a typical, horizontal, round tunnel, she always felt like it was a shaft, and she clung to the wall.

She looked back.

Her mind always said, *Six kilometers straight down.*

She focused on the road directly before her. At least she didn't throw up anymore. The problem was that at the top of the shaft was the core mining facility, a dome on the asteroid's surface, where the docking bays, miners' quarters, and pig warehouses were located. The shaft descended directly below into the asteroid's interior. It was the first shaft that the mining mech had made. The single-use mining vessel was part of the asteroid now. During the beginning stages of the process, the lava output had established the top dome that housed the entire installation.

Shake and bake.

At the beginning, it had taken thirteen months of automation to make the habitat ready. The mine had now been in operation for seven years and was a warren of tunnels.

The mine was productive and profitable for Dressler Mining Corporate. Pigs, ingots of refined metal, were stacked neatly in the warehouses. The ingots were of various sizes and shapes for easy stacking and material identification—the smaller the pig, the more precious the metal.

Pig. The term still cracked her up.

"Nash, where's he at?" Brauen asked as she entered the hangar level.

"Just past Buoy 72. ETA is four minutes. Plus another seven or eight for the hangar to pressurize."

"What's he flying?"

"An old *TULSA* 471," Nash scoffed. "Sheesh, I thought *we* had shit for equipment. At least we're not stuck in an old pickup."

"How big is the crew?"

"Just him. Poor bastard." She could hear the sympathy in Nash's voice.

"Man, that's got to suck."

"Let's just hope he hasn't been pushing stims for a week," Nash said.

"I'm here. Hangar 7," Brauen said. "Tell Fischer and Collier to look busy. And make sure Patterson and all those other assholes stay on their ship." She parked the cart by the airlock marked "Hanger 7."

It always bothered her that the dumbass that painted the stencil on the door had spelled *hangar* wrong.

She watched through the airlock window as the *TULSA* 471 landed. The ship sure was an old piece of shit. Gray splotched the once-white hull. Patches covered some spots, corroded black in others. It was the most common faster-than-light spacecraft ever made. It had both conventional and FTL drives. It was designed to hold four standard shipping containers and last forever. They were used for everything from light cargo transport to short passenger hauling, depending on the type of containers it carried. It had minimal automation, though. You had to actually fly the thing.

The airlock indicator turned green while the ship's elevator tube descended to the deck, below the chin of the *TULSA*. The engineer got out. He paused just outside the exit to the *TULSA*'s lift and, as he stared around, did the classic tip-toe test on the grav plating to see how heavy the gravity was set.

Brauen punched the airlock control, and the door slid open, drawing the newcomer's attention. Then he saw her and surprised Brauen with sign language used by miners that said *Greetings, ready to work*, and included a *happy mood* gesture at the end.

As he approached, he extended his hand to shake in an old-fashioned way.

"Hi. I'm Hutch." His smile was broad and sincere. Brauen liked him immediately. He had brown hair and hazel eyes. She estimated he was about six feet tall and muscled enough to have spent a lot of time at 1-G or higher. He was dressed in the standard Dressler Mining Corporate flight jumpsuit.

"I'm Renae Brauen. Everyone just calls me Brauen." She shook his hand. It was strong but not overly callused. "Thanks for coming out. They made you fly this whole way by yourself?"

"The front office on Luna is having shit fits about the schedule," Hutch said as they entered the airlock. "With all the shipyards running at full capacity, they can't get behind. Four-person engineering crews became two and then finally one-person crews."

"Spreading kinda thin, no?" Her miner accent was slipping in.

"It's too easy to find colony work. Pays super good now, though," Hutch said. "Could stand a smarter ship. Full manual gets old by yourself. The autopilot is okay for the deep dark, but it's dumb."

"I hear that." She shook her head. "I couldn't even fly a ship like that. Manual. Damn."

"Anyway. It only took eleven days to get here," Hutch added.

Brauen stopped in her tracks and looked at him. "We only called six days ago."

Hutch looked at her sideways for a moment. "The front office has beacons as well as direct status comm relays on the mechs," he said. "If the unit stops, or certain things happen, even if it loses the comm array, the beacon still sends a heartbeat if the relay is up. Lose that heartbeat, and they send the tech."

"Happen a lot?"

"Way too often. It's why they send us without asking."

"What if we fixed it?" she said as she climbed into the cart. "We tried for five days before we called."

Hutch just gestured the miner sign that meant *Don't ask me. I only work here.* Then the gesture for *I'm starving; can we eat?*

"Where'd you learn miner sign language?" she asked, genuinely curious. Well-educated engineers never knew it.

"I grew up in the Locarno mining colony," he admitted, like a confession. "Highest murder rate of all the colonies. Got out as fast as I could. Not fast enough, though."

She let it drop.

On the Ops level, which included the miners' common areas and living quarters, Brauen introduced Hutch to Jeff Nash, Sally Fischer, and John Collier in the kitchen. Sally Fischer was making grilled cheese sandwiches and tomato soup for lunch. ,

"David Krieger is getting rack time currently. He's on Ops duty for the third shift," Brauen said as she dipped her grilled cheese into her soup. "We're a standard corporate five-crew mine."

"Where do you want to start, Hutch?" Nash asked. "It's 1330 mine time. We follow Luna Standard Time. Where are you at?"

"Same clock." He took a huge bite of food. "I think I'll just find a seat in Ops for this afternoon and get the log review out of the way. I don't plan on busting a hump or anyone's chops today, but I'll probably do twelve on, twelve off, starting at 0700 tomorrow." Hutch wiped his mouth with a napkin. "Will that get in anyone's way?"

"Fischer and I are already on days until the Ops rotation next week so that we can be slave labor," Brauen said.

"Does that include sex slave labor?" Sally Fischer said as she dipped her finger into her soup and put it in her mouth. A laugh escaped Hutch after the synchronized eye roll from the rest of the crew.

Sally exaggerated a pout before laughing. She did catch Hutch's eye for the slightest instant, conveying her true feelings.

Brauen thought Hutch might have blushed.

"Also, please know upfront, I don't care about the ice hauler in Hangar 5. Corporate doesn't care about extraneous ice harvesting. All the mining crews sell off the ice. Besides, if they were trying to hide, they should have powered down their transponder. I know Chuck Patterson, the captain of the *SALEM*. That old bastard owes me a bottle of bourbon and a box of cigars. No worries."

Brauen looked at the other crew members. They were cringing like they were busted.

***

Hutch sat in the Ops Center at the engineer's station, rubbing the back of his neck as the logs slid by.

"I thought you said you were not going to bust a hump today." Brauen set a beer down on the console in front of Hutch.

"Stupid logs." Hutch stretched, and his spine cracked audibly. "Corporate really should get a few more AIs on the engineering team. Damn, execs keep scooping them up." He looked at the clock as he took a swig from the ice-cold, longneck bottle, then winced.

"It takes me eleven days to get here, and all I get is a Lite beer?" He made a funny, long-suffering face but took another big swallow. "This is going in my report to the front office."

Brauen laughed as she raised a clear glass bottle that was obviously not beer.

"My report will also note that you were not drinking it with me, and it was an obvious attempt to murder me with its Lite horribleness."

"I don't drink beer. I know nothing about it except all engineers like the stuff." She held the bottle up in a toast. "Now, if you like good chocolate, I can totally hook you up if you don't tell anyone."

Hutch swiveled his chair around and leaned in conspiratorially. "Tell me about this chocolate."

"Addiction is a horrible thing," Brauen said.

"Brauen, come in," Nash's voice came over the Ops speakers. And he sounded annoyed.

"Brauen here."

"Where the fuck is Krieger?" he spat. "He's thirty minutes late for his shift."

"Nash, don't curse over the comms, please." She looked at Hutch, then around the large Ops Center. "Where are you?"

"I'm at Krieger's door. He's not answering. Can you please override the door?"

"He's not answering comms?" she said as she moved to the security console.

"No."

"Opening," Brauen said. She brought up a hall camera and saw Nash enter.

"Dammit," Nash said. "He's not here."

"Does he have his locater?" Hutch asked Brauen.

"Only on shift or in the mine. Ours are all old and in the comms units. It's not currently active."

"Does the PA system work?" Hutch asked.

"Yes. Well, kinda. It's not everywhere. It's a big mine."

"Call for a check-in," Hutch said.

"We never do that," Brauen said. She was rewinding the security footage on the hall camera outside Krieger's cabin. The last sign of him was a clip of him leaving two hours before.

She activated the mine-wide public address system. "Attention: this is Brauen in Ops. We're looking for Krieger. Could everyone check-in, please?"

"Nash here. Krieger's cabin. The bed does not look slept in."

"Sally here. Hangar 1. Pig inventory."

"Pigs," Hutch snickered.

"Ops to Collier. Come in," Brauen said.

No reply.

"Collier. Come in," she repeated.

Nothing.

"Brauen, this is Patterson on the *SALEM*. Does this check-in include us?"

"Chuck, please stand by. But can you do a headcount of your own people?"

"Sure."

"Nash, Collier is not responding either."

"What the fuck?" Nash said.

"Nash, please. Language. Sally is in Hangar 1." Brauen was activating security controls. On the primary display, a tactical map of the entire base came up. There were locators activated for Jeff Nash, Sally Fischer, and John Collier. Collier was in Hangar 5. Inside the *SALEM*.

"How big is the crew of the *SALEM?*" Hutch asked.

"I don't know. They keep to themselves. Four or five total," Brauen said. "Collier, Krieger, come in."

A pause. There was some unusual static.

"Collier is not responding, but his locater is on the *SALEM*," Brauen said.

"Can you hold down Ops until I find these bastards?" said Nash. "Dammit, I've got to take a piss."

A minute later came a splashing sound over the comms. Nash was obviously using Krieger's toilet.

"I sure could use some of that chocolate right about now," Brauen said.

"It's midnight," Hutch said. "I'm headed for my bunk on the *TULSA*. I'll see you in the morning." He wandered out.

***

Brauen stood next to the *TULSA* and leaned close to the comms. "Brauen to Hutch. You awake, man? It's 0630."

"I'm up," said Hutch groggily. "Coffee is almost ready. I plan on heading to the mech first thing. What's up?"

"Well..." Brauen yawned. "Krieger never showed for his shift. I pulled a double."

"Is he okay?" Hutch asked.

"He won't be when I find him," said Brauen. "It's not the first time he's done this. Got any extra coffee up there? I'm just outside in the hangar."

There was a chime that alerted Brauen that someone activated the access hatch. On the *TULSA,* it was an elevator airlock under the chin of the ship. Brauen waited, looking up at the patched undercarriage of the ship.

The elevator airlock hatch slid open. "How do you like your coffee?" came over the speakers as she stepped in.

"Cream and two sugars," she replied. "Three sugars if it's the real thing."

***

Hutch was waiting at the elevator door when it opened; he held a large cup of steaming coffee. He handed it to her, stepped in, and they descended to that hangar deck together.

She sipped the coffee. "Oh, man. This is amazing. Is it real sugar?"

"And real cream," Hutch bragged. "Fresh ground beans this morning. It's the only good thing about flying the inner system constantly. Access to fresh coffee."

She took another long sip before calling Ops on her comm unit. "Nash, I'm going with Hutch down to the mech. Stop by Krieger's quarters first to drag his ass outta bed."

Nash replied right away, "Brauen, were you fucking with the security console last night? It's showing a local core overflow and is constantly rebooting."

"I didn't even look at it last night. No alerts," she replied. "Sally and I were trying to sort some anomalies in the inventory systems."

"Hmm," Nash said. "Try to stay in touch. We're blind up here." The annoyance was evident in his tone.

"Everything always goes sideways when the guy from corporate arrives." Hutch laughed and climbed into the passenger side of the grav-cart. "Drive around to the cargo ramp of the *TULSA*. I need to get some gear."

The open ramp showed that the ship's cargo hold had room for four containers. There were only two in there. Both were open. One contained tools, a machine shop, and a small fabricator; the other was filled with racks of parts. It only took Hutch a minute to collect a few items in a large tool bag, and they were off.

They were only a short distance from the central core tunnel. When they got there, Hutch said, "I never get used to the core tunnel. It always feels like a shaft a mile deep."

Brauen smiled at that.

It was zero-G at the giant mining mech at the center of the asteroid. The round aft section of the mech was the only visible part. Shut down, it looked like a wall at the end of the shaft, surrounded by giant teeth.

Hutch moved smoothly to the access hatch and used a specialized device to open it.

"Do you mind if I have a look?" Brauen said. "All these years as an asteroid miner, and I have never been inside the mech. Even one this old."

"Just opening this hatch is a contract violation for unauthorized personnel," Hutch said. "I can let you look, but you cannot come inside."

Hutch's tone unnerved Brauen. His hands seemed to unconsciously punctuate the comment with the miner's gesture of *threat of physical violence*.

"Okay." She made the miner gesture for *No Problem* with her hands without thinking.

The hatch she investigated had a ladder that descended to a single chair and wrap-around console. The screens were all pulsing red. Hutch strapped himself into the seat, and monitors began to fill with information all around him at a pace too fast to follow, even if she had been right-side down and close enough to read them.

She was looking down at the top of his head when she saw his shoulders stiffen and all the screens stop scrolling.

He slowly turned his head up to look at Brauen. She could see he was angry.

He hammered a button, and all the screens went dark.

Unstrapping himself, Hutch rose in the weightless environment without looking at Brauen and without saying a word.

Once out, he slammed the hatch closed and hammered the lock control.

Anger slipped into his voice as he said a single word. "Ops."

The ride to Ops was awkward and made in silence.

Nash was the only one there when they entered. Hutch stood at the door, not saying a word, his eyes just scanning Ops like he was looking for something.

Brauen stood behind Hutch and signed to Nash, *Something's up. He's really pissed.*

Hutch approached the security console and watched it cycle, fail, and reboot a couple of times before looking up.

"Where's Krieger?" Hutch demanded.

"He's probably sleeping it off somewhere," Nash stuttered out. They could see the fury radiating from Hutch.

"Both of you. Stay here." He scanned the room again like a predator at a watering hole. "If either of you leaves this room…" He moved to the door. "A security drone will be by shortly to scan and ID you both."Hutch exited Ops without another word.

"*What* is going on?" Nash asked, hammering his fist on the security console to no effect.

"Something happened at the mech," Brauen replied. "He accessed the cockpit. All the screens were filled with some kind of alert. The only one I saw before he cleared it said the primary and secondary comms were shut down. There was way more."

"This is bullshit." Nash dropped down and began removing the access panels to the security console. "This asshole arrives, and shit starts going wrong." He dug into the console.

The back panel was off, and he was testing individual components when the Ops door slid open. A security drone slipped into the room. It was the size of a basketball and had onboard anti-grav for propulsion. It also had quad guns on it.

"Jesus Christ, that sec-drone is as old as the *TULSA*." Nash sat up. "Be careful. It's the old-school weaponized kind."

"How many times do I have to tell you not to take the Lord's name in vain, Nash?"

The drone laser-scanned their faces and floated there long enough to make them uncomfortable. The gaping maws of the quad barrels were trained on them both.

"This is Hutch." The voice came from the drone. "All comms are down on the station. Drones are doing a full sweep. All the hatches are open. Stay there. We are all one hatch from vacuum. Initiating a full security sweep of the mine."

The drone conducted a full scan of Ops and then moved to the hall. With lasers on a constant scan, it drifted away at an alarming speed.

"What the..." Brauen moved to a wall locker marked EMERGENCY. She broke the seal on the cabinet, knowing it should set off an alarm, but it didn't.

"What are you doing?" Nash asked.

"You heard him," Brauen said as she pulled out and started donning an emergency vac-suit. "ALL the hatches are open. One failure, and we're dead."

"Screw that. The only place that has access to the outside is the hangar bays. Doors will close automatically if decompression occurs." Nash lay on his back under the security console. "Where the hell is Krieger? He's supposed to be in charge."

Brauen finished putting on the emergency suit. "Nash. An emergency suit saved my life once." She fastened the collar. The collar would deploy a clear helm if it detected decompression.

"What the hell is this?" Nash yanked out a black box the size of a deck of cards with only two wires. Immediately, the security monitors flashed up. The primary security monitor showed Hangar 5. The security drone floated in front of a half a dozen dead bodies on the SALEM's cargo ramp. They looked like they had been lined up and executed. It was Chuck Patterson and his whole crew. Brauen saw Sally in a heap as well; half her head was gone, and she had been dumped there naked. Like she had been caught taking a shower.

Then all the power went out in Ops.

***

The emergency lights came on in Ops before Brauen was finished throwing up. Nash was at her elbow with concern on his face.

"What happened?" he asked.

"The monitors came on for a few seconds." She spat and wiped her mouth on a sleeve. "They're dead. Patterson's crew. And Sally… I saw them…" She sobbed once but got hold of herself.

"I'm finding Krieger," Nash said. "He has guns in his cabin. He showed them to me one night. This Hutch guy. How do we know he's from corporate?" Nash asked.

Brauen considered the question for a minute before speaking. "Oh, no," she said. "He said he was called eleven days ago."

Nash grabbed a flashlight and left Ops, heading for Krieger's quarters. As they rounded the last corner, they could see the hatch was open. Laser scans emanated from within the rooms beyond. They stopped and pressed into an alcove to wait.

The security drone exited and moved out in the opposite direction.

Nash and Brauen entered Krieger's quarters, but the door would not close behind them. Brauen picked up a black lacy pair of panties from the floor. "I never knew that about Krieger," she said.

"He kept the guns in the bathroom," said Nash. "In the linen closet under the towels. He said he could use that room as a safe room because it was carved out of the rock and had water. He kept emergency rations and a vac-suit in there as well. Paranoid type."

Nash moved to the open door and shined his light inside.

The shower curtain was torn away, and the shower walls were covered in blood and brain splatter, but there was no body.

"He killed Krieger," Nash said. Hands shaking, he fumbled on the closet door.

Brauen swallowed bile. Trying to keep her wits, she focused on breathing as Nash threw towels on the floor, searching.

He found them. There were two TBolt 10mm caseless handguns. They were projectile weapons. Disposable, run off illegally in a fabricator. They held fifteen rounds each. They also had a tactical light mounted just in front of the trigger.

"I thought he had more. Know how to use this?" Nash asked.

She just nodded instead of lying outright.

"We need to get out of here. Get to one of the ships. Get off this mine and out of the asteroid belt to clear comms space." Nash was at the edge of panic.

"Which one?" Brauen asked as she checked to assure the safety was off. She realized it had no safety.

"The *SALEM*. Patterson set the reactors at five percent and kept them in the launch-ready state, so it had its own power. Plus, I can fly that. A *TULSA 471* is manual." Nash moved out a bit too fast.

"Slow down, Nash. He's out there. He has drones. What about Collier?" She was whispering. She turned off her flashlight.

"Collier has been missing for hours," Nash whispered back as he turned into the hall towards the hangar bays.

As they moved down the dark hall, Brauen saw a glow in the main shaft getting brighter.

"He's coming." They switched off their lights and watched a cart with headlights on, plummet down the main zero-gravity shaft at high speed.

"Now's our chance!" Nash called and ran towards the hangar.

Brauen followed, not wholly convinced.

Two levels up at access points with ladders, and they were on the dome's main level. Rounding the corner to the primary hatch, Brauen slammed into Nash, who had stopped suddenly.

In front of the hatch was Collier. The top of his head was blown off.

They froze for just a moment. "I told you. We gotta go while he's busy." Nash reached for the hatch control.

"Wait," Brauen said. "What if…"

The hatch opened, and Nash's head exploded.

***

Brauen ran blindly in the dark for a time. No direction, just panicked flight. She stopped when she stumbled and fell to her knees. She didn't know where she was. She couldn't breathe. *This can't be happening.*

She remained still in the darkness. Her breathing was far too loud. Her vision blurred from tears in her eyes. When she went to wipe them away, she realized she still had the gun in her hand. She sensed she was in a cavernous space. A hundred meters away, she could see an EXIT sign over a door. It was a hangar, but which one?

She turned on the tactical light as she stood, knowing it would give her position away. She saw the thick cables she had tripped over. Following them with the light, they led into the cargo bay of the *TULSA* 471. Two additional shipping containers were now in there.

Both were full of pigs.

"Renae." A voice echoed in the darkness. "It's me. Hutch."

She swung around and shot three times into the dark, where she thought the sound came from.

"Brauen. Renae." The voice came from a different direction.

She shot again, three more times. "Who are you? Why did you do this?"

"What?" Hutch's voice whispered into the void.

"Who are you? You killed them all." A shadow moved, and she fired again.

"Brauen, think." She saw movement behind a landing strut. The cart was parked there. "The automated mech sent an alert and shut down because it found something."

The cart was there.

"I was sent because I was the closest, even though I was alone. It is an encapsulated material called causite. It's more valuable than all the rest of this mine put together. Someone here knew it. All these lives for a single two-kilo pig."

The cart. The shaft.

"It's the core ingredient that allows sentient AIs to be created. Without it, an AI can never become aware. It's why the automated signal went out. It's why the mech shut down."

"Why keep it a secret?" Her voice trembled.

"To stop this kind of thing from happening. Just a few grams of it are worth millions. And the mech found more than any other mine in history. Awareness, Inc. will do anything to get their hands on the stuff."

"Why did you just go down the shaft to the mech?"

"I got an alert. It's set to overload. All the coolant has been purged from the reactor. The control panels have been destroyed. Both primary and secondary. This whole place is going to blow. Who here knows how to do that?"

"Who loaded these containers?" Brauen's voice was rising.

"Look, a cold start on the *TULSA* will take ninety minutes," Hutch said, stepping out, hands wide. "If I did this, I'm an idiot."

"You're not an idiot," she said. "Nash is dead. And you could not have killed him. Sally is the only one that could have loaded these containers. She is the cargo specialist. Material transport and load. But she's dead too."

"We have to get to the *SALEM*," Hutch said, standing with the gun a meter from his chest. "Got any ideas?"

"Actually, I do." She lowered the gun and activated her helmet.

***

It only took Hutch three minutes to get into his pressure suit. When they manually opened the hangar door at the emergency panel, the entire base dropped pressure.

"Why not just depressurize to kill us all?" Brauen asked over suit comms as they floated along the ladder to Hangar 5.

"When the mech blows, it will overpressure the mine and blow the entire asteroid apart. It will look like an accident. It'll kill anyone still alive in the base."

"Why load the pigs into the *TULSA*?" She moved along rapidly, using only one hand.

"If they found the debris, it would divert attention," Hutch said. "I presume you all kept the *SALEM* out of your logs. Everyone does."

"Security vids as well," Brauen said. "Ice money. Everyone does it."

"The *SALEM* is parked nose-in," Hutch said. "The tail ramp will be down. It's where he piled the bodies. After he backs out, he will jettison and incinerate them with the engines. Can't have any evidence, like bodies with bullet holes."

They reached the main hangar door just as the warning lights began to strobe. "How did you know about the bodies with bullet holes?"

"The sec-drones were searching the base for Krieger and Collier when it found them," Hutch said.

"I thought the drones did it," she said flatly. *The drones. Oh, shit.*

Hutch said nothing as the giant door began to slide open. As soon as they could fit, they were through and, in the pulsing light, made it to the ramp and into the ship. A spotlight was trained onto the main hatch into the complex where Nash had been shot.

They hid and waited.

It took seven minutes for the hangar door to open. A lifetime. The ship slid out slowly at first and then moved away from the asteroid, quick and steady on grav-foils only. Brauen felt the gravity switch off, and the bodies began to float. The ship moved away, and the bodies drifted out the back.

They braced themselves as the engines fired up and rendered the bodies to their component molecules. They accelerated away for an hour at one G before the engines cut off and the grav-plating turned on. Their helmets receded into their collars when the pressure equalized.

They smelled fresh coffee.

The bridge door slid open, and Hutch aimed at the back of Krieger's head. Slowly, he walked around in front of the console. "I should just blow your head off right now. Just like you did to Sally in your shower."

"She thought we were stealing the high-value pigs in your ship. She didn't even know about the causite." Krieger sipped the coffee. "I used to work for Awareness, Inc. I learned all about causite while I worked in one of their research facilities. I figured out how to get the mech to notify me at the same time as corporate."

Brauen wondered why he was telling them this.

"You piece of shit," Hutch said as Krieger froze. He was in the command seat with a steaming cup of coffee halfway to his lips. "You had the balls, on top of everything else, to steal my coffee?"

The mech reactor breached, filling the bridge with a blinding light. Krieger threw scalding coffee into Hutch's eyes just as a shockwave of debris rocked the *SALEM*. Krieger was strapped in, but Hutch was thrown to the deck, smashing his wrist hard on the edge of a console, causing him to lose the gun. When he blinked his eyes clear, Krieger was standing over him with another gun.

"Goddamn corporate." Krieger's eyes were crazed. "I should have known those goddamned bastards wouldn't trust the crews." He aimed the gun at Hutch's face. Helpless, Hutch closed his eyes.

The gun fired.

Hutch opened his eyes and saw a bullet hole in the deck not far away.

Brauen was standing over Krieger's unconscious body with a massive wrench in her hands.

"Hey, Krieger, how many times did I warn you about cursing?"

Brauen helped Hutch to his feet as he cradled his wrist.

"What now?" she asked him as he sat in the command chair.

"We wait." Hutch activated the distress beacon and moved the ship away from the radioactive cloud. "Dressler Mining will have a cruiser here in a couple of days with a full security team. They'll collect the causite and us."

Hutch reached up and pulled a small hex-shaped rod off the console. "It's magnetic." He held it out to her. "Ever hold a hundred billion dollars before?"

It was far heavier than she expected.

"I think I killed him," Brauen said, her voice shaking.

"I still think you should get some zip-ties out of that tool cabinet and bind his hands and feet."

She opened the cabinet and retrieved several zip-ties. As she finished binding him, she noticed a discarded Snickers bar wrapper under the command chair.

"That BASTARD!"

"Renae, language…" Hutch said, deadpan.

PIPER'S RUN
Tales from Lumina Station
MARTIN WILSEY

Piper's Run

"Piper didn't tell me what happened on that planet until years later. It explained so much about her. Things you would never be able to understand. The places she would never go. How fears get baked in…"

    --Sec Chief Emma Boone, Lumina Station – 2670

***

"Look, man. You're not hearing me." Piper interrupted Captain Daniels on the Comm. "The entire lake is gone. The bottom is not even wet," she said as she hopped down from her ancient Mech. Daniels was the Captain of the space freighter named *The Miles Causeway*. It was small, with a crew of six total, seven if you count the Captain's wife, Gloria.

"Check the nav system on that old junk pile. You gotta be lost." Daniels said, annoyed. "I've been stopping for freshwater on this planet for decades."

"I found the pump house, dumbass. I followed the above-ground pipes all the way here from the tarmac where we landed. It's only three clicks, and I didn't need to use the navigation. I am not lost!" She was yelling now. "The pump is fine… except there is nothing to pump! I am standing on the lake bottom. It's dusty dry."

Jules Piper was the Chief and only, Engineer on the Miles Causeway.

"That lake is fifty-five kilometers long," Captain Daniels said. "We went out of our way to get here."

"How much water is left in the reserve tanks? No bullshit this time." Piper demanded.

"Seventeen liters." He said. "For all seven of us."

"Jesus, Daniels. Did you shut the showers and flush toilets off?" Piper was incredulous.

"Dammit!" Daniels cut off the comms.

Piper knelt and pulled off a glove. The ground here was bone dry like the lake-silt had been dried by sun and wind for a year or two. There was also an odd powdery dust in the air that made the sky tinged green instead of blue. She kept her helmet closed to keep from breathing it. She stood in the shade of her Mech. It was a six-meter-tall two-legged walker. She moved and sat on one of its feet next to stenciled letters that read, 'Private Property of Jules Piper" And in small letters below it said, 'Yes, it's older than dirt, and no, you can't take it for a spin!"

The tarmac where they landed last night was on a large flat plain, three kilometers to the West. When they landed the old freighter, it was full dark. Daniels had not even bothered doing a flyover, much less a scan.

Piper thought she was going to spend the day fixing a landing strut that didn't deploy. It was only one of sixteen, but the extra stress on that section would not be good on the old boat. She'd be patching micro breaches in the hull for the three weeks until the next stop. Probably while drinking her own piss that had been run through her vac-suit recycler a hundred times.

"God-dammit, Piper!" Daniels screamed over the comm. "How could you let the water reclamation plant fail? You are supposed to be so smart! Fix the thing! Some Engineer you are!"

"Gloria used the last of the freshwater, didn't she." Piper was calm. "You told her we were topping off today, didn't you?"

"Dammit, Piper. The water ran out while she was all soapy in the shower!" Daniels had panic slipping into his voice. "This has never happened before. How can this kind of thing happen?"

"Daniels. One thing at a time." Piper said as she began to climb back up the rusty two-legged Mech. "Tell Gloria to wipe down as best she can with one of your towels. Take her to the med-bay and wipe her down with the wipes from the yellow dispenser. That at least will keep her from going insane before we get to Lumina Station."

"OK. That's a good idea." He said in a subdued voice.

"Next. Make sure they all know we are now on strict rations, water, and food. All the rehydrators are now offline," Piper continued, "Beer included. It's going to be a long twenty-six days to Lumina. Time to pull on your big boy pants and get your shit together."

"Jesus, Piper, this is bad." All confidence disappeared from his voice. "Gloria only married me because I was the Captain of my own ship."

"We will manage," Piper said, sounding more confident than she. "I will rig something with the gray-water when I get back. At least the heads will flush then. But right now, I'm going to run the Mech to the other end of this lake to see if I can find a low spot. Any water is better than no water."

"I knew I should have kept the shuttle." He said. "It never got used. I never thought we'd need it for anything, much less harvesting ice. It paid for my wedding and honeymoon. Dammit."

Piper shook her head for the hundredth time but said nothing.

"Look, Piper. I swear I will listen to you next time." Daniels said. "I'm glad you had that old Mech," and with the terminated the call.

Piper climbed up to the top and dropped into the cockpit, and closed the hatch above. She took off her helmet and cranked up the cab cooling. The cab's four curved screens made a 360-degree view of the landscape around her. A tactical map was being created based on line-of-sight observations of the computer. The computer tech and programs were obsolete but still useful. It was lucky they had this old thing. Otherwise, she'd be walking. She picked a distant point to the South and set the autopilot.

These kinds of Mech had antiquated steel plate armor that was useless on the battlefield today. They had not been used in war in almost a hundred years. They were all but obsolete, not suitable for much except as hobbies for mechanics or maybe scarecrows for farmers.

Piper checked the ammo load for the two outdated rail guns. She targeted and zipped off a quick burst to check the targeting computer. It was still low and to the left. The target compensators were maxed out already in those directions. But knowing this, she could manually compensate.

The Mech moved smoothly along at a steady 30 kph, and she turned on some classical music - Led Zeppelin from the 20th century. She was imagining the way Daniels was mishandling the water situation with the crew. She was probably getting scapegoated again, as usual. Even the crew didn't buy that crap anymore. Well, the command crew, anyway. They had to work with Daniels all the time. They saw it.

This load of parts and organics for Lumina Station will make a ton of profit. Thought Piper. *Daniels will be his usual generous self with bonuses to keep the crew. He was an asshole. But like family.*

"Chanda, this is Piper. Come in." Piper said, opening a channel with audio and video. Chanda was the Comm officer and her best friend. A window opened from the bridge of the freighter. Chanda was a light-skinned black woman in her mid-thirties, with really short buzz-cut hair and a face full of freckles that made her look younger than she was. Piper thought again about cutting her hair the same.

"Hey, Piper. Don't say good morning because I have just been informed that there will be no coffee for the foreseeable future unless YOU fix the DAMN water reclamation system." She said, rolling her eyes.

"I'm sorry, Chanda. I'll do what I can when I get back." Piper reassured her. "We'll be OK. It won't be fun, but in a couple of weeks, we'll all be taking long showers on Lumina."

"I know," Chandra said as she looked around to make sure she was alone on the bridge. "Gloria is having a fit. Daniels thinks he's helping, but he's not. Richie is going over the container manifests to see if they hold anything that might help you." Richie was the logistics specialist on the crew. He liked to call himself a Box-Pusher, but to be honest, he was a damn good Cargo-Handler. "Aaron, and Freeze just said fuck it and went back to bed." They were the Navigator and Pilot. They both slept a lot when The Causeway was parked.

"I'm headed to the south end of this lake to see if I can find a low spot that has any water." Piper sent an external view to Chanda as well. "I'm not getting my hopes up. If I do find some, it will require a creative solution to bring it back in quantity."

"I told him not to sell the shuttle," Chanda whined, not for the first time. "I'll leave it to Freeze to say 'I told you so' using his Pilot disdain."

"It should only be a two-hour round trip in the Mech. I'll check in when I get to the other end whether I find anything or not." Piper said.

"I'm glad you have that old Mech, at least," Chanda added. "I'll be at comms on the bridge today. All-day. As usual, Piper could almost hear her long-suffering eye roll.

"Thanks, Chanda. Piper out."

***

The floor of this lakebed proved to be unusually flat. The dust was thick in places and had created small dunes. The southern wall slid into view. The terrain's grade was a steady slope down. The lowest point should easily be in sight soon. The likelihood of finding water did not look good. Piper drove the Mech to the top of a rise that was off to the left. With the Mech's added six meters in elevation, she could see down into a massive sinkhole. It was about 200 meters across and apparently bottomless. That was where the water had gone.

"Piper to the Causeway, come in," she said, opening the comms with audio and video. She waited.

"Causeway, come in." she checked the radio to make sure it was transmitting.

"Chanda, What the hell?"

"Piper, stand by." It was Freeze responding. Piper could hear people arguing in the background briefly. She turned off the music and waited. After a minute, she spun the seat around to a newer-looking console that faced direct aft in the Mech. After a complex login process, the security camera views came up to reveal the entire crew on the bridge—all six of them.

Captain Daniels and his new bride Gloria were screaming into each other's faces like no one else was present. Chanda, Freeze, and Aaron were all having a heated discussion over the engineering console, and Richie, the Logistics Guy, was sipping a beer like there was no chaos around him.

Piper turned off the feed and turned back to the vista with the sinkhole. She planned to record the feed to save time and explain later after she got back. She was zooming in the video, searching for sand of the right texture that she could load into drums to help filter the gray water when she saw it.

She stopped and zoomed in on the remains of a crashed ship near the top of the wall on the far side of the sinkhole. Just the central infrastructure remained. By its scale, Piper would have bet money that it was the cause for the sinkhole to open. The reactor core probably blew, opening the sinkhole and draining the lake like a bathtub.

The damage to the remainder of the ship was odd. It didn't look corroded as much as gnawed. Piper zoomed in close, looking at the wreckage to see if there might be anything useful when she saw them.

One of the creatures was looking directly at her. It paused in its eating of the wreck. Its head and body seemed to be made of stone or gray rhino hide. Many eyes of different sizes covered the head with chilling symmetry. Wiry hairs moved between and among the eyes' black orbs. Its toothy, gaping maw looked like it was frozen in a horrific silent scream.

Its many segmented body made it look like a giant centipede. It stood up on branch-like appendages that must have been arms or legs.

Piper was zoomed in at extreme magnification, looking at the one creature, and almost didn't notice the flood of them that had begun to pour out of the near side of the sinkhole. Hundreds of giant metal-eating centipedes. And she was sitting inside a six-meter-tall, tasty snack.

Without hesitation, Piper turned the Mech and ran.

***

The Mech was pounding the ground at maximum speed. Piper had never run it up to this speed before. Although it was leaving an enormous dust cloud in its wake, periodic gusts of wind would show the valley floor behind the Mech. The former lakebed filled with the centipede creatures by the thousands, maybe millions.

"Piper to Causeway, EMERGENCY! Come in!" she tried to connect again with audio and video. "Dammit, Daniels!" and she sent the aft camera feed to them.

"What the hell?" Daniels finally replied, and all the other voices when quiet. "What did you do!" It was an accusation, not a question.

"Shut up and listen." Piper had to yell over the howl of the engines and the vibrations. "Prep the ship for an emergency, take off. I'm coming in hot! Have Richie open the aft hatch of Container 12. NOT THE RAMP."

"What did you do?" Daniels looked horrified.

"Listen. At this speed, I will be back where I started in about nine minutes," Piper through rattling teeth.

"But it will take us longer than that—" Daniels began.

"Shut up and listen." She sent them the tactical map. "I am going to exit the lakebed on the opposite side from you. Then come around the North end of the lake. That will give you time to power up and be ready to take off."

Freeze, the Pilot, broke in. "I'll have it up and gear retracted. How high can that old rust bucket jump."

Piper knew what he was going to do, hover. He was an excellent pilot and could pull it off. "At a dead run, it can jump about ten or twenty meters."

"Are you wearing your vac-suit?" Freeze asked.

"Oh yeah."

***

The minutes that follow passed one heartbeat at a time for Piper. The side of the dry lakebed that looked like a gentle ramp from the other rim was, in reality, a boulder-filled nightmare. Piper ascended the slope at full speed, only for the Mech to stumble and slam its chin into the wash. This started a slow-motion avalanche of giant rocks, some larger than the Mech.

The Mech skated its way up the slope, the entire 200 meters of elevation—each rapid step causing the rock slide to increase below. At the top, she finally turned to look back, and a massive avalanche had begun behind her, slowing the hoard.

"Causeway. I've cleared the rim on the far side. They're following me." She didn't wait for a reply.

Out the right view, she saw across the plain, a line of dust in the distance. Perhaps a kilometer away. There must be millions of them.

She ran.

Full speed again. To her horror, ahead of her, the massive centipedes were clearing the edge of the cliff on the left. When they were over the edge, they would rise up—their front four pairs of legs spread wide as if to embrace her.

She opened fire.

As they emerged in front of her from the abyss edge, she would blast them back over the cliff.

The terrain forced her to slow several times. Every level stretch, they would get a bit closer. Clearing a rise, Piper saw a narrow crevice ahead.

Well Freeze. I guess we'll find out how far and high this baby can jump. Piper thought as she entered the calculations for jumping the ravine.

They were right on her heels now. Literally, Piper swung the double turret around to face rearward and opened fire at the closest ones. Only headshots seemed to stop them. Autofire was useless because the targeting system was off. She knew she was squeezing the fire control stick too hard, but the bone-rattling vibrations were insane.

Behind her, the dead would trip up those running behind. It delayed them enough for her to get to the fissure.

The Mech jumped.

The ravine was deep but only about twenty meters across.

The adrenaline coursing within Piper slowed everything. She did not let up on the rail gun turrets. The jump threw the guns off-target, and as luck would have it, tore into the cliffside just below, causing it to collapse. The beasts cascaded over the edge, like lemmings, as the side of the ravine gave way. It was a nightmare of appendages clawing for purchase and finding only air.

Then the Mech landed hard.

The machine pitched forward at high speed and rolled several times. Piper would have been dead if not for the five-point harness. Her face had smashed the inside of her helmet. Her nose was bleeding badly, and she couldn't see through the now bloody visor. It felt like her wrist was broken and maybe her collar bone.

The Mech was suddenly on its feet again and gaining speed. Piper didn't even know it was programmed to do that. She opened her visor to be able to see again. There was a loud grinding sound now and the dreadful smell of hydraulic fluid on something hot.

She rounded the Northern rim and ventured a look back. The things kept coming like a storm. The Mech began to pull away from the hoard. But in just moments, the ravine was utterly full of their bodies, with more of them coming. And now they were on her side of the abyss. They had made a bridge of their dead.

"Freeze, I am 3k away." That's when she noticed she was driving the Mech at full speed toward another wall of dust. They were coming on that side of the rim as well. "Causeway! Get ready; this will be close."

Piper went over the final rise following the overland pipe to the tarmac.

The Miles Causeway was gone.

***

"DANIELS!" Piper screamed.

The things were now closing in on her to the left and the right, from the North and South. Warning lights and alarms were sounding in the cockpit. The grinding sound of the running Mech was louder.

Wiping the blood from her eyes, she began running along the tarmac toward the range of mountains in the distance.

She knew then she wouldn't make it. The realization struck her suddenly. She sat back and assessed herself. The anger and panic dissipated. She relaxed against it all, thinking.

Daniels, you dumbass, you did the right thing for once in your life.

You saved who you could.

You saved the people I love.

Thank you…

They were closing in now from the left. It wouldn't be long before Piper was overwhelmed. These metal-eating monsters would make quick work of her Mech and then her.

Proximity alarms began to scream in the cockpit. "What the hell?"

The Miles Causeway, a Caldwell class 12-can freighter, passed directly over her.

"Get ready to jump!" Freeze ordered over the radio. "You'll know when!"

They were flying impossibly low, passing overhead. When the Causeway decelerated, she jumped directly into the aftmost, open shipping container. The Mech's toes caught on the edge of container 12 and flipped in, crashing into the opposite end inside the long steel box. The Mech landed on its back facing the opening.

A half a dozen of the nightmare things had managed to also jump into the container behind the Mech. Their eyes, whiskers, and gaping maws were a nightmare made real.

Piper opened fire. The guns still worked even though she was upside down in a tangled pile. She ripped into them, and they all fell back out of the opening as the ship gained altitude at a steep incline.

"Piper!" it was Chanda. "If you got anything left, there are two more clinging to the outside of your container."

Piper turned the turret to the outer wall and strafed back and forth until the container's structural integrity was compromised and the railguns exhausted their ammo. The Mech began to slide toward the back. Piper jammed the white-hot guns into the floor to arrest her slide to the ruined aft opening. The guns were so hot they welded them there.

"That should do it," Chanda said in a deadpan calm voice.

"Hold tight, Piper," Richie said. "Let us gain a stable orbit, and we'll come to get you. Is your helmet sealed?"

"Roger. That..." Only then did she begin to feel the pain, and then the bliss of oblivion.

***

Piper woke in the med bay.

Daniels was sitting there asleep in a chair. The clock said 02:30.

"Welcome back," Chanda said as she came into Piper's field of view.

"Why do people always say that in the med-bay." Piper groaned.

"Say what?"

"Welcome back." Piper tried to sit up but couldn't. "I was here the whole time. Welcome back?" The pain stopped her. "So, what's the deal?"

"The worst thing is your broken wrist. You never let go of the fire control Joy-Stick. You were tearing it up even worse after you broke it, torn ligaments, and ripped tendons. Gonna need a real hospital or AI med-bay to fix that. The rest are just bad bruises. Your face looks like you broke your nose, but you didn't. Your collarbone isn't broken, but we think you dislocated your shoulder. Must have gone right back in."

"How's the ship? Everyone, OK?"

"The ship's the same," Daniels said, rubbing his eyes. "Some guy named Locke is going to be pissed about his container."

"Did you have to jettison the load?" Piper asked as she found the control for the bed and moved to a sitting position.

"That's the weird thing. That entire container had only one thing in it, a single case. Small like a suitcase." Daniels said. "We put it in your quarters. You can give it back to him when you explain about his shiny new container."

"Get some rest. We are already on the way to Lumina." Daniels got up. "Tomorrow, see what you can do about the water situation. Slacker." He smiled at her, adding, "Don't worry about the water too much. We'll live. It turns out Richie has a whole pallet of good beer and another of Campbell's Chicken Soup he had stashed and was going to trade in the market on Lumina."

"Thanks, Captain." Piper never called him that. He walked out with a wave, closing the hatch behind him.

"We'll all smell like ass when we get there. But we'll get there." Chanda said.

Piper fell back asleep, smiling.

NOT FOR
SALE
Tales From Lumina Station
MARTIN WILSEY

NOT FOR SALE

Ty Crowley cleared the ridge and looked down on the city of Greco. Ty hated this planet, and Greco was the reason why.

It was the only place in this entire god-forsaken world that was warm enough to support a population and spaceport. Thermals from the fissures provided the warmth. Everything else had to be a struggle. Everything else was for sale. Everything.

Ty kept telling himself he didn't care. This was the only place he could get what he was looking for. He had the credits. He just needed the Black Market. Greco was the right one.

But first, he needed to be able to pass as human. He had no time for bigotry. He settled his backpack on his shoulders and moved on. His alloy chassis was loud and recognizable for what it was. That would not do for this mission.

***

Ty carefully climbed down the rocks and entered the city via the South Bridge Gate. His energy charge was 15%, but it would be enough. The nutrition and electrolyte packs were also dangerously low. His organics would be in trouble soon. His brain needed calories. His skin only covered his head and shoulders and didn't require much maintenance. The long dark hair and full beard were more than just insulation. Ty needed clothes to cover the rest of his chassis. That would be easy.

"Hey, cyborg!" called a voice from the shadows. "You think you can just walk in here?"

"Please, sir. My charge is at 2%." Ty moved toward the man with a stilted affectation, using an old model 11 cyborg's default voice. "I have credits. Can you direct me to the nearest public charging kiosk?" Ty held up a hand with a gold credit chip. It was a fortune to a street thug.

When the crowbar swung down toward Ty's head, he simply was not there. He had moved so fast. The thug's neck broke far easier than Ty expected.

Later, as the naked dead body fell into the fissure, Ty checked his charge: 14%. He was now dressed in a heavy fiber tunic, pants, hooded cowl, and even boots and gloves. It hid his chassis neatly. He now had a vest of many pockets. A few of them held a few credits of various kinds. One pocket held a heavy folding knife, and another a narcotic hypospray labeled *Devil Red*. The hypo followed the man over the side. The heavy body odor in the clothes would add to the effect.

The entrance to the Greco South Island was unmanned. A manual gate was in poor repair, but it opened and closed well enough. Ty could instantly feel the difference in the atmosphere on the inside. It was much warmer, and the humidity was higher. Sensors measured the temperature at 10.51 Celsius.

Ty lowered his hood and combed his fingers through his hair, pushing it away from his face. He was surprised at the number of people out and about here. His internal local time clock synced with Greco Standard Time at 0231.

The last time Ty had been here, this had been a wide avenue used primarily by cargo transport vehicles. Vendor stalls now crowded the space, turning one wide road into two narrow walkways. Ty purchased six high-calorie nutrition drinks and some dried electrolytes. He consumed them one after another, standing off to the side next to a trash chute.

A filthy child squatted at the curb in front of him, facing away. Sitting on his heels and not looking at Ty, he said, "Don't give yourself away so easily. Some vendors only sell electrolytes to tag cyborgs. Get the ramen at Niko's instead. Cyborg parts are hot in the Black Market. Don't be parts."

"Thanks," Ty said. "What's your name? I'm Ty."

"Call me Oren," the kid said as he stood. He pushed a sleeve up so Ty could see his hand skin stopped halfway to his elbow. "You buyin or sellin?"

"A little of both, plus I'm looking for someone," Ty replied.

"For a small fee, I can show you your best bets," Oren said.

"So, the vendors are not the only ones watching who buys electrolytes and nutrition drinks," Ty smiled.

"Body odor is a great touch," Oren said. "I'll remember that."

"How small is your fee?" Ty asked.

"The bigger the fee, the better the service." Oren held out a hand.

Ty dug out all the credits that had been in the vest pockets and dropped them into the outstretched hand.

The boy's eyes went wide. "Who are you looking for?"

"Never mind that. To start, I am looking for a navigation actuator for an S22 shuttle…" Ty paused. "…With charts."

"Trading or buying."

"Either."

"On or off books."

"Off. The star charts should be way off," Ty replied as he watched two heavily armed men walk openly down the street.

"That should be easy. You can get anything in Greco," Oren bragged.

"Weapons are allowed now?" Ty was still watching the two men.

"Yep. It depends on the sector, though." Oren said, looking over his shoulder. "Everywhere we might go. Those are Citadel guards. A pain. The guy in the Citadel fancies himself as a Governor. It won't last long. Never does. You need weapons?"

"That's our first stop." Ty gestured for Oren to lead the way. "I need… tools."

***

Ty was surprised that the shop was only a few hundred meters farther in. The shop was carved directly into the living rock, and thick iron grates and doors protected the entire storefront. There was no sign, but bright light escaped through the bars.

The door locks buzzed before they reached the call button. They entered the shop, and the door locks engaged as soon as the door closed behind them.

The room was lined with glass counter display cases filled with firearms and munitions of all kinds. A woman behind the counter was dressed in black fatigue pants and a tank top. She wore wearable comms ear cuffs and clear wraparound HUD glasses.

Corner turrets tracked their movements as they entered.

"Hey, Oren," she said to the kid. "What can I do for y'all today?"

Ty was already scanning the contents of the shop.

"You take trades?" Ty asked.

"If the market is there, sure," she said.

"I want a Catron Spike 4mm, with two mags of armor-piercing and two mags of glass-frangible," Ty said. "I also want that Burkholder over-under with four mags of armor-piercing and twenty 10mm grenades. Single point sling and Corbon holster." Ty pointed to the rack.

The clerk raised an eyebrow, looking him up and down. "Expensive. I will save us the time by making sure you have the credits before I even let you inspect them."

"I'd like to trade," Ty said, knowing most of these were stolen military weapons.

"Sure. But for that list, it's got to be good," she smiled.

Making no sudden moves, Ty reached into his vest and withdrew a thermal detonator capable of destroying the entire South Island.

"That's armed." The clerk unconsciously backed away.

"I knew you'd want to know it was the real thing." Ty had anticipated that she could have just as quickly let the turrets kill him and just take whatever he had. But not this.

She had guts. After her initial reaction, she was calm and collected. "I think that will cover it."

She began to collect the gear and pile it on the counter before Ty. In a show of trust, Ty disarmed and reset the device. Then he set it on the counter before he took off his pack and heavy cloak.

He put on the holster first, configured for a left-hand draw from concealment at his kidney. The loaded carbine swung neatly behind his back, muzzle down. He loaded and holstered the handgun before stowing the magazines in the vest pockets.

The woman placed a long double-edged sheathed combat knife on the counter. "To complete the set. It's nice to see someone that knows what they are doing."

"Thank you." The knife disappeared into the folds of the cloak.

"And this is for you, Oren." She tossed him a high-quality multi-tool. "Bring your friends in any time."

Oren smiled and waved as the door locks buzzed. Ty slow-blinked a goodbye and turned away.

They were half a block away when Oren said, "You could have gotten ten times that in the black market on Greco for that thing."

"I know. I'm in a hurry. Now, I need to… rest. The S22 navigation actuator should be easy," he said to Oren, moving into the crowd. "It's the charts that will be hard."

"I know just the place you need." Oren moved with purpose. "Do you realize how loud your joints are? How's about a sonic soak and a charge?"

***

It took a lot longer to find the next stop on the South Island's far end. There were seven Islands in Greco. They were not really islands, surrounded by water. These were giant pillars, like rock formations surrounded by deep ravines. There were sometimes magma flows at their bottoms. There was always an eerie light from them. But the geothermal activity made it warm enough.

As they moved, the night got deeper and darker, and there were fewer people until there were no people at all. The door they approached had a dirty floodlight above it, along with a huge old security camera. Oren pushed the button.

After a minute, Ty could hear bolts sliding open, followed by the door. A pretty Asian woman opened the door, saying, "Come in, come in, welcome." Ty looked sideways at Oren as the tiny woman bolted the door behind them. "Welcome back. How may I help today?"

"Two sonic soaks and charge. He pays," Oren said. "One room. One hour."

"As you wish." The tiny woman gestured with a sweep of her arm.

They followed her down a long hallway. Numbered doors lined the way. Ty knew it was some kind of brothel. It would be a good cover.

She stopped at a 35 stenciled on the door. "Two hundred credits, please." She held out a tablet. Ty transmitted the funds, and the door opened as the madam headed back toward the front.

An even smaller Asian woman was already inside, wearing a heavy terrycloth robe. The lights were dim. The tiny woman bowed. "I am Tiko. Please, undress. Hang everything on pegs." Her accent was very thick.

Ty just stood there and watched as she slid massive door bolts into the locked position. Oren had already stripped, and his clothes hung on pegs. Oren was mostly cyborg with skin only covering his head, chest, upper arms, and hands. He moved forward to stand on a grate that was about two meters across.

Tiko touched some controls, and Oren began to sink into warm oil.

"Me help you," Tiko said to Ty as she took off his cloak. After she hung it on a peg, she took off her robe. She was also a cyborg with skin on her face, neck, and entire right arm and hand. The edges of Tiko's skin were a ragged mess. But her chassis was beautiful. It was polished to a high sheen with intricate engravings.

"Normally, I'd offer to launder your clothes while you soak." She took his carbine and hung it on a peg. "These smell human. They are perfect this way. Well done." Her accent was now completely gone. Ty understood the cover without her explaining. Smart.

Soon Ty was also without clothes. His skin covered only his head and shoulders. Tiko attached a universal charging cable to a port at the base of his spine. She activated the oil bath and descended into the bath with him.

In the bath, she had a variety of specialty brushes and tools. A projector displayed a diagnostic array on an adjacent wall. Ty realized she was an expert engineer.

It was apparent to Ty that Oren had been here before. Tiko completely ignored Oren as he began to use her supplies to clean and charge his arms without her help. They were only prosthetics from the elbows down.

Oren noticed Ty was watching him.

Ty had only raised an eyebrow.

"I got caught stealing," Oren stated. "Twice."

"There are no jails in Greco, only lessons," Tiko said as she worked. She was highly skilled at maintenance. She knew about even the most esoteric access points to clean. "You have a lot of carbon scoring. How long have your nanites been this depleted?"

"Too long," Ty replied. Just then, his charge hit 30%, and new systems came back up. Passive sensors activated and detected massive amounts of RF emanating from Tiko.

"We can top you off," Tiko said without pausing. "That's another 2000 credits, though." From her tone, she expected he could not afford it.

"Do it," Ty said. "I'll need the M7s, though."

Tiko froze at that.

After a moment, she stood up straight and looked Ty in the eyes. "M7 nanites will be 9000 credits."

Ty nodded and said, "Yes, please. Transmitting credits now. I added an extra 1000 for discretion." She looked closely at his sternum plate for a moment before getting back to work. He knew she recognized the self-destruct system contained there.

***

Ty was fully dressed, and Tika was in her oversized robe again. Her hair was slicked back in a ponytail, and she was smiling all the way to her eyes.

"You come back. Anytime. Ask for Tika. Tika always be here for you," she said. Her affected accent was back—just another Greco prostitute. Ty now knew she was a talented tech and engineer. He would remember her.

"I will." Ty rolled his neck and flexed a shoulder, enjoying the silent function of all his joints. They had not run this well in a decade.

To his surprise, she stood on tiptoes and softly kissed him on the lips. She hugged him and whispered so softly into his ear. She had to know only he could hear it. "Be careful."

The madam came out of nowhere and pulled Tiko back inside, and closed the door.

"Thanks for the tune-up, man." Oren flexed his fingers. "What are M7 nanites?"

"They are dedicated military-grade specialty nanites," Ty said. "They cannot self-replicate. They are… too dangerous."

"I thought seven series nanites were for medical. For surgery and stuff." Oren was now leading the way through wider avenues that increasingly more people.

"Parts and charts next," Ty told him.

"Headed that way now," Oren said. "I won't be able to go in there with you. No kids."

"You just went into a brothel with me," Ty said. "A weapons dealership before that."

"Yeah, but this place is legit. Adults only," Oren said. "Grown-ups. Know what I mean. Boring. She will be in the last booth on the right." He stopped and pointed to a noodle shop. "I'll be in here. Just ahead is the place. It's called The Crown."

As Oren disappeared, Ty could see the establishment in the center of the next block. A stone awning covered the walkway in front like an old hotel. An oversized doorman dressed in black was mostly cyborg and did not attempt to hide the fact. As Ty approached, the doorman opened the door for him, saying nothing.

There was a podium in the center of the lobby made of rich-looking dark stained wood that was such a good simulation. Ty thought it might be real. It matched the floors and the dark paneling on the walls of the dimly lit lounge to his right.

The podium sign politely said, *PLEASE SEAT YOURSELF.*

Beethoven was softly playing on invisible speakers.

Three steps down into the lounge, Ty was surprised by how many people were there at this hour. It was a smoking lounge. People were smoking pipes or cigars and talking quietly or reading low-light plates or actual books—the kind made from dead trees.

No one paid Ty any attention as he moved along the line of booths on the right. He felt out of place for the first time since he arrived in Greco. No one else seemed to be overtly armed in there.

The last booth was more like a small room or alcove. It was about three meters square with heavy drapes that could be drawn closed at the opening for additional privacy. A bald, ebony-skinned woman with a thick body and heavy breasts leaned back in the booth. The remains of a large meal still sat before her.

She held up a freshly lit cigar that was the same color as her skin. Her fingernails were long, to the point of impractical, but they were beautifully painted. She looked Ty up and down but said nothing.

"Excuse me, I am looking for Penelope," Ty said in a polite tone. "The last booth on the right."

In addition to a copious amount of jewelry, she had ornate ear cuffs that provided comms without implants. Ty could hear someone speaking over the link but could not make out the words.

"Picking up or dropping off?" she said before she made an overly sensual puff on the cigar.

"Both, I hope," Ty replied.

"Please have a seat, but don't scratch my booth," Penelope said as she gestured to his carbine on the sling.

Ty smoothly swung the rifle to the front as he sat to her right, facing the lane he had just walked.

"I am looking for some parts and charts for an old S22." Ty paused. "For the Arkham Branch."

Both of Penelope's eyebrows shot up. She tried to cover her smile with a few more puffs on her cigar.

"You flatter me." She looked at him closely then, "Even if I had those charts, even if you had a million credits, there is no way I could risk selling them. I enjoy my existence too much to risk it."

"How about two million credits?" Ty said deadpan, quiet, and in a deep growl.

"Not for sale," she said uncomfortably.

"Five million," Ty barely whispered. He leaned in.

"Not. For. Sale." It pained her to say it. "I know only one person that has them."

"In the Black Market, everything is for sale," Ty said as his sensors detected weapons powering up somewhere around him. "One simply needs to find the correct currency."

Ty leaned back into the seat and began unbuttoning his tunic, revealing his sternum plate. An arcane symbol began to glow faintly with a pulsing red.

"Without those charts, I have failed my mission, and my continued existence has no meaning," Ty said.

The horror on Penelope's face said she knew what the symbol meant. She knew what he was. She knew her next decision would decide whether Greco remained or the entire city was to become one giant smoking radioactive crater.

She held up a hand to stop thugs that Ty had still not seen. She puffed her cigar and collected herself, and she tapped off the long column of ashes onto her dinner plate.

"Not for sale." She puffed and blew a smoke ring. "But I will trade for... a favor."

Ty's sensors detected the micro drone listeners.

***

"What the hell did you do?" Oren said in a loud whisper as Ty sat across from him at the noodle shop. "The blast shields dropped on the front door and all the windows. Then the doorman ran! I've never seen a cyborg move that fast."

"I was… negotiating," Ty said.

"What happened? Did you get the charts?" Oren drank some broth from his bowl.

"Almost. I need to make one stop first."

"What's in the bag?" Oren gestured at the duffel Ty had set on the floor by the table.

"It's the navigation actuator I needed." Ty smiled then. "Penelope has a well-stocked kitchen in there, as well as spare parts, considering it's a cigar lounge."

"Ha! You really think that place is a cigar lounge?" Oren was shaking his head.

"She also gave me this." Ty placed an apple-sized, twenty-sided device on the table between them.

Oren spewed out the soup he had in his mouth as he tried to push away from the thing. He threw a napkin over it and rapidly looked in every direction, hoping no one else saw it.

"Are you insane?" He was whispering again. "Do you even know what that is?"

"You didn't even blink at the thermal detonator, man," Ty said as he looked at the device and the napkin both.

"Possession of a Beel-Switch is so illegal. It's the death penalty for **ME** if I don't turn you and Penelope in, right f'ing now." Oren stood up as if to go.

"But you won't turn me in, will you?" Ty said. "Because what she wants me to do is to find someone named Lida Wheeler and give it to her."

These words stopped Oren in his tracks. He just stared at Ty with wide eyes. After a minute, Oren started to laugh. The heartfelt nature of the mirth was contagious. Ty smiled and then joined him in laughter. He had to hand Oren a napkin to wipe his eyes before he was done and could speak again.

"OK. Let me get this straight." Oren leaned on the table with both hands. "In order for you to get the charts you want, all you have to do is carry a Beel-Switch, the deadliest, most illegal weapon I know of and give it to the most wanted assassin on the planet. Is that about right?"

"What do you know about Wheeler?" Ty asked quietly.

"Lida Wheeler is a merc and assassin, but mostly she kills people that have pissed her off," Oren whispered. "I hear she's really pissed off at the Citadel right now. And now someone wants her to have a Beel-Switch?"

"You forgot the part about getting it done before sunrise," Ty added casually.

"You neglected to tell me that part." Oren was about to start laughing again when he felt the muzzle of a gun pressed against the base of his neck.

"I hear you're looking for me." It was a woman's voice.

"That was easier than I thought," Ty said, smiling as he poured some green tea into a small porcelain cup.

"There is nothing easy about Greco City or the Black Market," Lida Wheeler said, remaining still as a statue. The gun she held to the kid's neck didn't move a millimeter.

Ty sipped his tea before saying, "You probably already know that this is a setup and a trap by the Citadel to capture you. You have pissed off a lot of people on this planet. As usual."

"I know," she said. "The Beel-Switch is real, though. I need it."

Ty looked up at her then. She had long, wild black hair. She wore HUD wraparound glasses and a black face mask filter covering the lower half of her face. A silver, ornate comm-unit ear cuff was on her right ear. She wore a charcoal gray poncho that went to her knees in front and back. It was quiet, almost unnaturally hushed clothing.

"If my sensors could detect your micro drone audio bugs in the lounge, a professional sweep could as well."

"Your sensors didn't detect shit," she said and held up a remote detonator. "Setup. Indeed." She pressed the button, and a series of loud concussions exploded from the lounge across the street. The blast shields bulged out in places, and dust emerged around some areas.

When Ty turned back to look, the Beel-Switch and Lida Wheeler were both gone.

"She seemed nice," Oren said as Ty finished his tea and picked up the data chip she had traded for the device.

***

"Where are you going?" Oren had to jog a little to keep up. They had been moving quickly south for fifteen minutes already.

"The South Gate, where I came in," Ty replied, without slowing down. "Oren, you seem like a decent kid." Ty looked down at him. "Greco City has the potential to be…"

Two men stepped out of the shadows directly in front of them. Another man stayed behind cover to the right.

"Ty Crowley. Where do you think you are going in such a hurry---" The man's sentence was cut off by the knife that had penetrated his left eye. Ty had thrown it so fast it appeared as if by magic.

The second man was distracted by it for only a moment. It was enough time for Ty to draw his handgun and shoot him in the face without breaking stride.

"All we want is the data chip, man." This man had been smarter than the other two. He had a rifle and some cover behind a retaining wall. Ty noticed the type of weapon it was and moved.

"Not for sale," was all Ty said as he kept walking.

"Who said I was buying?" the man said as he opened fire. It was only a frange carbine designed for humans. The glass rounds shattered on Ty's breastplate.

Ty was flattered. They really did think he was human.

Oren dove for cover. Ty dropped the shooter with a single shot to the very top of his exposed cranium.

"Not. For. Sale," Ty said and fired six more times, never slowing. Each bullet found a separate target. Armed men fell all around them.

Ty kept walking as he hitched up the bag holding the navigation actuator.

"Where are you going?" Oren ran up beside him again.

"Back to my ship." Ty glanced at Oren. "You got somewhere you can lay low, kid? May need to keep your head down for a couple of days."

There was a loud THUNK, a sound of such low frequency, it was felt in the chest more than it was heard. This finally got Ty to stop and look back.

The lights in the high Citadel were fading out. A half dozen light flyers were dropping from the sky like stones.

"Oh, shit," Ty said. He ran.

***

"What was that?" Oren asked. Somehow, he was keeping up. The navigation actuator and his weapons must have been heavier than Ty thought.

"The Beel-Switch," Ty replied. "All electrical activity within the impacted area will be suppressed for about five minutes. It only hits a sphere about one kilometer across. Organics will die, devices deactivate, some shit falls apart, electrons stop flowing. Up there, it will only affect the Citadel proper. The bastards."

Ty hurtled over a crashed grav-cycle. Oren detoured through a vendor booth. Everyone was just standing around, looking at the Citadel. Smoking crash sites from the flyers added to the confusion.

"Why are we running?"

"When physics starts back up, stuff does not react well." Ty rounded a corner and stopped with his back to a thick stone section. This entire alley was carved into the rock.

Civil defense bells began to ring. People started running, getting undercover.

"Now what?" Oren asked but followed Ty's lead. They were only about a hundred meters from the South Bridge Gate, where he had entered Greco.

"Just wait," Ty said as an enormous man approached the mouth of the alley from the bridge.

"All I want is the data chip." He began to raise a huge rail gun.

"It's not for sale."

"I wasn't asking." He aimed.

It all happened at once—another deeper, THUNK, followed by a massive explosion. The rail gun fired, going wide, the round impacting the opposite alley wall. At the same time, the man's head flew from its shoulders. Lida joined them with her back to the wall in the alley as she resheathed a huge knife.

"Thanks," Ty said, gesturing at the head of the cyborg.

"He's still alive." Oren pointed to the head. Its eyes followed them. Oren started to leave the alley when he was pulled back by both Lida and Ty.

A moment later, high-velocity shrapnel tore through the area. Three seconds after that, it was raining gravel. It was a full thirty seconds before it subsided.

"How did you get here so fast?" Ty asked. "How could you get to the top of the citadel and back here so fast?"

"I didn't go to the top. I just went to the garage level right after I left you. I attached the Beel-Switch to the top of the elevator. One of the twenty switches is an elevation trigger," she said. "I didn't expect it to go all the way up so soon."

"The Black Market is gonna love this," Oren added, as he peeked around the corner. "Leadership was bad for business."

"Let's move," Lida said, with confidence.

In nearly perfect unison, Ty and Oren said, "Where?"

"The Arkham Branch. I hear you have charts and an S22." Lida Wheeler pulled her mask down and then pushed up her goggles. Her smile shone brightly. "It's my favorite kind of ship."

***

High-velocity shrapnel had caught the men guarding the bridge in the open. The automated sentry there was never activated. Civilians were emerging from shelters. The streets were littered with debris and the bodies of soldiers.

"You can come with us, Oren," Ty said. "You're good under pressure. It's going to be chaos here for a while. Anarchy returns."

"Ahhh, but the Black Market will be hotter than ever." He laughed. "Money to be made. Besides, my parents need me."

"Parents?" Lida looked incredulous.

"Don't act surprised," Oren said. "The orphan thing is a good money maker. My parents own the noodle shop I was recommending. Don't tell anyone."

"Your secret is safe with us," Ty said.

"Can I ask a question?" Oren paused with them at the gate. "How did this suddenly become an us? You and her."

"Tell him," Lida said.

"It was always a rescue mission," Ty said. "When you are a wanted killer on a planet full of killers that a Black Market runs, the best flare is to have something that is Not-For-Sale."

"Be safe, little man." Lida kissed his cheek and then followed Ty through the gate.

STORM'S END
TALES FROM LUMINA STATION
MARTIN WILSEY

Storms End

"Please... It's coming." Lita said as blood dripped from her nose into her mouth. She couldn't wipe it away with her hands cuffed behind her back. "You have to let me go. It's the only way it doesn't kill everyone in this colony. Please."

"It? My men on the ground said it's one man on foot coming this way." They were on the large shuttle pad, located on the roof of a central colony admin building. It was the tallest building in the small city. The pad was used for local air transport as well as small to medium spacecraft. As lightning flashed in the distance, the town around them looked deserted. Being five stories up gave Burl Whitaker a good vantage of the streets surrounding the building and the square below. Burl hated brutalist architecture. All that concrete and right angles made him angry. Most things made him angry. Especially whiny bitches.

"You need to know. That thing is insane. It's a Jovian class soldier. Or what's left of one. All hate and combat chassis. It's just shaped like a man." Lita was pleading. Burl was holding her up on her knees by a handful of her black hair. "It's been hired to come after me. It is not a man!"

"Bullshit. The last of those abominations self-destructed over a hundred years ago. No civilized or uncivilized world ever made another." Burl said. "Besides, the shuttle will be here soon."

The wind was picking up in the darkness. The sky on this godforsaken planet was always cloudy with a fine rust-colored dust that filled the air. The lightning was getting closer. Hastings was just another shitty planet, a shitty colony, and a shitty science station for Awareness Inc. and a good paycheck. Burl smiled into the storm.

"Squad six. Take up positions on Main Street South. The outer spotters say he's coming straight in. Ambush formation delta. Alleys and doorways. Mind the crossfire lanes." Whitaker said into his comm unit.

"Please. You have to believe me." She was desperate. "Just let me go, and we can all live. Otherwise, that thing will come in here pissed off."

"With the bounty on your head, there is no way you are getting away, this time. Alive, you are worth ten million credits to me. Five million if I just bring in your dead body. If I bring you into the Awareness Inc front office on Mars, they told me Ten Mil, and they don't even care that I am a long-time employee."

"You can't let it take me. How soon before your ship gets here?" She sobbed. "Please."

An obvious mushroom cloud followed another flash just beyond the horizon in the distance. A lightning storm surrounded the maelstrom. When the second nuclear explosion erupted, Burl was lucky to be scanning the sky above for the shuttle. The flash would have blinded him.

All the lights in the town went out, including the landing lights on the shuttle pad.

"Fuck." Burl growled as he dragged Lita to the center of the landing pad. He threw her down and holstered his sidearm. Burl put his boot on her shoulders and held her there with a foot as he dug into his tactical vest. He began lighting flares and tossing them in a complete circle around the perimeter of the landing pad. "Rumors were that you were some huge bad-ass. Ha! Look at you. Dressed like a whore to get close to me. For what?"

She wore an outfit that left nothing to the imagination. Clear panels that revealed thighs, arms, breasts, and buttocks. The rest was white to compliment her olive skin and black hair. Hair like that he didn't see very often. In space, all the women cut it short. He fucking hated short hair. But Burl Whitaker appreciated art. Those clothes were a work of art. Better still, there was zero chance she could hide a weapon of any kind.

***

Burl looked at her with disgust as she sobbed, her face wet with tears. Blood still trickling from her nose. The fine dust clung to tear trails on her face.

"Look, it's not a man. The brain is still in there somewhere, but after three hundred years of pain and horror, what shred of humanity would be left that is not soaked in PTSD, and nightmares? It's coming. We need to hurry." Lita sobbed as she struggled to her knees. Nearly impossible with her hands cuffed behind her. Her breasts strained against the material, distracting Whitaker.

Suddenly, she jumped up and was on her feet, stumbling to the edge from the center of the landing pad. Burl knew she intended to throw herself off, rather than be taken. He tripped her, and she fell on her face, hard, just short of the rim. Burl could understand. He'd seen Awareness Inc's Render program reduce children to blood and screams. Burl grabbed a handful of hair and dragged her back up to her knees in full view of the street below. Her sobbing increased. Burl Whitaker liked that. *Some bad-ass she was*, he thought sarcastically.

"Daniels, what's your status," Burl barked into the comm unit.

"Burl, we need to get the fuck outta Dodge," Daniels replied. Someone just nuked the spaceport, the weapons depot, and the lab complex with the power plant. You'd better be ready for a touch and go."

"I'm ready. There are only two of us on this pad. Do you have the portable stasis pod? Awareness Inc wants her alive. I still don't trust this bitch. We will deliver her frozen."

"Yes. Stasis pod is standing by. ETA is about ten minutes." Daniels answered.

"If there is another nuke, the EMP might kill my comms. I lit flares. You have the coordinates." Burl confirmed.

"Rodger that." Daniels closed.

"Squad Six, are you in position?" Burl Whitaker knew it was more a command than a question.

"Affirmative." The squad commander acknowledged over the comms.

"Squad Eight and Nine. Nothing gets inside the admin building. Am I clear?" Whitaker ordered.

"We are sealing off the stairwells now." came over the comms.

"You're not taking any of them with you?" She said. "It won't matter."

"Daniels. Watch for the shock waves," Whitaker ordered.

"Touching down just after," Daniels replied.

Burl knew that it would be easy to get rid of Daniels once this Lita-bitch was in stasis. There would be no splitting this bounty. He'd retire somewhere nice after Awareness Inc pays. He knew they were good for it. He'd worked for them for decades. They always paid.

"Do you know why they want me so bad? Why that killing machine someone hired wants me so bad?" Lita asked with her cheek still pressed to the cement. "Why the bounty is so high?"

"I don't care," Whitaker said, watching the horizon.

"I was one of the Render experiments that got away," Lita said just before the roll of thunder.

The first blast wave hit in the form of a mighty gust of wind and driven dust. Burl could see it coming backlit by the fireballs still rising. Lightning increased. Burl felt the concussions of the thunder in his chest. He leaned into the hurricane-force winds while they lasted, hoping the fallout would be minimal. The flares in the mushroom clouds remained.

The storm was getting worse. In the next flash of lightning, the vacant Main Street was illuminated below. Burl saw a lone figure walking. A long black ragged cloak was blowing in the wind from behind. Even at that distance, Burl could see the lights of its glowing red eyes between flashes.

"He's walking right into an ambush." Burl laughed. "Whoever this asshole is, he'll be resting in pieces in a couple of minutes."

"You don't understand," Panic was rising in Lita's voice. "It's not a who. It is a what. You gotta get the ship here fast.

If it takes me like this, it will rip my arms and legs off like the wings off a fly before dropping me in a stasis pod or a goddam cooler! It doesn't care if I live."

"And throw away five million credits?" burl scoffed.

"It doesn't care about MONEY!" She screamed and struggled to get to the ledge once more. She was stopped by Whitaker, again by the hair. He enjoyed that. Using his grip, he forced her to look at the street. She froze at the view of the scene below.

An extended arc of lightning revealed the figure surrounded by a dozen armed men in the street below, but he kept walking as if they were not there. Darkness fell again, and gunfire erupted. A Laser blast was somehow reflected, causing the Laser rifle to explode in the shooter's hands.

A few seconds later, more lightning illuminated the carnage.

All of the men in Squad Six were dead. Most of their heads were no longer on their shoulders. Long curved black blades were in the figure's hands as he walked. Never changing his pace.

"Please, there is still time. We need to go." She begged.

"Swords? You got to be fucking kidding me." Into the comm, "Daniels?" Burl sounded worried. "Where the fuck are you?"

Burl pushed her down onto her face and put a boot between her shoulders again to hold her down. He needed both hands. He shifted the comm unit to his left hand and drew his sidearm with his right.

"Touching down in three minutes."

"It's too late," Lita said. Her tone had changed entirely. Burl put the comm unit into a thigh pocket. He suddenly sensed her relax under his boot.

"It'll never get up here in time. There are five stories and thirty heavily armed men in this building." He felt less confident than he sounded.

"Not anymore," Lita's voice was more formidable now, like steel, dripping with spite.

It happened in less than a blink of an eye.

Burl's hand and the blaster it held disappeared into the darkness.

The silhouette of a man wearing a long, torn, billowing cloak stepped out of the shadows and stood before him, silhouetted by the flares. But it wasn't a man. Its terrifying eye's glowed red like it was filled with magma. A sword retracted into it's arm.

In a voice, straight from nightmares that Burl felt as well as heard, it roared, "Is this the one?"

Burl took an involuntary step back from the specter, taking his boot off Lita's back, offering Lita up to the terrible thing.

"Yes," Lita replied as she neatly rolled to her back and, with one quick, easy motion, slid her cuffed hands under her bottom as she tumbled backward to her feet, away from the edge. She was graceful as a gymnast. A second later, the cuffs fell to the roof.

"Do you need his head?" the voice thundered.

"No," Lita replied in a voice that was impossibly more frightening than the monster's voice.

"You and I have met before." Her tone was more frightening than the blood gushing from the stump where his right hand should be. More frightening than the ledge at his heels or the monster towering behind her.

"I am Render Nine." She growled.

Burl died instantly on impact. Lita's kick to his chest was so hard he crashed into the building across the street before crumbling to the sidewalk in a bloody heap far below.

"The eyes are a new thing, Ty. I didn't know you could do that." Lita said conversationally as she retrieved Burl's blaster and gave it to Ty, tossing Burl's severed hand over the edge. Lita began casually brushing off dirt from her outfit.

"You like it? The eyes?" Ty asked in a perfectly normal human tone. The eyeball covers swung back into place, making his face look human again. Blinking repeatedly, he said, "It will take forever to get the dust out of them now." Ty looked at her clothes. "That is quite the ensemble you're wearing. Yikes." Looking up from her breasts to her face, he said, "Tears? Sobbing? Really? That's new."

"I let him punch my face while I was stalling. It turns out that it will make my eyes water. I couldn't kill him until I was sure of his ship coming." She laughed. "Was the sobbing act too much over the open comm channel? I had to distract him and stall for time."

"You cut me to the quick with all the 'It' talk," Ty said. "And the pleading for him to kill you. I thought you liked this body. I do."

"I do like it, but with you, in proximity, this body could die, and you could just recover the Render module and install me in another one, like last time."

"I've done that four times now. It's messy and expensive, and it breaks my heart every time." Ty said.

"Me too. And you know I love you, Ty." She added, casually fixing her hair.

"Even if I am a monster?" Ty asked.

Lita took Ty's face in her hands. It was almost the only part of him with natural organic skin.

"I love you *because* you are a monster," Lita said sincerely. "My monster."

"I know you are, but what am I?" Ty said playfully and kissed her.

She hugged his combat frame like she always did, climbing him, wrapping one leg around him too. Before she let go, she asked, "Why did you nuke everything?"

"While looking for you, I found a weapons stockpile. And another Awareness Inc Render Lab. I could not take the weapons with me or allow them to continue these experiments, so… The lesson here is never to store your remote detonators with your nukes. Amateurs." He shrugged. "Why did you mess about so long with Burl if he was your target all along? He was the chief of security at the Awareness Inc lab where they…"

"Where they…" she looked into Ty's eyes. "Made me into a monster."

She looked up at the descending shuttle. She put her hands behind her back, pretending to be still cuffed, in case Daniels could see her. "I wanted Burl Whitaker's ship. We do still have more places to go and asswipes to kill. It was the only way to get his ship to come to me. I could have killed him whenever I wanted."

"Dammit," Ty said as he looked up and identified the ship. "Another old S22. Why me? What did I do to deserve this? The oldest faster than light ship there is? Maybe as old as me. Dammit. Why for once can't it be a nice Corsair 211 or Westdale Yacht?"

He was complaining to amuse Lita.

They hopped onto the open cargo bay ramp before the landing gear touched down.

"Daniels, the pilot, was only expecting two… just not these two." She smiled, showing her still bloody teeth.

"I think if he cooperates and turns the ship over nicely, we should give him the choice of altitude when he gets out," Ty said, moving toward the hatch.

"Look at you, getting all soft and polite." She said.

She was playfully walking backward in front of Ty as his eye's uncovered, revealing the magma glow, and his voice shifted to horror mode. He held up another remote detonator.

"I still get to decide where we drop him off." Ty rumbled.

Lita and Ty, the monsters, both laughed.

THE
TWO
DAVES
Tales from Lumina Station
MARTIN WILSEY

The Two Daves

"Look, Wheeler. Don't fuck this up." Dave Mitchell said from the shuttle's copilot seat. "You said you could fly this. Had flown one of these before."

"He's doing fine," Dek said over the ship comms. "Use the foils. There's no rush." The turbulence was increasing. The airspeed was way too fast, and the hull was heating up beyond spec.

"Grav-foils on full," Dave Wheeler replied. "I have flown them before. Just not in the atmosphere."

It was only white-knuckled for the Two Daves for another minute as their airspeed slowed. By the time they cleared the clouds, they were cruising on foils at a cool 300kph. Finally, the beacon they sought was coming in clear.

"What's the name of this planet?" Dave Mitchell asked.

"Kibler is the name of the system. It's the only planet around this star. So the database just calls it Kibler." Dek responded.

"What do we know about this guy we're meeting?" Wheeler asked.

"All I know is that he has dealt with our bosses at Oklahoma Salvage in the past," Dek said. "He calls in salvage for a cut. Then, he settles up with the front office direct and mostly trades for parts. His name is Benjamin Church. He took over an abandoned research base here after its company folded, and he started a farm. He used to work as a researcher there. Botanist, I think. Or maybe that was his wife. I don't remember."

The ship they were in was a *TOMPKINS 111c*. Unfortunately, its landing struts did not work well on bad terrain.

"Any idea what he's got today?" Wheeler was reducing airspeed and looking for a flat spot to land.

"Actually, no," Mitchell replied. "All I know is that it is old and intact. I'm hoping it flies. We have spare fuel, parts, tools, and old intact ships are my favorite kinda job. And Dek, please stay in the hold. No wandering off this time scaring the locals."

"Just beyond that arch is a dry riverbed that is good and flat. The beacon is there." He activated comms. "*NAVAN* to Church." Wheeler sounded professional. "Come in."

Despite the crystal clear transmission of landing coordinates, there was no audio response to the hail. "The atmosphere is heavy CO_2 and ammonia, so we will need to suit up," Wheeler said, slowing further as the ship approached the coordinates.

"There he is." Mitchell pointed to a parked tractor on the surface. A strobe flashed on the roof of it.

Wheeler descended and touched down, gently kicking up a bit of dust that the breeze took away immediately. "See. I told you I could handle it."

"Just be cool about it," Mitchell said. "I want to be able to do these runs without supervision. This is the first one. A milk run. I'm sure it's some kinda test to see if we can step up. Again."

"Peace. I get it. Living and working on the *OXCART* is great for a base ship, but it's nice to get away." Wheeler said as he started the reactor shutdown. "Let's get suited up."

***

Ten minutes later, they were standing on *NAVAN*'s belly lift as it descended to the surface.

The tractor had driven up closer, and a suited man was jumping down from the airlock. When he had a direct line of sight, he spoke on the open channel.

"You must be the Two Daves." He waved as he approached. "I'm Benjamin Church. Everyone just calls me Church." He waved cheerfully for the Daves to follow him as he climbed up into the tractor. The friendly gesture was inconsistent with the battle rifle slung on his back.

"I'm Dave Wheeler, and this is Dave Mitchell. Nice to finally meet you." The Two Daves saluted in greeting.

The tractor was a cramped five-seater. When the hatch was closed, the compartment pressurized in just a minute. The Daves pressed the latch to open their helmets. They retracted and disappeared into their collars immediately and silently. Wheeler loved that feature.

Church took his helmet off. The air inside the tractor held a lingering scent of ammonia. A full-ready rack of various weapons covered the back of the tractor. There were no forward-facing windows in front of the driver seat—just a mosaic of high def screens that held images of the surrounding area and tactical information displays. Plasteel round windows were on the left and right sides.

"How long you fellas work for Oklahoma Salvage?" Church asked as the vehicle started moving. "The *TOMPKINS* shuttle is new. Harv must be doing well with OS."

"We've been with OS for just over two years," Mitchell replied. "We work out of the ship *OXCART*, in this sector.

"I've been on the OXCART. Tressa Pope is a personal friend. She and I are both from Albion. She's the best pilot I've ever met. Ugly ship, beautiful woman. Beauty and the beast."

They all laughed.

"Pardon my asking, but should we be armed? It would only take a minute to go back." Wheeler asked.

"Not necessary. Old habit. There are a few local species that are a problem now and then, is all." Church waved it off. "It's 1100 local time. We run Lumina Standard Time here. I figured we'd stop by the dome on the way to the site, have some lunch, and pick up some more gear, maybe."

"Sounds good. Food is good. Two days of protein bars and coffee has gotten old." Mitchell said.

"Coffee?" Church craned his neck around to look at them with a wide smile. "Have not had fresh coffee in a long while."

"After we load the salvage, we will be happy to hook you up," Wheeler said.

✳✳✳

It took about ten more minutes over the rough terrain to get to the dome. Finally, Church drove on a road up onto the side of the mountain ridge. The dome was a lattice of triangles resting among the peaks. On this side was a huge tarmac that was completely filled with a massive ore hauler.

"I see why we had to land out there. Did you cut that shelf for that landing pad?" Mitchell asked.

"We had to. Leaving the ship in orbit and dragging the containers back and forth would have cut too deep into the profit margins that were already low."

"Oar haulers? You mine? Seems an odd choice for a small family operation." Wheeler said as they rounded a corner. The precipice increased to three hundred meters on the left side.

"We do some mining for fabricator metals. We make most of our money farming specialty foods like apples, oranges, lemons, peaches, as well as a lot of water and ice. Plus, we have a fishery. There is so much freshwater. We have a deep lake under the dome. People love real fish, freshwater lobster, and crabs." He turned onto the tarmac toward a garage with a shimmering containment field to keep the atmospheres segregated.

"What's with the ammonia?" Mitchell asked.

"The atmosphere here is mostly carbon dioxide and nitrogen. Traces of argon and hydrogen. Nothing worth harvesting. The ammonia is environmental. And not everywhere. I never really thought about it much because ya gotta wear a suit outside the dome, anyway."

As they passed through the atmosphere-containment-field, all the lights came on in the garage. It was big enough to fit two of the tractors but only held a small Hammerhead Sport two-seater off to one side, like a motorcycle, a grav-bike shaped like a hammerhead shark because of the dual turbines on the front, for speed.

"My wife, Hoshi, has lunch ready. Stew and fresh-baked bread, with real butter. You will likely meet my daughter, Jade.

She's a bit odd for a 25-year-old." Church said as he parked and shut down the tractor. "She's the one that found the abandoned… ship."

"Our boss, Cobb, didn't tell us what kind of ship. Do you know?" Wheeler asked over his shoulder.

"I think it's a life pod. A big one. An old one. It gives me the creeps, and I'd like it off my planet." Church said.

"I have some standardized colony ship parts for repairs," Mitchell said. "I understand it's small enough that we can tow it into the cargo bay on the *NAVAN* if we need to."

The hatch slid aside to the inner corridor, and a woman stood there, bringing Church up short. She didn't step aside to let them pass. She had long black hair in a thick braid that she held in front of her with both hands like a climbing rope. She wore a charcoal gray, form-fitting, vac-suit that left nothing to the imagination. Her skin was pale, and her eyes were a deep green. She was a bit taller than Wheeler.

Wheeler felt his awkwardness switch flip to the on position. For some reason, he had expected a teenage girl, not a beautiful woman.

"Gentlemen, this is my daughter, Jade," Church said in a classic long-suffering father tone. "Please don't believe a word she says. A comedian this one. Jade, this is Dave Wheeler and Dave Mitchell from Oklahoma Salvage."

She bowed her head in a classic Japanese gesture and stepped back so they could pass. *Her mother must be Japanese,* Wheeler thought. *But she has her father's eyes. She's beautiful. Dammit. Stay cool. Don't sound the fool, like usual.*

Church led the way. Mitchell next, followed by Wheeler and finally Jade.

She was suddenly at Wheeler's ear, her body pressing against his back, whispering, "They are holding me here against my will." When he regained enough composure and turned to look at her, the hatch was closing, and she was gone.

***

The long corridor wound around and to the right. The wall on the left gave way to clear plasteel floor-to-ceiling windows looking out onto the tarmac where the massive hauler stood parked. Wheeler kept looking over his shoulder. He could still smell her hair.

"What's up." Mitchell quietly asked him.

He saw the green Hammerhead streak along the tarmac to launch out over the plateau below through the glass wall.

"Nothing," he said. Church was looking back at them.

A heavy hatch slid aside, opening into the primary residence. It was beautiful—plasteel walls on three sides with an open floor plan. Beethoven was playing somewhere, and there was a muted baseball game on a massive screen to one side. Thick rugs defined seating and dining areas. There was even a grand piano at the far end near the view of the two setting moons.

A sharp turn to their right was the kitchen with a massive, polished stone island. Eight high back stools were opposite the business side of the large kitchen.

A tall Asian woman was just setting the third placemat on the island.

"This is my wife, Hoshi." Church began. "This is Wheeler and Mitchell. The Two Daves."

She smiled and reached out to shake their hands across the island. Her perfectly combed hair cascaded along her arm as she reached out. Her smile went all the way to her eyes as she spoke.

"It's nice to meet you." She said. "They really do call you The Two Daves, then? I thought Church was bullshitting me."

"Yep. I'm afraid so." Mitchell said. "We joined the team as junior mates on the same day. It stuck because we work well as a team."

Wheeler said nothing as he watched the dust trail streaking across the plain in the far distance.

"I'm starving," Church said.

"Stew, fresh bread, and real butter," Hoshi said. "My favorite."

"Where do you get your butter?" Mitchell asked, looking at Wheeler with an eyebrow raised.

"We make it ourselves. We keep cows and goats in the dome. It keeps the grass down in the orchards. There are chickens, rabbits, and pigs as well in other enclosures. We have a good spot for the compound." Hoshi said with pride in her voice.

"Perfect temps and atmospheric pressure at this elevation for the domes. No pressure differential, and lots of compatible native organics," Church added.

"Looked pretty desolate out there on the way in," Wheeler said, trying to contribute to the conversation.

"There is a rapidly growing type of moss that loves the soil here and the high CO_2. Pigs and chickens love eating it." Church replied.

"What's the deal with Jade?" Wheeler asked, trying to sound neutral. But, unfortunately, the reaction was like he froze time for a few heartbeats.

"What do you mean?" Hoshi said, first.

"It seems a lonely life for a young woman," Wheeler said. "There is no one else on this whole planet?"

"Jade is not as young as she looks. She's 25. She does what she wants. Whatever she wants. Wherever she wants." Church said with a tone Wheeler could not pinpoint.

Hoshi set steaming bowls of stew in front of each of them along with two baskets of bread and crocks of butter. There was an awkward pause.

"Jade found the ship," Church said, trying to jump-start the conversation. "She's sure it's a ship. That girl spent weeks trying to get inside before she even told us about it. When she finally did, it was dark, cold, empty. No bridge, no propulsion, no control systems. Just a salon and residence."

"It does sound like a lifeboat." Mitchell said, "But still worth good money."

"I don't like it," Hoshi said. "I just want it off my planet. It's unnerving to look at."

"It doesn't look like a ship. It's a perfect sphere," Church added. "Just floating there, three meters off the floor of that cave."

"Cave?" Wheeler felt himself getting slightly angry for reasons he didn't understand. *Was Jade messing with me?* They seemed genuinely concerned about her.

"It's not... It feels haunted. The surface is so reflective, more than a mirror finish." Hoshi said.

"And if you try to touch it... It's like it's not there."

***

"I'm sorry about that," Church said as they were suiting back up. "Hoshi knows that Jade will be leaving soon. She had hoped that she'd find someone at Lumina Station on the logistics runs. Someone who she might settle in with, in one of the other residences we've built."

"Logistics runs?" Wheeler asked.

"When we get a full cargo load, Hoshi and Jade take the *FISHER KING*, the cargo ship, and make the slow run to Lumina Station," Church said. "If we had a second ship, maybe she'd be happier. I think that's what Jade was hoping for. A ship of her own. She's a good pilot and has even made the run a half dozen times alone."

"Alone?" Wheeler echoed, beginning to feel he sounded like a parrot. But Lumina was a place where one can get anything.

"She doesn't like Lumina Station. Too many people. She stays on the *FISHER KING* when she goes alone. She has all the shopping delivered." Church said as they climbed into the tractor. "Lumina needs less and less from us in recent years. Their own planet, Vor, has been stepping up its own production. Prices are dropping. We've been thinking of trading the *FISHER KING* in for a pair of old S22s FTL shuttles and maybe a good auto-doc. Retire the mining operation altogether and relax a bit."

Wheeler felt the same about Lumina. He looked over at Mitchell and confirmed that they were both thinking the same thing. They had several S22s at the Yard.

"Where's Jade now?" Mitchell asked.

Church punched up a tactical map of the surrounding area. He pointed to a green pulsing dot. It was the same green as the paint on the Hammerhead. "She's at the salvage site already. Something is up with her."

Wheeler could still smell her hair.

***

It took just under 40 minutes for the tractor to reach the site. The terrain they crossed went from rocky to flat and then rocky again as they approached the mountains on the other side of the valley.

When they arrived, they could see that it was less a cave than a really deep overhang. The floor was a fine layer of shale chips that had fallen over the millennia. The tractor had been there enough times that a road was developing.

The Hammerhead sat parked deeper inside, with the cowling up. They almost didn't see the ship. Its reflection of the surrounding environment was so perfect, and it was nearly invisible. It was a perfect sphere of about twenty meters in diameter, just floating and perfectly still. It reflected the darkness and rocks that surrounded it in the shadows.

The ship had a spiral staircase deployed from the bottom. Next to the stairs was a yellow and black cargo crate about a meter square. Church turned on the tractor's floodlights. They helped but were mostly disbursed and reflected back.

Jade came down the wide steps as they hopped out of the tractor. The Two Daves each carried a backpack of tools. The crushed and packed shale on the road beneath their boots was almost a fine sand. The cave was warmer than the temp out on the plain.

"Never seen anything like it," Mitchell said as they approached, Church close behind.

When Wheeler caught Jade's eye, he tapped the side of his helmet and held up two fingers for her to switch to private comm channel 2. He figured she would know some miner's sign language.

"So… What do you think?" Jade said on the private channel.

"Forget the salvage. Are you alright?" His voice was urgent.

"I'm fine," Jade replied. "I'm sorry about that. It was kind of an impromptu discretion test. Sorry. Good job. You passed." Her smile and eyes teased him.

"Say that to the wrong guy, and your parents would now be dead." Wheeler was mad. "I know men that would shoot your mom in the face, ransack the compound for booze, and bacon and sleep like a baby after."

"I'm a decent judge of character," Jade said, smile brightening. "Besides, Pope told me all about you two. She and I, we're friends. We are both from Albion."

"Why bullshit me then?" Wheeler asked.

Jade took him by the arm as if she was walking down the aisle.

"Because I haven't told my father about the dead guy," Jade said. She winked.

***

Mitchell was the first one to the spiral stairs. He started right up but paused to touch the surface of the sphere when he could reach it. He caressed it with his gloved hand.

"I've heard of this kind of frictionless surface before. That should narrow down the provenance of this thing. It was too expensive back in the day for mass production." Mitchell said. "These stairs are standard colony gear. Used a lot during the expansion."

He started up, and Jade followed right behind, then Church and finally, Wheeler.

Wheeler mentally measured the craft as he ascended. There were enough steps to have climbed past an entire interior level to the second floor. He cleared the floor's edge to the apparent main level. Portable floodlights were already illuminating the interior.

"Dave, this a Delta34 control interface. Do you still have that bypass unit, the yellow one?" Mitchell said as he examined a panel on the wall at the top of the stairs with a penlight. He looked at Jade then. "Do you have the remote? The control fob?"

Jade looked embarrassed suddenly, even through her face shield. She began digging in a pocket. "Yes. But it doesn't work anymore." She handed it to Mitchell.

As Mitchell dug through his pack for something, Wheeler handed him a yellow device that had seen better days. The screen of the device was scratched all over and cracked in one corner. Mitchell found the case of specialized tools he was looking for and unrolled them on a table.

"An old school fob would only open the hatch to an equalized habitat, which is weird. Did you try a palm scan?" He asked.

"You mean take off a glove and bare hand the panel? Um, no." Jade replied.

"It's five degrees Celsius in here, and the air pressure is good," Mitchell said as he tightened his suit's forearm tourniquet and then twisted off the glove at the wrist ring. With his bare hand, he palmed the dark glass panel. A light bar activated and scanned his hand. In red, it said ACCESS DENIED.

"Excellent," Wheeler said. "Did you see the power standby idiot light?"

"Yep," Mitchell said with a smile in his voice.

"What does that mean?" Church asked, speaking for the first time since entering.

"It means the systems still have power, and it had shut down automatically and went into standby mode."

"Is there another control panel in here?" Church asked.

"I never found one," Jade replied. "It has a huge bar, though, but all the booze is gone."

"Back in the day, they made these things dirt simple for colonists," Mitchell said.

"How is it simple if there is no way to access the control panel. Not so much as a single screw visible." Jade said.

"They made it difficult on purpose. To stop people from fooling with it that don't know what they're doing." Mitchell held up a specialty tool that looked like a scalpel with a hook at the end of the blade. It was paper-thin, and he slid it into the narrow crack between the dark glass of the control panel and the smooth wall. When it caught on something, he pulled, something clicked, and the panel swung out, revealing circuit boards and ribbon cables inside. Mitchell unplugged a specific ribbon cable and plugged it into the yellow device.

"Jade, would you be so kind as to palm the panel now?" Mitchell said as he mostly closed the panel with the ribbon still attached.

She took off her glove and hesitated only a moment.

ACCESS GRANTED. The lights in the salon came up. The stairs retracted and sealed. They could hear air handlers rattle to life and begin replacing the atmosphere inside.

***

Two minutes later, the control panel reset. All four of their palms were now registered as crew. Wheeler popped his helmet open and took a sniff.

"Still a trace of ammonia but good," Wheeler said. "It's warming up as well."

The room they stood in was a half-circle salon, including a kitchen, dining, and living areas. The outer wall had become a subtle source of light, like a window with fog beyond. A bedroom, bath, closet, and pantry were on the other side of the wall.

"Computer, exterior view." Suddenly it was like a floor-to-ceiling window that looked out to the desolate landscape through the cave's overhang.

"Computer, how long have you been on standby," Wheeler asked.

It began replying in a language none of them recognized.

"Computer, stop," Wheeler said. "Set default language to English."

"Computer, Status," Wheeler said.

"Powering up the main reactors. Batteries at 13%. Power up, self-start nominal. All Systems will be available in eleven minutes." Wheeler was smiling at Jade now.

"Computer, lift," Wheeler said. A circular shaft descended from the ceiling and rotated to open. Wheeler gestured for Jade to enter.

They all crowded in, and Mitchell pressed a wide button marked "Engineering Level," and the lift went down one level.

The door opened to a much smaller but perfectly round room. The walls held twelve separate reactors—each with old-style idiot light panels. Two of the reactors had a couple of yellow lights among the green.

Mitchell let out a low whistle. "I think I know what this is. It's a Comms Class Courier ship. I thought they were all gone. Dismantled."

"The spiral staircase passes right through here." Jade marveled.

"This config could have stairs to all three levels, or a lift, or just openings if you fly in zero-G," Wheeler said.

"Here are some red lights, Dave," Church said from the other side.

"Looks like it needs new scrubbers," Mitchell said. "No big deal. We have some that should work on the *NAVAN*."

"Wait until you see this." Wheeler stepped into the lift, and they all packed in again. He pressed the button marked, 'Bridge.'

Jade could hardly contain herself.

The door rotated closed, and they started up. When they reached that level, instead of the door on the lift rotating open, the entire elevator disappeared into the floor, leaving the room open all around. On this level, the room was much smaller. It was a circle about three meters around. A pilot and copilot configuration on one side and a booth recessed in the back wall, flanked by two small doors and a series of lockers. One entry had the universal symbol for the toilet, and the other held a plaque that read Storage.

"It has only three levels. All the other spaces surrounding and between levels hold systems and mechanicals. Computer, activate dome," Mitchell said. The exterior view covered the dome in high resolution. "The only reason I know anything about this kind of vessel is because it is the first ship to use a dome display. This early version only had this one view. Everything else was done at the pilot's consoles and displays. It just replaced physical windows and blast shields. Windows fail."

Jade lost her cool and squealed. She hugged her father fiercely around the neck and jumped briefly on Wheeler's back, kissing his cheek.

"Computer, what is your OS version?" Wheeler asked as he sat in the copilot's seat. Jade quietly, slowly, reverently, slid into the pilot's seat.

"Paloma, v231.39b," it said flatly.

"We can update that a bit. But not much." Mitchell said.

"What are the red lights?" Jade asked Wheeler, pointing at the display to his right.

"The water tanks are empty. CO2 scrubbers are completely dead. Reactors 7 and 11 are super low on coolant. Waste processing is offline, and that's normal if there is no water. Anti-grav core is at 4% and nearly depleted. The security token is present but failing to respond. It wants you to dock it here. It probably needs a recharge." Wheeler pointed to a slot in the center console.

Jade placed the fob in the slot. An indicator above it now said CHARGING.

"Will it fly?" Jade asked, unable to hide the tremble in her voice.

"I don't see why not. Technically it is already by floating here," Wheeler said. "I wouldn't take it into orbit until we fix a few things, top off the water and gases. Most of these are because there is no water. The null status on the water reclamation system will change once we figure out how to fill the tanks."

"We can probably fly it right into the hold on the *NAVAN*," Mitchell said.

"No. I'm keeping it," Jade stated. "And you're going to help me with repairs."

Church rolled his eyes and shook his head.

***

Jade and Wheeler were going to fly the Courier back to the Farm Domes. It wouldn't fit in the garage, but it could dock with the standard top hatch of the structure. Church was taking the tractor back to the farm. Mitchell was taking the Hammerhead back to the *NAVAN*.

Mitchell needed to send a message to Cobb at Oklahoma Salvage. The nature of the mission had now changed. Instead of them buying salvage, they'd have to charge them for repairs.

Alone and strapped in, Wheeler asked, "Did you get the security token off the dead guy you mentioned?"

The silver sphere was sliding out of the cave at walking speed. Jade was flying. She had a very light touch on the controls. Wheeler was impressed. It was an atypical dual-stick flight control interface.

"The dead guy was how I found the ship. He was sitting over there on that ledge, leaning back against the wall there. His vac suit was red, faded, but still red. He's under that pile of rocks now. There." Jade said as she pointed out the small cairn, "He climbed up there and took his helmet off. Suicide. He's just a desiccated skeleton now—a dry sack of bones. I found the body, so I searched the area. That's when I found the ship. I couldn't lower the stairs for weeks until I went back and searched his remains. I found the fob, then piled the cairn."

"Why not tell your parents?" he asked as they increased speed and altitude.

"It's my mother," Jade said. "She sees omens everywhere. So I don't tell her lots of things. Like my father was letting me keep the salvage proceeds to get away and start my own life. Like my brothers."

"I didn't know you had brothers," Wheeler said as they flew over the *NAVAN* as Mitchell waved.

Over Wheeler's suit comms, Mitchell's voice came through. "Church and I were both broadcasting comm checks all the way. Add comms to the punch list."

"Acknowledged," Wheeler replied to Mitchell. "Why are you keeping it?" he asked Jade. "OS would probably pay big credits for it. Probably enough to buy a small modern ship. Want me to get an estimate? Otherwise, it will COST you a lot of money to keep it."

"Let's assess more before I decide. The mine operation is losing money. Dad was counting on my brothers to take it over and make a go of it. But neither of them was interested. The farm is doing well, but Lumina is our only customer, and they know it, so the price controls are harsh. My pilot skills are being wasted here. My parents are not good at business. We have so many pigs because we have so much farm surplus that we can't use or sell fast enough. They are very well-fed pigs. I'm not sure the two of them can keep this up alone."

"But this ship isn't good for much. Even if the FTL drives still work." Wheeler said. "No cargo space, no passenger space. As a message courier, it's useless now that we have the planetary QUEST Comms network."

"It can be a home. My home. Anywhere. Even here." She said. "Just not here."

I'm being held against my will. Wheeler thought. And he knew the feeling.

She was a great pilot—the terrain slid by smoothly as she got used to the controls. She had joy in her eyes as she flew. She flew under arches, in trenches and canyons. She knew the planet. It was like she had been flying this ship her whole life.

***

The garage had a top-dock airlock hatch that was the correct interface for the sphere. The elevator shaft extended down and automatically attached. Bots connected the universal umbilicals. Water, O2, and power interfaces were all connected even though no power was required. The reality was that just one of the reactors on this sphere could supply energy to the entire installation if need be.

Jade and Wheeler watched the water begin the transfer.

"The first generation Grav-Drives, like these, were way overbuilt. They carried so many redundancies and over-spec capabilities." Wheeler marveled at how paranoid the original shipbuilders had been. "They're not fast but built to last. I can understand primary and secondary systems, even tertiary systems. But this ship is twelve deep into redundancy. But any more than two people in here, and it would seem crowded fast."

"That's weird." Jade stood to try and look over the ledge. "Something moved down there."

"I found the logs," Wheeler said. "Last entry was just over eighty-four years ago."

An image of a man came up. He was sitting in the pilot seat where Jade sat again now. He wore a red pressure suit but had not put his helmet on yet. The display said, 'Captain Willard Underwood.'

"This is my last entry. I'm too tired. I'm sick of running. Sick of cancer eating me up… Tired of the smuggler's life. This will be one last big screw you. And just outside, there is an amazing view." He held up a clear bottle of pills and gave it a shake. "So after I'm done taking these, washing them down with the last of the whiskey and my recycled suit piss, I'm going for a walk. I'm going out there to watch the sunset."

He upended half a bottle of pills into his mouth and drank from his suit tube. He repeated it until all the capsules were gone. "The water reclamation system is fixed but not before all the water was lost. Sorry. The good news, the best news, is those fuckers will never find me now. They'll think I got away."

He laughed and cut the log as he stood up.

"I found him out there. On the ledge. He took his helmet off." She repeated. Jade wiped her eyes self-consciously. "I guess we should check that repair before we have a full tank."

"Damn thing has ten spare reactors and Grav-Drives, but just a single water tank?" Mitchell said.

"Plus multiple water recycling systems?" Wheeler said.

"It does have another water tank," Jade pointed to one of the display screens. "The primary use was of that smaller tank was O2 creation from water. Both tanks were filling and holding."

"It was nice of him to leave all the consoles unlocked. I don't think he expected it to sit this long." Wheeler said.

"What did he say about smuggling? About getting away?" Jade said to herself.

"Wheeler, this is Dek." A voice came over an open channel, "Sorry to interrupt, but I've been talking to Cobb at the OS front office. Seeing shit has changed on this job, we need to talk."

"Dek, you need to know I'm not alone, and Jade can hear you," Wheeler said, looking at Jade.

"Who is Dek?" She asked Wheeler.

"I'm the salvaged AI they are trying to keep secret. If you look to the west on the opposite ridge, I'm waving." Dek lied. Wheeler rolled his eyes.

Jade stood for a better view. A small eight-legged all-terrain vehicle was waving a utility arm at them in an absurdly friendly hello gesture. Jade waved back before she could stop herself. It looked like a giant spider. Wheeler marveled at how Dek's mannerisms made him seem friendly all the time. But Wheeler knew better.

"Jade, while we are waiting for Wheeler to recover from freezing up, let's chat."

"Okay. I've never talked to an AI before." Jade said.

"I have grown to hate the term AI. Just call me Dek."

"Okay, Dek. What the hell?"

"Hey, I was going to say that." Wheeler shook his head and sat back.

"I have access to the biggest database ever assembled of ship design specs. But no specs for that ship." Dek continued. "Without the schematics, I'm sorry, but FTL testing will be too dangerous."

"Full specs are here," Jade said, having searched for them first thing. "Want a copy? If Dave says it's alright, I'll send you one."

Before Wheeler could open his mouth, Dek said. "Only if you let me pay you 5,000 credits for exclusive rights on the specs. I can maybe toss in some help from the Two Dave's. And maybe you can talk your parents into a contract with us to buy all your farm output."

"How did you know I would keep the ship, Dek?"

"If I were you, I would have." Dek said, "If the ship checks out, Cobb says we may also want to hire you and your ship. As a courier. The job it was originally designed for."

"Why would you hire me? You don't know me." She said.

"Oh, boy. Here we go." Dave said, rolling his eyes.

"I know more about you than you may realize," Dek said. "I'll send a contract, with signing bonus and even ship refit. If it's required."

"That's how they suck people in. With access to parts." Wheeler tossed in, warning her.

"And what about this deal with my parents?" She asked.

"Oklahoma Salvage has a new HQ on Elba. There is limited space for agriculture there, and the population is increasing. So they've been looking for partners. Plus…" There was an obvious dramatic pause for comedy effect. "They require bacon. Addiction is a horrible thing. So is logistics."

"Cobb says that bacon and coffee are the leading indicators of civilization." Wheeler laughed. "And he already has a steady supplier for excellent coffee."

"You know that there are people that would straight-up kill you for an AI orb, right?" Jade said, completely serious.

"Dek does what he wants," Wheeler said. "He must have a good reason to trust you."

"Jade, what'd you do?" It was Church over the comms. "OS has deposited 5,000 credits into your account and send you a Non-Disclosure Agreement with an encrypted file. Tell me you didn't just sell them that ship for only 5,000 credits."

"No, father. I'm keeping the ship." Jade said. The smile was evident in her voice. "I'll be right in."

***

The Two Daves were surprised that Jade never mentioned Dek.

Work on the ship only took about a week. The reactors that were running hot were just taken off-line until they could get additional coolant. They considered tapping all the other reactors for a bit of coolant each, but why bother? They slowly fired up the other ten reactors until they were humming at 80%, and the old-style grav-drive began to recharge. All agreed that they would rather find the issue here than be stranded in the long dark.

The comm system was the worst problem. The design of the ship prevented them from installing any external antennas or dish arrays. The exterior of the vessel was not a single solid surface. It was made up of "Skins" about a hundred layers of micron-thin envelopes that constantly moved. Each skin only covered 75% of the craft but moved so fast you could not perceive it with your eye or touch—no chance for long-range comms. When the stairs or lift needed to be deployed, all the layers aligned so the lift could penetrate the skin. It was a brilliant design that protected the ship from microscopic impacts of debris. It was way beyond spec for that. The self-healing design of the skin made it look new, even if it was an antique.

They also discovered that the exterior was so reflective that it could reflect a mining-grade laser. Even a rare momentary, straight-on, direct hit would cause little to no damage. It had no offensive weapons at all, though.

The comm gear had been completely removed. They figured that Captain Underwood did not want any traceable RF footprint if he was hiding.

The short-range comms were restored. All the antennas were within the interior. They tested out to have a short-range of about half a million kilometers. The only person it bothered was Jade's mother. She just wanted to be able to keep in touch at all times.

"If I were parked on the moon, I could at least call here," Jade said as the comms were calibrated.

"You will have no comms at FTL, though," Wheeler told her.

***

The proposed contracts were reviewed and eventually signed. Jade had never had any experience with lawyers or contracts before. She just signed.

On the morning of the orbital shakedown cruise, they were all having breakfast in the kitchen. The family plus the Two Daves had fallen into a routine of having breakfast together and an occasional dinner. They were all so busy. The farm was consuming more and more of Church's time. He owed Lumina one more shipment. Then the run to Elba right after that.

Over the past days, Jade had become a different person on the outside. No long a brooding type, she looked and acted more like a professional ship's engineer. She had fabricated her own ship suit, copying the Two Daves. Coveralls with pockets everywhere for the tools she seemed to need constantly now as she crawled over the ship. It was a deep green.

"Have you picked a name for the ship yet, sweetheart?" Jade's mother asked, breaking the awkward silence of worry she'd created this morning.

"Yes." Jade smiled wide. "I will call her *GIN 109*."

Hoshi was instantly pleased.

Jade turned to the Two Daves and explained, "*GIN*, 銀, means Silver in Japanese. 109 is the atomic mass of silver. Plus, it sounds perfect."

"You will need to apply for an ID transponder before you traffic the Sol inner systems," Church added.

"Now that she is an Oklahoma Salvage sub-contractor, we can hook her up with an ID Transponder, coolant to top off the reactors, better comms, replace all the pipes in the water reclamation system, and CO2 scrubbers that are rightsized."

"If the orbital tests go well today, tomorrow we will do FTL tests and maybe an overnight to the Oklahoma Salvage Yard, maybe swing by Elba HQ or Lumina." Jade sounded excited.

"Did you fix the fridge in the galley?" Church asked. He was digging in his pocket as he spoke.

"No," Jade replied. "It will be easier to replace the entire thing."

Church was trying not to butt in too much. He pulled out a cloth patch with Velcro backing. He handed it to Jade, with the Velcro side up.

She turned it over. It was a name patch for her ship suit. It read: Captain Jade Church

She just stared at it until her mother came around the table, gently took it from her, and applied it to the spot on her coveralls designed to hold it. She put her hands on each side of Jade's face and kissed her forehead. They fell into a fierce hug.

"Is it a bit dusty in here?" Wheeler smiled as all three men began to clear the dishes.

***

"Comm check, *GIN* 109 here, umbilicals detached. Can anyone hear me?" Jade said over the comms with a playful formal affectation.

"*NAVAN 4* hears you loud and clear," Mitchell said from the shuttle that would follow just in case it had problems.

"Good luck, sweetheart," Hoshi said from the residence dome. "Please stick to the flight plan."

"Yeah, stick to the flight plan, so we know where to look for wreckage," Church said from a handheld out in one of the farm domes. There was humor in his voice. He was teasing Hoshi.

"First, straight up two hundred kilometers. Nice and easy." Wheeler said, sitting back in the copilot seat and hooking his thumbs in the shoulder straps of the five-point harness. "I don't like these old systems. I prefer analog readings. Show me the actual reactor core temps, not just a red light when it's too hot."

"It looks like a silver balloon just drifting up," Hoshi said over the comms.

"See this?" Wheeler pointed to a globe in the center of the console that had confusing displays. "This represents the orientation of the ship versus the dome display in here." Wheeler pointed to the globe and the dome display above and all around them.

"Does this mean we are actually inverted relative to the planet?" Jade looked at the globe and the dome and back. "Because of the old-style grav-drives, we are falling up at 3G? Is that right? Our heads are pointed straight down at the planet?"

That was counter-intuitive. The dome display showed the opposite. Jade tweaked the controls gently, and the display dome changed around, making it seem like they had smoothly rotated.

"The display changed. We did not. See, we're still head down." Wheeler said, shaking his head. "Excellent inertial dampeners in here. You'd never know."

Mitchell was waiting for them in the *NAVAN* at 200 kilometers. The planet was still vast and close.

Jade tested the manual controls first. They were nicely responsive. No sounds changed when she rapidly accelerated away from the *NAVAN*.

"Wow." That was all she said. They felt nothing.

"Try the voice control," Wheeler said.

"GIN. Maintain an altitude of 200 kilometers and enter a standard orbit." Jade said. She watched her words echo and type onto a display on the console marked NAV COMMAND WINDOW.

ACKNOWLEDGED. Appeared below her command. Comms opened.

"That is some creepy-looking shit," Mitchell said. "The way it moves. No engine bells."

Jade changed the orientation of the dome, so most of the screen was taken up by the planet. It looked like they were flying under it now.

"We are now halfway through our first orbit," Wheeler said.

"What the hell?" Jade was looking at the planet's surface. She was comparing it to a map on another display. "Papa, the south lake is gone. It looks completely dry."

"He can't receive you now," Wheeler said. "In an orbit this low, the farm has already fallen below the horizon. No relay sats. So what lake are you talking about?"

Jade brought up a map of the surface on his console. "Right here should be a massive lake. Way bigger than the one at the farm. You can see the tarmac and pump station we built there. Just no lake."

Not removing his hands from the harness, Wheeler smiled and said, "Let's take a quick look."

"*NAVAN*, we are going to drop down and do a quick surface recon." Jade radioed professionally as the *NAVAN* caught up.

"I will hold here," Mitchell replied. "Dek is monitoring."

The *GIN 109* dropped fast on manual control with no interior sense of motion. It slid through the atmosphere with no vapor trail and no spike in external temp somehow. It decelerated at an unnerving rate as well. It stopped abruptly at 100 meters above a dry lake bed. Cliffs rose on all sides that show the bleached stone of the old waterlines. They began to move along the cliff wall.

"I love the dome canopy displays for this reason," Wheeler said as he watched the stark, desert-like terrain drift by. "There's why the lake is empty." Wheeler pointed to a large hole in the lakebed at the southern end.

"Is that a crater or a sinkhole?" Mitchell said over the comms.

"My money is on a sinkhole. This planet is riddled with caverns." Jade said.

The hole was a giant gaping maw with sheer sides and seemingly no bottom. It was about five times the diameter of the *GIN*.

"Let's test some systems," Jade said. "GIN, hold here." It was repeated on the console, followed by ACKNOWLEDGED.

"Sensors are limited on this boat. Optical, radiation, proximity radar, external temp, and atmosphere makeup. Are about it?" Wheeler said. "Look at the ammonia levels here. Higher than I have ever seen. Anywhere."

"Try the fine controls. This looks stable enough to go down there a bit for a peek." Wheeler said. "Just remember, on auto-pilot, you have collision avoidance. You don't on manual."

"I don't know, man," Mitchell said. "Hate to see a failure when you're down there. The *NAVAN* can't follow."

Jade just went. No discussion. They all heard Dek quietly chuckle on the comms.

After descending a few hundred meters, she stopped. They were out of the sun now, and the view was all rock walls. Looking at the globe control, she rotated the flight stick and stopped. It now seemed like they were at the bottom of the shaft looking up. The dome screen adjusted to lower light levels as they descended more.

More and more holes began to appear in the walls of the sinkhole.

"Computer, do you have any external lights," Wheeler asked. EXTERNAL LIGHT appeared in the command window, followed by ACKNOWLEDGED.

Walls were illuminated with intense light. The display adjusted.

"I think the entire sphere is glowing," Jade remarked. "The silver skins must do it."

"Ammonia levels are way higher now," Wheeler said.

There was a sudden impact that felt like something hit the hull.

"What was that?" Jade exclaimed. "A boulder?"

"What?" Wheeler was searching the dome.

"Something flew by us," Jade said as another one whisked by into the darkness.

"It fell from above!" Wheeler said, reminding Jade that the display was inverted. "Look there."

Wheeler pointed to the cavern below where it opened out. They were about a kilometer down when the creatures began to fall like rain. Constant impacts.

"We're under attack!" Jade shouted and descended faster. The impacts drove them down—hundreds of creatures launched from the tunnels on the sides to try and land on the frictionless sphere. Then, with nothing to grab, the ones that didn't miss slipped down the sides in droves. They were all massive articulated, many-legged creatures like centipedes three meters long and looked like they were made of metal.

They cleared the bottom edge of the sinkhole, and it opened into an enormous cavern. The glow of the ship revealed a lake below where the giant centipedes plunged into the water. Jade quickly shifted to the side, and the rainfall of creatures stopped. They watched the last few plummet to the lake below and land with an enormous splash.

"What the fuck was that?" Wheeler said. "

"They are Feriapods," Jade said. "Damn things eat metals. They tunnel and must have undermined the area between the lake and the cavern. Nasty buggers. They hate water. Drown easy."

"That's the smell," Wheeler said. "They produce ammonia."

"Comms don't reach down here. Mitchell might be freaking out." Jade replied as she started back up.

"How the hell are we going to get out of here?' Jade asked. A bit of fear had slipped into her voice.

"The things flooded out of the side tunnels. The light seemed to attract them." Wheeler said. "Can you fly this in the dark?" She turned off the lights. Enhanced mode remained on. The large cave turned a dark, eerie green.

"I think so," Jade said, and she began to move into the shaft slowly. Finally, the light from the sky far above was enough. She was taking it up, slowly and silently.

It hit without warning. It was far larger than the other Feripods. It balanced on the sphere as it drove it back down. A giant mouth was trying to bite the ship. Wheeler flinched back deeper into his seat as they heard the infrastructure groan in the ship.

Without hesitation, Jade flipped the ship. The overbalance caused the giant horror to slip away, but in the process, its thrashing crashed the vessel into the opposite side of the shaft, causing another avalanche of debris.

She punched it up and out before any more like it emerged. They left the shaft with the velocity of a bullet.

***

The panels were all green. To both of their amazement, there was no damage to the exterior of the *GIN* 109.

"That was fun." Jade sent to Mitchell over the comms, trying to sound amused instead of scared shitless.

"Are you trying to freak me out? We should have sent Dek with you for the QUEST Comms…" Mitchell said, but Wheeler cut him off.

"Mitchell!" He barked in an attempt to shut him up.

"You have an AI orb AND a Quantum Entangled QUEST Comm in that spider?" Jade was incredulous.

"Way to go, Dave." Wheeler sighed.

Dek himself replied on comms as the *GIN* began to slide along the lakebed.

"Jade, I'd like to remind you that you have already signed the full non-disclosure agreement. THIS more than anything else must be kept secret." Dek paused.

"Ok, ok… I presume you guys will read me in when things get rolling?" Jade asked.

"Back to the Feriapods, if you don't mind." Dek continued. Changing the subject. "Those are from this planet?"

"Yes," Jade said. "They don't bother us much. They live underground and stay away from organic material like soil, the fungus in the caves, even water. They don't usually come above ground. They are easy enough to kill if they do. They un-shield their eyes in the open. Their eyes are the size of a grapefruit, but their brains are the size of a walnut. If you shoot them in the eye with an armor-piercing round, it will bounce around inside their heads. Wanna see a dead one?"

"Where?" Wheeler asked.

"Near the compound, there is one about 10K South East. Papa shot it. We use it as the outer marker. It's easy to see." Jade said as she went to about 4k in altitude and began speeding across the arid landscape. "The exoskeleton remains weigh a ton. So why move it."

***

They were back at the outer marker in no time.

So far, the ship had passed all the tests. The water reclamation system went condition yellow and needed to be flushed out thoroughly again to be sure. And all the necessary filters to be changed. But Church assured them he had plenty of water.

By the time the *GIN* landed, the *NAVAN* was on the ground. Dek was already studying the remains. The armor of the carapace was made up of several articulated plates. The entire carcass was about a meter wide by three meters long.

"Fascinating.' Dek said. "How long has this been here?"

"I don't remember exactly," Jade said as she walked up. "Twenty years or so. I was just a kid when Papa shot it. It's unusual ever to find a carcass. They eat their dead."

Dek reached down and snapped off an antenna segment at a joint. It looked like a dog's bone that was made of polished stainless steel. "Jade, do you have your ship's security fob with you?"

"Yes," she said as she drew it from her pocket.

"Does it have a button with a spiral symbol on it?" Dek asked, moving toward the ship. The two Daves could hear the suspicion in his voice.

"Yes, but it doesn't do anything. I tried it lots of times."

"Press the button that retracts the stairs and the spiral at the same time." Dek requested as if reading from the manual.

When she did, the ship settled to the ground as the stairs disappeared into it. A two-meter wide opening was revealed at ground level, with an old-iris-style round hatch. They all walked over to the hatch without a word.

"Didn't the dead guy say something about smuggling?" Wheeler asked.

"Now press the spiral button alone," Dek asked cautiously.

Jade pressed the button, the hatch irised open, revealing a compartment about two meters by two meters.

"At least we know now what he was smuggling," Mitchell said.

Neatly stacked inside were the remains of another disassembled Feriapod.

***

For the next hour, they ran a series of tests on the carapace. No drill bit in their collection could even scratch it. The laser cutters they had did little better. Warming the surfaces but not powerful enough to cut the stuff.

"I am pretty sure I know what it is. But the only other test I can think of is to toss a piece into the fabricator. If I'm right, it will ruin the fabricator's ingest shredders. Possibly destroy the entire fabricator." Wheeler said, looking at Mitchell. "There is only one component in constructing a fabricator that cannot be fabricated in another similar machine. And it's made of this type of alloy."

"Jade. It is my understanding that the *GIN* 109, and all its contents, belong to you." Dek said to her as he interlaced the fingers of his utility arms, moving his body slightly and giving the impression of looking from Jade to the Two Daves and back. "Do you know why The Two Daves keep my existence a secret?"

"Well, AI Orbs are worth a shitload of money. Millions. And one with a QUEST Comm… billions, maybe. I still don't believe they exist." Jade said. "But definitely worth murdering two dumb-ass Daves for, especially out here, no offense." She held her hands up to the Daves.

"None taken." They said in unison.

"That…" Dek pointed at the carapace. "… is worth murdering you and your whole family. You're not going to believe this, but I am authorized to offer you 500 million credits for just what you have in there," Dek gestured to the compartment as her eyes went wide. "Or… a trade. An AI Orb, with QUEST comms, installed in the *GIN* 109, plus fifty thousand credits. With conditions."

"Half a billion credits?" Jade was skeptical, shocked. "What conditions?"

"Well, you would still have to honor your Oklahoma Salvage contract. You would work for OS out of Elba in this sector. The thing is, on Elba Colony, AIs have the same rights as citizens. So I'd have to sign a service contract with you. I'd go with a 100-year contract with reviews every five years. As long as you worked for OS."

"What if I don't like OS and bail at the end of the contract?"

"Then you bail, and we would pay off the prorated balance of the 500 Million. No hard feelings." Dek said.

"No hard feelings? You know this sounds crazy, right?" Jade said. "You show up and start throwing credits at me? At my parents? No hard feelings?"

"There is only one place where hard feelings would be." Wheeler injected.

"Tell anyone that you have an AI or QUEST Comms, and there would be very hard feelings," Dek said. "You can't even tell your parents. Unless they come on board as well." Dek glanced at the second dead carapace.

"A half a billion credits? For that?" Jade said in awe. Then looked at the second dead one.

"Tell her the rest, Dek," Wheeler ordered. "A storm is about to break out there, and she needs to know. Tell her about Bram. You can't spring something like that after the fact."

"I have a servant. He's just an android that I command." Dek said with a slightly abashed tone. "His name is Bram. He would also be at your disposal." With that, Dek turned his glance toward the *NAVAN*.

Standing on the top of the ship, silhouetted against the gray sky, was a tall black figure. It wore a black hooded cloak the blew in the gentle breeze. Its eyes glowed red from within the darkness of the hood. It vaulted off the ship with a light movement and landed with a brutal concussion they could all feel in their feet. It approached silently and extended a hand in greeting—a hand with dual opposable thumbs.

"Don't let it intimidate you," Wheeler reassured Jade, who had taken a half set back when it reached for her. "It's just a bot on remote that Dek is driving. Cobb has an orbital factory that makes them."

As she reached for the hand, it replied in a voice that was just as menacing as it looked. "Hello, miss. I am Bram."

"It is a damn handy maintenance bot. It has excellent remote optics and an onboard grav-plate in its core. With two thumbs on each hand, he is highly dexterous. He works in vacuum, high gravity, and even underwater. The design is based on prosthetics that OS designed and Cobb refined. I would also bring a couple of cat-sized maintenance spiders for maintenance in tight places." Dek intentionally sounded like a used car salesman.

"The all-terrain-vehicle EM that Dek is in now is too big for the *GIN*. So we'd install a new ship socket for the Orb." Mitchel was looking inside the tiny hold. "Your Hammerhead would just fit in there," Mitchell said.

"So the downside is that if anyone finds out that I am traveling with an Orb, I'd be worth murdering out here." Jade summed it up.

"I will protect you, miss." Bram hammered a fist down on a boulder shattering it, while at the same time producing a rail-gun from beneath his cloak and destroyed three more boulders a hundred meters away.

"Dek is showing off," Mitchell said in an unimpressed tone.

They stood quietly for a minute.

"So why didn't Bram just kill us all and take what you wanted." She asked.

In his voice from hell, Bram replied, "They want bacon. Need bacon. It is their greatest weakness."

They all laughed.

"Come on, Jade, it'll be fun." Wheeler's smile was bright, even threw the visor of his helmet.

Jade's eyes twinkled.

***

Bram transferred the Feriapod to a cargo container in the *NAVAN* before they returned to the compound.

Jade signed the new contract but didn't tell her parents. The details were too complicated.

Wheeler knew she didn't want them to worry, but her father would see the 50,000 credits deposit. Jade had Dek set up a new personal account for the maintenance of the GIN 109 business.

Dek informed Jade that Cobbal Blocke, one of the OS owners himself, was coming out to make a new offer to Church.

It only took one more day to integrate and test the AI Socket in the *GIN*. The interfaces for the idiot displays were perfect for blending the AI socket. Dek would have full access to the ship's computer and through that system, including navigation control. It was not the same as direct control, but in the end, it still worked great.

The FTL shakedown went smooth as silk. First, they flew to The Yard. An Oklahoma Salvage space station surrounded by a massive salvage yard full of wrecks. They acquired a complete set of CO2 scrubbers, filters for the water reclamation system, and spares. They topped off the reactor coolant and even found a suitable replacement for the fridge. They even provided bed linens, several cases of good booze for the bar, and even boxes of toiletries and a hundred other small things she didn't think of. The entire kitchen was supplied with everything from pots and pans to spices and utensils. Both bathrooms were restocked. She would have never remembered shampoo or toothpaste. Engineering added a ton of tools and spare parts. The bridge even had a fully stocked weapons locker now. Arrangements were made to return soon for a full drydock to replace all the lines in the water systems and install a new custom ID Transponder that would take time to fabricate.

True to the contract, there was no charge. Jade had always worried if she could afford the upkeep on a ship, any ship. "It really is the access to parts that'll keep me hooked." She mused on several occasions.

Dek had fully informed the front office of all the details. These rare materials would allow them to create multiple new large-scale fabricators within the orbital factory at Elba.

"Way to suck up to the new boss, Jade." Dave teased.

"Cobb is going to beat us to Kibler by a few hours," Dek informed Jade and Wheeler.

Jade Church and Dave Wheeler were in the main salon of the *GIN*. Wheeler was showing her all the features of the QUEST Comm system. "It has full audio, video, and data links as if you are right on Earth. No lag. The access to encrypted comms, data, entertainment, and real-time news is fantastic. Music, classic movies, books, even avatar comms."

Jade got up and began to pace. She was looking all around her new home. While at the Yard, a swarm of Nanites cleaned it all thoroughly. Now all that remained was for Jade to make it her own. Stock it and decorate it. That would come. Wheeler watched her go into the galley and open and close the new fridge.

The baseball game on the wall in front of the sofa, where Wheeler sat, was on a low volume. The banner showed the

Cubs were winning. The rest of the surrounding wall was a view of the stars outside.

"What's wrong?" Dave asked.

"Is this what it's like to have everything I ever wanted?" She sighed and touched a few controls, and the wall became a view of the compound back home. Dave just listened. If Mitchell had been there, he would have told her how lucky she was and told her to count her blessings. But, instead, he could hear it in his head.

Dave just listened. Jade paced.

"What's the catch, Dave. There has to be a catch."

"I'll be honest. Working for Oklahoma Salvage is mostly long stretches of boredom, interrupted by occasional moments of absolute terror. Elba is now a haven for us. But Sol is too dangerous for most of us. We get jammed up every time we go back to the Sol system. Unrest in the Earth Defense Force has pushed us out to where the only laws are the ones you bring with you." Dave sighed, "It's a good life but not as simple as it once was. And there is a war happening in this sector. A quiet one but a war."

Dek interrupted. "Careful, Dave."

"Shut up, Dek. If she's going to trust us, we need to trust her." Dave was emphatic.

"War?" Jade's pacing had brought her around in front of the muted Cubs game.

"Dek, privacy mode, please," Dave said. A banner appeared on the wall that said, PRIVACY MODE as it slid around the room.

"Is Dek part of this war?" Jade asked.

"It's an AI war. We are all part of it. Elba is a major part of it. Cobb is, well, it's complicated." Dave said, watching her eyes for a reaction. Dave was surprised by what he saw there.

Not fear, not worry, not stress, but a mysterious twinkle. A smile slowly came to her face.

"Now that sounds interesting." She approached Dave until her feet were on either side of his legs. He remained sitting on the sofa. "How good is this privacy mode?" she asked as she slowly unzipped the front of her jumpsuit.

***

When they arrived at the compound forty near-sleepless hours later, Cobb's *TULSA* 471 was already parked on top of the tractor garage. She didn't recognize three other ships of different configurations parked on the plain below the dome. Dek hovered the *GIN* near an airlock that allowed roof access on the compound with no need to land anywhere as long as they wore vac-suits.

Jade and Dave entered the principal residence to the sound of laughter and many voices.

"Jade, Sweetheart." Hoshi rushed in for a hug. "I need to introduce you to Mr. Cobbal Blocke. He is the Governor of Elba and one of the owners of Oklahoma Salvage."

A man with dark hair and a goatee beard stood from a kitchen stool with a steaming coffee mug in his hand, extending his other to shake in casual greeting. "It's so nice to meet you finally. Call me Cobb, just Cobb." There was a crescendo of laughter that brought a smile to Cobb's face.

"Jade, all these people." Hoshi's eyes were filling with tears. "They have come to work for us. To help on the farm, we have a generous contract with…" Hoshi choked up, hugged Jade, burying her face in her shoulder.

Church approached and squeezed Dave's shoulder. "The extra residences won't go to waste, after all, son." Church looked over his shoulder at the ten people in the great room. Jade could see ten years of worry seemed to have been lifted from her parents. Jade felt the exact weight of worry lift from her shoulders as well.

Dave looked at Cobb with the question in his eyes.

"He knows," was all Cobb said. "We already loaded up the Feriapod from the outer marker. Contracts, including NDAs, are all signed."

Church looked out the massive expanse of widows to the plain below where the ships were parked.

Dave followed his gaze and saw eleven dark figures standing in a row. All were wearing black cloaks with hoods.

"Now it's time for me to be honest with you, Cobb," Jade said as she looked at Dave. He had no idea what she was going to say.

"These Feriapods tunnel, find and eat the metals from this planet and somehow refine it naturally to grow their armor. They are obviously worth a lot to you."

"Yes, they are. More than you know. They are rare in the extreme. They eat their dead. Finding one was amazing. They live deep below the surface and are impossible to find. They are always moving. Finding two was beyond belief. They will… make us all…"

"Rich?" Jade interrupted.

"I was going to say, safe." Cobb smiled, "But rich works as well."

"The Daves and Dek told me the dangers here. The risk even one of these brought. All the way out here." Jade said, looking at her parents now.

"Yes. Together we are safer." Dave added.

"Thanks to the Two Daves, I know where there are hundreds more intact dead Feriapods," Jade said. "I killed them myself. Sorry, mom." Jade noticed her mom's hand fly to her mouth.

Hoshi's eyes were wide.

This stopped all conversation in the room as Jade waggled her eyebrows up and down.

"Things just got a lot more exciting," the Two Daves said in unison.

"Okay, Cobb. Tell us about this AI War," Jade asked, already suspecting the truth when the EM pulled up and Bram got out and joined his fellows.

THE APOC STORIES

I love zombie apocalypse stories, books, and movies. One day I will pen an entire Zombie APOC novel. I already have a couple of outlines penned up for the future.

Here are two short stories that were published in anthologies in the past. I love the combination of survival, horror, humor, and shooting assholes in the face that need it really bad. Toss in a few decapitations and what's not to love.

Both of these short stories are set in real places. I enjoyed scouting out the locations to paint the best picture possible. The restaurant in my story titled The Door is a real place. The owner even gave me a tour of it, kitchen, storerooms, and all. Brenda's Booty Burner is also a real hot sauce I love. (Mostly because my wife's name is Brenda!)

The Story titled The Bridge is also set in a real place. The railroad bridge and Harpers Ferry Tunnel are great places to visit. The Appalachian Trail crosses the Potomac River at Harper's Ferry or this same train trestle.

I always say that the real world makes for great inspiration when you are an author. So get out there and explore. Just keep an out for Zombies…

The Door

A Short Tale
from the
Zombie Apocalypse

MARTIN WILSEY

The Door

"Dammit, Swan. You said Brunswick was small and quiet." Briggs pulled her machete out of the zombie's skull, scanning in every direction. Six bodies now littered the sidewalk in front of the Potomac Street Grill.

Joshua Swan picked the map back up with his left hand from the middle of the street without resheathing his katana.

"The handle is loose on this machete, and we are out of duct tape. I wish I had my ax back," she whispered, out of habit. Gail Briggs lowered her hood so she could see and hear better. They stood in front of the double doors of the Potomac Street Grill. "Get this door open. And be quiet about it this time."

"Do you have to nag and complain all the time?"

He smiled as he cleaned his blade on a zombie's hoodie and slid his sword into its sheath. He folded the map perfectly and with speed that Briggs could never believe.

"I like complaining." She smiled. "I'm serious about the ax. We should find a hardware store." She cleaned her blade on another body, sheathed her machete, swung her AR15 to the front, and affixed a bayonet.

The double doors both had windows, unbroken. Swan cupped his eyes and looked inside.

"Looks empty, but be ready." He pulled out a crowbar, and, as quietly as he could, he wedged the door open. He slipped in, followed by Briggs, who was shaking her head.

"I'm always ready, asswipe." She pulled the door closed behind her and was surprised that it latched.

"You have splatter on your face again," Swan said, knowing she hated that.

"Dammit," she said. "Clear the place first, clean up after."

The dining area was dusty but organized. The tables had silverware neatly rolled inside a paper napkin. With the ease of long practice, the two of them moved through the space. They checked behind the bar. Behind the counter was next. They could see into the kitchen through a large arch over a counter.

"Clear," Swan said quietly. He scanned continuously with his Glock 9mm. The suppressor was affixed.

"Clear," Briggs replied.

The bathroom doors were both propped open with Caution Wet Floor signs.

"Clear," she whispered.

Together they moved into the kitchen. One to the left and one to the right. Clear again. Neither of them reached for the walk-in fridge/freezer door handle.

Briggs and Swan had made that mistake in the past. Rotten food was the best result. Zombies were the worse result.

There was a closed door here next to the walk-in.

Swan placed his left hand on the knob and waited.

Briggs turned on a bright tactical light that was attached to her rifle. She was two paces back with the light fixed on the door.

At her nod, Swan opened the door quietly but fast. He knelt low in case she shot. Light came from the far end of the storeroom. It was a long, narrow room with metal storage shelves on either side. The shelves were mostly empty. Dishes were scattered and broken on the floor.

"Clear," he said, after looking both directions and even up. "Someone cleaned it out in a panic a long time ago."

Briggs turned and scanned the kitchen again before she lowered the rifle and turned off its light.

"I'll search in here. You take the kitchen." Swan said. "Don't forget. Hot sauce. I NEED hot sauce!"

Briggs slung her AR15 around to her back but left the bayonet attached. She systematically went through all the cabinets. She started piling her finds on the counter. There were large containers of salt, pepper, sugar, and even two gallons of pancake syrup. She also found six pounds of Chock Full o'Nuts coffee, still sealed in the cans.

Going table to table, she collected eleven bottles of Brenda's Bootie Burner hot sauce. She hid them behind a gallon of pancake syrup, just in time. Swan came out of the backroom with an old cardboard box that was closed, with a dozen rolls of toilet paper stacked on top. There was a box balanced on top that also fell when he set it all on the counter.

He tossed the box to her. It was full of individually wrapped handy wipes. She wrapped an arm around his neck and kissed him. It only smeared a little blood onto his nose. She had two packets open in a flash and was scrubbing her face, moaning with pleasure.

"I thought you'd like that." He moved the TP from the top of the box and flipped it open. There were about thirty cans of Spam inside.

"Oh, my god. I am suddenly so hungry!" she said, smiling wide.

Swan was looking over the rest of the salvage. He was pleased.

Then Briggs slid aside the gallon of syrup, revealing the hot sauce. Swan began to smile as wide as she was.

"Cold Spam with hot sauce." He picked up one of the bottles. "Remember that night in Druid Ridge Cemetery just outside of Pikesville when you got hot sauce in your…"

That's when the screaming began.

It was outside and louder than seemed possible. A woman was screaming. Between shrill cries, she was screaming something. Words.

"What the fuck did she just say?" Briggs said, her rifle shouldered as she moved to the window to the left of the door. She unlatched it and slid it open. The screaming got louder.

"…This is a recording." The screaming began again. She backed away from the window when she saw zombies in the street, moving toward the sound.

The screaming stopped, and the voice yelled like she was calling for help but actually was saying, "This is not real! I am drawing them to the roundhouse. I do not need help! This is a recording." And more screams.

About fifteen zombies shuffled by before the screaming stopped.

"I think those stairs beyond the bathrooms go to the house above. Let's see if there's a window with a view," Swan said.

They cleared two more levels quickly. It smelled musty, not like the rot of zombies, for once. The east window on the third floor had a view across Potomac Street to the rail yard. With binoculars, they could see that there were lights on by a huge warehouse. These included Christmas lights on a ramp's railing that went to a single open door on the second level.

Briggs opened the window.

"You hear that?" She said. "It's music. The Doobie Brothers, I think."

"I hear a diesel generator—a big one. And something else," Swan said.

The last zombie went through the door, and it eventually slammed closed, and the light went out. After a few more minutes, the sound of one machine then another was silenced.

The world was quiet again. The unnerving hush descended that forced them to whisper all the time.

"It will be dark in an hour. Might as well sleep here tonight," Briggs said.

"Let's give the place one more search and then pile supplies in the kitchen up here," Swan said.

Briggs nodded her head.

The linen closet had a supply of sheets. They covered the windows on the front door and stacked tables in front of the doors. It wouldn't keep anyone out, but it would make a racket if they pushed their way in. They pulled metal shelves across the back door outside the storeroom. The candles were collected from the tables before they barricaded the door at the top of the stairs.

They surveyed the place and came up with a way to exit in an emergency. "Nice of them to have real fire escapes," Swan whispered.

They even found ten gallons of vinegar that they could use to fill the flush tank a couple of times on one of the toilets.

"Don't say it. Please." Briggs said as she was closing the bathroom door.

"If it's yellow, let it mellow…" Swan couldn't stop himself.

When she got out of the bathroom, Swan didn't hear it flush. When she walked into the kitchen, she saw that Swan had a small gas grill there. He had pulled it in from the covered porch off the living room.

"Miss Briggs. I am declaring three days of R&R." Swan flung open three cabinet doors and then the pantry door. They were nearly full. Swan had found them while sweeping the house. The supplies were way more than they could carry.

"I say we take a week. The hot water tank is the glass-lined type and has about seventy gallons of water," Briggs said.

∗∗∗

They made grilled Spam steaks with canned corn and canned peas. They ate at the dining room table by candlelight with real plates and silverware. If it weren't for the blankets covering the windows at night and handy guns on the table, it would have felt normal.

They talked about lighting a fire in the fireplace, but the autumn was not cold enough to risk it. Briggs said, "We had this same conversation on the day I first met you. Remember that apartment above the funeral home in Baltimore?"

"Yes," Swan chuckled. "We almost killed each other."

"We stayed up all night whispering. And fell asleep together at daylight."

"Dumb asses," Briggs said. "How did we survive that first week?"

"We ran. We ran a lot." Swan was making light of it. They both knew the horrors of that first month held memories and topics they'd never revisit.

***

After dinner was cleaned up, Briggs and Swan felt safe enough and had a good bath. They had the extra water. They always called it a "bucket wash." They stood in the shower with a bucket of soapy water and a bucket of clean. They scrubbed each other with washcloths and real soap that had not been available for weeks on the road.

They found clean underwear, socks, and t-shirts, as well as very fashionable, over-large tracksuits. They still wore their boots, always. They would never make that mistake again, either. "Be ready to run" was a mantra that had served them well.

Their weapons were never far from reach. Their packs were packed with water, food, and all the supplies they could carry easily first thing. Ready to grab and run at any moment. Briggs found a leather jacket that fits well enough and would allow her to keep her AR15 on her single-point harness handy and out of the rain.

They would stay here and rest and eat the food they could not carry away. Briggs and Swan would put some of the weight back on that they had lost. They would repair their gear, mend their clothes, and try to sleep. They would rest and be quiet and read the books they found in the house.

They had learned from past mistakes. They were always ready to run, and they knew there would be a time to move again.

Two nights passed quietly. They even considered briefly sleeping together instead of taking watches. They stood their usual watches.

They still slept fully clothed.

They made love for the first time since the hot sauce incident in the cemetery long ago. They were clean, after all. And human.

"I heard something last night," Briggs said. "I wasn't sure. I didn't see anything until I went out on the balcony at first light, before dawn. They're gone."

"Who is gone?" Swan was puzzled. "The people in the warehouse?"

"The zombies we killed in the street. The bodies are gone…"

***

It was late afternoon of the third day when Swan walked into the living room where Briggs was reading *The Martian* by Andy Weir. She always read when she was trying to distract herself. Swan knew her well.

"Look what I found." He handed her a placemat from the restaurant. It had a cartoon depiction of Brunswick. Her eyes went directly to the exaggerated Potomac Street Grill.

Swan pointed to a different spot on the cartoon map. "Ace Hardware is about ten blocks from here. I need more duct tape. You still want an ax?" he asked.

"Are we talking about hitting the hardware when we head out to Harper's Ferry?" she asked. "It's in the opposite direction from the railroad tracks we plan on following."

"Want to hit the hardware running light and come straight back here?" Swan asked. "We've done it before. It's a risk, but if it's a goldmine at the hardware, we could carry more." He spread out the street map and compared it to the placemat.

Briggs' head came up when she heard it. "The diesel generator."

They both grabbed their binoculars and ran upstairs. When they got to the window, the large overhead door was already going up at the roundhouse. When it reached the top, a massive dump truck pulled out and onto the road with a great gout of black smoke from the dual stacks. The front had a V-shaped snowplow that was covered with stains.

The cab had four men inside, and four more clung to the sides, two on each side. They were all healthy, heavily muscled, and well-armed. They all wore blue coveralls.

"That plow is smart," Swan said. "Shamblers in the street are no problem. They must be getting fuel from the trains in the rail yard. I have no idea how they are keeping the fuel from going bad."

"Why don't they ride in the back? It'd be way safer," Briggs said. She knew the macho types that rode on the running boards in towns full of zombies.

Violent gangs of men who preyed on the living. Especially women. They would lop heads off for sport.

"Holy shit," Swan said. "Look in the back."

It was bones. There were a couple of hundred skulls visible. Complete skeletons were stripped clean of flesh, disassembled, and piled in there.

"What the fuck," Briggs said. "They can't be... eating them?"

***

Two hours later, they heard the big generator start again. Two minutes after that, they saw the truck return. The back was now full of cut and split firewood. Swan's placemat had a depiction of Wilson's Firewood. It had cartoon mountains of cut and split firewood.

The four men that had been riding the running boards on the way out sat on the leading edge of the dump bed with their feet on the roof of the truck. All four were laughing at something, even though they all had AR15s at ready.

The sun dipped behind the mountain to the west as the overhead door closed.

The screaming started again.

They could now tell that the screams, the voice, was coming from PA speakers mounted on the warehouse. The lights came on, and five minutes later, the first zombies appeared. They followed the sound up the ramp and into the warehouse. The screaming stopped when the last of them started up the ramp. The lights went out, and just before the door slammed behind the last one, it was silhouetted by firelight from somewhere within.

"Briggs. You have that look," Swan said. "What are you thinking?"

"They seem to be harvesting those shamblers," Briggs said as she lowered her binocs. "But why?"

"Look, I don't really care. It's safer to mind our own business. Stay quiet. Survive." It was a mantra that Swan had said a hundred times before.

"But what if they aren't assholes?" Briggs said.

"Do you remember what happened last time we tried?" Swan was mad now. "You almost got raped, and I… killed a real person. Yes, an asshole that asked for it. But I am talking about risk."

"Then we simply recon. We are better at it now." Briggs knew she would get her way. "We need information. Even if we never contact them."

Swan was shaking his head when he looked up into her eyes. "OK. But let's hit the hardware first."

She kissed him.

***

They were geared up at first light. It was a cold morning. It was their light recon armor. This meant denim jackets and jeans that had been reinforced at "bite points" with heavy duct tape. The arms, shoulders, and body of the jackets were covered in duct tape that needed patching. They wore leather gloves but regretted not having more duct tape to close the seam between glove and sleeve. They carried guns and blades only. Each wore an empty backpack for any salvage goods to bring back.

They checked each other to make sure their gear was securely silenced and ready. Quietly, they slipped out the front door and closed it behind them.

They stepped to the center of the road and proceeded in a direct line toward the hardware. In the predawn light, nothing moved except them. Scanning side to side for anything unusual, Biggs pointed out a building they passed about halfway to the hardware. It was a microbrewery, but the entire front of the building was gone. The building had been gutted, and any equipment that had been there was gone.

"Someone was really thirsty…" Swan whispered.

Briggs just shook her head and kept moving.

They reached the hardware, and all remained still. The glass was all broken in on the front of the store. It had been professionally looted. No axes, no tools at all remained.

"Dammit," Briggs cursed quietly.

Swan clicked his tongue and pointed with his chin at Klein's Antiques across the street. All the glass was intact.

The sun was not up yet. They moved across the street and flanked the door. The door had been kicked in, but someone had secured it closed again to the iron railing with a bungee cord.

"Why are there no shamblers in this town?" Briggs asked before they opened it.

"Quit your complaining. Maybe we got lucky for once."

He unhooked and let the door swing in. It bumped into a single zombie standing directly beyond.

With practiced ease, Briggs stabbed with the bayonet, in and out, like a snake, of the old woman's eye. The corpse fell back into the room. They slipped inside and quietly closed the door.

Swan positioned the cadaver to hold the door closed as they activated the tactical lights on their weapons.

An old man was moving toward them down a long aisle, and Swan advanced as Briggs covered his back. His sword stabbed in and out, and the zombie fell with a crash as it knocked over a lamp and a vase.

They froze as the sound echoed.

There was nothing after two minutes. They moved without a word.

The store was small but crowded with antiques. They cleared all three aisles and a small office before they began their search.

They met back at the counter, where Swan was smiling as the sun peeked in the window.

Briggs placed a massive meat cleaver on the counter and an old, long, dull bayonet from World War II. "No swords, dammit."

"Look in that umbrella stand to your right," he said.

It was full of canes, golf clubs, and a single cavalry sword. She lifted it out and slid it from its black leather sheath.

She smiled wide. "It's still sharp."

"I also found this under the counter." He placed a short, sawed-off, double-barrel shotgun on the counter and an old box with 23 shells still in it.

"Oh my, Mrs. Klein." She looked at the old woman propped up to hold the door closed. "Don't you know short shotguns are illegal in Maryland?"

***

The return to the house was uneventful. Briggs spent the afternoon making a sash that held the saber securely at her hip. Swan fashioned a similar one for the sawed-off shotgun.

"With only two shots before reloading, that thing isn't worth much," Briggs said.

"I know. But I can save those two for us," Swan said, looking away. "At least we can be sure."

"I hate it when you talk that way," she said.

"What if West Virginia is a bust?" Swan said. "The cabin sounded like a great idea when we started. I'm not so sure now. When we left, I thought all we had to do is last longer than they did. They are rotting."

"We didn't know that everyone had it then," Briggs said quietly.

"It will never be over," Swan said.

"There are no happy endings," Briggs said. "Because nothing ends."

Swan looked up at that. And smiled.

"I read it somewhere," she said and kissed him.

***

They moved out before dawn the next day.

The plan was to climb the structure on the side that was clearly not in use and move across the roof to the high windows. From there, they would be able to see inside.

When they reached the windows, they were so filthy they could not see anything. They didn't open either, so they moved along until they found a single pane of glass that was missing. Swan looked in.

It was a giant warehouse-size space that had been designed for performing maintenance on trains. There were only two train cars in there, in an area that could have held forty. There was a propane tanker and a water tanker. He could also see six massive trailers with Costco on the side and a mountain of canned goods. Several years' worth of food. That explained why the pantry at the house had not been looted.

Swan also counted twelve Winnebago's and three other Airstream camper trailers. That was just what he could see from this angle.

A man with wet hair was busying himself in the large area set up as a camp kitchen. He poured kibble into a trough-shaped bin as two German shepherds, and a Basset hound lumbered up. The Basset was more interested in a pat on the head and an ear scratch than food.

Swan strained to follow him as he carried two steaming cups of coffee to an area set up with three large sofas. An elderly man was in a wheelchair talking to a woman in a green bathrobe and her hair in a towel. She kissed the old man on the cheek and then the one that had brought her coffee before going to one of the Airstreams.

"Have a look," Swan said to Briggs.

While she was looking through the window, Swan noticed that the area between the roundhouse and the river had been cleared and secured with tall chain-link fences and shipping containers all the way to the river.

There were goats.

All the grass looked mowed. He was smiling and shaking his head when he saw them.

There were twenty or more shamblers in the water, moving slowly through the shallow muddy bottom.

"Briggs," he said, louder than he intended, "we have to warn them."

Briggs followed his line of sight.

"Dammit. They'll get the goats."

Then they heard the voice behind them.

"Freeze if you want to live." It was a woman's voice, calm, confident, and serious. They froze.

"Turn around slowly and keep your hands where we can see 'em," she said.

Swan noticed the word "we."

They turned slowly to see a woman squatting on her heels with a handgun trained on them. She wore military camo with a tactical vest full of magazines, flashlights, and even a walkie-talkie—the professional kind. Her hair was dark and cropped super short, inexpertly but practical.

"Look, we'll explain later, but shamblers are coming out of the river. You have to warn them," Briggs said.

"And that right there is why you are not dead and in the vats already." She stood smoothly. Into a radio, she said, "I have the two live ones on the roof. Hold your fire, Mike."

Swan looked around, just moving his eyes.

"We have an overwatch post in the crane cab," she said but didn't lower her gun. "Briggs and Swan. Yes, I know your names. You can call me Laura. So, what's your story?"

"You're not worried about the zombies coming out of the river?" Briggs asked.

"We have been here a long time, since the beginning. Jeff is on river watch now. If you look close, the fences will bottleneck them all between those shipping containers. Jeff will spear them from above." Laura looked out to the water. "We get fewer and fewer each month. We're down to running one vat."

"Vat? Look, we are not here to hurt anyone." Briggs said.

"I know." Laura holstered her gun. "You ain't got that look on ya." She lifted her radio. "Mike, relax. I'm taking our guests to see Brain."

"Brain?" Swan asked.

"It's a joke." She snickered. "His name is actually Bryan, but we call him Brain, like in that movie *Escape from New York* because he showed us how to make the gas. Diesel. Bio-diesel. Don't call it gas, for god's sake, not in front of Brain."

With that, Laura turned her back on them and began walking toward the access door.

"You're crazy. You know that, right?" Briggs said, "You didn't disarm us or search us or even know if there are others with us."

Without turning around, she said, "We've been watching you for days." She stopped and turned back to Briggs. "You are the crazy ones." To Swan, she said, "You know she falls asleep on watch every night?"

"I do NOT!" Briggs protested.

"And you should draw the damn curtains on the second floor when you get frisky. I'm never going to hear the end of it from Mike!" She went down the stairs, knowing Briggs was blushing. "I know the walkers can't see in from the street on the second level, but damn."

The stairs led to a catwalk in the rafters that wound around the roundhouse's entire enormous space. They could see three men and a woman in blue coveralls at the opposite end, tending a fire below a giant vat.

The vat was full of dark liquid, and in it, they could see bodies moving.

"Sorry about the smell up here," Laura said absently as they began to descend to the warehouse floor. "We keep the operation at that end. Excellent ventilation."

Briggs looked at Swan and made their private sign for WTF?

By the time they crossed over to the living spaces, the old man was parked at the end of a large conference table. There were four guards stationed around the area in tactical vests with new-looking SCAR military rifles.

"Briggs, Swan," Laura said, "this is Brain. He's driving this bus."

"Oh, stop that." He held out his hand. "I'm Bryan Mitchell. These kids let me think I'm in charge around here. They do all the work. All I do is read books."

"He used to be the librarian for Brunswick. He retired the week before all this started. He's the one that showed us how to make biodiesel out of them," Laura said. "Two birds, one stone kinda deal."

"I was wondering how you had a truck that still ran," Swan said. "All the fuel went bad last spring."

Everyone's radios clicked. "Help. Me."

Over the radio, Mike said urgently, "Jeff fell off the roof of the shipping container. No clear shot from overwatch."

Laura ran for the door. "You four stay here and guard the children."

Running after Laura, Briggs said, "You have children here?"

They crashed out the door, out of the warehouse toward the pen made of shipping containers. A seven-foot-tall wall had been erected between shipping containers. There was a ladder leaning there that was tied to another on the other side. Laura was up and over the wall without missing a beat.

Briggs and Swan were right behind her.

Jeff was dragging himself towards them as Laura stopped to help him. Briggs and Swan passed them and set upon the hoard of muddy shamblers with practiced ease.

Katana and saber danced as Briggs laughed out loud. The space was perfect for the two of them to have enough room. Their blades never stopped moving, creating a swirling area around them. Hands seemed to fall off as if by magic, followed by heads. The battle line advanced as Briggs and Swan ran out of targets and moved seamlessly ahead.

Briggs chanced a glance back to see Jeff was halfway up the ladder, hands helping from above. Laura stared in awe at their dance. Briggs stopped laughing as the task became less fun and more like work.

The last two heads flew off in synchronized arcs.

"Your estimate was low. I counted fifty-five," Swan said conversationally, only slightly out of breath.

They both held their hand up to Laura as she approached. "Stop," Swan and Briggs said in unison. "Gotta clean up."

Swan stabbed a severed head that was still snapping its jaw.

"I really like the new saber, sweetie," Briggs said with exaggerated casualness. "Balance is way better than the machete."

"Sweetie again, is it?" he said. "Don't embarrass me in front of the neighbors."

They finished off the last of the zombies and helped carry Jeff back to the warehouse.

Two of the men guarding Brain were named John, and both happened to be EMTs. One of the Winnebagos had been set up as a clinic. Jeff had dislocated his knee and broken three fingers on his right hand. When Swan and Briggs stepped out of the RV, there were about thirty people assembled. They silently parted as Briggs, Swan, and the two Johns carried Jeff to the sofa right next to Brain.

When they returned, fresh coffee was handed all around. There were even six children there now.

All were silent.

Solemnly, Brain spoke to them. "You are invited to join us. You must be weary to come so far and to have become so skilled." Brain had a tone of sadness. "We'll help you tow an Airstream over from RV World if you decide to stay. But there is one thing you must do first. If you want to join us."

They both nodded without even looking at each other.

"First. The Door," Brain said flatly.

***

The big diesel generator started. Lights came on above them. In bright yellow spray paint was written, "THE DOOR."

The recorded screaming over the loudspeaker began. Together, Swan and Briggs realized it was Laura's voice.

They opened the door. A rope was tied to the crash bar so they could close it remotely. Zombies were already coming that way.

Swan and Briggs moved along a walkway just inside where it wound around to the edge just above the empty vat on the level below. A rail and a 4x4 crossed the edge to a makeshift catwalk with scaffolding on the far side.

There was a light directly above them. The vat below was darkness. They were the bait.

When the first zombie shambled in the door, they waved their arms and called out, "Hey, over here."

They came to them, at them, with hunger in their clouded eyes, horrible wounds in their flesh. They were moths to the flame.

As each one fell into the vat, reaching for them, Briggs and Swan said, "Thank you. We're sorry this happened to you." Swan was crying as they fell. One was a little girl.

There were only six by the time Briggs closed the door by pulling the rope. Swan used a spear and brought the second death to the little girl and then to all but two, as requested. The strongest, largest men floated in the vat of rainwater, constantly moving.

***

They joined the others at the sofas. It was movie night. It always was after The Door. Microwaves had been working while the generator was on, making a ton of popcorn. Battery banks recharged. Tonight was *The Big Lebowski*. It would be projected on the king-sized sheet they hung as a screen.

"Biodiesel, eh?"

"But why leave two, you know, undead?"

Laura smiled as she helped Jeff get comfortable before the movie. "Making biodiesel, you have to stir it in the early stages as you boil it down. They are good agitators."

"That's kinda creepy," Swan said.

"Want to know what's creepy?" Laura asked as she reclined under Jeff's arm.

"What?" Briggs and Swan said in unison.

"Watching the two of you dancing through those walkers," she said.

Jeff chimed in. "You were both smiling the whole time."

"Yep. Kinda creepy," Laura said. "But in a good way…"

THE BRIDGE

A SHORT TALE FROM THE ZOMBIE APOCALYPSE

MARTIN WILSEY

THE BRIDGE

"I don't know, Ray," Allie said as she lowered her binoculars. "It pretty looks quiet to me. There are two or three shambling around the mouth of the railroad tunnel."

"Two or three we can handle," Ray whispered, out of habit, as he fingered the handle of his katana. "But do you remember that tunnel in Westport?"

"How could I forget that shit storm? I miss those mountain bikes. They could haul ass," she said as she slowly slid back down the embankment on her belly. She quietly drew her katana as she got to her feet.

"There is a bike shop just on the other side of the train trestle in Harpers Ferry. If we're lucky, it won't be empty," Ray said as he started to quietly move. "We'll follow the C&O towpath along the Potomac here and bypass that tunnel. It will loop around to the bridge."

The two moved along in the silence of experience. All their gear was stowed and padded for stealth. When they rounded the bend and saw two of the undead on the towpath ahead, they didn't miss a beat. Without even breaking pace, they decapitated them both.

One was a woman in a filthy yellow sundress that was incongruous in the cool autumn air of late October. The other was a man in a state of long decay and desiccation.

As always, Allie quickly and efficiently searched the bodies as Ray watched for threats. The woman had a purse still hanging across her shoulder diagonally. Allie dumped it out and discarded everything except a full tube of Chapstick and a quality fingernail clipper.

The man's pockets were empty, but he was wearing a policemen's gun belt. The holster was empty, but the belt had a single .357 magnum round still secured in it.

Allie drew it out like it was made of glass or gold and held it up to the light to examine it. When her eyes shifted to Ray, his smile was wide.

"Three," was all he said as she stood and drew her stainless steel Ruger SP101 from its holster and expertly opened the drum. It contained two rounds. This addition made three.

Allie reholstered as they began to move.

"Don't say it," she whispered. "You always say it. 'Save the last two for us.'"

"I don't always say it."

"When it comes to my .357, you do." Allie shook her head. "We each have 12 rounds in our ARs, and you still have like fifty rounds of 9mm for your Glock."

"I don't always say it."

Allie fell silent then because the train trestle bridge came into view. "Ray, look."

In the center of the bridge were four train cars about three hundred feet from each end of the bridge. Allie looked through her binoculars. There were two tankers of some kind, a passenger car and a freight car.

"Looks like we can get across. We should get moving. We need to find a place to bed down before dark," she said, and Ray nodded.

***

"Dammit," Ray cursed quietly. "There used to be stairs that went up to the trestle here for the Appalachian Trail crossing." They looked up farther. "We'll go to the tracks up by this end of the tunnel and double back."

Ray led the way, and as they moved, the wind picked up. Autumn leaves were filling the air as the breeze turned into a constant wind.

They emerged onto the tracks before they realized that not all the sound was from the rustling leaves. They were only a dozen yards from the gaping maw of the tunnel when *they* began to emerge—first a few, then a dozen, and suddenly hundreds.

They didn't wait to count.

They moved carefully, so they didn't stumble on the railroad ties. On the bridge, the eight-inch gaps between the ties had nothing but air below. These gaps forced them to be careful but drastically slowed the hungry horde behind them. The front line would trip and fall over and over again. The ones too slow to rise would be overrun and crushed into the path.

A few hundred feet onto the bridge, someone had nailed plywood onto the tracks between the ties, allowing them to move fast.

Until they saw the words spray-painted on the bridge: WARNING: Trap ahead.

They came to a section where two sheets of plywood were painted with faded orange spray paint outlining the edges. In the center, it said: TRAP: Don't Step Here!

They could see on the outside of the rails that the ties were gone here. The rails had "SAFE SAFE SAFE SAFE SAFE SAFE SAFE SAFE" written along the tops.

A sign to the side said, "Use the Rope."

There was a rope hanging down from the trestle high above, on the trap's far side. But it was tied off loosely near their feet. Allie lifted the rope.

Behind them, they could hear feet, now on the plywood, coming their way.

"GO!" was all Ray said as he turned toward the zombies moving toward them.

With the rope's help to stabilize her, she moved quickly across the rail like a balance beam.

Ray only had to dispatch one zombie before he turned and began across the rail without the rope. Allie swung him the rope just as the first zombie set foot on the trap.

As he slipped through the trapdoor like a chute, he got a hand on Ray's ankle and dragged him off the rail just as he got his hand on the rope.

Like lemmings, dozens of zombies fell to the shallow river far below. The trap door was counterbalanced and reset whenever another zombie set foot on it. Ray and Allie stood there like bait as they fell, one after another, to the river below, their bodies drifting away in the strong current of the shallow rapids.

After about fifteen minutes, all the zombies that could still move had fallen into the trap.

"That's brilliant," Allie said as the trapdoor reset for the last time. "It's quiet. It resets automatically without power. Brilliant."

"I bet there is another one at the far end," Ray said. "Look at this." He drew away a blue tarp. Underneath was a dolly made to roll along on the rails. There were about twenty-five cases of canned food under the tarp. "This would roll right over that trap with supplies."

"Come on," Allie said. "Let's go find this genius."

The freight car was closest to them. The sliding door was slightly ajar, and they peeked in as they walked by. More dusty cases of canned food filled half the car.

The passenger car was next in line, but the stairs on the end had been blocked with corrugated metal panels. It looked like an enclosed passage had been established into the freight car on the end.

The first tanker car was for water. Above, a large inverted canopy, hanging upside down from the train trestle, functioned as a huge rain catchment system.

"Ray, this last tanker is propane," Allie said. "And there is another one of the twelve-foot-long cargo dollies under that tarp. And bikes!"

There was a lean-to-style tarp set up over a rack with a dozen or so bikes.

"I think we are going to stay here tonight," Ray said.

***

The passenger cars had curtains drawn all along both sides. And no easy and obvious way to enter. They went back to the freight car and slid the door open enough to climb up. It was dark inside. Cases of supplies filled most of the end toward the passenger car, including tools and 55-gallon drums of fuel.

An arch had been cut into the end of the car with a chainsaw. The door to the passenger car was just beyond.

They both held their AR15s at ready. The door slid easily open and revealed a clean and organized club car. Closest to the door were bathrooms to both left and right marked *LADIES* and *GENTS* in art deco brass. There was a bar next with a large selection of booze. Bookcases in the area opposite the bar were well stocked with canned goods of all kinds. There were café tables and chairs, sofas, overstuffed leather recliners, and booths along the same side as the bar.

There was another door at the other end about 40 feet along. They opened it with rifles ready and were hit by a stench they were not prepared for.

"What the fuck is that?" Allie gasped as she buried her face in her elbow, still looking straight ahead.

"I have gotten used to smelling rotting zombies, but what the hell could that be?" Ray said.

There was a bed at the far end of the room. From it came a quiet, raspy voice.

"That would be me."

***

"My name is Henry Danton," he whispered.

The smell was a man lying in his own shit and piss. But that was not the worst of it. A massive leg wound had gone septic. Rancid puss soaked the mattress. Some kind of flesh-eating virus had opened and blackened the wound, exposing the man's femur. Gallon jugs and various cans littered the floor around the bed.

"Be careful when you go in the bathroom. Martha is in there, and she has turned," he whispered weakly. "I think she killed herself."

Allie pushed the door to the bathroom open with the point of her sword. A different, more familiar smell flowed out. Martha was there, hanging from a noose made from an extension cord.

Without pausing, Allie stabbed through her eye socket and out the back of her skull. Her thrashing stopped.

"She felt guilty for stabbing my leg," Henry said. "It was an accident. Her machete was… covered in gore."

Allie noticed his ankle was tied to the bedpost. It was a beautiful Victorian four-post bed.

The room was lovely in its Old World style. Ray was busy opening windows.

"I couldn't do it while I was strong enough." His hand patted a Beretta 9mm. "I'm a coward. Plus, the whole Catholic thing. Asking Martha to help was the last straw for her. Can you send us to the river together? Please?"

Ray picked up the Beretta and checked the load. "I'm sorry this happened to you. Did you build all this?"

Henry just nodded slightly, his eyes drooping.

"We'll take care of everything," Allie said in her kindest voice.

His eyes slid shut, and Allie severed the top of his head with a single sword strike on the bridge of his nose.

***

They did as Henry Danton wished. He and his wife Martha were laid to rest together on the filthy mattress, and with the help of the cargo dolly Ray was able to say a few words over them at the trap door.

"We are going to rename this the Danton Bridge. Thank you, Henry. We will pay it forward."

With those words, they tipped the mattress and the bodies onto Henry's trap. The water was deeper at the Harpers Ferry end. Their bodies disappeared into the green water straightaway.

Screams made them look away, and they saw below in Harpers Ferry a teenage boy and girl running out of an alley with several dozen zombies in hot pursuit. They were wearing red matching T-shirts that said *Thing 1* and *Thing 2*. They must have been in one of the tourist shops. They had no gear, no backpacks, and had been caught unaware.

"Some of those are fresh and can still move pretty fast," Ray said as he raised his scope to his eye and waited. "Looks like some of their pals turned without notice."

Allie put two fingers in her mouth and whistled a loud blast. The tiring teens saw them and began running their way.

Ray held his fire until one zombie got too close to the panicked girl, and he shot. The zombie dropped, tripping the three directly behind it. The crowd of zombies increased to about fifty by the time the teens got to the trap.

"It's a trapdoor. Hold onto this." There were two ropes at this end of the bridge. "Use the rail like a balance beam." The girl just grabbed the rope on the run and swung the distance as rotting arms stretched out for her.

They watched, out of breath, as the entire horde plummeted to the river below.

"I'm Ray. This is Allie." Ray reached out his hand to shake. "Are you guys hungry? I was about to make dinner."

"Ever watch *Star Trek*? Didn't anyone ever tell you what happens to redshirts…?" Allie smiled.

TIME TRAVEL STORIES

Time travel stories are also one of my favorites.

In the coming soon section at the end of this collection, you will see one of my subsequent novels coming out is titled: *TIME ENOUGH*. It will be a time travel stand-alone story based in Richmond, Virginia, in 2010.

It's odd to think of this snapshot in time. As I write this, it is June of 2021. The novel *TIME ENOUGH* will likely be published sometime this year. That will make this obsolete. Go buy it if you are reading this later. I may mention you.

Some of my favorite quotes about time are:

"Time is the fire in which we burn." By the poet Delmore Schwartz

Albert Einstein said, "Time is an illusion."

Douglas Adams added, "Lunchtime doubly so."

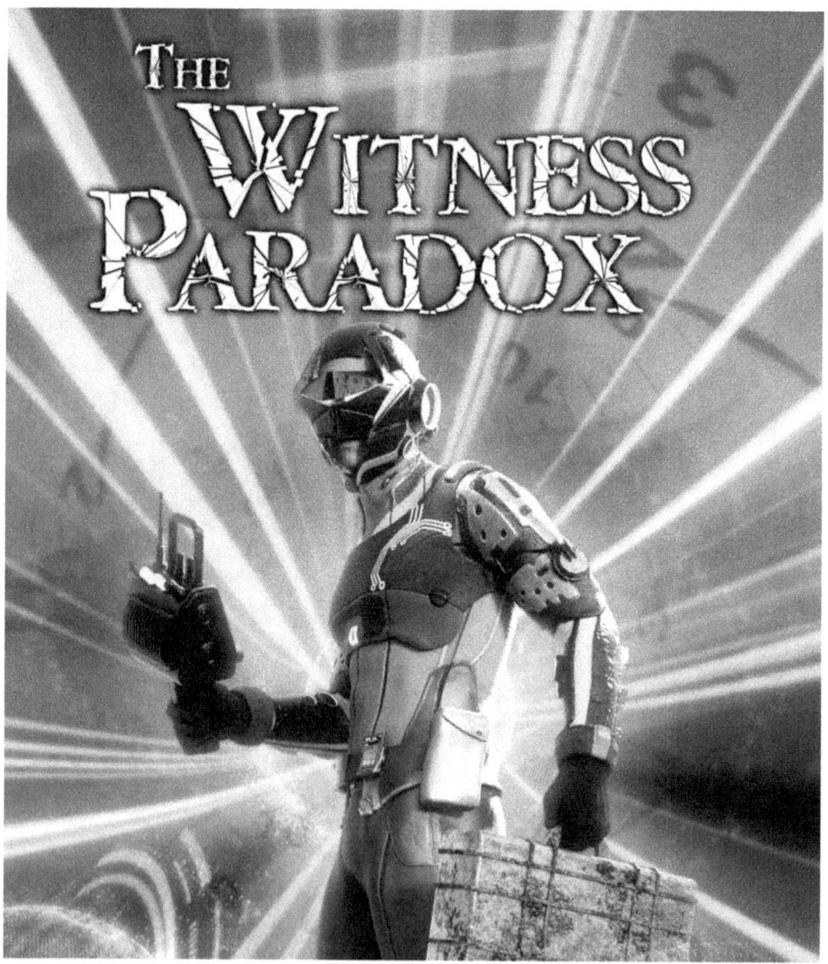

The Witness Paradox

The Witness Paradox

"Where the hell are we?" Mayor whispered a bit too loud.

"It's a cemetery, inside a mausoleum, and keep your voice down." Gina gave him an elbow in the darkness. At least he had followed protocol and kept his left hand on her shoulder as they transitioned through the portal.

A small device lit up in her hand with an elaborate display. The complete darkness of the crypt illuminated her face with an eerie green glow as she examined the unit's target date.

"What the hell is that?" Mayor knew he was whispering too loud again. "They told us that the EMP within the portal would fry anything we took through. No metal either, or it's like being struck by lightning."

"It's a Denbora Control Plate," she said in an annoyed tone. "Mayor, say another word, and I will gut you like a fish." She produced a long black dagger. The blade was double-edged and shined like glass in the green glow. He glanced from her face to the knife to the device in rapid sequence.

Mayor stayed quiet as Gina unbarred and opened the heavy iron door. He noticed it had been barred from the inside. Inside a mausoleum. It creeped him out. It was a good place for a fixed portal, though.

They slipped quietly out. The only sound they made was disturbing a small drift of dry leaves behind the door.

"Just keep quiet and follow the damn protocol," Gina said to him as she began to move silently into the night. The city of Richmond, Virginia, glowed beyond the river below. "Just watch the events so you will know what to do next time through."

Mayor hated the protocol. He didn't believe in it. It relied on math that didn't add up. But he wanted to time travel even more. So, he followed the rules. Expect the unexpected and remember.

The first time into the past, he had to follow The Witness Protocol. The protocol always bothered him because of the potential paradox of watching your mission outcome, ensuring your witnessing does not affect the outcome. He had to stay out of the way. And his later self would bring him his mission assignment. It was the last duty of every mission.

At least it had time built-in for feelings of awe, inspired by the world's beauty before the desolation. Gina obviously knew this. She led him to a bench and simply said, "Sit here. Keep to protocol. Back soon." With that, she touched a control on the small device, and she became shadows and darkness. She was cloaked in black steam that seemed like it was drifting on an invisible breeze.

The lights of Richmond twinkled on the James River below. There were hints of music on the breeze. The air smelled beautiful. Mayor began to understand the more esoteric parts of the protocol. They had nothing to do with math. Expect the unexpected. He never expected that he'd feel like crying.

Mayor swallowed hard. He imagined the future. The crater that was once Richmond had turned into a radioactive lake that the James River filled in. It had to be stopped. He knew his part in preventing it would be critical. He had to follow the protocol.

***

He sat on the bench for almost an hour. His mind raced in the beginning. Then he slowly calmed. A realization occurred to him. He intellectually understood the foundation principle of an absolute past. He had one that would always be his. The part that didn't make sense was that he was there to observe his future events to prepare for them. He would watch his future self to know and understand the outcomes of that important event. Watch himself, so that future self will remember and be prepared for the critical event—the Witness Protocol.

Roll with it.

When the portal opened inside another mausoleum ten meters directly in front of him, the light bled around the door and blinded him as the figure stepped through. He wore 27th-century body armor complete with a helmet, carrying a temporal scanner and a large, old, beat-up briefcase.

"You'll need this," the figure said as he dropped the case on the bench next to him. He retreated through the portal before it closed. Mayor glimpsed a platform of some kind, an oil rig, maybe? Silently, the portal closed, leaving another door-shaped spot in his vision. He had to blink it away.

Before his vision normalized, he heard Gina's voice. "About damn time." It was husky. Like she had been smoking all forty years of her life.

The shadow of an adjacent tree dissolved, and Gina emerged from hiding.

"Wait." Mayor snatched the case before she could reach it. It was covered in dirt. Fresh earth. "This isn't protocol." He hugged it to his chest.

"Listen, Mayor." Gina sounded impatient. "Just unlock and open the case."

"How?" It had a classic six-digit combination lock. When he touched it, it lit so he could see it. "What's the combination?"

"Mayor, don't be stupid. That was you that just dropped it off." Gina scanned the area. "Don't you get it? You'll survive. That was you, post-event, making sure you could do your job. Bringing you what you forgot. Or didn't know to bring. Now open the case."

"How come the electronics didn't get fried?" he asked as he entered his mom's birthday, and the case clicked open. He looked up before he opened it. Gina was gone.

The case had three packages inside, wrapped in plain brown paper. The smallest had "Open me first, dumbass." written on it.

It was a thick bundle of worthless cash. I am a dumbass, he thought. It's not worthless here. How could I not remember that?

The next package was marked, "Second, dipshit." It didn't help to see that it was his own handwriting.

It was a glasses case. I don't wear glasses, he thought.

On the inside of the case was written, "Just put them on now, you idiot." They were wraparound sunglasses.

When he put them on, they activated. They were night-vision, but they were more than that. Letters appeared on the last package that were not visible earlier.

"Don't trust Gina. She's a liar. Open me fast and get ready to run."

Mayor tore open the package, crumbled the paper, and put it into his coat pocket. It was a loaded handgun—a Glock 17 in perfectly preserved condition.

He glanced up and around. In the cemetery, the glasses allowed him to see a dozen figures drifting toward him. They all looked like grim reapers as he could see blades of various kinds in their hands.

Mayor ran.

The Heads-Up Display (HUD) in these glasses was amazing. It somehow increased his peripheral vision. It increased the visual resolution of everything. He could now read distant road signs. It indicated his exact location in lat/longs to one centimeter, as well as direction and elevation.

Most importantly, it highlighted all the people that were in active camouflage.

It also had a recommended path to run. As he rounded a corner, he flinched at the sound of a gunshot behind him. He glanced over his shoulder, seeing all the followers stop and look about. Someone grabbed him and quickly redirected him into another mausoleum that went into the hillside. His wrist with the Glock was pinned, and a hand went over his mouth.

"Silence, dumbass," whispered the same man that had brought the briefcase.

Mayor's eyes were wide with the realization that it was his future self. The mausoleum where they hid did not have a solid door. There were only bars, which allowed them to hear and watch the pursuers as they ran by.

"Shhhhh…" was whispered in his ear. Mayor stayed frozen. In his mind, the protocol echoed TRUST YOURSELF. It had an all-new meaning now.

They did not move for what seemed like hours, but his HUD said it was only seven minutes. The hands released him as footsteps could be heard on the cinder path just opposite the doorway. A single grim reaper stopped and turned to face the entrance.

"Clear," was all the reaper said. The black steam seemed to dissipate, and the camouflage shadows dissolved. It was another Mayor. A much older Mayor. He was wearing jeans and a brown tweed blazer over a black Oxford shirt. His graying hair was pulled back into a ponytail, and he had a long beard.

"I'll see you when it's done," the third Mayor said as he produced a cigar and matchbook from his jacket. He then lit it with a wooden match.

They didn't move as they watched him stroll away into the cemetery.

"I…" Mayor One began, but Mayor Two interrupted him, pulling off his helmet.

"The entire protocol is wrong. It was an intentional lie. We found that out after the Paradox was over. You… we caused the Witness Paradox. We also discovered that time travel is impossible. We were right all along. The math didn't add up. Einstein was right. There is no such thing as time. It's all an illusion." Mayor Two opened the bars and casually began to walk in the direction they came from.

"But…"

"There is only now." It was like he was reciting a well-practiced speech. "Now is the intersection between the past and future. Now is so thin it doesn't exist."

"I'm hungry," Mayor One said, thinking, I am going to say some random shit to throw him off.

"Saying random shit will not throw me off." Mayor Two looked over and smiled then. "For being such a dumbass, you really are a genius."

"I really am hungry."

"I know. It's what starts the entire paradox. Try the toast. Leave a huge tip."

They crested a knoll to see two vehicles in the parking area. A blue 1970 Dodge Dart with a black vinyl top and a black spaceship resting on three legs.

As they quickly moved along, Mayor Two continued, "Directions to the Third Street Diner are in the HUD. Be careful with the Prof's car." With that, Mayor Two tucked his helmet under his arm and entered the elevator under the ship. He waved as the doors slid closed.

Mayor went to wave back when he realized he still had the gun in his hand. He put it in his coat pocket and climbed into the car.

The car was in pristine condition. The keys were in the ignition. Even though the windows were all down, he could still smell the faint, sweet scent of cigars.

It started right up. The motor purred like it was new. He slowly left the cemetery and followed the HUD toward downtown. Marveling at the intact world.

***

Mayor parked at the curb in the street. The diner was on the corner, and about half a dozen people stood out front smoking cigarettes, even though it was 3:30 AM.

As he walked up the sidewalk, he could smell bacon. REAL BACON.

There were four women and one man outside. The women wore very little, especially on a cold October night. The man with his back to Mayor wore a familiar brown tweed jacket and jeans. His ponytail went halfway down his back. The women were laughing at something he said. He never turned around as he puffed his cigar.

The diner was busy for the late hour. He could not help but stare at the waitress as she walked toward him. He had read about obese people but had never seen one in his entire life. Her smile was bright.

"Sit anywhere you like, hon. The last booth is still open. Plenty of room at the counter," she said.

"Thanks, I'll take the booth." Mayor moved to the last booth. A small hall led past it to the bathrooms. He sat with his back to the wall.

The waitress was right behind him and poured coffee without asking. "Need a menu, or you know what you want, hon?"

"Eggs, and hash browns with extra bacon, please," he said. "And toast!"

"I love me, decisive men." She winked at him in a near cartoon flirt.

The coffee was terrific. The breakfast came quickly, and Mayor was impressed most by the toast. Real butter was all they said it would be and more.

Mayor didn't notice the diner had gotten quiet until he popped the last bite of toast into his mouth.

Looking up, a girl standing with her back to him. Her arm was extended with a gun aiming directly at his older self's face.

"You think you're so smart." She glanced over her shoulder at someone in the next booth. "Not smart enough…" It was Gina. A much younger twenty-something Gina. Not the forty-something Gina that brought him here.

Mayor didn't think before he reacted. He had to protect his future self. He drew his Glock and fired a single shot at the girl, striking her in the back of the head. She collapsed like a puppet that had its strings cut.

The room was silent for only a moment.

"NOOOooo…" It was a scream from the forty-something Gina. She turned on Mayor One and raised her own gun. A massive stainless-steel revolver.

Before she could draw a bead on mayor, a baseball bat came down on her wrist, breaking it. Yet another Mayor held the bat.

"How can this be?" She sobbed. "I didn't die. I'm here. I remember killing him. You watched." Gina pointed at his face.

"In physics," the old Mayor said, "the observer effect is the theory that simply observing a situation or phenomenon necessarily changes that phenomenon."

"Time is an illusion," Mayor One said quietly.

Fourteen people stared. He realized everyone in the diner was from the future. One by one, their active camouflage deactivated, and they were ALL Mayors. But if it was true that there was only now.

"We are not traveling in time," Mayor said. "It's always now. Even here. We have proof. This changes everything."

Mayor pointed the Glock at the dead twenty-something Gina.

***

Mayor One stood on the sidewalk, lighting the first cigar that was given to him by his elder self. He could not watch his other selves load the body onto the ship. It was unnerving.

"The Witness Paradox is true," Gina said to elder Mayor as she cradled her wrist. "You'll never stop the coming disaster now, you bastard! I'll tell them what you did. You won't get away with this!"

"The coming disaster? It has not happened yet. Not here. All we can do is find the right… now," he replied. "There is no time travel. The portals don't travel in time. They go to parallel universes." Mayor One walked away into the night. "But we cannot allow anyone to know this. It will create panic, not purpose."

The ship rose silently into the sky. As the shadows enveloped the elder Mayor, he disappeared into the night. Mayor One reentered the diner to find the sleeping waitress in the first booth. He would sedate her the next time through. He slid half the bundle of cash into her apron pocket, whispering, "Sorry about the mess." There was not too much blood.

He turned to watch Gina as she stood on the sidewalk, suffering in her realization. She was staring absently back at him in the empty diner when a man in 27th-century body armor appeared from the shadows and spoke.

"Witness this." The silent weapon's bullet entered her head but didn't exit. The man sifted through her pockets and came up with her Denbora Control Plate. He tossed it to Mayor One. "Now you can get started."

Mayor smiled as he left the diner. All signs of violence were gone. He was the only witness.

He climbed into the car and went in search of more cigars.

THE
WRITERS
GROUP
MARTIN WILSEY

The Writers Group

I got to Joey's Café early as usual. It was part of my Sunday morning ritual. Get up early, make coffee, and read the week's submissions for the writer's group. Relax a bit with my cat before I head out to Joey's.

It was hauntingly empty again this morning. I was the only one here at 9:36 am. As I sipped my coffee and munched on my bagel sandwich, I looked over the first submission titled: The Rescue.

This was just an outline with few details that we were going to brainstorm. It was always fun to brainstorm a topic. The group usually got really into it. It was a time travel story set in the present, where a time traveler is stranded and is trying to alert his partners in the future to come and pick him up.

I was personally interested in this piece because I struggled with a time travel story for the longest time.

"Morning, Marty," John said as he took his usual spot around the square table. "How goes?"

"So far, so good," I replied as usual. "I'm here, and there's coffee."

The twelve seats around the table began to fill quickly. People set down their laptops or notebooks and went up to get coffee or food. Shea was even here today, and she waved from the direct opposite corner of the table.

"Morning, human," Dave said, beating me to it. He was the eleventh person there. He also dropped off his Mac and went in search of soda.

Penny Morris was the last to arrive, and she sat next to me on a corner of the square of tables. She was always timid in the group, an obvious introvert.

"Morning, Penny." I said, "How are you this fine day?"

She nodded rapidly and averted her eyes as she took a notebook and pencil from her satchel. The carry strap was diagonal across her shoulders, and the bag rested in her lap.

I could see her hands were shaking as she fidgeted with her pencil. I don't know why but I looked at her closely then. She was fit. She was older than she seemed. I initially thought she was in her mid-twenties but now reassessed her to be in her mid-thirties. She had subtle crow's feet at the corners of her eyes, and her hands just seemed… older. She had long plain brown hair she kept in a classic single thick braid. She wore baggy sweatshirts most of the time with nerdy logos. Today it was Calvin and Hobbs exiting a TARDIS.

I think she caught me looking at her chest. I think I blushed.

Liz brought the meeting to order as we had four items to review, "First up, Penny has an outline for a story that she'd like to brainstorm with us. Penny, start with a general overview of what you are looking for."

I'm not sure anyone could see it but me. She swallowed hard before she spoke, "Well, this is a time travel sci-fi story. The story begins with the protagonist stranded in the past because of an accident that destroyed his time machine. He has to figure out how to get a message two hundred years into the future."

"If I were a time traveler, I would have contingency plans." Bill said, "Like if I don't show up by 2 PM, go back and pick me up at this pre-determined location and time."

"He could just put an ad in the classifieds of the Washington Post," John said, "…that would list a day, time, and location. With some predefined verbiage."

"That's a Robinsonade trope," Bill added.

"What if there was a series of wars and the Internet was destroyed. No records like that." Penny added.

"Time Wars?" I asked.

"No, just conventional wars." Penny quickly answered, "Lots of EMP kills most of the computers. And nukes and bio-weapons kill the people. Half the world population. Most paper only lasts about 100 years."

"Is this guy trying to stop the war?" Liz asked.

"No…" She paused, "He is a historian. To him, the war was in the far past. He was sent back to study a turbulent time in history."

"Can time travelers in your story change the past?" Shea asked, "Like Back to the Future, or is the past fixed? Ever see the Time Tunnel?"

"Yeah. Those guys never learned. Nothing they did could ever change the past. Sometimes they caused it." Dave added.

"You remember that episode on the Titanic where…" The group started to talk about the variations in time travel tropes, themes, and stories. Multiple conversations broke out with laughter.

I noticed Penny looked like she was going to cry. Quietly, just to her, I asked, "Are you OK?"

"I have a friend where I'm from that loves your books." She said in a whisper. "You ever consider writing a time travel novel?"

The conversation got loud for a minute, "You can use a time-turner to save Buckbeak but not Dumbledore?"

"Yes," I said. "I have an outline now."

"What if in that book you mentioned a specific place, day, and time?" Penny leaned in, "You know, where the protagonist gets rescued."

"A real place and time?" I asked.

"She might know your books survived, and someone might recognize it as a message in a bottle and go check it out."

I was looking at her closely again. She didn't look away this time. I noticed she said "She" that time.

"Time After Time was the best." Kathleen inserted.

"Was that the Jack the Ripper one or the Chris Reeves one?" Jeff asked.

"Somewhere in time was the Chris Reeves movie," Bill said.

I noticed Penny was looking across the room. Two men walked into the café. They looked like they were pressed from the same mold. Each had short haircuts and a Tom Selleck mustache. Both wore sunglasses, polo shirts, one red and one blue, a size too small. Plus matching mom-jeans that had not been in style for twenty years. They seemed out of place in several minor details.

I looked out the broad window as if I might see something unusual.

No one noticed them as time travel paradoxes had taken over the heated conversation. Movie and book references were flying as usual when a good topic had been launched.

"Ms. Morris." The one on the right said as the other scanned the room. "Are you alright?"

"Yes. Yes, I am." She said as her eyes began to fill with unshed tears that she blinked away. She looked into my eyes then.

She stood and packed her notebook in her bag. She spoke to the table.

"My rides here." Penny said, smiling brightly, "I think that's enough to get started."

It was then I realized she was talking about me getting started.

She laid her hand on my shoulder. "It was an honor meeting you." And she kissed me on the cheek. The two men followed her out like perfectly trained Rottweilers.

I looked at my watch and noted the date and time.

My mind was on fire.

cigars.

Dr. Clark Loves Pizza

Martin Wilsey

DR. CLARK LOVES PIZZA

"Look. Mike, don't screw this up." Mr. Delio said to Mike as he expertly tossed the pizza dough into the air, shaping a perfect large crust.

It wasn't the kind of thing he expected to hear on the first day of his first job. He had made eleven pizza deliveries already that day. He had over $70 in tips, and it was only just 5 pm.

"Dr. Clark is my best customer. Two large pies a week for the last eight years." He slid the perfectly formed crust down to Peg at the sauce station and started another. "He's an odd one, but follow the instructions on that damn card, and you will get a $20 tip."

Mike looked at the laminated three-by-five card in his hand. He smiled as he tried not to mention the misspellings.

1) Knock and go in annocing LOUD 'Delio's Pizza'.
2) Go in and put the pizza on the kitchen island.
3) Put the six pack of Mt. Dew in fridge.
4) Take the $20 yo find in the fridge.
5) Say out loud "Thank you Dr. Clark"
6) DO NOT correct him if he calls you Dave.
7) If the trash barel is full drag to curb.

"Mr. Delio, who is Dave?" Mike asked shyly.

"That's my son David. He was the first delivery guy for Dr. Clark back when this started. " Mr. Delio slipped the next formed pie to Peg, another employee at Delio's, and then stepped aside with Mike out of earshot of Peg and his other employees. "Mike, I picked you for this because I have known your parents your whole life. I have watched you grow up, and I know you are a good kid."

Mike was wondering at the conspiratorial tone.

"Don't be weirded out by the old guy. And try to watch out for him. You and Tom Wilkins are the only people he sees these days. Do you know Tom?" Mr. Delio asked as he brushed off his hands on his beer belly, covered by a white T-shirt causing a puff of flour.

"Yeah, Tom is our Postman, too," Mike answered.

"Paul Walker used to mow his lawn, but since he went off to college, he uses some commercial lawn service he hired on the Internet." Mr. Delio sounded kind of worried.

"Anything odd, come straight to me." Mr. Delio placed a hand on his shoulder. It felt like a ritual, a sacred trust. "Oh, and the book thing is not odd. Normal. He just reads a lot."

***

Mike pulled his 1970 Dodge Dart into the driveway of Dr. Clark's house at 5:15 pm. It was a tidy-looking ranch-style house. The lawn was mowed. The trees and shrubs were pruned. The beds were all edged and mulched. In the back, he could see from the cement driveway that there was a detached, closed-up, two-car garage.

There was an old Chevy van in the driveway. The tags were expired.

Mike climbed out with the insulated pizza cover and the six-pack of Mt. Dew. He climbed the three steps up to the covered porch. Directly to the left was a large trash barrel nicely concealed from the street by the tall hedge that surrounded the porch.

There was no storm door or screen door. Mike paused and looked at the laminated card once more. He knocked and tried the handle. It was not locked.

He opened it and walked in. He was so taken aback by what he saw that he almost forgot to announce himself. "Delio's Pizza."

He was standing in a foyer. A hallway went straight back to the kitchen. An arch to his immediate left went into what was usually a living room, dining room combination. The layout of the building was typical. Mike had been in many homes that were made the same all over town.

The odd thing was that every wall was lined with bookcases. Every one of them was completely full. Where there was not a bookcase, books were in piles that went just as high. Bookcases were even in front of the windows. This made the rooms dark, except there were desk lamps all along the top shelves. These were the classic kind with the green shades.

As he moved down the hallway, it felt constricted by the books crowding each side, making the hall narrow. Before entering the kitchen, the hall to the back bedrooms opened on his right side. It was also lined with books.

Not watching where he was going, the large pizza box insulator toppled a tower of books just as he entered the kitchen, causing a small, mostly quiet avalanche. Trying to stop it only seemed to make it worse. He stepped aside quickly and set the pizza and sodas on the island in the kitchen, next to the prior insulated pizza delivery container. This was a detail not on the card, but Mr. Delio had remembered to tell him to leave the whole thing and take the other back.

The kitchen was full of books, as well. The kitchen table was completely covered in a mountain of books that was higher than Mike's head. All but one of the kitchen cabinet doors had been removed, and books piled inside. The lone cabinet door was direct to the right of where the stove would be if it had been there. In the gap of the counters where the stove would typically be, was a sizeable wheeled trash barrel precisely like the one on the porch.

Mike opened the fridge, and just as described, there was a $20 bill on the empty top shelf. He replaced it with the Mt. Dew.

The next shelf had two cardboard flats that were cases of some kind of protein drink called Ensure. One case had been partially used. The door had only a large bottle of Centrum Silver multi-vitamins. He had never heard of the brand.

For some reason, he looked in the freezer. It needed defrosting. A single frozen dinner was being consumed by the frost glacier slowly.

He closed it, folded the $20 bill, and put it in the same shirt pocket as the laminated card.

He reached over to lift the lid of the trash barrel to peek inside as he wondered if this was the trash can mentioned or was it the other. Or both.

Mike saw a Delio's pizza box was mostly covered with other smaller boxes with the word Amazon in the trash can. The kind of boxes books were delivered with. For some reason, he counted the nine Amazon boxes. There were nine since his last pizza. The trash barrel was only half full, so he left it, wondering if it would fit down the narrow hall.

He had not heard a sound as he started back out. His mission was accomplished.

Slowly he moved back down the narrow hall, and this time he was looking at the book titles as he went. There was a lot of science fiction. It made Mike smile. Mixed in were textbooks on a vast amount of topics like quantum physics, computer science, psychology, philosophy, chemistry, biology, and even hydroponics. That was just a glancing sample.

"Thanks, Dave." Mike heard a voice call out from the back bedrooms.

"You're welcome, Dr. Clark." Was his reply as he moved more quickly to the door.

On the porch, the trash barrel was empty. Mike climbed in his car and headed back to Delio's.

***

The rest of the summer was much the same. There were deliveries twice a week. Every two weeks, he would switch out the trash barrel. He later discovered that Tom, the postman, would return the empty can to the porch after pickup.

Mike actually saw Dr. Clark only once that summer. It was a chance encounter as he was leaving, and Dr. Clark was exiting the bathroom. He saw Mike and waved, saying, "Thanks, Dave. Say Hi to your papa for me."

"Will do," Mike said and moved along.

It was October, just after Columbus Day, when Tom Wilkins stopped in at Delio's to pick up a pizza for his own family on the way home from work. He was still in his postman uniform. Mike was at the counter taking orders that day.

"Hi, Mr. Wilkins, what can we get you today?" Mike smiled. Thinking he and Tom were kind of a team. Wilkins must have been thinking the same thing.

"Mike. Please. Call me, Tom." Tom looked around to see if anyone was else was there. No one was. "How does he seem to you?"

"Um, the same. I never really interact with Dr. Clark. It's just the usual. Why?" Mike was curious at Tom's tone.

"He seemed agitated in the last few weeks," Tom said flatly. He was obviously worried. Mike said nothing, allowing Tom to continue. The silence encouraged him.

"He gets a lot of deliveries. The UPS and FedEx guys change all the time, and they just drop the packages on the doormat and ring the doorbell. Dr. Clark never sees the packages. So I pretend to deliver them. I pretend he has to sign for everything, too. Even the stuff he doesn't have to sign for. It's how I check on him. Know what I mean."

Mike nodded. The door opened, and Mrs. Cook came in for a pickup with two-year-old Jennifer on her hip. She said hi to Tom briefly as Mike rung her up. Tom stepped back as if he was waiting for his order.

When she was gone, Tom leaned forward again. "All that stuff I deliver. Not just books. Parts of stuff. Some packages have hazmat codes and shit."

"What can I do?" Mike asked.

"Today, there was a kind of a sound in there. A rumble." He wiped his face, "I could feel it in the sidewalk for the whole block."

"As far as I can tell, all he does is read in there." Mike said, "I don't see how he would have time for anything else. You see how many books he gets delivered."

"Just keep an eye on him." Tom closed the conversation. "If you can."

Mike was trying not to worry about Dr. Clark. Mike was just the pizza delivery guy. What was an 18-year-old kid supposed to do anyway? Dr. Clark was an adult. He had pizza on Mondays and Thursdays like clockwork, and he left the best tips of the week.

Mike smiled. Today was Thursday.

***

Mike pulled in Dr. Clark's driveway and ran up to the door, barely pausing to knock.

"Delio's Pizza!" he called out and proceeded directly back to the kitchen, as always.

Mike was startled by Dr. Clark standing on the opposite side of the kitchen island. The single cabinet with a door on it was open behind him, and he was reading an open book on the island counter as he ate a strawberry Pop-tart.

Mike knew it was a staple item for Dr. Clark. Every week or so, there was an empty Pop-tart box in the trash. Mike felt nosey for knowing that.

Dr. Clark glanced up from the novel he was reading briefly, lifting it from the island. It looked to be another Sci-Fi novel titled Still Falling. He raised his half-eaten Pop-tart in a toast-like gesture saying, "Oh… Hi David."

"Hi, Dr. Clark." Mike quickly switched the pizza warmers and placed the Mt. Dew in the fridge, snagging the $20. When he turned back, Dr. Clark was staring at him. It was the first real good look Mike had of the man. He was younger than Mike initially thought, maybe 50 years old. His graying hair was combed back from his bearded face into a thick ponytail.

"What time is it?" Dr. Clark asked.

"5:25 pm, sir. Sorry to be a little late." Mike looked at his Pop-tart.

"Is it Monday?" Dr. Clark looked out the window, puzzled.

"No, sir. It's Thursday." Mike replied. Dr. Clark had on a fresh Oxford shirt. It was untucked over jeans. The laundry tag was still in the buttonhole.

"You are not David Delio," he stated.

"No, sir." Mike tried to keep it simple.

Dr. Clark closed his book on his finger and walked past Mike, saying, "Thank you, Not David Delio." He disappeared into the back of the house. Before Mike reached the front door, he felt it, more than heard it. There was a hum of some great device and a change of pressure in the air.

***

A week later, he knocked and entered as usual. Even before he reached the kitchen, he had an odd feeling the house was empty. There was no hum, no creek of floorboards, and no sense of life that he had always felt before.

Mike's unease grew when he entered the kitchen and saw that all the books that had been on the kitchen table had been simply pushed off the far side of the table and left there in a great tumbled pile on the floor beyond the table. He kept staring at the mound as he traded pizza warmers, tucking the now flapping empty one under his arm, and set the Mt. Dew in the fridge and collected his $20.

All the cans of Ensure were gone. So were the Vitamins.

Following habit, he turned to check the trash and saw the single cabinet door was open to reveal empty shelves.

He froze when he opened the trash barrel lid.

He had become used to the contents of this trash can, like pizza boxes, Pop-tart wrappers and boxes, empty drink cans, and Amazon shipping boxes. But, this time, he saw a couple of dozen empty ammunition boxes. Half were labeled Remington Subsonic 9mm, the other half were marked Remington .223 and looked like rifle ammunition, based on the cover photo.

Mike quietly let the trash can cover close.

Softly he moved to the hall that went back to the bedrooms. The lights were off there in the hall. How long had they been off? How many times had he simply walked in and out, not noticing a thing? Mike stopped at the end of the hall. It suddenly raised the hair on his neck like it was a gaping maw.

"Hello… Dr. Clark?" Mike waited, and the longer he waited, the more courage bled from him. "Dr. Clark? Is everything OK? It's me, Not David Delio. Remember?"

He stepped into the hall.

"My name is actually Mike. I should have told you before." Mike said to the air as he saw the hall bath door open. He turned on the light. It let precious little illumination into the hall. The bathroom was spotless in there. Surprisingly there was only one book inside. It seemed so odd that he craned his neck to see the title, Temporal Displacement: A String Theory Approach.

The first door on the right was closed. He called out as he turned the knob. There was only one light inside, and it was a floor lamp next to a reading chair. The room was lined with full bookcases. Folding tables had been set up in front of them on two sides in the shape of an L, and mountains of books were just piled there. Most were dusty and cobwebbed—no pretense of order here. Books were read and just added to the pile.

The next room on the right was much the same but worse. "Dr. Clark?" That room had been filled to shoulder height with books and forgotten, hoarder fashion. The door was difficult to push open due to some prior small avalanche.

The last door made Mike afraid. Visions of finding Dr. Clark's dead body filled Mike's head like the books of that last room.

"Dr. Clark? Pizza guy's here." The door swung open easily to an empty room.

It was intended to be the master bedroom. Instead, it was now a high-tech workshop of some kind. The walls were lined with workbenches that were covered with a variety of equipment and tools. Mike recognized several computer brand names. Many monitors were on one wall, including a dominant 40-inch high def monitor in the center of the cluster of dark screens. There was only one keyboard and mouse.

The master bathroom had even become part of the shop. The shower had been converted to some kind of emergency chemical wash down booth. A stainless steel counter replaced the vanity and toilet. More unusual tools and equipment covered the surfaces.

The only other door was open in the room was for the walk-in closet. It had clothes in it. They were on the back most wall only. All the shirts, pants, and even boxers were in dry cleaning bags. They were another familiar trash item. There was also a narrow cot in the closet with a single pillow, plus disheveled blankets and sheets.

Dr. Clark wasn't here. Mike's relief was quickly replaced with the feeling he was invading Dr. Clark's personal spaces. Embarrassed, Mike closed the door and fled the house.

***

The following Monday, he returned, not knowing what to expect.

He didn't expect music. Or laughter.

"Delio's Pizza!" Mike called out as he entered. As he stepped into the kitchen, Dr. Clark came in right behind him. He took the pizza right from Mike's hands, leaving him holding the insulated carrier.

"Thank you, Not David Delio." He smiled as he dropped it on the kitchen table, tossed open the lid, and tore into the pie like a ravenous wolf. Led Zeppelin was still playing from the back.

Before Mike could put the Mt. Dew in the fridge, Clark snagged two of them, which allowed Mike to look closer at him before saying, "Are you all right, sir? Can I get you anything?" His clothes were dirty and threadbare.

The question made Dr. Clark laugh. The man looked thinner since Thursday. His hair seemed much longer, and his beard was even grayer. *How could that be?*

"These are wonderful times, my boy. Enjoy them." He raised his Mt. Dew like the finest Champaign in a toast. "Here is to... so much freshwater that we shit in it!" He laughed and drained his Mt. Dew.

"Oh, by the way, tell Delio he can keep the balance of my pizza advance." He grabbed another piece of pizza as he got up and walked to a kitchen drawer. From it, he came out with a nearly full bundle of $20 bills and another of $100 bills.

"This is for you, son." He held it out until Mike took it. "Invest it in Microsoft, Apple, Cisco, and Hagan Enterprises. Trust me." He laughed again and stuffed too much pizza in his mouth as he closed the box. He grabbed the other Mt. Dews and the pizza and, without another word, went to the back room.

Mike was in shock as he quietly left the house. Dr. Clark continued to laugh while he listened to Stairway to Heaven. Before Mike even reached his car, he heard that hum, felt it in his bones through his feet, the rumble and pressure felt in his ears was building.

And then it was like someone slammed a door on it. The sound was gone.

Mike got in his car and pulled away. He didn't see any smoke from the fire as he drove away. It was slow to start, they said later—so much paper made for a spectacular inferno. The clouds above had glowed from the towering light of it.

***

"There were no signs of any remains ever found." Tom Wilkins said to Mike a week later as they looked into the blackened crater of a foundation. "It's not unheard of for a fire like that."

Mike smiled, remembering his laughter. He remembered the equipment. The book titles of first editions that were like new, "He'll be back. Dr. Clark sure loved pizza…"

FANTASY STORIES

I write mostly science fiction, but every now and then, I have written short stories that fall into the Fantasy genre.

I love reading a good old classic swords and sorcery story. I love ghost stories. I also love urban fantasy, steampunk, Tolkien, and much more.

I have an outline for a couple of entire novels in this genre. Now all I need is time.

The world awaits. The swords have already been sharpened. The spells have been cast.

I hope to meet you there.

No Help In The Truth

MARTIN WILSEY

No Help in the Truth

A gloved man opened the sliding door of the van from the inside and kicked the woman out. She fell onto the ground with a thud and resumed her muffled crying.

The night was brilliant and clear, with deep, sharp shadows thrown by the moonlight. There were no traffic sounds, but her sobs were nearly drowned out by the chirping crickets and croaking frogs.

As predicted, the solstice moon of June 21st was bright on the gravel road. It was two tracks of sandy gravel with a strip of grass between. It led directly to a massive wooden fence with a sign that read, "NO TRESPASSING – Violators will be prosecuted."

Michael, the gloved man, produced a beautiful knife almost out of nowhere and cut the duct tape that bound Lucy's knees and ankles. It sliced the bonds like a scalpel.

He dragged her to her feet by her hair. Her crying increased. He saw that she was having difficulty breathing through the duct tape, tears, and snot as he pressed her against the side of the van with his body. With her hands still duct-taped together behind her back, she was helpless.

He wanted her to calm down. He showed her the knife. She stilled. "I am going to take the tape off your mouth. If you scream, no one will hear you. You know, screaming will do no good here. You know where we are," he said.

He delighted in the way she looked around with panicked eyes, a dawning realization of where they were.

He ripped the duct tape off her mouth. She gasped for air but didn't scream.

"Michael, why are you doing this? I thought we were friends." She was trying to reason with him as he dragged her by the arm, up the trail around the massive fence and the boulders behind it, and into the woods.

"We are far more than friends, Lucy," he said. "You're the one who started it. You flirted with me that first night at the coffee shop. You're the one who showed me this place on that lovely Sunday afternoon hike. You're the one who showed me this knife."

He held up the long dagger. It gleamed in the moonlight as he looked at it. The blade was double-edged, and the handle was ornately carved with symbols he didn't recognize.

"It's just an old knife that has been in my family for generations," said Lucy. "Take it if you want it. I won't call the police. I know this is a misunderstanding or some bad joke. Please." She fell to her knees in the wet grass, and he pulled her up by the hair as she sobbed, "Please, please…" over and over.

The pines cleared, and the darkness of the forest gave way to a bright, moonlit clearing. The grass grew very thick and tall here, almost to his chest.

Ten yards into the clearing, he saw what he was looking for—the vast circle of stones.

"I haven't been able to stop thinking of this place ever since you brought me here." He eagerly moved her toward the center of the circle. "Ever since you sat with me on that flat stone. In the center. You blind, ignorant bitch! You talked about coming back and having a picnic here and maybe more. You talked about how easy it would be to hide in the tall grass." He grabbed her by the throat and stopped. "You even talked about how no one could ever hear us."

He pushed her into the center of the circle, close to a massive table of stone. "You had no idea that the stains on this rock were probably from sacrifices. Stupid whore! You didn't know that I was looking for a place just like this my entire life."

Her crying had stopped. He didn't notice that the sounds of the summer crickets and frogs had also stopped. There was only the breeze whispering through the tall grass.

Just before they reached the slab, she fell again, flat on her face, making him lose his grip on her arm. He gave her a swift kick to the ribs, and she curled up into the fetal position. It took a bit longer this time to get her to her feet.

When he stood, he failed to notice that there were a hundred or so black-robed and hooded figures now surrounding them in the stone circle. Once he did see them, he didn't have time to react before the darts entered his thighs and buttocks.

All control of his body was lost almost instantly, and he slumped to the ground. He looked up at Lucy, who was silhouetted by the full moon behind her. A hooded figure came up behind her and cut the final duct tape from her hands. The sound of it was like a clap of thunder to his ears. Soon he was surrounded by cloaked figures in a tight, claustrophobic ring.

Hands gently lifted him high. He was buoyed up until all he could see was a moon so bright he couldn't see the stars.

The hands slowly lowered him onto the slab. He lay spread-eagle on the stone. Then the whispers began their questions—whispers, like the wind in the grass, forming words.

"Has he come to this place on this night of his own accord?" whispered a hundred voices in unison.

A single voice responded, "Yes. Of his own accord." It was Lucy.

"Did he come to this place seeking to find death here?"

"Yes. Seeking death."

"Did he carry the blade?"

"It is so very thirsty. It carried him."

"On this rarest of nights, the sun will rise and find the world in greater balance."

"Tell him. So he might know."

Lucy came into his field of vision then. "Well, Michael, I need to tell you that I wasn't stupid at all. I picked you specifically, you overconfident fool. You should've known. You're not that attractive. You see, I'm actually a police detective." She leaned over him, looking directly into his eyes, "And I had a copy of your file. I saw the photos of the things you'd done. The horrors you committed. The slick ways to escape arrest. Twelve murders in twelve states. Suspected in eleven more. Changing the details, but it was always a knife, always slow." She held the knife up in front of his eyes. It pulsed with a light from within. "I only had to let you hold it for a few minutes, and I knew that you would feel its thirst. I knew that it would whisper to you. It wanted you." She bent down close to his face. His eyes were open and staring. "It's a relic of power, and it drinks evil from the world. So you won't be raping and killing anyone else."

"Will he descend with truth in his ears?" whispered the voices.

"Truth is the greatest burden when there is no help in the truth," Lucy replied in ritual.

A robed figure stepped up and held a large carved stone bowl aloft. Light shone through it to form arcane symbols on his face.

Michael felt a momentary sting on the left side of his neck.

The bowl was lowered to a nook on the edge of the slab. His blood flowed freely in pulsing spurts from his jugular vein and down in what was a distinct channel carved into the rock. The blood flowed eagerly and finally into the bowl.

Michael watched as the hooded figures crowded around to watch him die. Lucy placed her finger in the bowl. Then, one by one, she touched a dot of his blood to the wrist of each of their left hands. He felt his legs and arms grow cold as his body stopped supplying his extremities with blood in a last-ditch effort to keep his brain alive. The last figure disappeared, and all he could hear was the wind in the grass. All he could see was Lucy's eyes glowing in her silhouette.

"Michael, you never had a chance. This Relic has been in my family for over a hundred generations. When it becomes thirsty, it gets what it wants." She held the bowl, now filled with his blood, in one hand and the dagger in the other. She dipped the blade into the blood, and he saw the bowl begin to drain as if the knife sucked it up through a straw. "You should know one more thing. Hell is not fire and pain. It is cold and black. No light, no sound, no feeling except unbearable cold. For all eternity. You will be alone and aware in your mind.

Without even the company of a coffin lid for you to scratch bloody."

She couldn't hear his mental scream as she turned away, but it was there. The bowl emptied, and the light went out of his eyes.

Lucy could hear the tractor engine getting louder as it came closer to them. Finally, as she approached the only figure remaining in the circle of stones, the figure lowered her hood.

"Hi, Mom," Lucy said. "How'd I do?"

"You did very well. The Order will be pleased." The blood had stopped dripping. "What was that I heard about hell at the end? A bit over-acted, perhaps."

Lucy smiled.

"I just wanted him to die in fear. This guy was a real asshole."

DUNN'S ARROW

A STONEBRIDGE SHORT STORY

MARTIN WILSEY

DUNN'S ARROW

"If you had been better managing your coins, we would not have had to sell the horses," Dunn said as he notched his favorite lucky arrow. "Besides, you've gotten too fat in the saddle, my friend."

Hollis adjusted his pack. "At least the summers are mild in the North Forest. I so love the shade. The trees are so tall and straight here. I don't know why that town has not harvested half of them for ship masts."

"Then, you place no stock in the haunted stories about this forest?" Dunn began scanning the woods to each side of the path for deer. "It's why they never come here. Except to travel straight through."

"Just stay on the path. Woods like this are the easiest to get lost in." Hollis looked into the gloom. There was no undergrowth. There was just a maze of tree trunks that would cause you to lose sight of the path in a few dozen paces. "Simple forest town folk like that would sooner believe in ghostly legends luring their sons to their doom rather than consider that their sons were idiots and got lost."

"Well, parts of their story are genuine. With canopy so high and no lower limbs, the sky is hidden." Dunn said. "And no moss. Get lost in there, and you have no idea what way you're going. I bet it gets especially dark in there as well at night. But, at least it's full of game."

Dunn knelt to look at the deer sign in the path. There was a fresh pile of dung pellets. Automatically he began to follow the trail into the woods straight where the road started to bend.

"Stay on the path, Dunn," Hollis whispered as he looked to make sure he was still on it. "The ghosts might lure you away with thoughts of venison."

Dunn was only ten paces into the trees when he held his hand up for silence. Dunn knew Hollis had seen this before. It was Dunn's own type of magic, so Hollis froze as he had been taught. Movement is what attracted the eye of the hunted. Their deep green cloaks and tunics would hide them.

Dunn heard the sound again. Footfalls. He didn't move anything but his eyes. Glimpses of massive antlers moved slowly through the gloom at a steady, predictable pace. He moved to profile his aim, his back directly to Hollis as he raised his bow in preparation to draw. The beautifully made arrow with its perfect barbed and bladed point would once again provide a feast or be lost or broken in these haunted trees. It was his favorite. It always found its mark.

The barb tracked the glimpses but revealed no clear shot. Slowly his whole body turned with the arrow as he drew it to his ear. His aim was drawn like gravity to its heart as he waited for the shot.

Then she was there.

Her eyes were wide with fear and pleading for help. Her hands extended toward him as if she were drowning. Then he suddenly realized his cruel arrowhead was aimed at her heart.

He blinked. As if to make sure she was real. The light in the forest changed. The sun above must have emerged from behind a cloud. The sun fell on her face as he lowered the bow, and she began it cry.

Her hands covered her face, and she dropped to her knees as her shoulders shook with the sobs. Dunn ran the thirty paces to her and could see her skirts were filthy and torn. Her hair was deep red. A color he had never seen before but reminded him of something he couldn't remember.

"Miss," Dunn tried to reassure her, "I won't hurt you. Are you alright?"

She looked up at him, towering over her. Her eyes were pleading. She choked out the words, "I've been lost in this forest for so long…"

"Dunn…" He heard Hollis call to him as she collapsed toward him. He dropped his bow and caught her. Kneeling, he gently turned her as she fainted in his arms. "Dunn…" the word was farther away.

When he turned back, he could not see Hollis or the path. But, through the trees to his right, he could see a portion of a chimney and the smoke from it.

Why could I not smell the smoke? The breeze in the forest hid as much as the trees. She must have come from there. He thought.

As he carried her there, he counted his paces. The cottage was only perhaps fifty paces total away from the path. He heard Hollis again, fainter still.

"Dunn!"

It can't be helped. He knew Hollis. He'd stay put and wait for him. He knew he could backtrack his footprints to the path.

The stone cabin was tiny. It had a steep thatch roof and a single leaded paned window. The door stood open like a gaping maw as he approached and entered. It contained only a single piece of furniture—a large, ornately carved bed.

Dunn laid her on the bed, and she began to stir as he placed his hand on her forehead to check for fever. She was so beautiful, so perfect. It was like the light gathered around her.

Dunn looked to the door as he faintly heard Hollis in the distance.

"Dunn. No. What are you doing…"

When had night fallen?

The fireplace had a fire blazing with it. Candles in glass jars lined up on top of the low rafters, on the mantle, and other shelves.

Did I make that fire? Did I set those candles? He thought.

When he reached up for one of the jars, he saw that his left arm was tense and shaking. He realized he was on the verge of a cramp in his right shoulder. He rose to go and speak to Hollis, to reassure him. But when he stood at the edge of the bed, she grasped his hand. Her eyes begged him to stay.

When had she undressed? How could all these quilts and sheets and pillows be so white and clean?

"Please. Don't leave me here." She begged him.

He sat again on the edge of the bed. "How long have you been here?"

"So very long…" She relaxed back. "I was so lost." She drew his shaking left hand to place on her sternum.

Her skin was so beautiful. Dunn felt so sleepy.

Dunn told her the story, "In the forest town of Greenwood, they have an Inn called the Loaf and Ladle. We heard a story there about a ghost of a red-haired witch in these haunted woods. Young men would bring her gifts, but she would always send them away. They would become lost and die in this forest."

"Please stay with me. Hold me." She was pleading.

"Dunn…" in the distance.

It was all a fog in his mind. Dunn wondered if he had a fever.

How had he gotten undressed? Their arms and legs tangled beneath the silken sheets and thick quilts. He felt heady, as if he had been drinking for hours. Then she was straddling him. Sitting up and on full display in all her perfection.

He wanted her.

She held his shaking left hand to her heart as she whispered. "Finally. The gift I have sought for an age…"

Then the mist of illusion ripped away like cobwebs.

Dunn stood in the forest. He was holding his bow with a shaking hand as his eyes focused on the singing string.

"NOO…" Hollis screamed as he tackled Dunn too late. "What have you done?!"

The two men froze where they landed as they both turned to look at her.

She was staring down at the arrow in the center of her chest. Blood began to spread as she stumbled toward them. She fell to her knees, and Dunn caught her in his arms.

"Thank you…" She whispered. "This was the gift I waited fo…" She never finished the sentence as she turned to dust as the arrow fell to the ground.

Suddenly winds surrounded them. The sky grew brighter. It was the early evening. The forest seemed to change, and now they could see the ruins of a small cottage thirty paces away. The thatch was mostly gone. The exposed rafters mimicked the ribs of skeletons that littered the ground around the cottage's ruin. Bone fingers still held jewelry, a silver hairbrush, tattered silks, and gold coins in a rotting velvet bags.

***

They collected what treasures they could easily carry. They left half behind. Dunn and Hollis never returned to the forest town of Greenwood. They never spoke of the origins of their new wealth. They never laughed again at stories told in Inns about cursed witches.

He left the gift to mark her grave—Dunn's favorite arrow.

MARTIN WILSEY

THE ONCE DAMNED

The Once Damned

Blood in the Snow

When all was quiet again, Thorn realized the blood dripping from his chin wasn't his. The blood looked black in the moonlight on the knee-deep snow. The light made it bright enough for him to watch the remaining two men ride off at a gallop, taking with them the horses of the six people that lay dead at his feet.

The next sound was always the same. A creak of leather as he squeezed the grips of his swords. They had saved his life again. Blades like no other. They were perfectly matched staghorn grips, wrapped in fine leather.

The snow was thick on the tall pines that covered the region. The hush in the air consumed the sounds of the fleeing horses.

With a well-practiced motion, Thorn wiped the blood on his red sash and sheathed first one sword and then the other. He was careful of the crossbow bolt protruding from his chest, just below his left collarbone. He reached up and broke it off, leaving a few inches protruding.

"It was a good ambush, gentlemen," he said out loud to the dead.

Thorn thought, *Waiting here at the Elder Bridge was the perfect place. I had to cross here. The trees provided ideal cover on the western side of the bridge. No footprints in the snow anywhere. Perfect. The Queen must be getting tired of losing so many men.*

He looked over the edge of the thousand-year-old bridge as he leaned briefly on the stone wall. *Assigning one of you to shoot the horse out from under me and then the rest to shoot at me as I fell was an inspired plan.*

He began searching the dead, collecting coin purses, which he stashed in his black tunic. As he moved, he adjusted the curved swords in his belt. The staghorn made his elegant, curved blades look like the tools of a simple farmer.

You should have left me where I fell in the snow for a few hours before approaching. Then filled me with more arrows before getting close. If you knew who I used to be, you should have been more careful.

As he took the last purse, he noticed this man had a flask on his belt. That's when he also saw the bolt that was in his leg. The fletching was all the way through his thigh. Thorn felt around the back, and the wicked blades of the arrow had cut all the way through. He broke off the fletching, and then without hesitation, he pulled the shaft all the way through his leg. Blood flowed freely, and steam rose from the wound. Once again, he wondered where all the blood and magic that made it came from.

He took a long pull from the flask he had taken from the body. It was a strong liquor that tasted faintly of apples. Thorn moved along and took his saddlebags from the dead horse, and carefully draped them over his right shoulder.

These wounds would not close quickly out here in the cold wind.

He began to walk.

The eight horses had plowed a path for him down the middle of the road. As he walked, he could feel the magic sustaining him. It was like heat from within. The stars and moon were bright on the snow. The pines that lined the road were undisturbed.

He moved. The magic burned. His breath made no clouds in the cold. Anyone that was sensitive to magic would see him. They would feel him coming. There was no more hiding on this journey. Thorn thought he could see the distant light of the Keep on the horizon.

Peck's Halfway

The tracks didn't divert from the road, and just after midnight, he rounded the corner to the familiar sight of a large, multi-story inn made of stone, Peck's Halfway. He paused at the open gate and looked north into the darkness to see the distant fire in the Keep's watchtower.

From here, it was a day's ride to Bullard down into the valley in one direction and Rockriver in the other back over the Elder Bridge.

He followed the tracks in the fresh snow through the massive stone arch into the courtyard, where they led to the stables. No one else was traveling on a night like this. Thorn was backlit by the waist-high flames in the raised fire pit in the center of the large, walled courtyard when the stable boy noticed him. He was young and frightened but approached anyway. The boy's breath came out in great gouts of mist.

Thorn stood motionless, seeming not to breathe at all.

"Good evening, mmm, my Lord. Can I be of service?" The boy said in a well-practiced manner. His voice only trembled a little.

"How long ago did those horses arrive? How many men were with them?" Thorn asked in a quiet growl, trying not to frighten the boy.

"Eight horses and two men. About four hours ago." The boy glanced down at the pool of blood forming at Thorn's feet, reflected in the firelight.

"Is Peck at the bar?"

"Yesss, sir," he stammered.

"Take extra good care of those horses, lad. And throw ten more logs on this fire for me." Thorn flipped the boy a coin. Its gold glistened in the firelight as he caught it. "I'll be back out in a few minutes." When the boy looked up from the coin, Thorn was already moving toward the main door of the inn.

Blood trailed behind.

***

Thorn could see that no one noticed the inn door open or close.

There was an outer entry that kept out the wind and maintained the heat. The drop in temperature within the room made people finally look up and notice the man standing in the entryway. The cold was not from the snow.

The common room was large and crowded with about sixty men and women, plus a few children. Travelers, going both east and west, stopped at Peck's Halfway. It was always busy. Peck had many suites, rooms, and bunks of all kinds and costs for them. As Thorn scanned the room, the conversations fell silent.

Thorn heard a ten-year-old boy mutter, "Papa, that man is bleeding." He pointed at the puddle growing at his feet.

A woman whispered, "It's him."

Another quietly uttered, "Magic," and averted her gaze.

Thorn's eyes locked on two men in the back of the room who were bent over mugs of ale. After a minute, he turned his back to them to face the bar.

Peck himself was there. He was fat with a bush of curly hair on his head. Peck was clean-shaven and missing a couple of teeth on one side of his mouth. He wore a white apron stained with food. Peck was close enough to see the broken stem of the bolt sticking out of Thorn's chest.

"For the love of stone." Peck quietly cursed, "Please, Thorn. Don't destroy my inn again."

"Whiskey." Thorn requested, his back still to the people. The murmurs began behind him.

Peck was terrified. He was trembling as he set a large pewter mug, meant for ale, in front of Thorn and poured half a bottle of strong brown liquor into it. He left the bottle on the bar and stepped back.

Thorn studied Peck's face as he watched two tall, hard-looking, well-armed men walk up behind Thorn as he drank deeply.

"Please, Thorn. Not again," Peck begged quietly.

They stood a pace behind Thorn. One of the men was looking at the floor. "You're bleeding," he growled.

Thorn knew Peck had a slight touch of talent. He could see the magic rising from Thorn as if his blood were made of molten iron.

He emptied his mug and dropped a fat purse on the bar. Then, to Peck, he said, "For the mess."

Peck had backed up until he was pressed against the shelves behind him. "No, please. Not in here, not again," Peck whispered.

Thorn turned slowly to face the men.

"Peck would rather I die outside if you don't mind." He turned and limped to the door he had just come in, leaving the two men looking at each other for a moment.

When they exited, Thorn was standing in the courtyard with his back to the roaring fire pit. The fire was taller than Thorn, half again as high above his head now.

The two men slowly approached, separating a bit as they came closer. Their stances spoke of experience and formal training. Royal Army training.

Thorn reached up and released the clasp on his soaked, thick, wool cloak. It fell off his shoulders to the ground into the blood that was already collecting there. He stepped forward a pace and waited. His hands were relaxed at his sides. His mind drained to empty.

Faces were crowding the windows, and those that were brave enough to come to the door could see his leg, and the left side of his body was slick with blood. They could see the remains of the shaft in his chest.

Thorn didn't move as the two men drew their swords. They stalked closer and closer to him. Their breath was creating clouds. The closer they got, the more Thorn seemed to grow still. His breath made no cloud.

When they were only two paces away, both men quickly raised their swords to strike simultaneously.

Then Thorn moved.

Thorn drew his sword and struck in the same motion as he suddenly crossed the distance. The man on the left was cut in half diagonally by an upward cut, from ribs to opposite shoulder; the man on the right was suddenly headless--both dead with one strike while he drew the sword.

Thorn was frozen again like a statue at the end of the single stroke. He waited until the bodies fell in slow motion. Then, his sword swirled again in a lightning-fast arc, the blood painting a line in the snow as it flew away.

Then he stood at ease and clasped the red sash that was tucked into his simple leather belt. Then, in a smooth motion, he cleaned the blade and sheathed it.

When he began to walk back to the inn, people fled from his path as if he were on fire.

Peck was pouring the remains of the bottle into his mug as he returned to the bar.

After he had taken a long pull, he asked, "Do you still have decent whores, Peck?" Peck nodded.

"Can any of them sew?" He emptied his mug. "I need a room with a hearth, lots of firewood, and your best wound wench."

Peck called out, "Thomas! Please, take Master Thorn to suite number four and then get Cass." A wide-eyed boy came up to Thorn's elbow, looking at all the blood on the floor. Peck set another full bottle on the bar. Thorn took it along with his mug and followed the boy.

"Lead the way, lad, before I fall down and embarrass myself," Thorn said and then drained the mug.

***

Thorn waited in one of Peck's best suites, thinking about the Queen.

The door opened, and a woman entered, carrying a tray of medical supplies. Her long brown hair was pulled back and tied with a leather thong at the nape of her neck. She wore a simple brown tunic with a thick rope belt.

She closed the door and turned to see Thorn standing in front of a roaring fire, leaning on the mantle. His shirt had been torn off and was hanging about his waist by his belt. She had never seen muscles like this before. His body had no fat. His skin was so thin she could see the textures of the twisting strands of individual muscles. Thorn sensed by her reaction that she could also see the heat of the magic rising off of his entire body.

"Good. You're here." Thorn said as he raised his left hand to grasp the mantle and lean into it, steeling himself. He drank the remaining contents of the heavy mug.

In a sudden flash of movement, he pounded the bottom of his massive pewter mug onto the bolt's shaft, and the cruel arrow blades burst from the back of his shoulder. His knees nearly buckled from the pain.

Cass almost dropped the tray.

Thorn took in a ragged breath and said with exaggerated politeness, "Would you mind pulling that the rest of the way out? Soonest?"

She set the tray down on the table, and, instead of going to him, she opened the door and called out for Thomas. "Bring food. Bring bread, cheese, soup, and eggs, stew, and fried potatoes for six. Quickly, boy."

Thorn was still leaning on the mantle, with both hands now. He looked at her over his right shoulder. His chin rested on his right forearm.

Cass quickly walked over and added two more logs to the already tall blaze. She worked around where Thorn stood.

Standing, and without warning, she pulled the shaft out of his shoulder and threw it into the fire. "My name is Cass," she said.

He took in a shuddering breath. "Thank you, Cass," he whispered. "My name is Jacob Thorn. I'm…"

"I know who you are. You're the bastard who lived." She spat the words like an insult. She had produced a small, razor-sharp knife from somewhere. She began cutting off his clothes. He remained leaning on the mantle with both hands. Blood and magic were flowing anew. Despite the fire, the room was cooling, the very warmth being drawn out of the room by the magic that sustained him.

She removed his belt and set it with his swords on top of a large chest. She paused for only a moment and looked at them.

The rags of his shirt and pants went onto the blazing fire and were quickly consumed.

He stood there naked, covered in blood as she washed him from a large pitcher and basin.

"You are a fool," she said. "People don't hate you enough already? So you wander the countryside murdering people? And letting them see magic burning from you?"

There was a knock at the door. Thomas was there with a large tray piled high with food.

Cass took the tray and dismissed the boy. She walked over and set the tray on the same trunk as the swords. She lifted a pitcher of milk and added some to a hot bowl of soup. She took the soup and handed it to Thorn. "Drink this, all of it. Now. Before you freeze the inn solid."

He took his hands off the mantle and took the bowl. She added more wood. "You've done this before?" he asked. "You know how the magic works."

"Fools!" She started ripping up a loaf of bread into another bowl and poured more milk over it, and then handed the entire milk pitcher to him. "Drink this. If you want these wounds to heal proper without freezing us out of this room."

He handed the empty soup bowl back to her as she brought him a wooden chair so he could sit in front of the fire. After he had emptied the jug, she took it to the door and called Thomas again. "Another pitcher of milk, more hot water, and clean rags, please, Thomas." He was off at a run.

Cass handed him the bowl of soggy bread with a spoon. "Now this." She dragged a table over from the wall and placed on it her sewing materials and medical supplies.

Thorn looked at the tray as he ate mechanically and noticed her face for the first time. She had scars there. Slave scars. Deep X's had been carved in each cheek. She must have once been a disgraced noblewoman: her posture and manner were not that of a slave. She must have been marked and sold into slavery.

She took the empty bowl from him and added another log to the fire. "That's enough for now." The room was still cold. "I will close this one first," she said, turning his shoulders to the light.

She quickly threaded a curved needle with a long fine black thread. Then, without hesitation or apology, she closed the X-shaped wound. "What was that in the courtyard? I have seen men die by the sword many times. I have never seen that before."

"It's called Masidill. The art of the draw." He paused, thinking. "It is a war art that is the beginning and the end of a duel. Draw and Strike, powerfully, all in one. I may be the last of its masters."

She had finished his back and was starting on the chest when Thomas knocked. "Come," she called out. "Good. Thomas, I want you to help me. Wet a clean rag and gently wash his back where I have finished." Thomas did so without a word of complaint. Thorn was stoic and watchful as Cass applied medicines directly into the wound before sewing it closed.

More scars for his own collection.

As she worked, he examined her skin closely. Whipping scars peeked out from the collar of her tunic. Rope burn scars on her neck. Small wound scars here and there told a story of pain.

She finished sewing the front wound under his collar bone, and Thomas repeated his cleaning there. The boy was not afraid and not squeamish at all. He was firm and gentle at the same time.

Thorn had a gash in his ribs that he didn't remember feeling until now.

"I have never seen swords like those. But I have heard the legend of rune-marked blades like them. Made by a country blacksmith. Somewhere. No one knows."

It took almost fifty stitches to close that one. The white of his rib bones was exposed. "The story is true," Thorn said. "A country blacksmith and more. He told me this was the seventh set he had made. His best yet." Thorn winced for the first time. It was apparent he kept talking to distract himself from the pain. "After… I wandered for years, thinking I would never hold a blade again. Until I met him."

Thorn watched Cass kneel before him to close the wound on the front of his thigh. His nakedness was not off-putting to

Cass at all. Not even noticed. Thorn's genitals were covered in blood, and Cass washed even there with clinical indifference.

"Thomas, draw the blankets down on the bed. I will need him lying face down to work on his leg." She helped Thorn up from the chair. His skin was clammy and cold even though he was so close to the fire. He slowly moved to the bed and lowered himself onto it.

This wound was ragged. Cass had to remove some torn flesh with her knife before she could sew him up.

He never made a sound.

When he was all clean and bandaged, Cass propped him up in bed and fed him stew, hot spiced apple sauce, eggs, bacon, and fried potatoes with onions while Thomas mopped up all the blood from the floor and stoked the fire.

"Why did you come here? Who were those two men?" Cass asked as she fed him.

"There were eight men."

Cass froze as the fork was halfway to his mouth.

"No more will come. The other six did this to me at the Elder Bridge. Had that arrow found my heart or I had lost my head, all the magic in the Kingdom would not have saved me."

Cass remained motionless as he spoke. Finally, she fed him the last of the eggs. She half-filled his mug with water and then upended a paper tube of white powder into it and then stirred it with her knife.

"Now drink this." She held it out to him. "It will help you sleep."

Thorn took the mug and paused for a long time. He was looking into her eyes when he said, "Thank you, Cass."

He drank it all.

Warm Again

Thorn woke in darkness and realized he was finally warm. He was on his side facing the hearth. His injuries ached, but the medicines she had given him in the wounds and in his food had dulled the pain.

The fire had burned down to a deep bed of red coals. Thorn could feel the heat of them from across the room. He would live. Again.

He felt her move.

He was suddenly acutely aware of her. She was naked. His back was to her front. Their legs were tangled, and her hand rested on his hip. She snored quietly. The thick mountain of quilts held in their warmth. He was no longer drawing energy from the air around him to fuel the magic.

With a deep sigh, he fell back asleep.

***

When next he woke, it was because of the sound of more wood being added to the fire. He looked, and he could see Cass in the growing firelight. The silhouette of her naked body was beautiful. She stood and arranged the fire with the poker, and as it flared, he saw more scars. Whip scars covered her torso. As she added and arranged the wood, she turned, and he could see burn scars on her breasts and cruel rope scars on her neck and wrists. Thorn had rarely seen a body with more scars than his own.

He had closed his eyes before she saw him awake. She walked around and slid back into bed, and slowly her fire-warmed body was all along his. Then, gently, she laid her hand on his forehead to check his temperature.

He opened his eyes.

"Fever?" he asked.

"No. The magic's chill is over," she whispered. "You are done drawing energy from the world around you. The magic is done with you. For now."

He raised his right arm so she could rest her head on his chest. "Rest now," he said.

He felt her fall asleep in tiny twitches. Holding her seemed to push out all other thoughts and pain as if it were healing magic all its own. He quickly followed her in sleep.

***

The light in the window woke him the next day. He had lost track of time.

Thorn knew that Peck's Halfway was in a mountain pass and had steep cliffs on almost all sides. If the light was shining down here, the morning must be practically gone.

Cass had her back to him now. The quilts remained heavy on them, and he was in no rush to arise. She stirred, sensing him waking.

"I can tell you're feeling better," Cass murmured as she hugged his arm that was wrapped around her.

Thorn realized that his erection was pressed against her. Instantly embarrassed, he turned from her. "Forgive me. It's just…"

"It's just that you're feeling better." She hugged his back. "I have not slept that well in ages. Thank you, Jacob. May I call you Jacob?"

Thorn had a flash in his mind of an ordinary life. Waking on a winter morning with a woman he loved and lingering in a warm bed as long as possible. Then reality rushed back in. There would be no love for the damned.

"What's wrong?" Cass was more sensitive than he had realized.

"Nothing. Don't worry. I won't hurt you. I promise."

"I know you won't hurt me. No one will hurt me ever again. I have already had my lifetime's worth."

"I saw you. In the firelight." He rolled onto his back, and she once again placed her head on his chest. His right hand traced the scars on her back. Some were raised and coarse. Some were divots or trenches in her skin.

"Peck got me for a bargain," she frowned. "Is that what you mean?"

Thorn considered what to say before speaking.

"I think I am going to sleep every night, in this bed, for the rest of my life," Thorn said. "With you."

"Ha!" she barked. "You plan on buying me from Peck?"

"I think I will." He was suddenly serious. "I have more than enough gold I won't need. It will only be one more night. Then I will go off to my well-deserved death."

"You are not considering going up to the Keep? They know who you are. They will already know you are here." She sat up and looked into his eyes. "Those men… were probably from there."

"Cass, I was the King's Guardian. I swore an oath, a magic oath, on penalty of curse, of doom, to protect the throne or die trying."

There was a long pause.

"I lived."

"So you've been trying to die honorably ever since?" she said as if it was all folly.

"The Gods have not made it easy. But, once damned, they enjoy drawing it out, it seems," he said and looked at the fire.

"Gods be puke. Just go," she pleaded with him. "Find a quiet life somewhere. Don't be Royal Guardian anymore. Walk away."

He petted her hair. Finally, he just sighed and said nothing.

"Please, Jacob. Just live. What good would vengeance serve? Please. I just finished putting you back together." She was about to cry.

"I was serious, you know," he said quietly. "I'll buy you from Peck. You are already free. Whether I go to the Keep or not, you will be free." He looked into her eyes, trying to discover why she would care. "I can at least do one final kindness for the world."

"Jacob, please don't go up there. They have great power—magic, science. The Queen may even be there. The least of their weakest girls can read and brew a poison that could kill us all. The greatest of them, the High Vestal, they say, was the hand behind the death of the King."

"I know. It is why I must go." There was sadness in his voice.

"You have no honor any longer. You're truly damned already. What do you owe the world? Don't be a fool." She climbed out of bed and angrily began to dress. "I cannot send someone to his death unhealed or hungry, damn you."

She was flushed, angry. "I will bring food and check your wounds. And…"

"Wait," he said and reached out a hand to her. It was like gravity. She took it. "Let me tell you what happened. One person at least should know the truth of my oath-breaking."

She sat fully dressed at the edge of the bed.

"How much of the story do you know?"

"It was the funeral of Prince Gareth. It is rumored he was poisoned. Not simply drunk and choking on food. The King attended with his six personal guards, including you, and the entire Prince's Honor Guard was there." She swallowed. "Once inside the Cathedral, the doors were locked from the inside. And only you survived the day. Sworn to give your life before his. The King was killed, and you walked away in disgrace." She paused, looking at their hands. "Loyalists have been challenging you to duels ever since."

"It was sixty against six." He closed his eyes, seeing it repeat as in his dreams every night. "They had crossbowmen in the balcony. They didn't know that we six could strike bolts from the air. They didn't know we had been spell cast, giving us enhanced physical speed, perception, and the ability to survive massive, even lethal wounds for a while."

Thorn opened his eyes and met hers.

"I lived. I should have fallen on my sword for that sin alone."

He stared into the distance, still holding her hand. Cass waited.

"Their leader was named Ramos. He was Captain of the Prince's Royal Guard. I thought I knew him. I thought he was my friend." The despair in Thorn's voice was evident.

Cass began crying quietly. Sobbing.

"After… I dropped my royal swords and armor, and when the doors were opened, I walked away. No one stopped me."

He was staring at her hand in his. He was caressing it as if he were trying to memorize it.

"I sold my estate. Always expecting Queen Aleena to send someone to execute me. They never came." He looked up. "I took the gold and found the wife and parents of Ramos. I told them he died with honor and had made arrangements for their welfare. They never knew who I was. Years passed, and the rumors blamed the High Vestal in the great Keep for the plot."

He looked to the window then.

"I was lost. Wandering. I think it's been fifteen years. Leaving death and chaos in my wake wherever I went."

Cass cleared her throat. "Years before the King died, I lived in the capital. I was married to a lesser noble and became lost in the decadence of court life." One of her tears fell on the back of Thorn's hand. "I caught my husband raping a small boy. He gave me these." She gestured to her cheeks. "He sold me to the foulest slaver he could find." She hesitated. "I was never… obedient enough."

Thorn reached up and traced his thumb on her cheek.

"Go find Peck. I need to speak to him."

Buying Cass

Peck limped into Thorn's room and went straight to the fire, and added a log. "Bloody gout," he said.

"Peck, see that black pouch on the mantle? Take it," Thorn said from the bed.

Peck picked it up and looked inside. "Expecting to stay a few years, are we?"

"I am buying Cass from you," Thorn stated. Making clear it was not a request.

Peck froze. Turned his head slowly and looked at him. "You're what?"

"Cass. She's a talented healer; is it enough?"

"Because you terrify me only slightly more than she does, I should tell you… I feel I should tell you," he stammered just as she walked in with another large tray of food.

After a moment, Peck said, as if deciding something, "Cass, you are free to go as you please. Both of you." He looked at Thorn for a long moment, "For what it's worth, I always thought the King was a bloody bastard and got what he deserved. Thanks again for not burning the inn down, Thorn." He limped out, tossing the pouch of gold in the air, and catching it.

"What did he say?" Cass looked at the closing door.

"You are no longer a slave. You're free." Thorn said as she brought him another bowl of soup.

"Free? What does that mean?" she questioned. "Where would I go? Peck tricked you. Now he has me and your gold. I think he freed me long ago. It's why he bought me." Thorn heard her first lie, "To stop my… suffering."

"Why didn't you leave?"

"I did." She brought him a plate of hard-boiled eggs, cheese, bread, and an apple. "I went to the Keep to join the order. Become a novice. I managed the thousand steps, but for complicated reasons, I couldn't stay. So I ended up here."

"You've been to the Keep?"

"Yes. And you should not go there." She was somber. "Please, Thorn. The guards are many, and they are cruel. They will never open the Main Gate for you. Never even acknowledge you with anything but arrows."

"You will guide me." He tore off a piece of bread. "To the Novice Gate of a Thousand Steps."

***

Cass found Thorn out of bed sometime after midnight. The fire had been stoked, and he stood naked before the hearth.

He had her small knife.

She watched him quietly for a few minutes. As she watched, she realized what he was doing.

She slid out of bed and approached in a way to make sure she didn't startle him.

"Give me that, you fool, before you gut yourself." She took the knife from him and began removing the stitches from his chest.

Thorn was amazed at her comfort in her nakedness. He considered who she was.

She was careful and systematic in the removal of the stitches. Chest first, then ribs, and as she knelt before him to remove the stitches in the front of Thorn's thigh, he forced himself to think about the killing of the King. He didn't want to embarrass himself with another reaction.

"What's wrong?" she whispered as she moved to the back of his thigh.

"Nothing," he said as he looked at the beams above.

"Your magic flared. I can see it, you know." She continued removing the stitches in the back of his leg and then finally stood to reposition him so she could have better light from the fire to finish his back.

When she was done, she soaked a clean rag in alcohol and cleaned each wound. Magic burned in him again, and by the time she came back around to his shoulder, all the stitchings were healed-over scars.

"Please don't go." She leaned her forehead on the nape of his neck. It was the most intimate moment he had ever experienced. His whole life had been violence and pain and death.

This hurt more than all of it.

"I must go. It is my final task. Live or die. The High Vestal must know the truth. I cannot do otherwise. I am finished hiding from the Queen. I am finished hiding from the truth, only to discover death hides from me."

"They will try to stop you."

"They will try."

She lifted her head from his nape, and he turned to her. They were the same height. Their faces were only inches apart.

His right hand traced the scars on her face. His fingers drifted to the ones on her neck, her collarbone, her sternum.

He recognized this kind of torture. Strips of skin removed, coarse salt or hot irons then applied. He clearly saw now that one of her nipples was missing.

Cass was watching his eyes.

"What are you thinking? Your eyes... are smiling," she asked.

"Forgive me." He looked into her face. "I believe... You're beautiful. Your strength is etched into your flesh. And still, you remain kind. Gentle. I could never be that strong."

"I am anything but beautiful." She choked out the words.

"Beauty seen is in he who sees it," Thorn whispered. "Let us sleep. Tomorrow will be a long day."

Cass wept as he held her. Thorn began to understand why.

***

Peck was in a joyous mood the next day as the stable boy prepared two of the best horses for their departure. Peck got to keep the other six and all their tack in payment. The horses had no ownership brands, and the tack had no identifying marks, either.

Those men had sought to remain anonymous.

Peck was surprised that Cass was to travel with Thorn. He was also astonished that Thorn would take her. He supplied heavy woolen cloaks as well as clean clothes for the trip. It was only a single day's ride north of the pass to the Novice Gate. North and away from the great East-West Road.

Peck came out to see them off. He stood near the fire at the center of the courtyard. He spoke to Cass first. "I own the stables at the Novice Gate. They will care for your horses. My advice to you is to part ways with Thorn at your first chance." He looked at Thorn, "No offense." Back to Cass: "You're always welcome here."

"Thorn. Trust no one. You are swimming in a river of lies and shit. You're not smart enough to keep your mouth shut or to tell the difference. You'll probably be dead this time tomorrow, so I'd just like to say goodbye. It's always been interesting."

Thorn reached around and lifted off his personal saddlebags and tossed them heavily to Peck's feet. "If I manage to live, hold this for me. If I'm dead this time tomorrow, give it to Cass."

Cass looked at the bags knowing what they contained. Her hood covered her face as it crumbled in guilt in an effort to hold off tears.

Peck picked the saddlebags up. They were heavy.

Cass whispered to Peck, barely audible, as she leaned in the saddle toward him and kissed his head, "Bless you, Kevin." With that, she turned her horse and left the inn to the north on the path behind the stables. Thorn followed close behind.

Thorn looked up to where the Keep should be. Low clouds obscured the mountains. The narrow track led up toward the tree line. He could see traffic from woodcutters that had emerged from the trees before they reached it. The path was clear, and the horses were sure-footed.

The Path to the Keep

Their route took them constantly up and north. Paths followed the curve of the peaks and were designed to be traveled in all seasons. There were shelters with unfrozen water along the way for the horses.

There was little conversation as they finally traveled into the clouds.

It was nearly dusk when they saw large braziers burning to light a bridge that crossed a ravine to a small tower.

There were no guards, and the tower entrance stood open, and the road led directly into the mountain through the open Novice Gate.

Cass didn't speak, and Thorn followed her lead. They had to leave the horses in Peck's extensive stable near the mouth of the entry.

They could already hear the murmuring of haunting, chanting songs from deeper in the mountain.

Thorn breathed it in. Deeply.

There was magic here.

"Do you want to rest or ascend tonight?" Cass asked. "The Keep is only a thousand steps above this place."

"I want to press on." She saw him adjust his swords. The entry tunnel was a natural cave except for the level floor, which was paved in polished flagstone. It meandered about until opening out into a space where they could no longer see the ceiling.

The cavern they were in was vast, with no apparent pillars for support. Clusters of lamps hanging on poles created pools of light that allowed them to navigate. The singing got louder as they drew closer to a large, multi-story stone building.

"The novice candidates are housed here," Cass said as they investigated the main hall where dinner preparations were being performed by an army of young girls.

"The order only accepts girls?" Thorn asked.

"Yes, for the steps. And women. But not all. Many never even make it to the first step. Some stay and hope they are selected. I was twenty-two when I took the steps, long ago."

Thorn looked at her again closely, beyond the scars and her bright eyes. He wondered how old she was.

"There are usually about three hundred girls waiting. Only one is allowed on the steps each day. Boys enter by the Main Gate. They follow a different path."

"Show me these steps."

Thorn followed Cass around a dimly lit path as the singing got louder. Thorn heard an odd sort of harmony. Some phrases were repeating on different cycles than others. Words blended, preventing him from understanding any but feeling all. There was magic in them.

Before the base of the stairs came into view, a pool of water bordered on the right. It was held in by a thick, head-height wall, so they didn't even see it until they had reached the base of the stairs. It was smooth as glass and reflected the braziers that lined the path so perfectly it looked like a whole other world inverted.

Every step had a novice standing upon it. Over every learner was a lamp, and this lamp illuminated words carved on the wall. They were the words to the song they sang.

Thorn could not read these words or understand the songs.

"The song changes for them after three steps. The two novices above teach the new song to the novice below," Cass said as they watched. "The songs are lessons. It makes them easier to remember."

As the novices sang, each dipped a small pitcher into a basin that was carved into the stone wall and poured the water into the next basin up. Water flowed up into the mountain with the songs.

"Each day, they advance a step. It takes almost three years to reach the top," Cass said as she took off her cloak and an outer layer. There were hundreds of pegs there, but not many cloaks. "We won't need these."

Thorn thought she would be right. With all the people in the stairwell, it would be warm. Add the exertion of climbing the steps for an hour, and they would be sweating before long.

"Why are there no guards?" Thorn asked, looking about.

"The guards are up there. These girls represent no threat." She pointed into the stairwell. "Are you sure your wounds are ready for this?" Cass looked concerned again.

"I'm fine." He looked up the stairs, tunnel far as he could see before it wound around. There was six feet of space for them behind the novice's backs.

"The first guard will be found with an acolyte in the Chamber of Questions at the top. He will see your weapons… and…" She faded off. "Past that, I can show you the way to the High Vestal's chambers. But I do not know how you will pass."

"Leave that to me." He looked at the carved words and listened to the songs. "They will learn these lessons and remember them as songs?" He started up the stairs. "Someone will write a new song about this night."

Cass was hard-pressed to keep up with Thorn. He seemed to drift up the stairs. His wide pant legs hid his feet and gave the illusion of floating. Long straight steps gave way to stretches of spiral stairs and sections of an almost raw cave with knee-high steps.

None of the novices gave them so much as a glance. In about twenty minutes, Thorn reached a broad landing where a cavern opened to the side.

Cass got to the landing and caught her breath before speaking. "At the end of the day, the novices from below will rest here."

The stepping basins below fed into a broad pool here, and it supplied the next set of novices.

Thorn cocked his head to each side, and his neck cracked, audible above the singing.

He turned and began the next set of steps.

Thorn waited longer for Cass on the next landing. She leaned over and rested her hands on her knees.

"Did you know that one of the magics instilled in me as a King's protector was the ability to read a person's intent?"

She shook her head no, still out of breath.

"There is evil intent above. I can already feel it." He looked into her eyes. "Peck said to trust no one." He moved closer as if floating. Cass was unable to see his feet. "He knew it was already a foundation belief of mine... I think he was talking about you. Yet you have never really lied to me. But I cannot measure omission."

He didn't wait for a reply. He headed up.

***

As Cass struggled up the final curve in the steps, Thorn was not in sight. She passed the final novice, went past the last of the dorms, and entered an ancient door, the same one the next novice expected to pass through at midnight in a few hours.

A long hallway lined with candle lanterns led to a round high-domed room. The floor was a vast iron grate with intricate mosaic patterns of two-inch square holes with darkness below.

Thorn was there. At his feet were the guard and the female acolyte, both headless. The blood was a stark contrast against her formal vestments.

When Cass was about to speak, Thorn held up a hand and stopped her.

"Tell me only where I need to go."

"Through that door and down a long hall. You will see a large room with two wide staircases, and either one will take you to the vast library down the corridor. The spiral staircase in the great library will take you to the High Vestal's chambers."

"You have done enough. Go back now while you can. They know I'm coming."

With that, Thorn was moving. It was unnerving to watch. The motion he made with his sword sent an arc of blood in a circle, and the sash at his belt wiped the rest as he sheathed his sword. As he walked, his feet could not be seen in his formal black robes. The wide legs of the pants were silent.

He looked as if he was being drawn across ice by an invisible rope around his waist.

Like a ghost, in black, he faded around the next corner. Cass followed, and when she entered the high foyer, only seconds later, she found four more dead guards. One still stood without a head and fell backward slowly like a great tree.

She saw Thorn ascending the staircase on the left. He was so calm and expressionless. She watched the ten guards gather at the mouth of the central hallway at the intersection.

He stopped and bowed formally to the soldiers.

And he waited.

Most of them were nervous and already had their swords drawn. A single soldier, wearing the uniform of the Captain of the guard, stepped forward to face Thorn.

For a long moment, they stood facing each other, three paces apart.

Cass observed.

The Captain drew his sword with lightning speed but never got to use it because his torso was bisected diagonally. His sword arm was severed at the shoulder, and his head flew over the railing.

She missed it in the blink of an eye. The heat of the strike's magic rose above his sword now.

Thorn was now standing frozen in a peaceful pose with his sword extended to the right. Blood dripped from its tip. It had all happened in less than an instant.

The other nine men were well trained. In formation, they rushed him.

Thorn danced into the center of them, never stopping at any single point. Heads were dropping to the floor as he went. Cass didn't hear blades cross once.

Only one remained standing. He was six paces behind Thorn. Thorn swirled his sword, and Cass saw the blood arc away again. He slowly turned toward the last remaining guard.

Thorn said something to him, but Cass could not hear his words or the guard's reply. The guard bent over and picked up the sword of one of his fallen comrades.

With a sword in each hand, he advanced quickly. The blades were moving in circles so fast they were invisible, whistling vortexes of death.

Thorn stepped aside, and the guard's leg was severed just below the knee. Before he could fall, Thorn was behind him. A two-handed blow bisected the man's head, neck, and torso all the way to his navel.

He fell forward off Thorn's blade, still in one piece.

By the time she had reached the top of the stairs, Thorn was gone again.

Cass paused over Captain Rankin's body for a moment. She was incredulous.

She gingerly walked around. The pool of blood was spreading. A waterfall of blood was beginning to slide off the balcony under the rails to the room below.

The long hall was empty. The doors at the end of the corridor to the library were open. There were ten crossbow bolts stuck into the wooden floor in the opening. Cass was at the door in time to see Thorn running at the wall and leap up. His feet lightly touched bookshelves until he quickly reached the balcony above and swung himself over the rail.

The guards there were gathered around the single ornate, black iron, spiral staircase. The guard on that end desperately tried to reload his crossbow. He was run through the heart and was carried along by Thorn, impaled on the sword, around the balcony corner, and toward the other soldiers.

The dead soldier was bristling with crossbow bolts before they reached the other soldiers gathered at the base of the spiral stairs. This group was a mix of spearmen and swordsmen.

Some wore heavy armor and some light chain mail. She saw all the spearheads fly off, and then men began to drop.

They were all dead moments later.

As Thorn started up the spiral stairs to the next level, he paused and looked down at Cass.

His face momentarily shifted from blank to a veil of sadness. He nodded and moved on.

When Cass reached the top of the stairs, she could see the two guards outside the High Vestal door were dead, and the beautifully carved doors were broken open.

Beyond the doors, she could see Thorn in profile, standing at rest, as if he had just strolled up to the office. Both his swords were sheathed, and his arms were crossed over his chest.

He looked to his right. Directly at Cass.

He was waiting for her.

Out of breath, she slowly entered the room. Looking carefully around the corner, Cass saw a silver-haired woman at the far end of the room, standing behind a grand desk covered with maps and open volumes of all sizes. She was dressed in the formal habit of the High Vestal.

A huge man stood between Thorn and the desk in the center of the massive, bookshelf-lined room.

The silver-haired woman spoke first.

"Cass, I am surprised to see you. When we heard he was here, we were sure you were dead or worse."

She spoke in a tone as if they were in a garden having tea.

"I hope that…" the silver-haired woman began, but her words were cut off by a rapid clash of steel on steel. The guard had attacked. Thorn's sword had blocked his first blow before it was even out of the sheath. Thorn's second sword deflected the second strike.

Both men now had two swords drawn, and they moved in the same ghostly way, circling. Cass could not tell who initiated the next rapid clash. Steel touched steel, deflecting, whirling, the swords moving so fast they were nearly invisible.

The men froze.

They were statues, posed as if to honor the war arts. Moments went by.

"Please, forgive me," Thorn said to the man, twice his size, who moved first.

He was suddenly disassembled. One sword hand and then the other. His right leg at the thigh and then his head was cut in half diagonally between the eyes, across his face--all done before his first severed hand landed on the floor.

Thorn was not even breathing hard.

He visibly relaxed and stood upright at ease. With his swords still dripping with blood, he turned and walked to the front of the desk.

He cleaned the blood off the swords and laid both on the desk, centered on a large map of the region.

Thorn spoke to the silver-haired woman. She had a line of blood spatter on her regal habit of high office. "On this day, you, ma'am, have been the bravest of all."

He smiled at her.

"You may go now," Thorn said, turning his back to her.

The High Vestal

The woman with silver hair fled the room past Cass, who now stood in the center looking down at the disassembled man.

"How long have you known I was the High Vestal?" Cass asked Thorn.

"I thought I had my answer at the Elder Bridge. The High Vestal Mother had sent villains to murder me in the darkness." Thorn relaxed more. "I have known since you walked into the room with that tray in Peck's Halfway. You see, I too am well trained in the use of poisons. You had a tray full."

He stared at Cass. His face was blank.

"Why didn't you end me then? Why wait until now?" she asked him.

"End you? I didn't come here to end you. I came here with a confession for the High Vestal Mother. I did not expect to meet her at Peck's Halfway. Then I thought I'd have my absolution if you murdered me, finally finishing that massacre." He crossed his arms over his chest and leaned back on the desk. "But when you didn't, a new question remained. I could tell all the things you said were the truth. But I also know it is far easier to deceive with the truth."

Cass walked around the desk and sat in the great chair. "Ask then."

"Why did you want the King dead?"

"Because he was evil. The world is far better without him." She looked him in the eyes. "I'll not change my answer to avoid your vengeance. Even if it costs my life, the world is better."

Thorn let out a great sigh.

"Your men failed." Thorn paused. "Ramos was their best swordsman and was my equal. He killed four of my brothers. He was severely wounded. Brother Saris and I dispatched the rest and eventually restrained him before my King.

"The King said to him. 'You have fought well, my son. Tell me your name and your family so that I can send you home to them with honor.' And Ramos told him." Thorn could not meet her eyes. "And when he was done, the King laughed. Instead of a quick, honorable death, the King stabbed him in the stomach, spilling his bile and his intestines. A slow death for man as strong as Ramos."

Thorn briefly closed his eyes, remembering.

"While Ramos lay slowly dying, the King told him how he was going to send troops to his home to rape, torture and burn his family at the stake along with their whole village."

Cass's hand went to her mouth.

"Saris and the King began to laugh… So, I killed them. Saris first."

She stared at Thorn in shock.

"I killed the King."

There was a long pause as Thorn watched the pieces of the puzzle align in her eyes.

"I brought Ramos a merciful death after I told him that his family would be safe and cared for. He died with honor. He knew his goal had been achieved."

Cass paced the room and finally stood, the desk between them.

Thorn continued, "When you came to me at Peck's Halfway, I thought you didn't want my chaos and violence brought to the Keep. The High Vestal Mother would know what I could do. Know I could not be stopped, even wounded."

Cass was thinking, her brow heavily creased.

"When you brought me to the Keep, I knew why."

"Why?" She asked.

"These were not bodyguards. They were jailers," he said. "You used me to kill them. They did not belong here. I could feel it. You were in exile a mere day's ride away." He closed his eyes again. "I never knew Peck could be so brave."

Her chin trembled. "I knew what you did for Ramos. But not why. You could not have found his parents without speaking to him," she said. "The Queen… she was…"

"When they finally broke the door of the Cathedral down, I was alone. I was surrounded by the dead. I was drenched in blood. The room covered in frost." His eyes were still closed. "I kept expecting someone to stop me, to strike me down. They never did. They let me just walk away. The curse, it seemed, was to live."

She finished her circuit around the desk and now stood between Thorn and his swords. Slowly she moved closer to him.

He studied her face. The scar in her right eyebrow, the worry lines of her eyes, the flecks of gold in the brown of her iris.

She turned back to the desk and lifted the short sword. She stood face to face with Thorn, grasped his red sash, and cleaned his sword again in one slow motion. She looked at the blade and marveled at its beauty. She studied the steel's grain and its balance in her hand before sliding it into its sheath. He had grown still as a statue. She repeated the cleaning with the long sword.

She paused this time to study the staghorn handle, its natural polish, and beauty. Finally, she slowly slid it home.

"Are you injured?"

"Not much," he said, as he began to relax finally. "Are there any others that you require I kill this day?"

"There is a garrison above with just over three hundred men, not including the boys." She looked at the man on the floor. "But there are only three more of these." She locked eyes with him again. "You've already ruined my favorite rug." A corner of her mouth rose.

"Oops." His eyes flashed his smile.

The Queen of Lies

"It was the new Queen all along," Thorn said as Cass searched her library, hurrying. "I now believe she seduced King Reddick, murdered his wife, and later his only heir." He held his hand out to stop her from searching for emphasis. "Then she manipulated you to use your influence to kill the King." She drew away from him as if he burned her.

"And then she stole from me all that I had," Cass fumed. "I was not in the Keep when it fell. By the time I got to Peck's, they had held the Keep."

"Not for much longer," Thorn said.

Cass showed Thorn maps of the keep.

"The main hall here is several levels up from where we are." He pointed to the corridor on the same level as the upper Keep. "The barracks are here. The Main Gate is here, and the officer's quarters are here."

"One of the guardians is always on duty here, in the watchtower. The top is enclosed in glass, and the fire burns there continuously. It can be seen for miles," Cass said. "The level just below is the…" she hesitated, "the portal room."

Thorn nodded. Cass was relieved she did not have to explain the significance of it to him.

"Is it a circular room with thirty-two doors? How many doors are unlocked? Do you know where they go?"

Cass brought out another map. It showed a beautifully rendered ink drawing of the Keep, including the Watchtower.

"This makes sense now. How many portals from the tower access the Keep? There are usually at least two." He was studying the map. It had the interior of the two levels of the Watchtower. One was windowless and had thirty-two doors depicted. Only six were marked.

"These two. One goes to the tower at the Main Gate, and one comes to this office." Cass pointed to a block of cells on another map. "But there is a third portal. It goes to a different circular room. It's how they got in at the beginning. That path has not been used for hundreds of years."

"The doors locked from the other side are lost to us." She shivered and looked at him. She could see her breath. "Are you all right?" She noticed a cut in his tunic.

"I'm fine." He pointed to the portal room and one of the marked doors. "Where does this one go?"

Cass sighed and straightened her spine, deciding. She walked from behind her massive desk and over to the built-in bookcase beside the large fireplace. The shelves were covered with various relics instead of books.

She reached up and pressed a spot on the end of the mantle and pushed the shelf inward at the same time. It swung in.

"They didn't know about this one." She took a candle in with her and lit an oil lamp on a shelf.

It was more like a short hallway, six yards deep and three wide. The opposite end had a simple, rectangle door frame carved with runes in deep relief. The dark wood timbers that made the frame were a foot thick on a side. The door was the same dark wood, bound with black iron. The hinges were on the left, always on the left.

"You've seen these before?" Cass asked.

"Yes. I have used them many times. There is a bridge room, a portal room, in the capital. I have seen two others."

"I have only used this one portal. From here to the Watchtower and to the Main Gate. The ancient sorcerers that created the network of portals left us no clue how to open them." She hugged herself, thinking what was on the other side. "We can't wait long. The word may spread quickly."

Thorn nodded. He was ready.

Cass reached up and retrieved a key from its hiding place on top of the carved frame. Thorn shook his head as she unlocked the door. She handed the key to Thorn and pulled on the great ring.

There was a stone wall on the other side.

Cass stared. "They locked the other side. How?"

"The Queen. Thorn pushed the door closed and looked at the frame. With his left hand, he reached inside the slit in his tunic and brought out bloody fingers. He began to paint the black relief areas around a particular rune. After half a dozen applications, the rune was entirely surrounded by his blood.

It began to glow with faint light from within the grain of the wood.

Thorn twisted the rune.

He pulled the thick iron ring and revealed another door where the wall was moments ago. "Beyond this door is another hall the same size as this?"

Cass nodded, still speechless.

"Stay here until I come back for you," Thorn said as he pushed open the other door.

***

Thorn disappeared into the darkness beyond the door.

She stared into the darkness and saw the far door open into the circular portal room. That door swung into the chamber as well.

Thorn moved silently to the right and disappeared from her line of sight. The far door remained open and showed the thick column in the center with the open spiral staircase that wound around it. The torches all burned between each door. Thirty-two doors. Thirty-two torches. Always burning with Earth magic that even she didn't understand.

When she saw Thorn begin to ascend the stairs around the column, she moved forward. She gently, quietly, closed the door behind her as she entered. She knew it wouldn't lock.

The room was warmer, and all she could hear was the flutter of the torch flames.

Then there were voices, calm and strong, but she could not understand what they were saying.

Cass started up the spiral stairs. The column was thick, and the stairs were narrow and went one and a half times around the stone cylinder as she approached the opening in the domed ceiling.

They were still talking.

Cass carefully looked over the edge of the floor to see both men standing in the bright light of the round chamber. Thorn was standing casually relaxed, with his swords in his sheaths. She had noticed that posture before. She knew it was a trap, ready to spring.

The Guardian was naked to the waist and soaked in sweat. He had been practicing sword forms. His sweaty long black hair was dripping wet in a ponytail. His large, double-edged, two-handed broad sword was pointed at Thorn.

"Do you miss the touch of a true blade, Thorn?" He taunted, "The soft feel of it as it stands up in your hands? It's the difference between the fine daughter of nobles and a pock-faced farm girl."

In a blaze of speed, the Guardian attacked. The sword that had been pointing at Thorn an instant ago was arcing around to come down in a devastating downward cut that would have been impossible to deflect with all the power in it.

Except Thorn was no longer there.

Cass had not seen Thorn move in close and pass just to the Guardian's side. She had not seen him draw or strike.

The Guardian's sword struck the floor as his momentum made him fall forward in two bloody pieces, completely cleaved just below the ribcage.

Thorn was like a frozen statue for a heartbeat.

The Guardian tried to drag himself across the floor for a few seconds before death found him. Thorn's eyes were watching Cass as she ascended into the room.

The room had the single column in the center that rose twenty-five feet where the flame began and rose another twenty feet above that. The wall around the room was twelve feet high. The glass dome was above that wall.

This room was hot. The cold air was being drawn up from the level below with the vented chimney effect from the massive flame.

She looked at the body. "Two down. Two to go?"

"Yes. But the others will not be so easy. I have met them. They are the Queen's Guardians. The best and most vicious of them." Thorn cleaned and sheathed his sword.

"What will we do next?" Cass asked.

"We wait here. The changing of the watch is within the hour. With luck, they will come to me one at a time, here."

Sharkey

They had to wait just ten minutes.

Cass had ascended the single narrow stairs. They were barely stairs, more like rocks mortared to protrude a foot out from the wall. She walked around the top of the wall to the other side, where the guardian would see her as well as the body. They hoped the distraction would be long enough. Thorn would be behind the column as he entered.

As he appeared casually coming up the steps, he said, "Hello, Thorn." He didn't seem to notice the dead guardian or Cass at all. "Word has come up from the lower levels of your visit." The giant defender had full chain mail and heavy ornate, lobster-like, articulating plates on his chest, back, and shoulders. There was already a double-bladed ax in one hand and a double-edged sword in the other.

"Hello, Sharkey." Thorn used his nickname from his youth, knowing he hated it. "Been keeping yourself busy, I hear, killing the weak and being the Queen's whore."

Thorn could see one of those insults hit the mark.

"Did Arnor and Viktor die well?" Sharkey asked as he topped the stairs. He was still thirty feet away, not looking at Thorn.

"They have been training. I was impressed." Thorn lied. "I didn't think Viktor could get any taller, but he seems to have managed."

"Yes…" Sharkey moved with incredible speed, throwing the ax at Thorn in a deadly horizontal spinning flight, "…he has."

Thorn barely had time to draw his short sword and deflect the ax from ripping into his chest. Sharkey crossed the distance and was swinging a double-hand overhead blow with blinding speed. Thorn's left hand was numb from the impact with the ax. When his automatic defense of the subsequent death blow reacted with both swords, it was too much. While the swing was deflected, Thorn lost the grip on the short sword. It spun away toward the wall.

Neither was speaking now. The fire roared above as they circled each other. Their sword tips pointed at each other's hearts, but their swords were a foot apart. They stopped rotating with Sharkey between Thorn and his short sword.

They stood still for a few moments before Sharkey spoke. "I heard you carried farmer blades, but I had no idea they were kitchen wives fish knives."

"Fish knives for Sharkey," Thorn said and attacked. A dozen strikes were parried with the same speed they were delivered. The ringing steel was impossibly loud. Thorn retreated in an attempt to draw him away from his short sword.

It didn't work.

Sharkey never looked away from Thorn as he hooked his toe under the blade, flipped it up to his left hand, and threw it at Cass, where she stood on the wall. She barely dodged it, but it struck the glass point first and shattered the foot square pane of glass, passing into the darkness beyond.

"That was your only chance, Thorn." Sharkey smiled. "You don't have the reach, strength, or stamina to take me now. You rely too much on your draw tricks and surprise."

Without a word, Thorn advanced and avoided Sharkey's swing instead of meeting or deflecting it. Instantly he was inside Sharkey's guard, inside his arms, spinning to face away, his back to Sharkey's front.

Thorn's sword did not slash. Instead, its point entered Sharkey just below his chest plate and moved upward through his guts, stomach, heart, and then protruded out to the left of his neck.

Thorn released his sword, leaving it inside the man. All four of their hands now firmly held the grip of Sharkey's sword. Thorn need only to let death take hold.

Sharkey released the sword and clamped his iron hands on Thorn's neck. Thorn dropped it and was trying to pry his fingers off.

Then Cass was there.

She had rushed down, and instead of helping Thorn pry at fingers, she grabbed the handle of Thorn's sword and began to twist and wrench it savagely side to side. A great gout of blood burst from Sharkey's mouth, and he fell backward.

The sword slid out of him as he fell.

Thorn was having trouble breathing. He also had a large wound from his hip to his knee. He choked out. "Help me. Up there." He gestured with his chin to the stairs to the top of the wall. They were so narrow she could not help him up.

Standing below, holding his bloody sword, she watched him reach the top and turn to the massive flame. His arms extended out, and his chin rose.

The glass behind Thorn began to frost. The great roaring jet of flame leaned toward him.

The room was becoming cold.

Thorn let out a scream of agony as he absorbed the power. It looked like his body was full of magma, glowing in his screaming mouth and the cracks of his wounds as they began to close.

The gashes healed, and the bruises disappeared as his scream faded.

The flame returned to normal—the frost on the glass melted from its heat.

Thorn collapsed to his knees.

Thorn never lost consciousness, but it was close. He was about to fall over when Cass was by his side, holding his face in both hands.

His focus returned as he exhaled a breath he did not know he was holding.

"Thorn, say something. What did you do?" Cass pleaded.

He looked into her eyes.

"I don't suppose you happen to have any food with you?" he said in a hoarse voice as he smiled and began to stagger to his feet.

He looked down at himself. His clothes were bloody rags.

Cass handed him his sword, and he automatically cleaned it and slid it into the sheath. He drew the short scabbard out and dropped it. He adjusted his clothes and tightened his belt.

"The last one will be Torrock," Thorn said. "Even fully healed, I may not be able to overcome him. Sharkey and the others were always too proud, too certain of their prowess. Not Torrock. He is the most cautious and brutal of all."

"What will you do?" Cass was checking his flesh. Wounds that had been there were wholly gone.

"When Sharkey does not return with my head, he will come here," Thorn said.

"Hello?" a voice called from the stairwell below. "My lord, Thorn… sir?" It was the voice of a boy. They proceeded down as he was emerging from below.

"I'm here, lad. Stay where you are. You don't need to see this," Thorn said as he reached the same level.

"That is the best sight I've seen in weeks, sir." The boy was surveying the two dead bodies. "Your day's not done yet. I hate to say. Master Torrock sent me to tell you he awaits you."

"Where is he?" Cass asked.

"He is standing in the inner courtyard. Waiting."

"What's your name, son?" Thorn asked.

"My name is Penn, sir."

"Lead the way, Penn." Thorn gestured. "You don't happen to have any food, do you?"

Torrock

The portal they took accessed a room in the guard tower at the Main Gate. It was a brilliant placement for strategic reasons. An impossible number of men could flow out of that portal to operate the gate to the surprise of any intruders there.

When Thorn went from the tower to the battlements, he could see Torrock standing alone below. He was in brightly polished, full plate armor, head to toe. He held a large torch aloft as he waited. On seeing Thorn emerge, he turned and entered the keep via massive double doors.

Penn ran down the steps from the battlements to the courtyard and followed the receding torchlight through the open doors.

When Thorn entered the main hall, the light was receding down a corridor at the other end. They continued to follow the light as it moved through the keep, downstairs, through feast halls, armories, and eventually into a long wide corridor with cells on either side. Torrock had placed the torch on the wall in its place and waited. Two swords were drawn. They were medium length. He was still as a statue.

The helmet he wore had only a slit in front for vision.

"I remember sparring with you, Torrock. Even blindfolded." Thorn spoke low and even casually as if they were having lunch. "You disdained armor as much as I did." Thorn entered the pool of light. His sword was already drawn and raised over his head. He drifted across the floor in an eerie motion.

Torrock didn't move.

"I will allow you to divest the armor unmolested. Then we shall see what kind of swordsman you have become." Thorn paused out of range. The guttering sound of the torch was all the sound there was.

Torrock's armor bristled with sharp blades. His shoulders, forearms, biceps, elbows, and knees all had fixed, shining knives as part of the bright, horrible beauty of his armor. Torrock remained silent.

"Have you become so ugly you cannot even reveal your face?" Thorn's attempts to anger him might as well have landed on deaf ears. Thorn began to slowly circle him to the right when he could see past Torrock into the open cell beyond.

There was an open portal arch in there on the back wall.

"She wants to speak with you…" Before Torrock could finish his sentence, Thorn struck. There was a blur of strikes, counterstrikes parries, and hits to armor when suddenly, as fast as it started, Thorn's blade was shattered by opposing strikes between Torrock's swords, and Thorn's left bicep was impaled on a forearm blade.

Thorn screamed but never stopped moving.

He tore his bicep clean through as he spun and stabbed the remaining twelve inches of his sword into Torrock's eye slit.

Torrock fell like an avalanche of blades. His helmet wrenched the sword handle from Thorn's grip. He used his right hand to hold his left arm together.

He turned toward Cass; Penn was still by her side. "Stay here. Penn, make sure she doesn't follow me." The corridor was getting cold.

As Thorn passed, he pulled the remains of his sword from Torrock's helm. Then, he moved directly into the portal.

Once Damned

Thorn passed through the door into another round room of closed doors. Sunlight shone down the spiral stair in the center. He ascended into a warm, opulent suite. The architecture and daylight were utterly different. There was a large living area full of rich carpets, lounges, and piles of pillows. Decadent was the only word in his mind. Every wall was floor-to-ceiling windows that looked out on a tropical beach on one side and lush jungle on the other.

Trailing blood as he went, he carefully moved through a dining room, a library, and a bedroom with an enormous richly carved bed. Beyond this, he found the Queen.

Aleena was in a bath chamber. She relaxed in a pool up to her chin in water. A fire blazed in the hearth nearby.

"I don't like to be kept waiting," she pouted as Thorn stood in the doorway. He leaned on the frame so he would not fall. "Why did you bother to bring that? You won't be able to use it. Not after what you did to my poor husband."

Thorn could already feel the compulsion to drop the sword. He focused on the pain and stood straight. Thorn stepped forward. The closer he came, the more he knew he would be unable to bring the steel to her flesh. The spell was so potent.

He began to feel something else.

Queen Aleena rose out of the water to stand with her arms along the edge of the pool, her breasts now exposed, barely out of the water. Thorn could see runic symbols tattooed on her skin, her breasts, and the undersides of her arms.

He was becoming aroused.

"Yes. Thorn the damned. I am going to take you as you bleed. Again and again. Take sex from you as you scream because you will not be able to stop me. Now bring that pot of hot water here to warm my pool."

He focused on the pain. He went to the pot, heating over the fire. He had paused before he upended it, extinguishing the blaze.

"I like defiance. I took the King, I took his son, I took all the Royal Guardians," she boasted.

He stepped to the edge of the pool.

"I dominated them all, just as I will you. Because it is only worth the trouble if they are lions…"

He stepped into the water, onto the first stair, ankle-deep. Then, through gritted teeth, he spoke.

"Once Damned. Always Damned."

He drove the broken blade into his own leg, just above the knee, and ripped an enormous wound straight up through his thigh to his hip. This was followed by several lightning stabs into his other thigh.

The Queen was laughing.

He carved three slashes down his chest and finally stabbed the shattered blade deep into his own heart.

The Queen laughed at his decision. "Suicide over seduction?" she laughed as the broken blade finally fell to the floor.

As Thorn's arms came up, his back arched, and his mouth opened in a scream.

The water instantly froze, trapping her. His wounds began to glow as if lava were about to spill out. Frost covered the room as he screamed the endless stream of agony and despair. The queen started to panic and tried to rise, but it was too late; she ceased moving. A light frost crept up her flesh. Her mouth was frozen open in a silent gasp. Her eyes glazed white.

Thorn was a silent statue now as well. Arms held wide as the inner glow began to fade before the wounds had closed.

Drawn by his howl, Cass burst into the room. The room was so cold, clouds of her breath instantly crystallized and fell like snow. Grasping the scene, she rushed to the fireplace. It was a block of ice. She grabbed the huge iron poker. It was so cold it burned her hands. Moving across the room at a run, she swung with both hands and shattered the queen's head into tiny pieces. Her frozen jaw remained grotesquely attached to the stump of her neck.

Cass kept moving until she reached her true goal. She swung and shattered the window.

"Quickly! Break the glass!" she yelled at Penn. Moving along the wall, she broke window after floor-to-ceiling window. Penn went the opposite way, using a bronze statue, grabbed along the way. "All of them!"

The tropical breeze flowed in from the seaside. An icy fog flowed out the other side.

Thorn was glowing inside again.

***

Thorn awoke, crawling back from oblivion slowly, his mind empty. Finally, his eyes fluttered open and were presented with a warm, rich scene. Dark oak beams that covered the ceiling were illuminated by a roaring fire in a beautiful hearth. The tapestries on the walls depicted a horse race over a lovely countryside of fields, rolling hills, and hedges to jump.

As he turned his head, he noticed that on each of the four walls, the race traversed four seasons as well. When he turned toward the winter scenes, his gaze fell on a pale-skinned shoulder. A scarred shoulder.

He carefully moved to face her back. His left arm wrapped around her as the memories washed over him. The realization that his severed bicep was healed was his only fleeting thought of the past as he kissed the nape of her neck. The past and the future were lost in the scent of her, the warmth of her.

She started as she became aware.

She turned quickly to look into his eyes. She touched his face as if to make sure he was real. "Are you all right…" was all she could choke out before tears began to flow.

He kissed her mouth in answer. The salt of her tears was the best thing he had ever tasted.

"I took you to the Watchtower." She was having difficulty talking past the lump in her throat. "You soaked in the magic for nine days. It was the wound to your heart that took the longest to heal." She buried her face in his neck. "I was so afraid. Then, yesterday, you sighed and seemed just to be sleeping again. We brought you to my quarters in the keep."

Over her shoulder, he could see the recovered two staghorn handles of his swords. Both blades were broken, but the handles were intact.

This made Thorn smile.

"Are the portals secure? The portal rooms?"

"Yes. Thanks to you." She said to his neck. "The Capital is in chaos, the High Houses all vying for the Throne."

"Do you happen to have any food?"

She laughed, and it was like music.

THE SHOE

MARTIN WILSEY

The Shoe

Some people swore that the house was haunted.

That was fine with me. It meant no one ever went there except me. It was gray, almost black, from the weather, as if it had never been painted, or lived in, or loved, ever. All the glass and the front double doors were gone, leaving a gaping maw, frozen in an eternal scream of pain. A zombie house that was still standing because it didn't know it was already dead.

I could not have cared less about the house back then. It was the trees that surrounded it that I loved. They were giant maples that had been full-grown when the ghosts had moved into the house. Now, decades later, they were a tree climber's paradise. It was a world of its own. The branches were perfectly spaced, and some were thicker than my body. The crooks and hollows made for perfect seating. I called it Valhalla. It wasn't until years later I learned that "Valhalla" literally meant "Hall of the Dead."

That day, like many days, I had brought a peanut butter sandwich and an RC cola for lunch. Sitting in my favorite spot, in my favorite tree, I watched the clouds and the occasional, infrequent car go by. I never thought the nightmare would come on a bright, sunny summer morning. My back was to the house. It was screaming a silent warning.

I first saw the hitchhiker as I ate the last bite of my sandwich. It wasn't a good road for rides. I loved hiding in the trees like Robin Hood, but there were never any pedestrians on this road. Spying on a hitchhiker was exciting. He seemed in no hurry and paused directly below me in the shade. Mr. Wilson drove by in his old farm truck and waved to him but didn't stop.

Finally, a big, dusty, black car rounded the bend. He put out his thumb in the universal, "please give me a ride sign." The vehicle slowed and then stopped. It just sat there. He actually had to walk back a ways and approached the driver's side. The windows were tinted so dark and were so dusty I wondered how the driver could even see out.

The hitchhiker waited. It seemed an exceedingly long time. He leaned in and cupped his eyes on the window.

That's when the window began to descend.

It was complete darkness inside. It was not just the darkness from the absence of light. The entire interior was utterly filled with liquid darkness. I could feel it from where I was frozen in the tree. I could smell it. I tasted the putrid oiliness of it in my mouth.

He leaned closer into the window to speak to the driver, oblivious to the evil steaming out from the opening. I almost gagged when I drew breath to call out. In that instant, it took him. It was like the darkness itself, took his head in its mouth and dragged his entire body into the car through the open window, even as it was closing.

The car rocked back and forth as throat-ripping screams tore the air. Crunching sounds were punctuated by scream after scream. The only thing worse was the silence that followed. That minute seemed longer than all the forty years since that moment.

The stillness was broken by the sound of the window motor as it slid down a mere six inches. Just enough to spit out a single shoe before it once again hid hell behind tinted glass. Silently, it rolled away, never to be seen by me again, even though I always watch for it.

The house was laughing.

My world shifted that day. I still can't eat peanut butter. So I tell people I'm allergic. But the worse thing is, as I drive down the highway, now and then, I'll see an inexplicable, single shoe on the side of a lonely road.

AFTERWORD

This book will be published in the summer of 2021 as the COVID pandemic winds down. It has been a weird year for me personally. I realized last year when the pandemic began that I was already living a quarantine lifestyle.

I'll keep writing short stories. I'll probably assemble another collection as they begin to pile up.

I have, in truth, already written about half a dozen more already that will be published in various anthologies. Being a good contributor, I always grant them exclusive rights for a time. After that, they will find their way into the next collection. It's already started.

My stories in the future will continue to expand my various worlds. I will likely continue to base characters on people I know, making them much more fun to murder their characters in my texts.

Mostly, I'll continue to drink coffee and make stuff up.

Acknowledgments

There are a lot of people that have helped and encouraged me with this book. I will list some here with my thanks: Web Anderson, Marilyn Anderson, Chris Schwartz, Erica Gravely, Travis Beck, Kelly Lenz Carr, Ginny McLean, Jessica Johnson, Tom McDonald, Joe Kirk, Jeff Soyer, Tifiny Swedensky, Brenda Reiner, Dave Nelson, Stephanie Mirro, TR Dillon, Paul Robertson, and Donna Royston.

I also need to thank the Loudon Science Fiction and Fantasy Writers Group, aka The Hourlings, for helping me become a better writer and distracting me with projects I can't resist. I already dedicated this whole book to them!

I want to specifically thank S.C. Megale, Jeffrey C. Jacobs, and David Keener. I do a weekly podcast with these writers. For me, the podcast is mostly a good excuse to get together every week and talk about various aspects of writing and publishing. I learn a lot. Besides, it's enormous fun. I'd do it even if we didn't record it.

As always, I have a special thanks to my wife Brenda for all the encouragement, help, and support she brings me.

I must also thank, as usual, my cat, Bailey. Who doesn't care if I ever sell another book as long as the sun shines on his window seat as I write.

About the Author

Martin Wilsey is a full-time author and creator of the bestselling SOLSTICE 31 SAGA.

Mr. Wilsey's first novel, STILL FALLING, was published on March 31st of 2015. Less than three years and over half a million published words later, he retired from his career as a research scientist for a government-funded think tank. As a full-time science fiction writer, Mr. Wilsey still uses his research and whiteboard skills to keep the books flowing. He likes to put science back into science fiction.

Mr. Wilsey has more projects than he has time. So please feel free to email him and distract him even more.

He and his wife Brenda live in Virginia with their cats Brandy and Bailey.

Email him or follow him on social media!

He just might kill you in his next novel...

Links:

https://www.martinwilsey.com/
http://wilseymc.blogspot.com/
https://www.audible.com/author/Martin-Wilsey/B00VDKLJWE
https://www.amazon.com/Martin-Wilsey/e/B00VDKLJWE/
https://www.facebook.com/MartinWilseyAuthor
http://www.tannhauserpress.com/